The Mark of the Tala

THE TWELVE KINGDOMS

Books by Jeffe Kennedy

The Twelve Kingdoms:
The Mark of the Tala

The Twelve Kingdoms:
Tears of the Rose
(coming December 2014)

The Twelve Kingdoms:
The Talon of the Hawk
(coming June 2015)

The Master of the Opera
available as an eBook serial
Act 1: Passionate Overture
Act 2: Ghost Aria
Act 3: Phantom Serenade
Act 4: Dark Interlude
Act 5: A Haunting Duet
Act 6: Crescendo

Published by Kensington Publishing Corp.

The Mark of the Tala

THE TWELVE KINGDOMS

JEFFE KENNEDY

KENSINGTON BOOKS
www.kensingtonbooks.com

To David
Who puts up with so much

ACKNOWLEDGMENTS

Many thanks to my agent, Pam van Hylckama Vlieg, who knew how to sell this story, and to my editor, Peter Senftleben, who knew to embrace it—and who came up with the perfect title.

As always, gratitude to my long-suffering critique partners: to Laura Bickle and Marcella Burnard, who helped me tease out this story from my tangled dreams, and to Carolyn Crane, Kristine Krantz, and Carien Ubink, who read fast and furiously at the exact moment I needed it most.

Thanks to the Kensington team, especially Rebecca Cremonese, for making this such a special book.

Finally, thanks to my family—especially my mom and stepdad, Dave—for all the love and support.

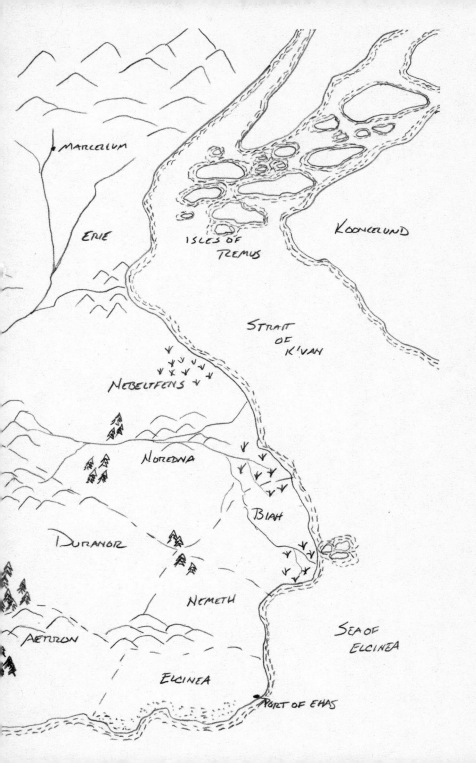

1

My version of the story goes all the way back to the once upon a time with the three princesses, each more beautiful than the last.

That's me, there, in the middle.

Of course, the history books usually cite the Assault of Ordnung as the beginning of this story. Or the Siege at Windroven, with all the drama and glory of it. Everyone knows what the books say happened at Odfell's Pass.

The smell of blood saturates my memories, the crimson circle widening in the snow around his body, just as I'd seen it, over and over in visions.

But the story I want to tell you starts with me and my sisters.

I suppose I'm lucky not to be the oldest and least beautiful. Ursula, however, is our father's heir and couldn't care a whit for things such as prettiness. Sharpening her sword, yes. Studying the law books, of course. Always planning her strategies.

I confess, I sometimes envied Ursula's dedication to ruling. But even when she reminded me that something could happen to her—making me next in line—so I should learn my role like any good understudy, I didn't do it. If something happened to both our father and Ursula, then the world would have fallen apart beyond repair. It would save nothing to stick my butt on a throne.

Then there's Amelia. The youngest, breathtakingly beautiful. They called her Glorianna's avatar when she was born and started composing sonnets to her by the time she turned twelve. Hair the color of sunrise, eyes like twilight, skin like moonbeams. Ursula used to have to shoot me mean looks and tap the cabochon jewel in the pommel of her sword to remind me not to roll my eyes.

The worst part: you couldn't even hate her for it.

Amelia has always been the sunshine of our lives, inside and out. She's not the fake-nice of the courtiers and the ladies-in-waiting, either, with that kind of happy chatter that grows louder and louder the more they're trying to cover their motives. Lady Dulcinor, for example, yakking on every day about her flowers and whether or not last night's chill will have frozen their petals. When I grumbled over dinner, for the umpteenth time, about her endless, empty-headed nonsense, I found the next morning that Amelia had taken Lady Dulcinor into her retinue and traded me the young Duchess of Gaignor.

When I thanked Amelia, she fluttered her red-gold lashes.

"I'm not martyring myself for you at all, Andi. Dulcinor is kind of sweet. I ignore the sillier things." She hugged me with pure affection, violet eyes alight with humor. "Besides, it's worth it to see you happy. Gaignor loves to ride almost as much as you do. I worry you don't have enough friends."

See how she is?

We grew up the cherished and protected daughters of the High King of the Twelve Kingdoms, our lives as carefully ordered as all of Uorsin's lands.

Until the day Prince Hugh of Avonlidgh walked into court.

He was meant for Ursula. She would need an appropriate consort, our father declared, and she should choose one so that Uorsin could see him trained in the skills of government, also.

Hugh, naturally, fell head over heels in love with Amelia.

If Amelia's strawberry-blond hair meant sunrise to the poets, then Hugh was blazing noon. He strode into the formal audience chamber that day like a prince out of the old stories. His chain mail, studded with rubies, glittered in the light pouring through the chamber's clerestory windows. The velvet of his sleeves echoed his eyes, blue as the summer sky, and provided the perfect foil for his swept-back hair.

He bowed, low and deep, to Ursula. I swear to Moranu every female in the room sighed.

Ursula looked fine, too—make no mistake. Her ladies wouldn't allow otherwise. She cleaned up well when she went to the trouble. But Ursula's beauty is in the clear, firm lines of her jaw, the sharp eyes that miss nothing, her incisive intelligence. She sat at our father's right hand, while I sat next to the queen's empty chair on the other side, Amelia to my left. I'd spent pretty much my entire court life one chair divided from my father and older sister, ever since our mother died at Amelia's birth. All told, I suppose it's better to have an empty chair than to fill it with someone who might create a bigger rift in the kingdom's rule than this aching hole of a reminder.

Not that High King Uorsin would marry again. Some said he kept the queen's throne empty as a reminder that he didn't need anyone's help to keep his crown.

At any rate, my point is that Hugh had to look quite a ways over, away from Ursula, then across the King, another large throne, and invisible me, to see Amelia and fall in love. We were caught in the harp string that thrummed between them. Even as he brushed his lips over Ursula's lean brown hand, strong from sword practice, Hugh's eyes arrowed to Amelia, his head following with a snap.

The click reverberated through the foundation of our world.

Amelia gasped and clutched my hand.

I knew then we were in for it.

"Absolutely not!" Our father, in full king mode, stormed about his private office. We three stood in a row before his desk, Amelia still holding my hand as if she were the wounded party.

Tears ran down her cheeks, likely more for Ursula's pain than for her own heartbreak. "I cannot approve a marriage between Amelia and Hugh of Avonlidgh. Ursula—how can you suggest it? He's *your* betrothed!"

"You would have me wed a man who longs in his heart for another?" Ursula's face was composed, her profile clean and sharp, her clear eyes staring down our father. "You'd consign me to a fate of waking every morning to a husband who doesn't love me? To watching a beloved sister pine for the man I took from her? My solution offers happiness to two people, while yours condemns three people to lifelong misery."

"Love is a myth trumped up to make people feel better about themselves." King Uorsin leaned his hands on his desk, returning Ursula's challenge with his own hawkish gaze. "I don't believe in it and neither should you."

"It's irrelevant at this point." With an impatient sigh, Ursula pushed past me and laid her hands on Amelia's shaking shoulders. "Look at her, Father."

He did. Grave, King Uorsin examined his youngest. His favorite. We all knew it. Even with her face crumpled in sorrow, Amelia looked lovelier than the orchids in the hothouse.

"I'm so sorry," she gasped. "I can go away. I could go to Glorianna's temple—become one of the White Sisters."

I couldn't feel my fingers, she gripped my hand so hard.

Father raised his eyebrows. "You'd go study with the priests and priestesses of Glorianna? Take their vow of silence?"

"Yes." Amelia firmed her soft lips. "I will. It's just this face. Once he doesn't see me, Hugh will love Ursula as is meant, and . . ."

"No."

They all looked surprised that I spoke. I guess I tended not to. Frankly, with both Father and Ursula in the room, I seldom needed to—or *could*—slide a word between their fencing barbs, even if I had something to say. On the rare occasions I did, our father would give me that look, full of some unnamed distaste.

"No," I repeated, tasting the word, surprised at my own

certainty—and at the sudden pinprick headache. "Ursula is right. Rational or not, whatever 'it' is—love, infatuation, lust—it's done. Pairing either of them with anyone else would be an exercise in futility. This is how it will be."

Even Amelia's tears stopped while they all considered me. I nearly checked my shoulder to see if I'd sprouted a second head.

The King opened his mouth to say something, reconsidered, and shook his head. He sat. Turned away from the sight of me to Ursula. "What of the alliance with Avonlidgh? The whole point was to throw Old Erich a bone, so he'll stop his plotting."

"Amelia is a Princess of the Realm—she can seal the alliance."

"Erich wants his son—Avonlidgh's heir—on a throne, not married to a third child."

"His son would never sit on the throne as High King, even if he married me."

"Erich doesn't know that."

"Better to disappoint him now. His heir married to the most beautiful woman in the Twelve Kingdoms might please him and the people of Avonlidgh sufficiently."

"Poems and songs aren't power."

"Power isn't the chair you sit in."

Amelia and I stepped back, fading behind Ursula as she and our father engaged in their familiar back-and-forth. They could argue each other into the floor and frequently did, sitting at the high table into the wee hours, drinking wine and debating politics.

Some less discreet courtiers whispered that my father need never remarry because Ursula made a better queen than any other woman out there—and was the only woman likely to put up with him, despite his many, very temporary lovers. Watching Ursula delight in the debate over what Erich of Avonlidgh might or might not do with his wayward son, I understood that no man could match our father for her.

"This is serendipity, My Lord King," Ursula insisted, stabbing the polished wood of his desk with a pointed finger. Still in her rose-colored court gown, made of brushed silk in the hopes that it would soften her sharp edges, she should have looked silly. Instead, she burned with magnificence. "Let Hugh and Amelia marry. Make it splendid. Commission an official *Ode to True Love*. We have our alliance. Old Erich will have something to chew on besides you. Hugh and Amelia get to be together. The people get to feel good about what a happy world we live in."

"And you, my heir?"

Ursula smiled in a firm line. "I will decide for myself."

The Royal Wedding was a magnificent event—it's in the history books, too. Pretty much everyone in the Twelve Kingdoms took that entire seven-day off. It was the first Royal Wedding in the High King's family, since Uorsin and our mother had married before he consolidated the Twelve Kingdoms and established his seat at Castle Ordnung in Mohraya. Besides, a party is a party.

The wedding also coincided with Glorianna's Feast Day in the spring, which made the temple happy, as they'd always regarded Amelia as their own.

Father, determined to dissolve any hints that this might not be the wedding originally planned, threw treasure at the event. Delegations scoured the corners of the Twelve Kingdoms for the finest of everything. We wore nothing but velvet for the entire week—over-the-top even for the High King's family.

Really, it all went blissfully. Flags, ribbons, trumpets. The horses smelled of roses and the goats of jasmine.

Amelia, of course, looked spectacularly lovely. Hugh nearly fell over himself when he saw her in all that white lace that a thousand women had crumpled their fingers to make, night after night. Ursula and I waited with our father and King Erich of Avonlidgh on the raised dais in Glorianna's grand temple, which the High King had built along with Ordnung. Amelia's ladies escorted her through the thronging crowd on either side of the aisle. Like little pastel fairies, they bustled about her, protecting the priceless lace that snagged on the least little thing. Ursula and I would not attend Amelia for this ceremony, King Uorsin decreed, to celebrate that Hugh and Amelia created a new era between them.

Ursula said that he sought to save our dignity. We might watch our baby sister wed before us, but at least we didn't have to trail behind her down the aisle. Small mercies.

I doubted that was Uorsin's motivation, however; rather he wanted to keep me out of sight as much as possible. Which was fine by me. Though Ursula brought it up again, later in the summer, when I mentioned how lovely the wedding had been.

"As if we hadn't figured out we've always been in little Amelia's shadow," Ursula observed, taking a break to examine her sword—and giving me a chance to catch my breath. After years of trying to teach me to be a fighter, she'd given up on nagging me to spend more time in the practice yard and settled on weekly sessions to make me reasonably capable. Instead of getting better at it as I grew older, I seemed to do worse. Where Ursula was all strength and speed, I was a clumsy mess. But then, I just needed to keep myself from getting killed before a bodyguard could save me.

"You could never be in anyone's shadow," I told her, admiring the complicated parry, turn, and thrust she executed in the air, as if she danced with her sword.

She turned her gaze on me. Her nose might be too hawkish for beauty, her jaw too like Father's, but those steel-gray eyes looked silver in some lights, keen as the edge of a blade.

"Whereas you're twice shaded, Andi—is that what you think?"

I shrugged, sliding my sword into the ratty leather sheath, since it seemed Ursula had finished tormenting me for the day. "I don't try to fool myself, Ursula. Amelia might be lovely, but you are . . ." I paused.

"Trying to choose an appropriate word?"

I wrinkled my nose at her. "So many to choose from. No, I was going to say 'powerful,' but that's not right. Not yet. You have a way of mastering everything and making it fall into place for you, Ursula. I think you'll be possibly the best monarch we've ever had."

"Faint praise for Father."

I shook my head. "No—Father brought lasting peace to the Twelve Kingdoms. He will always loom large in history, the first High King. You, though—" I squinted at Ursula, who watched me with a curious look on her tanned face. The sun blazed behind her, hot and bright, starting a headache behind my eyes. "Something tells me your reign will be extraordinary."

The word fell between us, sizzling with all the implications of good and bad it carried.

"Father expects me to take his throne." Ursula felt her way through the words. "Are you saying my task won't be easy, despite his groundwork?"

I laughed, trying to soften the harsh shadows gathering around her thin lips. "We're only talking. I don't know what the future holds."

"I wonder." Ursula missed very little. Just by looking, she seemed to dig my secrets out of me. As if I had any. Still, I turned away from the uncomfortable stare and stripped off my protective gloves. If I hurried, I might have time for a ride before afternoon court, which would no doubt be more complaints about crops failing and arguments over which of the kingdoms should have to assist the others. Riding my horse, Fiona, was both my joy and my refuge.

On horseback, I never felt that weakness in my limbs, the odd, shooting pains. Away from court, I escaped the strange looks or, worse, the way most people seemed to look right through me.

"When you were born, Mother said you belonged to Moranu—did you know that?"

I shook my head. Our mother had died when I was but five, and I remembered only bits and pieces about her. No one ever spoke of her, not if they wanted to avoid angering Uorsin. Which, of course, everyone did.

"They say Moranu's priestesses can see the future, is my point," she continued.

"You mean, the ones forbidden to enter Ordnung? You know full well that none are to worship Moranu or Danu. I'm surprised you even know that."

"Do you know why I stopped nagging you to practice your sword skills?"

"Because I'm hopeless?" I quipped, but she didn't smile back.

"That's the thing, Andi." She pointed her sword at me. "You're not hopeless. You could learn if you wished, just as you could be as lovely as Amelia if you ever stepped out of the background. I think you like our shadows, because they let you hide."

A frisson ran through me, something dark, with an edge of flame, the kind of hot that leaves you shivering.

"Not much to hide here," I tossed at her, letting the foreboding roll off me and spreading my arms to indicate my shabby working leathers. "Unremarkable me is all you get."

Ursula lowered the point of her sword, slid it into its sheath with a hiss.

"We'll see, won't we?"

After that, the princes came courting Ursula. Ever hopeful, they made their plays for power. When she turned them away, a few turned their intentions toward me. It amused me, to watch them realign their courtly praises and scramble to find ways to praise my beauty, my intelligence, my courage—none of which were in evidence. I tried to be pleasant, especially when Ursula sentenced me to ten laps around the stables for any time she caught me rolling my eyes.

Somehow she managed to be kind and firm to the hopefuls, sending them packing with smiles on their faces. Before much longer, the supply thinned, then trickled off altogether. They called Ursula the Sword Princess, and some of the pub songs wickedly suggested that her blade satisfied her at night better than any man could.

When an impertinent minstrel sang one of the ditties for us, late one night after dinner and after Father had retired, Ursula simply laughed and acknowledged it could be true. She stroked her sword, resting in its formal jeweled sheath on the table, her fingers brushing the cabochon topaz in the hilt.

"My lover," she mused. "It certainly gives me all I could wish—companionship, protection, an edge over the competition."

The minstrel toasted her and strummed a few lines.

"And what do they sing of Andi?" Ursula refilled my goblet with dark-red wine.

The minstrel glanced at me as if he'd forgotten I was there. Likely he had.

I smiled at him, one of Amelia's sweet expressions to show him I didn't expect to be noticed. I was accustomed to falling through the cracks.

"That's mean, Ursula," I stepped in while the poor man stammered. "I've never done anything to merit a song and you know it. Our minstrels need more inspiration than I provide."

He plucked a few strings on the lap harp, making that liquid sound, water running over rounded pebbles, a horse clipping lightly along a mountain trail. His blue eyes studied me while his fingers flickered in the firelight.

"Forgive me, Princess Andromeda"—he bowed his head to me—"but it occurs to me that those who are overlooked are like the waters of our deep mountain lakes. They seem only to reflect what's around them, but in the depths lurk the great mysteries."

"Sea monsters?" I replied with a laugh, imitating one of Amelia's delicate shudders. Hopefully that covered my flinching at his use of my full name. Only my mother had ever used the whole ungainly thing. It both annoyed me and picked at the scar over my old, aching sense of loss.

"Ah, but Mohraya has no seacoast. Let me sing you a song of the ocean, then. If it pleases you. Of lost treasure. Or paradise." With that he launched into a winding ballad I'd never heard, of a land with turquoise waters and white cliffs, where fish fly in the air and birds swim in the waters, bringing back pearls to nestle in the petals of tropical flowers. And lovers walk hand in hand along the shimmering sands.

Ursula smiled, her face smoothing into relaxation, and closed her eyes to listen.

The song stuck with me.

Silly, I know. Still, there's something about a handsome young man singing a song just for you. Or that you can pretend is just for you. It creates this nostalgia for love you've never experienced. I know you can't be nostalgic for something that hasn't happened, yet I felt it. As if I already loved someone and he was out there somewhere, moving around in the world. Someone who would see me for me and not as the space between my sisters.

The sense of searching drove me to longer rambles, exploring trails I hadn't ridden before in the forested foothills that rose behind Castle Ordnung.

Technically that land was out of bounds to me, and probably was outside the boundaries of Mohraya at some point. The boundary with the Wild Lands wasn't clear. Very few people lived there, mostly hunters, trappers, and hermits. The Wild Lands were forbidden, the warnings laced with tales of roving demonic creatures. Restless, driven by a need to see more, I skirted those boundaries, pushed them.

In all truth, Fiona and I had been riding out farther west each day since the wedding. I missed Amelia and her happy presence.

In the quiet of my heart, I could admit I envied her. Hugh had been kind even to me. He would cherish our Amelia as she should be. As she deserved to be, our little motherless sister. But the envy worked on me, and I found myself wishing that people—that our father—looked on me with admiration. That Hugh had seen me and fallen in love.

These were ugly feelings to have, and they plagued me.

The farther I rode from Ordnung, though, the more the dark thoughts dissipated, and the more right I felt. So I went farther than I should have, had anyone known. Sometimes too far for me to easily make it back before I was expected, and we would return in a headlong rush, racing against disapproval.

That day, moody with the song, I rode farther than ever. Fiona's hooves tapped along the trail in a cadence that echoed the minstrel's song.

> *Under the waves, under the water*
> *All the days of his life he sought her.*
> *Mermaids danced in blue coral ballrooms*
> *While she watched from the dark of the sea.*

The longing in it made me a little teary, and I shook my head briskly at myself, nudging Fiona into a canter. We'd reached the top of a hill we'd never before climbed, finally emerging from the close, shadowed woods. A high meadow, filled with waist-high grass the color of green apples, lay before us in unspoiled splendor. With a snort of horse-joy, Fiona leapt under me, racing across the grassy bowl that curved up to the cloudless sky.

A laugh tore from me, even as my hair escaped its coils, whipping free behind me like Fiona's pearly white mane lashing my face.

This.

This was real. The smell of the air, a hint of snow sliding down from the high peaks, promising winter to come after glorious summer. It thrummed through me, filled me. I sank into the solid muscle of the horse, savoring her sleek strength. I didn't need more than this. Formless longings meant nothing.

Then Fiona screamed.

I heard it after we were already falling. I fell with her, tumbling to the grass—not soft, but brutally hard under the bright dressing. Fiona's great supple weight rolled over me, crushing my breath. Long practice had me kicking free, so her ungainly lunging to right herself left me behind, grateful not to be dragged by my foot as she galloped out of sight.

My lungs struggled against paralysis, grasping at the bits of air they could drag in. Knife-like pangs shot through my muscles. The image in my head throbbed with stark shock.

A man, standing there with a pack of dogs, in the fold of a wallow. Hounds bigger than wolves. No wonder Fiona had shied and lost her footing.

They would be on me in a moment.

A man with dogs where they shouldn't be was never a good thing. As far as I'd gone, I was surely still in Mohraya, where Uorsin owned all hunting rights. And my sword still strapped to the saddle, racing off to nowhere. Only my little dagger remained, in the sheath on my belt. If I survived this, Ursula would kill me.

The hissing grasses as he strode toward me sent panic through my veins. Gasping, forcing my rib cage to flex, I struggled to my hands and knees.

"Should you move just yet?" inquired a low voice.

The air burned like fire. I looked up through the dark tangle of my hair. He stood a short distance away, black leathers, black cloak. Seven wolfhounds ringed him, sitting on their haunches, an avid audience with uncannily blue eyes.

"I'm fine," I managed to say evenly, thinking of the times Ursula had knocked me with the flat of her blade and taunted me until I stood. Of course, she hadn't done that in some time, since it took me so long to get up again. "You startled my horse."

And you shouldn't be on King's Land.

I didn't dare say that, though. Because I shouldn't be on King's

Land either, unless I came from the royal family, and he didn't need to know I was Uorsin's relation.

"Yes," the man agreed, dark eyes steady. "Do you need assistance standing?"

Definitely not. The man shared the lean, hungry, and lethal look of the wolfhounds, even with his careful distance. I wiggled my knees and ankles. They felt okay. Hopefully nothing was so damaged as to make me stagger when I stood. The cold congealing in my stomach told me I couldn't afford to appear at all weak.

I stood, slowly, brushing grass off my riding pants as I unfolded, to give myself time to test my weight. Nothing gave way, thank Moranu.

"I'm fine," I repeated, returning his assessing stare, deliberately slowing my heaving lungs.

One of the wolfhounds sniffed the air in my direction, raising its russet ears. It growled softly. A hushed word from the man settled it.

"Not often one finds a princess unattended in the wilderness," the man observed, as if commenting on the weather, but his face burned with an unholy, acquisitive light.

I scoffed. "I wish! I imagine those royal brats have soft lives of silks and candies. No, I'm only hunting rabbits for my family."

He took a step toward me, flattening his hand to signal the dogs to stay. I steeled myself not to step back. Predators always became more dangerous when presented with a chase. Two horse lengths between us still gave me room. To do what, I didn't know. I could never outrun those hounds.

"Lies don't become you, Princess." His gaze drilled into me, evaluating, calculating. "Now, which one are you? Not Ursula the heir, I don't think. Rumor says she looks more like a man than a woman."

"No closer," I commanded.

"Or what, Princess Amelia—you'll scream?" He held out questioning hands to the empty sky, but he stopped closing on me.

"I'm not Amelia," I said on reflex. Idiot. I closed my hand

over the hilt of my dagger and drew it. "And I was thinking more of using this."

He smiled, eyes glittering. A breeze wormed through the meadow, sending a wave through the grasses and lifting a strand of his long black hair, tied in a tail at the nape of his neck. He took another step closer and stopped, watching me to see what I'd do.

"You'd have to get quite close to me to use that," he purred. "Are you certain that's wise?" He flicked long fingers, and the wolfhounds stood to attention, ears and tails high, surging around him in an eager sea.

"What will happen is that you'll go your way and I'll go mine."

He took another step. One horse length.

"Even if I hadn't recognized Salena's look about you, I'd have known you for one of Uorsin's by the way you give orders. I am not, however, one of your subjects."

At the sound of my mother's name, I lost the little breath I'd gained. The name no one spoke. This wasn't bad. This was catastrophic.

"Who are you, then?" I gritted out, my thighs tensing. One more step and I'd be within his reach. His looked to be a good six inches longer than mine. I was outmatched in every way. I'd have to get inside and do damage quickly, before he could inflict any on me. "Besides a bully and a trespasser."

He raised a defined eyebrow at my words, taking a half step. Barely outside the boundary where I'd have to act, which he had to know. He moved like a warrior and used the pressure to discomfit me. He stared me down, the hounds shifting restlessly behind him. From this close I could see his eyes weren't black at all, but very dark blue.

"Is that how you name me?"

"Care to argue the points?"

"If you're not Ursula and not Amelia, then you're the other one."

"Flawless logic."

He grinned unexpectedly, a flash of white teeth unsettlingly like his hounds'.

"What shall I do, then, with this amazing piece of serendipity, Princess Andromeda?"

"The wise trespasser would let me leave in peace. The foolish bully might find himself gutted like a pig."

He shifted, leaning his body a hair closer. I sank into my feet, shifting my weight into my back leg, which gave me a bit of space and made me ready to spring. Big men seldom expected a smaller opponent to jump in close, but it was the only choice for someone like me, who couldn't afford to stay at the devastating perimeter of a larger opponent's weapon. I kept my gaze on the center of his chest, where any movement would start.

"Ah. Or, since I am already judged and condemned, perhaps I'll trespass just a bit more for my trouble. If this is the opportunity I think it is, we can't afford to waste it."

Don't think. Watch for the window of opportunity.

His hand snapped out to grab me—Moranu, he was fast—but I confused him by moving in. *Men always try to grab,* Ursula's voice reminded me. *It gives you time to strike if you keep your head.*

Using my momentum and holding the knife pointed down in my fist so the power of my shoulder drove it, I sliced the blade across his cheek, whipped the arc around into a circle, and slammed the hilt against his temple. My sleeve tore in his grip as I sprang away, and he dropped to his knees, clutching his face, bright blood sliding through his fingers.

The dogs ringed him, anxious, forming a suspicious guard. I backed away, reestablishing distance. Careful to test my footing. *Don't you dare trip, or those dogs will be on you in a flash.* I'd never be able to fight them off.

The man was woozy from the blow. Ursula would have knocked him unconscious. His dark eyes found me, blazing.

"Point to you, Andromeda."

"This isn't a game." I kept stepping back. My arm stung. "I'm leaving. Keep your dogs to you or I'll kill them."

"Brave words." He climbed to his feet, unsteady, but intention coiled through him. "But you've only made the test easier."

Blood laced down his cheek and over his throat. Three horse lengths. Where was Fiona? I'd trained her to return to me if I got unseated. If I survived this, I'd have to teach her to come to me even if there were wolfhounds involved.

"Now that I have you, I cannot let you go until I know for sure if you have the mark."

I pointed the knife at him. "You do not have me. And you never will."

"Ah, lovely Andromeda—I think you're mistaken in that." A wry smile twisted the bloodied side of his face. "You surprised me with your little sticker, I'll admit, but I dare you to come that close to me again."

His face darkening, he strode toward me. One pace, two. Too fast.

I panicked.

I ran.

Run. Run for the forest.

The grasses tore at my hips and thighs, whipping my arms with stinging tips. My heart gasped for blood, the cool mountain air searing into me and providing no sustenance. I wasn't a strong runner, but I prayed to Moranu that the blow and blood loss would be enough to slow him.

Just let me reach the forest.

A thundering weight hit my back, throwing me down into the green cave of grass, my body shuddering with the second impact in only a few minutes. I held on to the dagger, though, striking out wildly at the man, who tried to pin me, a howl screaming out of me, something animal, feral.

He ducked the blade and grabbed my wrist in an iron grip, holding it to the ground. I struggled to get a knee up to his man-jewels, but he pinned me under heavy thighs. With my left hand I stabbed stiff fingers for his eyes. He caught that hand, too, closing strong fingers over mine, crushing them together and pushing my hand down tight against my breast.

I screamed. Fought.

To no avail.

After forever and a few minutes, plus a massive effort of will, I stilled myself. Time to rethink strategy. My thoughts, shattered into pieces, began to fit together again.

"Finished?" the man pressing me to the ground asked. He sounded grimly amused. Probably feeling triumphant. I could use that.

I opened the eyes I'd held squinched shut since my fall. His face loomed a hand's width over mine, the knife cut I'd given him welling blood that smeared down his face and neck, contrasting with those fierce midnight-blue eyes. His black hair had come loose from its tie during the struggle, and now it rained down around us.

"Let me go," I whimpered, wriggling against him in what I hoped was an enticing way. It worked in that I managed to reposition a knee to the inside of his thigh. I'd likely get only one chance at that, but even a glancing blow might distract him long enough for me to plant the dagger in one of those blazing blue eyes.

Like you should have done in the first place.

His dark lips twisted in that half smile. "Nice. But you don't play the damsel in distress all that well. And if you go for my balls, I'll break your wrist."

"If you plan to rape me, you'll have to get them out at some point—I'm sure I can find a way to injure the precious things," I snapped back.

He blinked at me, his face curiously still.

"Rape?" He examined me, as if the thought hadn't occurred to him, his gaze lingering on my lips. "Isn't that rather prosaic?"

"I've found most men are."

"Have you?"

I didn't answer. It had sounded good.

"You mistake me, Andromeda. My plans reach farther than a bit of a tumble in the meadow, enticing as the thought might be. Our current position is simply serendipity."

His words chilled me in a way that the prospect of attempted rape hadn't. Rape I could fight and likely win, if I kept my head.

"You'll have a hard time taking me hostage," I sneered with deliberate contempt, "unless your pack of mutts will help you drag me off to whatever prison you have in mind."

The right side of his mouth lifted in a half smile, creasing the blood.

"It's true. I hadn't expected this opportunity and I'm ill prepared. I hadn't thought that—" He sighed. Amused chagrin crossed his face. "Is it too late to woo you into coming with me willingly?"

I laughed, the sound harsh as the cawing of a crow.

"Do I look feebleminded to you?"

He examined me, considering. "Foolish, perhaps. Certainly overconfident. But no"—he sighed again, as if pressed by a great weight—"not likely to trust me. Yet."

"Trust!" I spat. "You're the feebleminded one."

"Look at me, Andromeda," he commanded, sapphire glints hypnotic in his dark eyes. "I've been looking for you. Don't you recognize anything about me?"

I couldn't help but look. The press of his hard body, the searing heat of his skin, the eyes like midnight and twilight wrapped together—they reminded me of something. A wolf howled, lonely, my mind. The ocean surged, swirling blue depths sinking into deepest black.

> *Under the waves, deep under the sea*
> *Sands dissolve the cicatrix of thee.*
> *Cobalt crabs pluck at deep-frozen lies*
> *Eating the corpses of what she denies.*

The images, as with the words of the song, ate at me, blurring the edges of who I knew myself to be. Salena. He'd mentioned my mother. What did that mean?

"I've never seen you before in my life," I whispered. It felt like a lie.

Was that Fiona's nicker in the background? I seized on that. My horse, my life at Ordnung. That was true. Real.

"No. But I thought you would know me anyway."

"You didn't recognize me—you thought I was both of my sisters."

"Did Salena teach you nothing?"

"My mother died," I snapped.

"Believe me, I know. Her death caused a number of problems."

"I'm so sorry that the greatest tragedy in my life gave you annoyance."

The half smile twisted his lips. "More than you can conceive. I'll make you a deal. Give me a kiss."

I didn't reply. My dagger hand had gone numb, but a flex of my fingers reassured me I still grasped the hilt.

"One kiss," he repeated, "and if you still don't want to come with me, if nothing happens, I'll let you go."

Seemed like a bad bargain on his part, but I wouldn't point that out.

"Fine."

"No arguing?"

I shrugged as best I could. "Whatever gets me closer to freedom. Either you'll keep your word or you won't. Either way, I've given up nothing of importance. And I seriously doubt your kisses are that spectacular."

"No?" he murmured, lowering his head. "We'll see."

Mesmerized, I watched his lips descend to mine. The blood still pulsed, oozing out of the cut, fresh and bright over the dried tracks. Despite his nonchalant words, I felt the tension shimmering through him. This was the moment Ursula had described, when lust clouds one's thinking.

"Blood," I murmured the moment before he touched me.

"What?" His voice rumbled through me, soft, gravelly.

"You have blood on your lips."

"I know. That's the point." With a certain grim determination, his mouth fastened on mine, though I tried to turn my head at the last moment. A bright flash of pain and I realized he'd bitten my lip.

"Thrice-damn you!" I tore my mouth away, struggling.

"Watch," he ordered, holding me still.

On his lips, the blood seemed to shimmer, then move of its own accord. A tiny bird formed, darkening from the scarlet of fresh blood to black.

Then flew away.

Aghast, enthralled, horrified, I watched it go, an impossible pinprick disappearing against the sky.

"That's impossible," I whispered.

The man's joyful and triumphant smile crashed into disappointment at my words. "You really know nothing at all."

"Then let me up and you can explain."

Resigned, he nodded and moved just enough to loosen the grip on my hand.

Not my dagger hand, but the one between us that he'd pressed to my bosom. I pushed my fist through his hand, up in a short jab to his larynx. He jerked back, howling, and his blood spattered my face, warm salt on my tongue. I pulled my dagger hand free and plunged the knife into the only target I could reach, his muscular shoulder.

The knife stuck and I had no time to tug it free. I yanked away. He grabbed my ankle and I stomped down on his wrist with my boot and ran.

Straight to Fiona, who waited right there, thank Moranu.

The dogs gave chase and I couldn't separate their excited

barks from the man's angry howls. I heard him ordering them to stand down, as if they'd understand his words.

I scrambled onto Fiona, expecting the sharp bite of the hounds at any moment, but they only spun around my horse, sniffing and yipping. I dared to look for the man.

He knelt in the grass, rage, pain, and blood distorting his fine-boned face, black hair a wild cape around him.

"This isn't over between us, Andromeda," he punched the words at me through his pained throat. "Don't think for a moment that you've escaped me. I am your fate. *I have the taste of your blood now.* Run now if you're afraid, but I will come after you. I will always find you. You will be mine."

"Never!" I shouted at him.

"Always."

It sounded like a vow.

2

I kicked Fiona into a gallop, tearing back across the meadow, leaving that man behind to his threats and his dogs. My mind whirled in a windstorm of reaction, my thoughts racing as fast as the trees whipping by, yet making no more sense, as if it all moved too fast for me to get a good look.

After a time, my heart and lungs slowed their panicked pumping. Fiona read my gradual relaxation and slowed our wild flight. My stomach hurt, I noticed, cold and congealed, and a headache throbbed in my temples. We limped home, Fiona no doubt banged up from her sudden roll. My arm stung where the man had scratched me, but I thought I had escaped pretty much unscathed. When we drew near enough to see Ordnung's searing white towers, I dismounted and walked Fiona in, studying her gait for any sign of injury. Now my body ached in every joint. I could feel the bruises blossoming.

"What happened to you?" Ursula, wearing a court gown, came from the direction of the castle and gave me a scorching look.

"Don't you have things to do?" I muttered, unstrapping my

sword from the pommel. "Ruling kingdoms? Digging up obscure laws?"

She narrowed her eyes. "Amelia and Hugh have arrived for a visit. When I heard you'd been spotted riding in, I thought you'd want to know. You should keep your sword on you, not strapped to your saddle. Especially if you're going to take off for Glorianna knows where without a bodyguard."

"Yes, Your Highness."

"Nice attitude—what happened?"

"Nothing. Fiona took a fall, is all."

"So I gathered from the grass all over both of you. That's not what's bothering you."

I shrugged, careful to hide my wince at the shooting pain across my shoulders. "What—you're the only one who gets to be crabby around here?"

"You should be thrilled that Amelia and Hugh are here and you barely acknowledged it." She drew a long stem of that acid-green grass from my hair and examined it thoughtfully. Bit it lightly. Settled a hard gaze on me. "Where in—or outside—Mohraya did you get to? And is that blood on you?"

"I never left King's Land, Highness," I snapped. "I know my boundaries." More or less.

"That means nothing and you know it. You went over the foothills, toward the Wild Lands."

"Which is still King's Land."

A young groom started to lead Fiona away. "Check her over, would you, Jemmy? She took a bit of a fall."

He nodded at me, eyes wide.

Ursula held up the blade of grass, blocking my way, gray eyes hard as steel. "I've seen this while hunting. It's at the border of the Wild Lands, probably over. Have you lost your precious mind?"

"Clearly *you* have been there."

"With about fifty other people, not gallivanting by myself!"

"I need to get cleaned up. I cut myself up a bit—that's the

blood." I shouldered past her and she grabbed my arm. I hissed at the pain. Ursula softened her grip and flipped up the torn fabric.

"That's a bruise and scratch from a hand—not a fall. And you have a swollen lip." Her voice sounded clinical, but I could see the fury building in her. "You're going to tell me what happened right now, Andi. Or I'll tell the High King and let him drag it out of you."

Tears unexpectedly pricked my eyes. Maybe it was her fierce concern. Or the aftereffects of the whole incident. I felt as young and fragile as Ursula saw me. Her face softened instantly when she saw me crumple.

"Oh, honey . . ."

She started to embrace me, but I put up a hand to stop her.

"Please, no, Ursula. I don't want to get into it now. I need to take a bath. I want to see Hugh and Amelia. We can talk later."

"I need to know if you—or any of our territory—is in immediate danger."

The man's severe face and dark words scattered through my mind. Long-range plans, he'd said. "I don't think so." I hesitated, then added, "Not yet, anyway."

Ursula cursed, her hand twitching for her sword. She tossed the blade of grass aside and pointed at me. "Tomorrow I'm taking a scout team up there. You're coming with us and you'll tell me every single detail."

"And if I'm too sore to ride?"

"Serves you right for being so careless. I know you don't pay much attention to such things, Andi, but you're no longer a tomboy who can ride everywhere. You're a pretty young woman and second in line for the throne. You dangled yourself like a juicy snack in front of a pack of wolves, endangering yourself and your kingdom today. Trust me—my methods of punishment won't come near what Uorsin will do when he hears of this. And don't mistake me. Once I've dragged everything out of you, then you get to tell him."

She spun on her heel, her strides too long for the gown, spine a rigid line up to her tightly braided hair, and left me in her dust.

Lady Gaignor waited for me in my chamber, already marshaling the maidservants to fill the bath and lay out a gown.

"Her Highness Princess Ursula sent word you'd need help." She held out a basket of liniments by way of explanation. "Bad fall? Is Fiona okay?"

"She seems fine, Violet." I smiled at her. "If you get a chance to sneak off later, would you check with the grooms about her?"

"I'll look her over myself, if you like, Princess."

"I'd be grateful."

The hot bath settled me considerably. Between that and Gaignor's competent massage with the liniments, I felt more like my usual self. She also shared the gossip that had arrived along with the Avonlidgh entourage.

"King Erich is giving them Castle Windroven? That's a surprise."

Gaignor shook her head in my peripheral vision while the maidservant coiled my hair into an elaborate pile. "No, it isn't. It's tradition for Avonlidgh's heirs to be born at Windroven. King Erich is clearly expecting grandchildren, and soon."

I tried to listen, but my mind found its own way to the man in the meadow. Did Ursula think he represented some kind of incursion from the Wild Lands? Now that I thought about it, she hadn't been terribly surprised. Angry, yes. With me and more. Already more sentries were stationed at the castle's outer perimeters—so quickly and in such an obvious way that I had spotted them from my window before I ever got into the bath.

I watched myself in the mirror, not seeing the woman Ursula had described. She wasn't given to exaggeration, but I had nothing like Amelia's beauty. Instead of her winsome heart-shaped face, mine was my mother's oval, my chin too round and soft. I shared Ursula's gray eyes, but where Ursula's shone clear like steel, and Amelia, of course, had eyes like pure violet twilight, mine were as dark and muddy as storm clouds. My hair looked fine spruced up like this, but the color, neither Ursula's rich auburn nor Amelia's strawberry-gold, was simply dark brown, or rusty black, as one of our nurses used to say. I possessed neither Amelia's delicate dancer's body nor Ursula's athletic physique. Sometimes I worried that this advancing weakness meant that I had some terrible disease. Rotten in the middle. No one had ever said I resembled our mother. I couldn't recall much of her face, after all these years.

The borders of my mind blurred again, as they had when those feral blue eyes had captured me. Once he knew I wasn't my sisters, he'd looked at me differently—and not in a bad way. As if I was someone—not just the space between them.

"So we're all waiting to see if Hugh is carrying a message from King Erich or if this is purely a social call."

"Oh?" I answered Gaignor, scrambling to catch the words I'd forgotten to listen to.

She wrinkled her nose at me. "I don't know why I bother with you, Princess."

"I don't either," I sighed. "I don't know why anyone does." Melancholy crept in with the headache. I could lie down and sleep the entire afternoon.

Gaignor patted my arm. "It's the fall. You'll perk up when you see your sister."

Amelia squealed when she saw me. We weren't in formal court, since Hugh was family now. Still, Ursula frowned at Amelia's lack of decorum when she leapt out of her chair and ran to me with her happy laugh. Or maybe Ursula just hadn't stopped frowning. Amelia could usually get away with most anything.

"Andi!" Amelia chirped, hugging me. I swallowed the flinch.

"I've missed you so. How dare you be out riding when we arrived!"

I tugged one of her tumbling locks of shining hair. "When you grow up someday, you can send a note ahead."

She pouted. "I wanted it to be a surprise. And darling Hugh was kind enough to indulge his spoiled wife." She looked over her shoulder, reaching a hand for Hugh, who waited a respectful distance back.

He stepped up, took her slim hand, and kissed it. "You're a delight to indulge, my love." He bowed to me then. "Princess Andi, you're looking lovelier than ever."

"And you, Prince Hugh, are a dreadful liar and likely the most charming man in the Twelve Kingdoms."

He chuckled and winked at me, his summer-sky eyes friendly, warm, without calculation or shadows. Taking my hands, he kissed my cheek. He smelled like vanilla and sunshine. Amelia beamed at us.

"Princess Ursula mentioned you'd taken a fall—you're unharmed, pray Glorianna?"

A little knot formed between Amelia's delicate eyebrows and she pushed her finger against it, so she wouldn't get wrinkles. "I didn't hear that! Oh, I wish you wouldn't ride that horse all over beyond."

"She won't, anymore," Uorsin rumbled.

My stomach dropped. Father strode into the room and settled himself on his throne, Ursula beside him. Twin pairs of steely eyes observed our little reunion. It did not bode well at all that Father had announced such a thing in open court, informal or no. Our attendants provided ample witnesses that the King had instructed me. In one sentence he'd robbed me of my freedom and any opportunity to present my case.

I curtsied to him, low and formal, my sore muscles protesting. "It's my pleasure to serve the King's wishes."

He nodded and glanced away, avoiding looking at me, as always. I took the opportunity to flash Ursula a mean look. She only raised her eyebrows at me in bland accusation. How could she think I brought this on myself? Yes, I'd ventured too far, but there was no way to know that man would be up there . . .

Amelia slipped her arm through mine. "Don't worry—I'm sure he doesn't mean for always. Come, let's eat and I'll tell you how wonderful Hugh is."

"Yes." I smiled to make her happy, pretending everything would be okay. "I hear you two are getting a castle all your own."

"With a suite set aside especially for my favorite little sister," Hugh assured me with an easy grin, offering his arm on my other side. Sympathy shadowed his smile. Hugh would understand about losing freedom. He leaned to whisper in my ear, "When you come visit, you can ride all you like."

"Now that my free-roaming daughter has seen fit to join us," Uorsin announced, "we shall retire to enjoy a feast celebrating the first postnuptial visit of my beloved Princess Amelia and her noble husband and treasured liege, Prince Hugh."

Smiles and clapping all around. Not for me, sandwiched between the golden couple. Amelia whispered in my ear, "What on earth happened to make Father and Ursula so angry?"

Even they didn't know. I opened my mouth to tell her—

The stained-glass window of Glorianna's rose flew apart with a great crash.

A wave rippled through the room as everyone flinched from the explosion of sound, then from the rain of rose-colored glass. An enormous bird, bigger than a hawk, smaller than an eagle, so black it absorbed the sunlight, swooped around the room in a great circle. Ursula, Uorsin, Hugh, and the guards all responded like a second wave splashing back, thrusting whatever steel they possessed at the ceiling.

The bird swept another circle, turning its head to glare at us with a baleful blue eye.

Then it dropped a small cylinder at the King. A guard deflected it with his blade. Another tracked the bird's flight with the tip of his arrow. The zing of the bowstring drew a strangled cry from me. The arrow sliced through the edge of a wing. The raptor screamed in rage but recovered its flight. A single black feather wafted down in front of me, taking its time in a rocking pendulum descent, while guards called orders and ladies covered their heads and shrieked.

The feather landed at my feet, iridescent now against the white marble floor.

I thought no one saw me pick it up—their attention was so riveted on the circling bird. Several more arrows flew, embedding themselves in the priceless carved ceiling. The raptor cawed out a laughing sound and soared back out the broken window.

I turned the feather over in my hands, the rigid edge nearly as sharp as glass. Terror slid through my veins, leaving paralysis behind. Like a hunting dog, I'd run home with the bear on my heels, exposing everyone I loved to the predator. *Silly*. I tried to calm myself. *He knew who everyone was already. This isn't necessarily to do with what happened today.* Still, the back of my neck crawled, as if his intense midnight gaze still focused on me.

Not knowing what else to do with it, I tucked the feather in a pocket of my dress.

Several of Uorsin's advisers clustered around the tube. One donned metal gloves and carefully took up the tube, calling out that it held a message. Amelia slipped her little hand in mine, lacing our fingers together. Hugh stood with Ursula and Uorsin, forming a loose semicircle of our protectors, overseeing the advisers while they argued about magical taints.

"Do they really believe it could hold a terrible spell?" Amelia whispered. "I thought that was only stories."

"That was no natural-born raptor," I murmured back, thinking of the tiny bird that had formed from the blood on the man's lip. "You saw it. It should never have been able to break that window. And it was . . . intelligent, somehow." A shiver ran through me and she clutched my hand tighter.

"Such a strange day," she mused. "First you, who never fall off your horse, take a bad spill, and Father is so worried he tells you not to ride anymore, and now this."

I loved her for not putting it all together right away. Ursula certainly had, judging by the flinty look she cast me over her shoulder. She had her queen face on now, so I couldn't tell if it was anger, fear, or worry that made her tap the point of her sword restlessly against the toe of her soft court slipper.

The message was placed under a glass dome and the court priest of Glorianna said prayers over it, dusting it with powdered pink rose petals. I didn't point out that Glorianna's window hadn't held much power to keep the bird out.

With a show of great care, the advisers used thin prongs to extract a parchment roll from the cylinder. My vision darkened and I realized I'd been holding my breath. My heart beat hard, like the glass-edged wings of the raptor. Derodotur, the King's senior adviser for my entire life, and for a long time before, stepped forward to read the missive.

> *Greetings, King Uorsin and Family,*
>
> *It's been many years since our realms have communicated. Indeed, though our families were once joined, an unfortunate separation has splintered us. As you well know, Uorsin, this was not the agreement.*
>
> *Therefore, I call upon you to live up to your promises and repay blood for blood. You will deliver your daughter to me, specifically, the very lovely Princess Andromeda. I had the pleasure to become acquainted with her today and was delighted to find her heritage is true. I have reason to believe my dear Andromeda will accept my offer with pleasure, and I send her my fondest regards.*
>
> *With all due respect, etc.,*
> *Rayfe*

Amelia fainted dead away.

I kind of caught her, but my own muscles would barely hold.

Fortunately, the ladies who perpetually follow us about made themselves useful and jumped in to support us both. Amelia's ladies, several of whom I didn't know and who must have come from Avonlidgh, fluttered about Amelia, fanning her with lavender-wafting handkerchiefs. The too-sweet scent turned my already-queasy stomach.

Violet Gaignor, ever practical, held my elbow like she'd steady one of her horses and handed me a cup of wine.

"Drink it," she muttered, "you're going to need it." It was a mark of her own distress that she forgot to use the honorifics. I gulped the wine gratefully, embracing the burn that warmed my frozen blood.

"Her Highness Princess Andromeda!" King Uorsin thundered. "Attend me at once."

I stumbled a bit, my body too numb to obey him and too well trained to respond to that title to refuse.

"Explain yourself." Had it bothered me that he never looked at me? This withering, contemptuous glare nearly melted my bones. This was the High King who'd carved tiny Mohraya out of the foothills, built Castle Ordnung to be the seat of the Twelve Kingdoms, and accepted tribute from the rest. I'd seen kings and battle-worn commanders wither under that glare. "Tell me what secrets you've been keeping."

"Here, Your Highness?" I gestured to the court, now full to bursting with guards and the curious.

"Perhaps you'd prefer to wait until Rayfe and all the Tala have descended to storm the castle, so you can fling open the doors for your lover." Uorsin pounded his fist on the jeweled arm of his throne. Even Ursula flinched.

"With all due respect, Your Highness." I released the teeth I'd clenched to keep from shouting back at the King. "I have no idea who Rayfe or the Tala are. I encountered a man today, yes, who tried to take me hostage. I have no idea if this is the same person."

Oh, but I did.

Ursula knew it, too, given the incredulous stare she fixed on me.

"She was too young to remember," she murmured to our father, "since you forbade mention of them after . . . *she* passed."

Uorsin stopped her with a flick of his hand. "And you chose not to report this to me."

I gritted my teeth again. "It just now happened, Your Highness. I thought to wait until we were private and—"

"You thought to betray us to the Tala!" he roared. "You were born a monster and now you show your true face before us all."

Stunned silence crushed the air out of the room. No one moved, afraid to draw the King's ire. Ursula caught my eye, stricken. Even Hugh, who'd moved to the cluster of ladies around a groggily sitting-up Amelia, stood frozen.

"If I may, Your Highness?" Derodotur stepped forward with a deep bow. "It's entirely possible the shock of the events today affected Princess Andi's constitution. Her emotional state is likely delicate and the young lady could be injured, if indeed it was Rayfe who approached her. I would be willing to work with her, question her, to find the truth of things."

Uorsin clenched his jaw, studying me like a deer strung up for skinning. "Exactly what did you do with that demon?"

What was the right answer? Ursula shook her head infinitesimally, but no to what? Would the fact that he hadn't really hurt me make me seem complicit?

"I fought him off, my King," I replied, hoping he wouldn't notice I'd ducked the question, "thanks to my sister Princess Ursula's excellent instruction. Should you see a man with a knife cut from chin to cheekbone, that's the one I met."

A flicker of a smile passed over Ursula's face. Now that I thought about it, I had done surprisingly well. In fact, that last burst of strength when I escaped him had been amazing.

"But did he kiss you, Princess?" a thready voice demanded. Lady Zevondeth, leaning on her cane of gold-wrapped oak, pushed through the circle of advisers. She thumped the cane on the marble with a crack. "Did his blood pass your lips in any way?"

"Uh, no, Lady Zevondeth," I stammered. How had she known? And why ask this? Not was I raped, but was I kissed. The blood. Mine mingling with his and that impossible bird flying away. I slid my gaze to Ursula, still impassively of no help.

"But he tried, didn't he?" She peered at me, milky eyes sharp with perception. I nearly squirmed under the relentless attention of everyone there.

"My King," Derodotur inserted.

"Yes, yes." Uorsin waved a hand at his adviser, steeled gaze never leaving me. He sighed. "I shall abide by your advice for now. Derodotur, Daughter—attend me. The rest of you can go enjoy the feast."

He heaved himself out of the throne, as if impossibly fatigued.

"My King—" Ursula started.

"No," Uorsin growled. "You shall host the feast in my stead."

She rolled her grip on her sword hilt then, seeming to remember suddenly that she still held it. Ursula sheathed her sword, bowed to the King, and set about dispensing orders to get the room cleaned up and inviting the lords and ladies to please proceed to the feast.

"With me." Uorsin strode from the room, Derodotur and I trailing in his wake.

The King quickly outpaced Derodotur's stilted steps. An old wound from the wars made one of the adviser's legs rigid. Derodotur used to tell us stories of the Great War. He had been another general's page on the battlefield, which had been always difficult for me to see in the carefully formal adviser.

With an eye to the King's back, Derodotur took my arm, something he did for balance, but it allowed him to speak quietly to me.

"Tread carefully, Princess. He is not himself at the moment. And you are not you in this story, but a game piece in someone else's. He's fighting ghosts. Don't let him make you the target."

"I don't understand." I was tired. My head pounded. That was why my voice sounded so weak.

"No. Nor were you meant to. Uorsin thought to duck this . . .

consequence, though he well knew this day would come." He flicked a glance at me from the corner of his eye. "Salena said it would be you, but then she died, and, well . . ."

The King reached his study, flung the door open, and wheeled around, impatiently waiting for us. Breaching protocol, he gestured for us to enter ahead of him. As I passed him, my father looked at me like he'd never seen me before in his life. Like he was seeing some sign of contagion in me that would spread through the kingdoms. And an avid lick of hunger lurked within him. For what? Uorsin already controlled the known world.

A little piece of me broke off under his unspoken accusation. I'd always known that I wasn't his favorite, but I hadn't thought he hated me. I had thought I was done longing for my mother. Not so. Suddenly and dreadfully, I missed her.

"Sit," he commanded and sank behind his desk. "Tell me everything. Leave no detail out. And I shall know if you are lying."

I told them the story in humiliating detail. How he pinned me, how he teased me and tried to kiss me, which had seemed like a minor point at the time. Their grim expressions said otherwise.

I didn't mention the blood bird.

"You are certain he did not actually kiss you?" the King demanded, steepling his fingers.

Since they all cared so much, I lied. "I'm certain."

"And his blood, child," Derodotur asked in a gentle tone. "You said you cut him—did any pass your lips? Or mix with yours?"

A wave of cold dread washed over me, settling in my stomach. My face felt numb, all sensation drained out of it. Both men watched me, tension high while they awaited my answer. Another lie. "No. No blood."

The King sat back, tapping his sword-calloused fingers on the arms of his chair, clearly relieved. "How many times have you met with him?"

What? "I told you, this was the first time I ever saw him."

He frowned at me.

"Your Majesty," I amended hastily, but it did nothing to alleviate the dark expression.

"You went there to meet him, then."

"No, sir."

"How did you know to go to that place at that time—have you been exchanging messages?"

"I didn't know!"

"You just happened to walk straight into his arms, by happenstance."

He made it sound ridiculous.

"Why did you ride to *that* meadow, today?"

I shrugged helplessly, at a loss to give him what he wanted. "I felt like it. I wasn't even thinking about where I was going. I was just riding along and thinking . . ." I trailed off.

He pounced. "About what?"

"Songs and poems," I replied, far more tartly than I should, but I wasn't going to own up to girlish thoughts of love and a nameless longing to these two men. Especially given what had happened.

"Uorsin," Derodotur interrupted, yet again.

The King's black glare landed on his adviser. I'd never heard Derodotur call the King by his name to his face.

"May I speak freely?"

"It appears you already feel comfortable enough to do so, Derodotur."

"I stood by your side the day you wed Salena and sealed your bargain." Derodotur raised his eyebrows, waiting for my father's curt nod. "When Princess Andromeda was born, Salena said she was the one. How Rayfe found out, I don't know, but he clearly thinks Andi knew. That means this is beyond our ken—which we thought even then."

You really know nothing at all.

"Do you have a point, Derodotur?"

"Yes, I do. It's entirely possible, and likely given the evidence, that Andi did not know and still does not know what drew her to that meeting place."

Uorsin studied me. My skin crept under the scrutiny. As if Rayfe's blood even now crawled through mine, tainting me in some horrifying, irreparable way. I gazed back at my father, wondering how to ask him to save me from it.

"There were no others with him?"

"Just the wolfhounds."

They exchanged significant looks.

"My King." Derodotur's voice was soothing. "It doesn't mean—"

"You may go, Princess," Uorsin interrupted him.

The surprise held me to my chair a moment. Apparently my interview had ended. I stood, curtsied. Neither of them said anything more. The weight of the words they needed to say to each other outside of my hearing lay heavy in the air.

"Do not leave the castle," the King added as I reached the door. "Inform Ursula that you are to have a guard and be watched at all times. Consider this a test of your obedience and loyalty. And stay away from the windows."

"Yes, my King," I replied. Inside, that little piece of me that had broken off withered up and died.

3

I slipped into the banquet hall, trying to be my usual inconspicuous self, but a hush rippled through the room, suppressing conversations that then started up a bit louder than before. With new topics that weren't me, apparently.

Holding my neck straight and face relaxed, I stopped by Ursula's chair. The arrangement echoed the throne room, so she sat three seats removed from Amelia, who had Hugh on her other side—a new addition to our lineup. For the first time, it occurred to me that if I did marry, my husband would have nowhere to sit. Likely the thought that I might wed had never occurred to anyone.

But then, the idea of the wolfish Rayfe sitting down to dinner with us carried enough absurdity as it was.

Ursula had watched me cross the room with a gimlet gaze, and I steeled myself to report my instructions to her. To my shock, she stood and embraced me. The open show of support shook me, and I clasped her gratefully.

"I apologize to you," she whispered in my ear. "Had I handled things better, it would not have gone this way."

"No, I should have gone ahead and told you what happened. I wasn't thinking that—"

"It would follow you home in such a spectacular way?"

I could hear the wry smile in her tone. It thawed me a little. "I'm to tell you to assign me a guard. That I'm to be watched at all times."

Ursula sighed and released me. She nodded, serious. "I swear that you'll be protected at all costs, my dear sister."

She said it in a carrying voice, too, and only raised her eyebrows to my rueful look. Ah, well, what's done is done. Hopefully the King wouldn't be too angry at her declaration of loyalty. Ursula beckoned to the captain of the guard, so I went to sit in my chair.

Amelia slipped her hand into mine, squeezing it, her violet eyes swimming with tears. Hugh leaned forward, giving me a nod of solemn approval. Then we all fell silent, focusing on our plates while the careful chatter of the room washed over us.

I picked at my food, having absolutely no appetite, though I hadn't eaten since breakfast. Too much had happened. I couldn't digest it all. My gorge rose and I thought I might vomit in my plate.

During most of the meal, I resisted slipping my hand in my pocket. The feather must be in there still, sharp as broken glass. It worried at me like a canker sore that you want to poke at with your tongue to see if it still hurts, even though you know it will and you'll be sorry you didn't just leave it alone.

After an interminable time, and after it became quite clear King Uorsin would not be joining us, Ursula offered a short toast to Amelia and Hugh's visit. She made no mention of the afternoon's events. There was no need.

Hopefully the feather hadn't fallen out, to lie in the hallway where a servant might pick it up and discard it. I felt the fabric of my skirt for its outline. Panic burst bright when I couldn't feel it. Gone. I'd lost the cursed thing. To be sure, I reached in. Ah, there it was.

I closed my eyes with the relief, the flooding reassurance, and a flash of a midnight gaze smiled at me with warm affection.

"Andi?" Amelia's worried voice awoke me to her hand on my shoulder. "Are you all right?"

Everyone was drifting out of the hall, Hugh and Ursula off to the side, discussing security, given how they touched their sword hilts and surveyed the broken window. My sister glanced over her shoulder, a line between her clear gray eyes. I stood, carefully extracting my hand from my pocket as I did so. As if I'd been doing something illicit. Consorting with the enemy. It had an ugly sound.

There should have been dancing for Amelia. Music to celebrate her return. Not people slinking away and the clash of guards changing over.

"I think I'll turn in," I told them, and they nodded at me, unsurprised.

"Hugh, darling." Amelia kissed his cheek. "Would you mind if I met you in our chambers a bit later?"

"Of course, my love." He smiled at her. "Princess Andi—rest well and know that we shall all be here to protect you." He kissed my hand with a gallant bow. My heart lurched at that and at Amelia's pleased smile. I felt small for ever wishing he could be mine instead.

"Thank you," I muttered, withdrawing my hand, not putting it in my pocket to check if the feather was still there.

Ursula and Amelia fell into step beside me as I walked to my own chambers, where there would be no handsome prince waiting for me with love in his eyes.

"What—are you two my escort?"

In answer, Ursula jerked her head at the men behind us. Three lieutenants of the Royal Guard trailed behind, in full armor. "No, they are."

"We are coming to your room so you can tell us *everything*," Amelia supplied.

I opened my mouth to protest, then glanced at the sober lines around Ursula's mouth. "Perhaps Ursula could fill us in on a thing or two, also." *She was too young to remember*, Ursula had said.

She rolled her head on her shoulders, neck popping with a loud crack. "Yes," she sighed, "perhaps that would be the thing to do."

Wine awaited us in my chambers. Amelia poured while the ladies-in-waiting withdrew. Ursula instructed the guards at their stations outside the door and in my antechamber, then checked the window.

I looked out, too. My chamber sat high in one of the turrets because I liked to see out. It helped that no one else particularly liked to climb so many stairs. From there, the whole front of the castle grounds was visible. The arched white stone bridge over the river and the outer walls bristled now with soldiers. Had I known we had so many?

"Where did they all come from?" I marveled.

Ursula snorted. "I swear to Danu—you pay attention to nothing at all, do you?"

"I just didn't think we kept a standing army."

"Yes, well, you don't think much at all, do you?"

"You know, Ursula, I'm really not in the mood for being beat up any more today," I snapped. "I'm sure everyone will be lining up tomorrow to tell me in excruciating detail every single thing I did wrong—again. You'll have ample opportunity then."

Her lip curled and I braced for her snarling response. Then she stopped herself, rolled her shoulders again. "You didn't do anything wrong."

"What?"

Amelia appeared between us, jeweled goblets of wine in her hands. Ursula took hers and stared at it. I cradled mine, grateful for something to keep my hands busy.

"I would never criticize our father, as King." Even though she knew we were alone, Ursula automatically glanced around for eavesdroppers. "But, had you been warned"—she gulped the wine—"perhaps this could have been avoided."

"Let's sit," Amelia suggested. She fetched her own wine and crawled onto my high bed, arranging herself on it comfortably. She'd taken her hair down, and it spilled around her like fiery gold, her eyes luminous. "Andi can tell us her story, and then Ursula can tell us what our mother has to do with all this."

That's the thing about Amelia: she's so lovely and sweet, you forget how clever she is and how little she really misses.

Though we'd only rarely done this as girls—Ursula was already fifteen by the time Amelia turned five—it felt familiar and cozy to sit cross-legged on my bed with them. Ursula reclined back against the pillows, watching us while Amelia pulled the pins from my hair and brushed it out in long, gentle strokes, something she did to her own hair every night and swore by. I told them the whole story, just as I'd told our father while he glowered at me like I'd stuck a knife in his heart.

When I finished, Ursula reached for the pitcher and refilled all our glasses, frowning.

"Why was the kiss so damn important?" she demanded. "And the blood thing?"

"I was hoping you'd tell me." I felt guilty not mentioning the blood bird, but I couldn't bear for them, too, to look at me with revulsion. If they even believed it.

"It has to be a magic thing, right?" Amelia mused. "Lady Zevondeth was all worked up about it, and you know how she goes on about the old stories. Except that there's no such thing as magic."

"The kiss and whether his blood passed my lips," I agreed. I'd told them about the meeting with the King and Derodotur, too. "So, now, Ursula—please. What does our mother have to do with this?"

She dropped her head back and stared at the canopy overhead. "Salena was of the Tala."

She said it as if she expected us to gasp in realization. Instead, Amelia and I frowned at each other.

Then Amelia smoothed her frown away with the tip of one finger. "So the Tala are real? Father said Rayfe was of these Tala, too. I thought they were a myth, like white bears or sea monsters. But Hugh says they talk of them in Avonlidgh—stories of the Great War."

Ursula contemplated us, clear gray eyes troubled, then uncoiled to her feet to pace to the window. As if the sentries needed checking.

"See, this is a good lesson—history is written by the victors. Never forget it. What you believe to be true is exactly and only what the people who won want you to believe."

"But Father stopped the Great War," Amelia protested. "That's why the Twelve Kingdoms made him the High King. He's brought lasting peace."

The line of Ursula's shoulders grew tight, and I put a cautionary hand on Amelia's slim arm.

"Tell us what really happened, Ursula," I asked of her, quiet, somber.

She glanced over her shoulder at me with brows raised. "Oh, Uorsin triumphed all right. No denying that. But I have reason to think he had help from Mother's people: the Tala."

Those wolfhounds. They had reminded me of something. Tales from the Great War. Giant dark eagles filling the skies, black wolves with blue eyes—those were in the songs, too. Fobbed off as bits of fantastic glory to dress up otherwise dull battles.

"Shape-shifters and wizards." The words escaped me before I could pull them back. Amelia looked astonished, her rosy lips pursed in a giggle, but Ursula nodded crisply, turned so she propped her lean behind on the stone sill. So many torches flamed outside, her hair—still tightly pinned up—looked like it burned at the edges.

"That's what they say. Not all of the books have been cleaned up."

"But those things aren't real." Amelia tossed her hair over her shoulder. "They're stories only."

"If they're only stories," I pointed out, "why do we pray to Glorianna to protect us from them?"

"Glorianna is the pure, the protectress, She who banishes the dark." Amelia looked at me like I lacked all sense. "Everyone knows that."

"Yes, but how do we know that?" I pressed.

"You wear the rose of Glorianna like we all do, Andi." Amelia tapped the intricate gold rose hanging from the chain around my neck. "Why?"

She had a point. "Because Father gave it to me, as he did to both of you. Glorianna's protection. From what?"

Amelia blinked at me, long red-gold lashes sweeping across her twilight eyes. Something in them stirred, not quite so sweet. I handed her the hairbrush again and she automatically pulled it through my hair. It soothed me while I turned it all over in my head.

"So, Ursula, I'm guessing you heard a lot of this from Mother, since no one else speaks of it."

A pang of the old loneliness shivered through my heart. I remembered only a few things about her. All that long, coiling, dark hair. Her sorrowful eyes. Mostly I had a feeling for her, not a face. That sense of love. With her I'd felt wrapped up in it, like a velvet cloak that protected me from the world. Losing it had left me forever chilled.

It just about killed me that Ursula had memories of talking with her.

She nodded, grave, like she followed my thoughts. "Before you were born, but after Father issued the edict that the Tala should never be mentioned. It wounded her, I think. She was pregnant with you, Andi, and I came upon her watching the full moon and weeping. I'd had a bad dream and went to look for her, I think." Ursula shook her head free of unnecessary detail.

"It doesn't matter why I was up. I went to Mother's chamber and she was curled up on that big padded window seat, remember? Where she'd always sit to stare out. And she watched the full moon setting over the mountains."

"To the west," I whispered.

"Consistent, no? Yes, the Wild Lands west of the castle. She told me that her people came from there, that she left them to marry Father. She rubbed her belly, so swollen with you, and said that the first of her daughters to show the mark of the Tala would return to her people and take the place she'd left empty."

"She said those exact words?" It was uncannily close to what Rayfe had intimated.

"If she was pregnant with you, Ursula was five," Amelia said gently. "She's not going to remember the conversation word for word."

"Oh, but I do, Ami." Ursula, however, studied me. "I remember because I started to cry, too, thinking I'd be sent away. And Mother took me in her arms and said I was my father's daughter and would not be the one. She promised me that. All the time she told me this, she stroked the round curve of her belly. I knew, even then, what she wasn't saying."

"She thought it was me," I whispered.

"She knew it was you," Ursula corrected. "What's more, Father did, too, though he pretends like he didn't."

"He spoke of it today. Derodotur, too."

Her lips thinned at the confirmation. "I would have told you, but Mother told me never to speak of it. Not that she had to tell me that—Uorsin flew into rages even then, when the Tala were mentioned. So much so that not even Mother objected when he forbade discussion."

"What is the mark?" Amelia asked.

Ursula shrugged, restless, unhappy. "Who knows?"

But I knew.

"Rayfe told me he could tell it about me. He wanted to know if I had some mark." I got up, too, setting my wineglass down. I didn't need my head any fuzzier. "Am I so different?"

Amelia glanced away unhappily and Ursula simply returned my gaze, as she would in swordplay, waiting for me to decide upon my next attack. I knew it, didn't I? The way everyone had always done their best not to see me. Not to see the monster inside.

"Why didn't you tell me?" I tried to keep my voice steady, but even I could hear the fear in it. The trembling hurt of the betrayed. "How could you look at me and see"—I gestured helplessly at myself—"whatever it is you've been seeing, and not say anything?"

Ursula glanced away finally, fiddling with the hilt of her sword.

"Fine," I breathed, slipping my hand into my pocket for the reassuring knife-edge of the black feather. "So. Uorsin made some kind of deal with Mother's people. They let him marry Salena, help him win the war, and the first daughter with this Tala mark on her forehead gets married to one of theirs in return. Sounds pretty straightforward. Except Father reneged on his word. Not so straightforward."

Ursula reflexively glanced toward the antechamber. "Really, darling, you might lower your voice when you speak treason against the King."

"What?" I snapped. "Rayfe already doomed me by saying I'd be receptive to his offer. No wonder Uorsin thinks I've been consorting with the enemy."

"Technically you have," Amelia pointed out, "rolling around in the grass, kissing."

"I did *not* kiss him."

Ursula stilled. "And his blood did not pass your lips."

Not much, anyway. I ducked the question and regretted the wine. It hadn't helped the headache, only tightened it like an iron band around my temples. I pressed my fingertips into the bones around my eyes. "They all made a big deal about that. Those things must seal the pact somehow." *Or make tiny birds.*

"The old ways." Ursula nodded.

"We don't recognize the old ways," Amelia argued. "You might not think much of Glorianna's temple, but our laws don't recognize a marriage outside of that. Not even Moranu or Danu can seal a marriage."

Not anymore. But they did in the old ways.

"True." Ursula tipped her head at our little sister. "If the Tala want the High Throne of the Twelve Kingdoms, then Rayfe would have to marry you legally."

"Okay." I let out a long breath. "So, it's not enough to whisk me off. The King has to agree to the terms."

"The King has already agreed to the terms—before any of us were born. Now he has to get out of them."

"Continue to get out of them." Amelia blushed when we looked at her. "I mean, none of us knew about this, right? So they're all in collusion, like Ursula said. Rewriting history, avoiding a political alliance."

"What's important," Ursula said to her in a stern voice, "is protecting Andi. That's all Uorsin ever wanted to do. Protect us, protect his kingdom, protect the peace."

"What if there had been sons," I wondered, "did they get nothing in that case?"

Ursula considered that. "Mother didn't say. Surely any agreement would have covered that eventuality."

"What if"—and this possibility bothered me greatly—"what if the Tala don't want the throne?" Rayfe had wanted to take me somewhere beyond the Wild Lands. Away from my sisters and the only home I'd ever known. My heart clenched with dread. "What if there's some other plan?"

"What do you keep fiddling with in your pocket?"

Guilty, I yanked my hand out of my skirt. "Nothing."

"It's that feather," Amelia tattled. "I saw you pick it up. Is that really wise?"

Flinty anger sparked in Ursula's gaze. "What in Danu are you thinking, Andi? Burn the damn thing!"

"No!" I couldn't bear the thought, though I couldn't understand why. It tangled up with the terror that I'd be taken away. Cast adrift with no one and nothing. "I'll get rid of it, but I refuse to burn it."

Ursula held out an implacable hand. "Give it to me, Andi."

I shook my head.

Her face went to stone. "That's an order, in case you missed the concept."

"It's mine. It doesn't matter to anything else. I just want to study it."

"You understand nothing of the Tala," Ursula hissed.

"Like you do?"

"That bird was a creature of darkness—you saw how it behaved. A feather from it is a totem that ties you to them. Is that what you want, Andi? Because if you wish to be a traitor to your people, your kingdom, and your King, then you'd better tell me right now."

"My people?" I gasped it out, my heart thudding at her words. "We're all half *her*! I might bear this mark from our mother, or whatever it is, but these Tala are your people, too—did you somehow gloss over that part? Maybe I have it the strongest, but both of you have at least some of her blood." Always back to the blood.

"Andi." Amelia scrambled off the bed to stand between me and Ursula. "We understand how difficult this is, but—"

"Give me that cursed feather, Andromeda," Ursula demanded, "or I will take it from you by force."

"No."

"You stubborn git! Give it now."

"Andi, just give it to her—it's only a little thing."

But it wasn't a little thing. I didn't know why, but I hated to give it up. The certainty filled me and overflowed, digging me into the earth. "I won't let you have it."

Her jaw strained, teeth tightly clenched, hand fisted on her sword hilt. Ursula leaned in, hawk nose flanked by flaring gray eyes. She topped me by a head, easily. For a wild moment, I thought she'd draw her sword, and I wished for my knife. The one I'd left in Rayfe's shoulder.

We each had a piece of the other, then.

"This is about me," I said. I felt cool now, reasonable, explaining this to her. "My curse, my fate. Whatever happens, it affects me most of all. I decide how to handle things. And I feel keeping this feather is important."

Scorn filled Ursula's face. "You fool," she hissed. "This is not about you. You're a blood pawn. A baby maker to be traded between political alliances. The Tala don't want *you*—they want to fill you with little shape-shifters and wizards to populate our throne and overrun our kingdoms. And you'd hand it all over to them on a whim? Because you have a *feeling*?" Contempt dripped from every word.

A small sound escaped Amelia, and I saw tears running down her face.

"You asked me what I see in you, my little sister?" Ursula continued, relentless. "I see someone who is never truly a part of this royal family. I see you riding off to be by yourself, not listening to important policy matters. You care more for your horse than for any of us. Now I'm wondering if I see a traitor."

"It's a feather, Ursula, not the keys to the kingdom."

"Prove it."

"I shouldn't have to prove myself to you."

"No, you shouldn't, should you? Anyone else would have never picked up a stinking relic like that—why did you?"

"I don't know," I whispered.

"Oh, I think you do know. I think somewhere deep in your mind, there is a reason. Is it him?"

"What?"

"Oh, you watched Ami fall in love, you gaze at Hugh with such admiration, and now you think to have a prince of your own. But contrary you, it has to be someone different, doesn't it?"

"You're wrong," I told her, but my voice wasn't steady. Rayfe's midnight-blue eyes filled my mind. My body pulsed, remembering his weight on me. How I'd wondered where his chair might fit in the throne room. *Traitor.* It's an ugly word.

"Oh, I don't think so," Ursula said, soft, deadly.

"Give her the cursed feather already, Andi—please!" Amelia sobbed out the words.

I slid my finger along the glassy edge of the feather. Just a thing. It didn't mean anything one way or the other. I pulled it out and the firelight caught it, gleaming indigo-black. Amelia made a little sound. I laid it across Ursula's calloused palm. Out in the night, a wolf howled and I shivered.

Ursula didn't hesitate. Of course, she never does. She strode to the fireplace and tossed the feather in. For a moment it gleamed there, perfectly black and glossy. Then it burst into flame, a flash, a tendril of blue smoke rising and fading away. And it was gone.

Ursula folded her arms, watching the fire burn with her back to me, a long, lean silhouette against the bright fire.

"Don't give me cause to doubt you again, Andi."

"It seems to me that doubt is something that rises in your own heart and mind, Ursula, regardless of my actions."

She turned, a line between her brows, and surveyed me as if she'd never seen me before. "Our actions define us. They speak who we are more clearly than any number of words."

"I gave you the feather to destroy, didn't I?"

"What else happened in that meadow, I wonder?"

"I told you everything already." Mostly.

"But not how you felt. You haven't said how you felt about it all."

"She was hurt and afraid—it's hard to put that into words," Amelia defended me.

"Are you feeding her the correct lines, Amelia?"

"I don't need lines, Ursula." My arms were folded, too, a mirror of my sister. I unwound them, holding them deliberately still by my sides. "If you judge me by my actions, then note I left my dagger buried in that man's shoulder. I defended myself and succeeded. And you know full well that wasn't easy for me. Don't stand there and accuse me of dreaming after love from my attacker." Though, hadn't I? Imagining him as my husband. That longing churned with the fear in my stomach.

"You two are my entire world. Don't push me away—I can't bear it." The emotions pushed up into my throat, making my eyes sting. "What do I have if I don't have you?"

Amelia slipped her arms around my waist, leaning her shining head against my breast, as soft and sweet as when she was a child. "Don't cry, Andi. We love you. We would never let those awful people take you."

"Thank you, Ami." I wrapped my arms around her but kept my gaze on Ursula.

Ursula nodded slowly. "So be it, then. We'll keep you safe, Andi, whatever it takes. We won't give you over to them, to him. I give you my solemn word on that."

I should have felt reassured by that. And yet, with the sudden gulf yawning between us, it still somehow sounded like a threat.

A chill of loneliness frosted my heart. It knew what I didn't yet understand.

4

After they left me, I dreamed of Rayfe.

Hard to imagine I wouldn't, given the way his advent into our lives had turned everything upside down. I did my best to clear my mind before I slept, mouthing the words along with Gaignor while she led the ladies in a prayer to Glorianna for Her divine protection against the dark forces, to uphold and protect the Twelve Kingdoms and me.

Sometimes I wasn't sure which they referred to.

But even as Gaignor repeated the ritual praises of Glorianna, invoking Her inviolate strength, I kept seeing the shards of Her window raining down, like so many sharp drops of watery blood.

I fell asleep mesmerized by the declining flames in the fire-place, fending off the chill night air. Their falling dance lulled me into rest, the interplay of light and shadow a silent music. Even the noise of the sentries ceaselessly pacing the ramparts had quieted. Blessed, sweet sleep welcomed me and drew me down.

The brush of black wings on the stone sill yanked me awake.

My window didn't have even Glorianna's feeble glass to keep it out. I sat up, heart pounding, almost afraid to look. The raptor sat there, cocking its head so one bright eye fixed on me. The deep shadows in the corners shifted. Moved and seethed. The restless bodies of the wolfhounds churned in a dark swirl, tossing up the gleam of fangs, a flash of fulminous blue. The satin quilt shifted under my fingers like sand, whispering of blood and death. Someone laughed. Soft. Regular.

I was a child again, alone in this big bed, crying for my dead mother. No—that was Amelia wailing. Thin shrieks echoing through the castle. Coming closer. Her nurse carried her into the room and set the baby in my arms.

I tried to tell her no. *No, keep the baby away from the dogs.* But I couldn't speak.

"You have to quiet her," the nurse said. "Stop your weeping and care for your sister."

Amelia's enormous twilight eyes blinked at me. "I'm hungry," the baby said. "Feed me."

My breasts were a flat child's. I had no milk.

She screamed at me. "Feed me!"

I tried to shush her, but the dogs had heard the cries. They surged up, with barks and growls, fangs tearing at the infant blanket. I held the baby tight against me. White teeth sank into my arm, shredding my flesh.

"Rayfe!" I cried, finding my voice. "Help, oh, please!"

Why I called out to my enemy to save me, I didn't understand. But, in the way of dreams, it was my only path.

A whispered word and they were gone.

The infant, who both was and wasn't Amelia, the wolfhounds, the giant black bird, all gone. Only Rayfe remained.

He stood by my bed. His black hair spilled loose over his shoulders, his midnight gaze on me, his face grave.

"Beautiful Andromeda—don't be afraid. I'm here."

He sat beside me and stroked a finger down my cheek. It felt real and warm and I wanted to lean my cheek into his palm, for comfort.

"You're not real," I whispered, willing myself to wake up.

"I am real. The other things are not. They're just . . . fragments tossed up by your mind because of the changes in you. I would spare you this pain, but I cannot. Let me soothe you."

He ran a hand over my hair and his scent wrapped around me, warm, enticing.

"I apologize, Princess, for this morning. I bungled things. I thought once our blood mingled, you would understand. Come to me and I'll make it all up to you. You need to. It's your destiny. Neither of us can change that."

"I cannot. I never will." I clung to the covers, as if I could keep from being dragged away. "This is my home, my people."

His fingers twined in my hair, possessive, impatient. Tugging me close. For a moment I thought he'd kiss me, and my heart pounded in fear and elation. "Your true people await you. Your home is Annfwn and it needs you. Won't you see? You only wound us all by resisting."

He turned, showing me the dagger that stood out from his muscled shoulder, blood soaking his sleeve dark.

"You injured me, Andromeda. Won't you take it back?"

He took my hand, unfolded my fist, stroking my open palm, and wrapped my fingers around the hilt of the knife. It filled my hand, hard and hot with his blood. I cringed. It had seemed so right at the time.

"I was defending myself."

"I know. It was my fault for frightening you. But now I need you to pull it out."

"I can't."

"You must."

"Have someone else do it."

"Don't you understand yet, my Andromeda? It has to be you. No one else can. I need you. Annfwn needs you.

"Please." He whispered the words, insidious. "Please, Andromeda, do this for me."

I tried. I tugged, but the dagger wouldn't come free. It was stuck, deep in the bone. Rayfe threw his head back, howling out a scream of agony, and I snatched my hand away.

He was gone. I sat alone in bed, the fire cold, dawn barely lighting the sky from black to dark blue. The dim light, though, was enough to see the blood covering my hand. Feeling sick and sorry, I dashed to the washbasin, stumbling a little in my haste, and scrubbed my hands in the chilly water until they gleamed white and stainless.

If only I could do the same for my heart.

By the time I awoke again, this time to midmorning overcast and drizzling rain, impossibly sore and feeling a hundred years old, Ursula had already left on her scouting mission, leading her special squad of soldiers—Ursula's Hawks—to the meadow of acid-green grasses. Despite the previous day's threat, she not only didn't force me to go along; I was forbidden to leave the castle. Rumors of war whispered around every corner. For a while I lurked in my chambers. I ate what breakfast I could choke down and sent all my ladies away because they seemed unable to talk of anything else. But the constant clatter of soldiers drilling in the yard, sentries changing guard every hour . . . it wore on me.

Enthusiasm sang in the very air. Mohraya had been birthed out of the blood of the Great War. Uorsin was a warrior, first and foremost, and a general hard on the heels of that. Twenty-five years had passed since the final victory. The warriors of Ordnung thirsted for more.

It ran through their voices, the desire to fight, to triumph. My sentries in the antechamber told one another stories about their fathers and grandfathers. About this siege and how that city fell. They reminded me of women telling one another childbirth tales, each story more agonizing, painful, and horrifying than the last.

I itched to be outside. To ride Fiona beyond all the voices and the sideways glances. To be free again, if only for a while.

By late afternoon, Ursula had returned and the High King summoned us for formal court. Not a good sign.

I let Amelia dress me to her satisfaction. She always seemed to think our father would be happier with me if I looked prettier.

More like, well, Amelia. Now I knew, however, that I looked like Salena—and like the monstrous people our mother came from.

We all convened, sitting in our array of thrones and looking out over the assembled nobles, representatives of the other eleven kingdoms arrayed in the front. None of the kings would have had time to travel to Ordnung. Of course, Uorsin alone represented Mohraya. The lovely room sang with tension, the boarded-over window where Glorianna's rose had shattered like a blackened eye.

"People of the Twelve Kingdoms." Uorsin intoned the words, at his kingly best. He wore his formal robes and the crown. Not at all a good sign. He rarely did, complaining to Ursula that it itched. It was an ugly thing, crafted of unpolished iron, with twelve points, one for each kingdom. "Many of you know that we face a trial greater than any since the Great War. To spare the gentle hearts among us, we have not spoken the name of our ancient enemy in all these years, but now we must. The Tala—demons, every one—have escaped into the Wild Lands."

He let the aghast murmurs run through the crowd. They all acted shocked and surprised, as if every one of them hadn't heard what happened the day before.

"We face a grave peril indeed. They seek to undermine our peaceful and united kingdom with their black magic and evil ways. Worse, they think to destroy us by taking our beloved Princess Andromeda and bending her to their devilish purposes. We shall not let them!"

He pounded his fist on the arm of his throne, and a weak cheer went up at the signal, gaining strength from there. Until then, they hadn't been sure how to respond. It would have been comical—I almost expected someone to say *Who?*—except my head was pounding. Amelia took my hand. Hers was cold as ice.

"We have no recourse but to defend our precious homeland. They shall not have our princess. We will destroy them and send them running back to their stinking burrows like the animals they are.

"People of the Twelve Kingdoms, we are at war!"

They cheered in earnest at that, the soldiers and guards sending up a roar that reverberated against the walls, making my ears ring.

After that, the true nattering began, the various representatives arguing over whether they should provide additional troops. Avonlidgh and Branli, in particular, preferred to keep their forces at home, to defend their own borders with the Wild Lands. Hugh stepped in to negotiate for Avonlidgh, Amelia trying not to look bored at his side, while Ursula seemed fired with a new light, arguing with the envoy from Branli.

I didn't understand any of it. Why would Father go to war for me? While I appreciated the sentiment and greatly preferred not to be thrown to the wolfhounds, it seemed unlike Uorsin to fight for me, his least-favored daughter. Something more was going on, and I needed information.

As usual, everyone had now forgotten my presence, except in principle, so I took advantage of the moment. I fled to the library.

At least the only people there were the ones who weren't so fired up to get out and defend my honor. Books were never high on Uorsin's list of priorities, unless you counted law books, which were kept in his study chambers for easy reference. The majority of Mohraya's archives were relegated to a series of dank cellar rooms, part of the previous castle's foundation, most of which had served as dungeons or cells for prisoners before the Great War. After Uorsin took power, he had prisons built throughout the Twelve Kingdoms, part of the Plan for Peace. The librarians complained regularly of having to keep the wood fires going constantly to keep the mildew away. Uorsin finally told his field engineers to make them pipes to carry the smoke away, but he wouldn't give up good aboveground space to books.

On days like today, the fires snapped with welcome warmth. I didn't miss windows since all they showed was preparation for war. One I seemed to have caused.

"Can I help you, Princess Andi?"

All that had happened must have left me rattled, because I jumped inside my skin. Lady Mailloux blinked at me, her cinnamon-brown eyes concerned. "I did not mean to startle you, Princess."

"No, Lady, I am . . . a little on edge." I surprised myself, confiding that so readily.

She smiled, a soft curve of understanding. "If half the gossip is true, I'm not surprised."

"I feel quite certain that far less than half is true."

She quirked an eyebrow. "That does not surprise me either. So how may I assist you? You don't often seek your answers in my books."

Oddly phrased. "Where do you think I usually seek my answers?"

"If you don't know, how would I?"

Somehow I suspected that was a dodge. Up until now I hadn't thought I had any questions. "I'm looking for books, histories on the wars, especially the Tala. And the Wild Lands." And my mother, though I couldn't yet articulate that.

She twitched, smoothed it out. "So that bit of gossip carries merit, anyway. I'm sorry, Your Highness, that subject was interdicted many years ago. The official records were all destroyed."

She shifted under my gaze, demurely dropping her eyes so she looked off to the side, a sweep of red hair dropping over a white cheek.

"And the unofficial records?"

"I wish I could help you, Princess, but I cannot offer what I do not have."

"But you can show me the place where I might accidentally unearth something. Something overlooked, perhaps?"

"I'm sure I—"

"Look, Librarian Mailloux, I may not have spent much time down here, but I hear the petitions in court. Every one of these is precious to you." I waved my hands at the towers of shelves, neatly

stacked with books and scrolls. Beyond our circle of firelight, another room glowed, and a series after that. Endless cubbyholes of
accumulated learning. "I've heard you say it before: *all knowledge
is worth having.* I'm asking you to let me have it."

She tapped restless fingers on her brown trousers. Her nails
were broken and stained with ink and dust.

"What can I do in return?"

Her canny brown eyes sharpened, and I knew I had her.

"If there's war, they'll want their dungeons back again. For the
prisoners," she prompted at my blank response.

"But there are prisons now."

"High King Uorsin will want to keep his prisoners of war close
by, for questioning," she countered.

I imagined Rayfe in a cell, stuck back in one of these corners.
All these cells, filled with the tortured, the ones unwilling to give
up their secrets, the others too dangerous to release and yet not
important enough to execute outright. Surely that would never
come to pass.

"I don't think I could stop King Uorsin from reclaiming his
dungeons. Perhaps you overestimate my influence."

"No, Princess, I feel sure you're correct. But if you could put
in a word for the library. Ask for space for us. We've never really
had a champion at court. It's a great deal to ask, I know, but perhaps now you see how important these stories are."

"Well, I haven't seen yet, have I?"

She flashed me an unexpected grin, a dimple gracing one
cheek. "Leave your men here and I'll have one of my girls provide
them refreshments. Follow me."

The guards didn't complain. Though it was a warren of rooms
and cubbies, the former prison possessed only one way out. With
grave bows and assurances of my honor staying safe in their
hands, the men settled by the fire to wait. I followed the librarian.

"Never before have so many been so interested in my honor,"
I muttered to myself.

Lady Mailloux cast me a look over her shoulder. "Your people love you and wish to protect you—would you throw that back in their faces?"

Are you kidding me? The people barely know I exist. But I couldn't say that. "I beg your pardon, Lady, I did not intend to sound ungrateful." I had to duck under a low archway. Ursula would have had to bend almost double.

"No, I beg your pardon, Princess. I was out of line. It is a failing of mine."

"Well, this particular failing makes you the ideal person to help me now." She didn't comment. I didn't blame her. Before yesterday morning, I'd never thought about treason. Now it seemed to become an issue in every conversation. And here I was, making my way through a maze of rooms I'd never known to look for. "I won't betray you. I feel like I should say that out loud. I appreciate the risk you're taking here."

She stopped to pull a lantern from a cubbyhole and lit it. The waxing flame cast an odd shadow across her face. "My risk is also yours, Princess Andi. That evens out the obligation. Besides"— she gave a one-shouldered shrug—"you're promising to help me save the library. Nothing is more important to me than that."

"Nothing?" It sounded good, but really? "Your own life? Family?"

She laughed, sounding genuinely amused, and handed me the lantern. She shoved aside some dusty crates—now her dirty trousers seemed most practical and I regretted letting the ladies dress me up in their idea of innocent-victim-princess—and wedged open a creaking door.

"There's something unusual about you, Princess Andi," she said, taking the lantern back. She preceded me into the room and hung the lantern on an overhead hook. "Princess Ursula would know that I am a ward of the King's, since I lost all my land and my family in the wars, and Princess Amelia would have pretended to know and offered kind words. It's far too damp in here, Moranu curse it."

"I'm sorry," I offered, unable to think of kind words and feeling like a lame horse. "I didn't know."

"Damp is our eternal enemy. But it's hard to keep something both dried out and secret with these accommodations."

"I meant about your family. I've lost only a mother—I can't imagine what it would be like to lose everyone, along with your home."

Lady Mailloux lit the little fire already laid in the woodstove. "There's not much good ventilation in here, so you'll have to be careful. I miss them, but over time you forget the details, which is a mercy, and very little looks the same. I remember your mother, the Queen. She was kind to me. Her death grieved us all."

"Did you know she was . . ."

"Tala?" Lady Mailloux squinted at the shelves as she drew on a pair of soft leather gloves. With nimble and unbearably gentle fingers, she pulled a scroll down and laid it on the table. She kept working, finding and laying out for me books and parchments organized according to some arcane system of her own. "Yes, I knew. Not everyone did, I don't think. High King Uorsin, even during the Great War, didn't like it to be discussed. But because I grew up here, bordering the Wild Lands before the war, I knew more than most. I remember my father saying that the Tala and Uorsin both had made a deal with the devil."

"You said you grew up here—at Ordnung?"

She cocked that eyebrow at me. "At Castle Columba, on whose ruins Ordnung was built." Her gaze wandered over the old walls. "In some ways, I never left home."

She drew down a large and dusty tome, reverently setting it on the table. "I built this collection from my family's library. If you were one of the young scholars come in here, I'd threaten to break your fingers if you so much as smudged a page." She studied me, chewing her lip.

I held up my hands. "I value my fingers. May I borrow your gloves?"

Lady Mailloux smiled, drew them off, and handed them to me.

"I'd like to sit here with you and guide your research, but I'd best oversee my staff—and make sure your sentries don't feel the need to check on you. This"—she pointed to the huge tome—"is an annotated history of the Tala. It's quite dense and would take you weeks to get through. I suggest you use it as a reference. There's an index in the back. For recent events, look through these scrolls. They'll give you tales of Tala during the Great War."

"What about any . . . contracts or legal treaties that might have been . . . drafted, here and there?" I picked my way through the question, but she raised her brows with a look that told me she knew exactly what I asked after.

"Derodotur keeps all treaty documents in the King's study, Princess." She had her formal demeanor back now. "You would have to apply to him or Lady Zevondeth for that information."

"Zevondeth? Why would she have the information?"

"Why, Princess Andi"—Lady Mailloux widened her eyes, all innocence—"I thought you knew that Lady Zevondeth arrived here as your mother's attendant. Indeed, she was your mother's most devoted companion and was at her side even unto her death."

My world shifted again, realigned.

"I'm indebted to you, Lady Mailloux."

"Dafne. Call me Dafne, Princess."

"Thank you. I'd tell you to call me Andi, but I imagine you won't."

Dafne glanced around the confines of the little room. "In here I will, Andi." She turned to go. "It means a great deal to me that someone will see these documents. I want you to know—" She hesitated, made a decision. "No matter what you may read or hear, your mother was not evil. Nor do I believe the Tala are demons. Salena was . . ." Dafne trailed off, considered me.

"Sometime I'd like you to tell me more about her. I remember her as kind."

Dafne laughed a little. "Oh, she had a temper; don't mistake that. But she loved life, in this brilliant, passionate way, before she declined. And she loved you. She would be proud of you."

That brought me up short. I'd thought before about making my father proud, and Ursula—though I had never really suc- ceeded with either of them. But my mother?

"Proud? I've done nothing with my life."

"Actions may speak who we are, but first we have to be that person. She would be proud of who you are. I suspect she would be proud of what you will do, too."

"Hide in the castle and let armies die for me while I read books?"

She sobered. "Is that your plan?"

"In point of fact, I have no plan. Nobody seems to feel that I, personally, need a plan here." The bitterness edging my voice took me by surprise. Hadn't I always gone along with what Uorsin and Ursula recommended? What Amelia coaxed?

"It seems to me," Lady Mailloux said thoughtfully, "that we drift along in life without particular plans until a point of crisis occurs. We find we want something we can't have. Or someone wants from us something we don't want to give. Only then do we have to really wake up and make decisions for ourselves."

"The voice of experience?"

She nodded. "Unfortunately, yes. And if you want another bit of advice with that?"

I did.

"The people around you who are accustomed to you going with their plan won't like it if you no longer are."

"Duly noted."

"Good luck with those documents. I'll come back to see how you're doing."

I wanted to look for a name like the one Rayfe had said in my dream. It had sounded like "ohna-fn," but I had no idea how it might be spelled, so I started with the longer ballads, thinking I might find the rhyme. These were the songs that had stuck in my head from childhood. The fierce battle tales set to music that left nightmare images in my head.

One song told of wolves pouring like black ink over the hillsides, tearing apart friend and foe alike. Another spelled out in gruesome detail how giant ravens descended on besieged castles, plucking out the sentries' eyes or sometimes ganging up to knock them from the parapets. Sometimes wilder beasts, like the tigers of the tropics, only black on black, with blazing blue eyes, or even dragons, snarled and laid waste through the stories. Though these beasts seemed to behave in ways that showed more than animal intelligence, none of the ballads mentioned shape-shifters or demons. Nor did the more staid descriptions of the Wild Lands and the Great War.

Until I got to the history of Uorsin himself.

It's funny: though I knew my father existed as a man before he was King or my father, I'd never quite conceptualized it. That he wasn't from Mohraya because Mohraya hadn't existed before he created it. Instead his history began in the least likely of the Twelve Kingdoms, in peaceful and pretty Elcinea, with its sandy beaches and fertile waters.

He'd been a sailor, which I hadn't known—first for fish and then for treasure. When neighboring Duranor attacked Elcinea, he joined her defense. He sold his boat and all his equipment to buy himself a horse, armor, weapons, and a squire to feed. The history didn't name Derodotur, but I knew that's who it must have been, this "squire of uncertain lineage but excellent survival skills," as my father had been quoted to say.

Uorsin rose in the ranks, though Elcinea quickly folded to Duranor's greater might and avid determination. Instead of going back to fish and hunt treasure to fill Duranor's coffers, Uorsin stayed with the conscripted army. It was unclear how much of that decision was voluntary, however, as Duranor cheerfully took possession of all Elcinea's bounty, including the dubious cream of its military.

The soldier who'd found himself field promoted to lieutenant went on to captain the cavalry, and then served as general to defend Duranor when its vassal states rose in rebellion.

Ursula would likely swat me on the head for not really learning this history, but names, dates, places, and battles? Not so interesting. But now I followed Uorsin's rise in the Duranor military with intense personal interest.

Especially when things changed.

Duranor had overreached, the supply lines failing and battles waging on all sides. Even Elcinea, encouraged by the success of its neighbors, had managed to generate credible difficulties for her liege-country by bottlenecking the ports. Uorsin lost a crucial battle—right on these very grounds, where Castle Columba had stood. The siege of Columba took too long, and though General Uorsin overcame the Mailloux family in the end, he and his forces found themselves besieged in turn. Uorsin was wounded in the final battle that broke the original siege, then disappeared from view—presumed dead or captured.

A seven-day later, he staggered out of the Wild Lands. With a bride.

"How's it going?"

I nearly tore the scroll, Lady Mailloux's voice startled me so.

"Moranu!" I exclaimed. "Don't sneak up like that."

"You were absorbed," she said in a dry tone, "and your sentries wanted lunch, have been replaced, and now the new lot want to lay eyes on you, to ensure your safety and their duty."

"Are there descriptions of Salena?" I held up the scroll. "This one goes right from Uorsin returning with a 'bride,' description apparently unnecessary, to him suddenly becoming a god on the battlefield, winning the hearts of young and old alike, then finally transforming himself into the High King of eleven kingdoms that had hated one another, but suddenly and joyfully proclaimed peace and carved out a new spot just for him."

"With his Queen at his side, who gave him three daughters, each more beautiful than the last."

"Apparently you've read this one."

"I've read them all." She held out her hand for the gloves and I stripped them off. "And no, there's never anything more about Salena than that."

"What about the Wild Lands? Nobody describes them. It's like no one has ever been there."

"I agree. And your men are waiting."

"Yes, but I—" I sighed. It would be worse than unfair to Dafne if they should come looking for me. "May I come back tomorrow?"

"This is your library, Princess Andi. You don't need my permission."

"In this I do. I don't wish to jeopardize your hard work. What you've done here—I admire your tenacity."

She studied me. "You are very like her, you know. That same sense of being far away. Then suddenly your attention shifts and it's as if a magnifying glass focuses."

"I was told I look like her."

"You do. More—you *feel* like her."

"How so?"

"Can we walk and talk? I'm really worried that your men will—"

"No. It can't be that long of an answer and everyone is ducking it. Just tell me and we'll go."

"It isn't a short answer!" she flared. "There are no words for this. And it's not . . . flattering, maybe."

"Tell me."

She pulled on the gloves and began efficiently returning the scrolls to their nooks. My fingers had grown chilled and numb, so I went to warm them by the stove.

"When I was a little girl," Dafne said to the shelves, "I saw a butterfly feeding on a flowering vine. So beautiful, with great orange and black wings. I tried coaxing it onto my finger, though I didn't think I could. To my utter delight, it worked. I held it up close so I could see the gorgeous colors. And it clutched my finger, crawling up my hand with those pricking hairy legs, this enormous insect. Before I thought, I shook it away as I would a spider."

She shuddered in remembered horror. "It flew away and I was glad to see it go."

I didn't know what to say. But it explained the looks, the uneasy sidling around me in the halls, as if I were some breed of insect. Perhaps I'd learned to be invisible because of that.

"I'm sorry." Dafne laid a hand on my now very dusty sleeve. "You look so sad—I should have found another way to describe it."

"No," I breathed out, brushing off my dress and her hand with it. "That was a perfect way to tell me. Not quite human. It's not like I haven't seen how they look at me."

"People don't think it." Dafne caught my sleeve again, her cinnamon eyes earnest, serious. "It's a feeling. A raising of the hairs on the back of the neck."

"Somehow that doesn't sound any better." She flinched and I sighed. "I asked you to tell me the truth and you did. I asked you to show me—at the risk of your life—interdicted materials I need and you did. I am indebted to you. But I have one more question."

She looked resigned, waited.

"Have you heard of a person or place called Onnafen?"

Her eyes opened wide. "How did you hear that word?"

"Would you believe me if I said in a dream?" I answered weakly.

But she nodded, solemn. "I would. Annfwn is beyond the Wild Lands. Ancient homeland of the Tala."

"I need to know more."

"There's very little written about it."

"Can I see what there is? Please?"

"Yes," she decided. "You should know what you can. I'll show you tomorrow."

"Thank you."

But I didn't go back, because that was the night the Tala attacked Ordnung.

5

Despite the preparations, the increased guard, everyone seemed taken by surprise.

After all, no one attacks Ordnung. No one with any sense.

Ursula's scouting expedition had found nothing. The meadow of the acid-green grasses apparently turned out to be only a meadow, which I could have told her. It wasn't like Rayfe lived there. Or that Tala would have come swarming up out of the vegetation like flesh-eating insects.

No, when they came, they came at night.

I thought I wasn't sleeping. I'd tossed and turned for a long while, afraid the nightmare would catch me up in its claws again. The stories at dinner hadn't helped. Once again, Uorsin remained closeted with his advisers. Freed of his firm presence for a second night, the court fell into serious tale telling. The anticipation of the day, the thirst for excitement, and the building lust for battle got them dredging up stories from the wars. And before.

One stern old soldier—the one who taught the younger kids basic defense skills because his missing legs were an excellent cautionary tale—told how he saw a pack of black wolves destroy a farming village. How they went for the bowels, tearing the guts from women and children alike while arrows bounced off them or went wildly astray. They'd knocked him down and chewed through his ankles, leaving him helpless to move while he watched them toss an infant around like a chew toy.

"And then"—he took a deep drink of the soldier's brew, a harsh liquid I could never abide—"they turned into men. I saw it with my own eyes," he insisted to the scoffing murmurs. "The wolves were gone, and dark men with black hair stood in their places. They built a pyre and burned the bodies."

I wanted to ask how he'd survived, then—the blood loss first and the scouring of the village for bodies after, but someone had chimed in with tales of demons visiting the old kings in their beds and leaving them dead.

"My gran told me this tale," one of the younger ladies from Amelia's retinue chimed in. "Old Erich's father, who was king before him in Avonlidgh. He retired one night, hale and hearty. Some say his valet saw it. A black shadow crawled in the window—not an animal, nor a man. The valet was frozen to his chair, where he'd sat to keep vigil. The shadow had wings, like a great bat, and blue eyes that shone in the dark. It crawled over the king like a lover—and drank blood from his throat."

A few of the more timid ladies squealed and clutched the arms of their escorts. Amelia's lovely eyes grew wider and glistened as she drank in the wild tales. Ursula raised her eyebrows at me in faint disgust. She wasn't one to credit these stories much. Of course, no one mentioned our mother, not even glancingly. It didn't do to imply the queen had been part demon, even now.

Still, the lurid stories stuck with me, images of blood and wolves chasing one another through my mind, winding through the stories I'd read, some every bit as horrifying. Sleep would drift over me and start to take me under; then the covers would shift under my hands, sliding away like sand, and I'd jerk awake once more.

But I must have slept, because Rayfe sat on the edge of my bed again. He stroked my cheek, calling my name in his husky voice. I opened my eyes, seeing him, black hair blending into the dark behind him, the stone walls of my chamber misting away into dream fog.

"Andromeda—wake up, my bride."

"I am not your bride."

"You are. Always. Come to me."

"Leave me alone," I whispered.

"I can't." He shook his head, his long hair falling forward as he leaned over me. The scent of dark spices filled my head. He cupped my face in his long-fingered hands, midnight-blue eyes brilliant with intensity. "You're the one. I don't want to fight, but I will if I have to. The need is too great. You are the only one who can stop all this."

"I can't stop it. You started it—you stop it."

"I promise I'll treat you well, but you must come to me. Annfwn needs you."

"I'm afraid," I pleaded with him. "I want to stay here."

"Why? There is nothing for you here."

"My sisters are here." Well, at least Ursula was. Amelia would be gone again soon. "My horse. My home."

"They will still be your sisters. Bring your horse. Annfwn will be your home. Trust me—you'll be happy there."

"Even if I believed you—and I don't because I know you care nothing for my happiness—my father will never agree. You don't know him."

Rayfe laughed at that, leaning back. He hissed in pain, and my heart lurched. The dagger protruded from the center of his chest now. Fresh blood radiated in a circle, like an archery target over his heart, bright crimson. He saw me staring at it and cocked his head.

"Will you remove your dagger now?"

"Why don't you do it? Or one of your surgeons?"

"I told you. Only you can. Take back the wound you gave me. Please."

Shouting arose outside the window. A clash of steel. A shriek of terror.

"What's that?"

He didn't even glance. "We're coming for you, Andromeda. To rescue you. I told you I'd fight if I had to."

"I don't need rescuing!"

"Then exercise your free will and come to me. We'll distract your guards so you can."

"I can't." I tried to scramble away from him, my heart pounding in terror that he'd somehow grab me and drag me out the window, carrying me away, screaming, into the night. But I was trapped between him and the tower wall.

His face fell, disappointment followed by anger. "You can and you will." He took me by the shoulders, strong hands biting into my arms. His hair draped around me, curtaining out the world. "If you won't come to me, I'll come for you. Wherever they hide you, I will find you. This I swear."

Lady Gaignor, blond hair spilling in a wild tangle around her, shook me by the shoulders.

"Princess Andi—wake up! We must get you to safety."

Behind her, my three sentries ranged in the doorway, swords gleaming deadly in the torchlight from the antechamber. Men in armor poured into the outer room with much clashing and banging. Sounds poured in from outside. Horrible shrieks and angry cries.

I rolled across the bed to the window. Below, dark shapes swarmed over the bridges, climbing up the outer walls with spidery strength and speed. Archers picked them off here and there, but ten times as many spilled over. The sword-bearing soldiers fared no better—more seemed to be chasing after furry, long-legged shapes than skewering any. Great black raptors dived from the sky, harassing soldiers and archers alike.

Everywhere, bodies were strewn about, human and animal, blood pools glimmering in the light of the torches on the walls. In the brief moment I caught, an enormous black wolf took down one of our soldiers, jaws locked on the woman's throat.

"Princess!" One of the sentries grabbed me around the waist, placing himself between me and the window. "It's not safe for you to look out."

"I just wanted to see—"

"Put this on, Princess." Violet Gaignor looked as panicked as I'd ever seen her. She threw a black cloak over me and knelt to slip boots onto my feet, lacing them tightly.

"Boots? Do they really go with my nightgown?" It was all so absurd.

"In case the enemy manages to penetrate the inner walls. And believe me, you'd be glad to have them then."

Ursula came striding in, steely eyes glinting as she surveyed me. Some kind of shining black liquid spattered her boots. "Why isn't anyone on that window? Moxon, Din—get over there and cover it. Andi—why in Glorianna aren't you out the door already? I taught you better than this. I swear you can sleep through anything."

"My sword is on the press by the window—would someone allowed to go near the window hand it to me?"

One of the soldiers—Moxon, maybe—leaned around the open arch of the window and snagged my sword where it lay in its sheath, the leather belt snaking around it. With a blush and a nod, he handed it to me. I buckled it on over my nightgown.

"You should keep it closer than that."

"Not all of us sleep with our swords, Ursula."

Someone sniggered and I regretted my sharp words until she replied.

"Not all of us are so lucky as to lie about while others give their lifeblood to protect us. Speaking of which—why aren't you in the safe room yet?"

"If you'll get someone to gather up some real clothes for me, I can change in whatever room you're hiding me in."

She nodded at me and I let Gaignor bundle me out of the room. Tall soldiers surrounded us, so all I could see were backs and shoulders. Between their striding legs, I glimpsed the hallway, the floor flooded with a pool of shining black. They took us to an inside holding room, several floors up from the ground level, but not in one of the towers.

"Did you see anything?" I asked her. The sounds roaring across the castle seemed far worse for coming from invisible sources. What made that peculiar howl?

Gaignor shook her head. "No. Nor do I care to." She dashed tears away, stifling a sob.

"Hey—don't cry. They're probably just making a show, to get the King to hand me over. Posturing. You know how the fighters do."

"If they breach the outer courtyard—what of the horses?" she choked out.

My stomach congealed, cold with dread. The horses would be killed. I imagined the stables on fire, Fiona screaming as she burned. Midnight-blue eyes flashed in my mind, Rayfe smiling that cocked half smile, his wolfhounds milling around him while he dug his long fingers affectionately through their fur.

"They won't hurt the horses." My voice carried conviction and Violet blinked at me through her tears. "They love animals. It's the soldiers who will die." Faceless men and women in their armor. I didn't know the names of most of them. Not like Ursula did.

The door opened with a crash and Amelia came rushing in, a vision in creamy lace that barely concealed her lithe-limbed body, largely because she'd neglected to fasten the emerald velvet robe she'd tossed on over it.

She flung herself in my arms, twilight-blue eyes wide with concern.

"Are you all right, Andi? Those horrible creatures haven't hurt you?"

"No—have you seen them?"

"Yes." She shuddered, shaking her hands as if they were spattered with night dirt. "They swarmed our tower. Hugh had to fight them off to get me through. Horrible. But he carved through those beasts like they were nothing."

Gaignor and I exchanged glances.

"What *were* they, Amelia? We haven't seen anything."

"Haven't you? Oh! I thought surely if they were in our tower, they would have been in yours. Of course, they can't know where we each sleep, so I suppose it was chance."

Except I knew it wasn't. Rayfe knew where I slept. Those weren't just dreams; they couldn't be. My arms ached where he'd grasped me, and I still smelled his scent on me, never mind how impossible that might be. My head throbbed.

"The creatures, Princess Amelia," Lady Gaignor urged, "what are they?"

Amelia bit her lip. "They're not like anything. Rats, maybe. Yes, like large rats with no tails and sharp teeth. And they're black as midnight. When Hugh cut them with his sword, black fluid poured out, leaving them these empty sacks. Hairy bags of nothing, strewn everywhere. But their blood poured over the steps, coating everything. Hugh had to carry me over it."

The black spatter on Ursula's boots, the slick pools covering the white stone floors.

"Rats don't howl." I couldn't sit, so I stood to pace the small chamber, feeling silly in my riding boots and white nightgown, cinched around my waist with the sword belt. "Did you see dogs? Like wolfhounds?"

"No one breeds wolfhounds anymore, Princess." Lady Gaignor said it gently, like I might be delusional and in need of soothing. I realized I'd dug my fingers into my hair and was pressing my skull. The headache that had never quite faded spiked, hot and cruel. The howls from outside seemed to be crying my name.

"You're thinking of Rayfe's wolfhounds, in that meadow," Amelia breathed. She cocked her head, listening. "I don't hear howling. And I didn't see any dogs—just those rat things."

"You're wrong." I paced faster. This room was far too small. I needed to see outside. "They're out there. Can't you hear them? They're in pain. They need me."

Come to me.

"Did you hear that?"

Gaignor and Amelia exchanged looks. Amelia slowly rose to her feet, holding out a slim white hand to me. "Come sit down. We need to be quiet and wait."

"No!" I screamed at her. "Don't you see? I should never have left my dagger in his shoulder. In his heart. He's bleeding. Can't you hear him howling?"

I grabbed the latch and flung the wooden door open. The surprised guards spun, swords flashing silver up to my face. I ducked beneath, making it only a bare stride before one wrapped his mailed arms around me, lifting me from my feet, crushing me while I screamed incoherently.

"Don't hurt her," Amelia sobbed in the background.

"She's gone mad," Gaignor called. "Restrain the Princess. Do not harm her."

More shouting, and a flock of small blackbirds filled the hallway, warbling so sweetly that the screams, the black ooze pouring down the nearby steps, seemed impossibly vulgar and wrong. I stilled, watching them. They swirled a perfect spiral and vanished. When their song ceased, the howling had stopped also. And the pain in my head miraculously eased.

All the tumult from outside ceased, leaving an unnatural silence heavy in the air.

The guard set me down.

We stood there, pretending nothing odd had occurred, while I adjusted my gown around the sword belt and drew the cloak tight around me. A chill breeze speaking of more rain poured in, meaning that the great front doors of the castle were open again.

Ursula's boot steps came snapping down the hallway. I heard her calling out orders for scouting parties and renewed guards. "My sisters—are they all right?"

She rounded the corner and raised a sardonic eyebrow at me. Shining black drops spattered her high cheekbone on one side. Some of my and Amelia's ladies scurried behind her—including the garrulous Lady Dulcinor, who threw me a scandalized look disguised as sympathy—thankfully carrying better clothes for us.

"Your clothes, as ordered." Ursula's tone was dry—though for my telling her what to do or for something else, I couldn't be sure.

Amelia's ladies slipped past into the little room, drawing the door shut behind them. Gaignor took my clothes and starting shaking them out for me.

"I can't change in my room?"

"You're not going back to your chambers—too dangerous."

"What's going on?" Amelia called out.

"The enemy"—Ursula gave me a curious look—"suddenly fell back. They appear to be in full retreat. Our forces are in pursuit, but we must take advantage of this opportunity. Andi, change your clothes—the King is on his way."

Too late. Uorsin's bellowed orders rattled down the hallway, bouncing off the marble floors and soaring ceilings. Ursula stepped back a pace, setting herself apart. Not a good sign.

Uorsin came around the corner, clad in gleaming golden armor, scarlet cape swirling with the vigor of his stride. His grizzled hair bristled in disarray from the helm he'd yanked off, the one the young page trotting at his side carried like a shield. Hugh followed, off Uorsin's left shoulder, his bright armor spattered with red and black blood. Uorsin held his naked sword still, the bright silver length dripping with shiny black. I'd never seen my father so radiant, so brilliantly present. His eyes flared with battle fire.

Then he pinned me with his gaze.

I drew myself up, acutely conscious that, with Amelia having changed, I alone now wore my nightclothes, topped as my gown was with a riding cloak. Surrounded by these armored people, I felt suddenly alien to them. Whatever had woken in me to the presence of the Tala around me still prowled in my heart. I was part Tala, and Tala wore no armor. My defenses came from inside. I would not quail in imagined guilt before my family.

I had done nothing wrong. I only wanted to stay in my home.

"My King." I curtsied, trying to steady myself against the soul-crushing fear. "Prince Hugh and Princess Ursula. We offer our undying gratitude for your defense of us tonight."

Hugh's face changed, passing from the grim lines of the warrior to such a glowing expression of joy and tenderness that it was almost embarrassing to look upon. I knew that meant Amelia had slipped out of the room behind me. She joined me in the curtsy, slipping her delicate fingers through mine.

"Indeed, my King, my sister. My husband and prince—we are grateful. And thankful for your continued well-being." Amelia's voice held a question, and I saw Hugh's slight nod. Her breath sighed out in a rush of relief, as if she'd discovered that she, too, would live.

"We were victorious," Uorsin declared. "The Tala fled before our superior forces. They are no match for us."

A pair of servants passed down the hall then, one pulling and the other pushing a wooden wagon piled high with furry black bodies, the empty sacks Amelia had described. My stomach clenched for all the death and suffering, and I yanked my gaze away to find Uorsin still staring at me, calculating. Angry, yes, but he also loved every moment of this.

Uorsin, the hero of the Twelve Kingdoms. I could see that young man in him now, the one who'd emerged from the Wild Lands with a bride—nowhere was it mentioned how willing she might have been—and proceeded to take over the known world. Remaking it in his image.

"We fought bravely tonight," Uorsin declared to no one in particular. He handed his sword to the page. Another popped forward with a cleaning cloth. Uorsin stripped off his gauntlets and handed them to another page without taking his gaze from me. "And our cowardly attackers failed in their foolish quest to take what belongs to me. But this is far from over."

He seemed to be waiting for an answer from me. I waited him out. Something not quite sane rode through his voice. No one seemed to hear it but me.

"You do have the look of her," Uorsin mused. "I wonder what else of hers you got."

He closed the space between us, raised his hand, and I braced myself. But he only lifted a long stream of my hair where it flowed thick and loose over my shoulder. "This is her hair, too red to be black. Never mind your witchy eyes. Somewhere in there you are mine as much as your sisters are. You will give me what your mother denied me. I see it now. They will regret this attempt to take what's rightfully mine. You belong to me. Your power is mine, not theirs! They think to have you as I had her, and I won't allow it, do you hear? I would see you dead first!"

His voice ended in a thunderous roar, his meaty fist bunched in my hair so my scalp screamed with it. But I refused to flinch. Amelia clutched my hand so tightly, she crushed the bones together. I hoped she wouldn't cry even as I marveled that she didn't cringe back from him.

"You are to be sent away, Daughter. Now is the ideal time, before those unclean vermin summon up the dregs of their pitiful courage again. I shall question the prisoners and discover their strategy. Then we shall eliminate every last one and you shall help me take possession of their lands. This is the price they will pay."

Uorsin released me so suddenly, I staggered against Amelia. She held me tight. Hugh and Ursula both maintained diplomatically polite faces.

"Set your ladies to packing your things. Take whichever among them you wish to. No telling how long we'll have to hide you away. We shall make them believe you are here, inviting them to try their pitiful attacks until they have nothing left. They think I don't know that once they come out, they cannot return." He smiled unpleasantly and glared, clearly waiting for my reply.

"Thank you, my King." I stammered the words somehow, from behind the fist in my throat. A day ago I hadn't imagined myself as anything but the invisible middle daughter, living my cozy and uneventful life. It seemed my mind had great trouble catching up to all the changes. I couldn't quite conceive of who I'd be, in this new place I'd never seen. *I don't want to leave my home.* Had I told Rayfe that only hours ago? And now I would anyway.

Amelia squeezed my numb hand, reminding me I still had sisters. Dafne Mailloux had survived without that much. I could be at least that strong.

"My King and Father?"

Ursula stiffened with a steely warning glare, but I ignored her. I knelt at Uorsin's feet, ignoring the gore encrusting his boots. I bowed my head and waited.

"Speak." His voice was gruff, but not so angry. I raised my head and he offered his hand, the one he'd wrapped so cruelly in my hair. I took it and leaned my forehead against it, following a vague memory of my mother doing this very thing.

"I shall take Dafne Mailloux with me." I thought it best to sound as didactic as he. Uorsin understood that. "I know you will need your dungeon space because of all the trouble I've caused. I'll have her remove her books and so forth from that space and store them in my empty chambers for the time being."

"That is unusually thoughtful of you, Daughter. Though I had thought to use those useless tomes and silly scrolls as fodder for the bonfires."

"As you think best, of course, my King," I murmured to his hand.

"Ech," Uorsin pulled his hand away and lifted my chin. His glittering eyes surveyed my face. "You were never one to care much for books. Why now?"

I tried to keep my face impassive. Desperately I wished for Ursula's cool steel.

"They do matter to you. How interesting. Fine, then. Ursula— rouse Lady Mailloux, if no one has done so. Inform her she'll be traveling with Princess Andi"—he flicked a glance at Hugh—"to parts unknown. Direct her staff to remove all the texts to the Princess's former chambers, which shall be stripped of her belongings."

"Thank you, my King," I told him, when he paused to hear it.

"We will keep them for you. Along with that horse you love so well. Should I have any reason to doubt that your loyalty lies with me and me only, I shall make a bonfire of those precious books and burn your horse alive upon them."

He smiled, a grim warrior's smile that savored his hold over me.

He'd been the one to set me on my first pony's back. It was my birthday, the last one before my mother died. She'd given me a doll, so excited to show it to me. She'd suggested I name the doll Garland. I'd kissed her and handed the doll back—it wasn't a very pretty thing—and my father had promised to show me how to ride, giving me attention I rarely received. Happy, I realized now, that I liked his gift better than hers. I cheerfully named the little black pony Garland, instead. My mother never said anything that I recalled. She set the doll on the shelf near my bed, to watch over me, she said.

This memory, so vivid, hurtled through me like a shooting star in the aftermath of my father's threat and his clear pleasure in my suffering.

Uorsin turned and strode off to question his prisoners, unholy glee in his eyes.

And I, hollow inside, prepared to leave the only home I'd ever known.

6

After that pronouncement, no one dared speak.

I took my clothes from Gaignor while Hugh drew Amelia aside, murmuring to her and cupping her lovely face in his hands. She leaned against him, red-gold hair streaming nearly to the floor, and he laid his cheek against the top of her shining head. They looked like a painting that should be called *The Lovers*. Ursula watched them too, and for the first time I saw the longing in her. She caught my look and hardened her face, raising her eyebrows at me.

"I don't think you really want to dillydally," she said.

I could have said a lot of things to that, but I didn't. I stepped into that close little room and Gaignor helped me strip and don what they'd brought me. Servants' clothes—trousers, rough shirt, leather jacket—probably a good choice. Gaignor braided my hair for me. She sniffed and had me hold the half-done braid so she could wipe her nose.

"Why do you weep, Violet?"

"How can you not be weeping, Princess Andi?" Her voice trembled and she yanked on the braid. "We're leaving everything we know. Everyone we love."

"You don't have to come with me."

"My place is by your side. Would you shame me by refusing my service?"

I waited until she tied off the braid, then turned and took her hands in mine. Her face showed lines of fear and grief. I wondered if she regretted leaving her home at Castle Gaignor to serve at court.

"What I ask of you is to stay here and care for Fiona."

Her face whitened. "I wouldn't be able to stop the King if—"

I shook my head to stop her. "I know. Just . . . do what you can. Ride her and love her, so that if—" Unexpectedly my throat closed, unshed tears running down the back of it. Suddenly it all rushed up and strangled me. I had to push hard to get the words out. "If these are her last days, I want them to be happy ones."

Violet understood that at least. She clutched my hands and nodded. "I can do that much. I'll care for her. Besides, you're as loyal as the day is long. Nothing will happen to her."

I nodded, feeling the weight of all the lies I'd told. The restlessness that had begun prowling my heart lately snarled at Uorsin's tactics. Had he used something like that to bind my mother to him? There was something, given what I'd seen of his methods.

I embraced Gaignor and thanked her for her service. Hugh, Amelia, and Ursula waited for me, my sentries still discreetly down the way. The castle clattered with activity, the sounds of carriages and horses heavy from the yard.

"We're sending out conscription notices to the villages—and warnings to be on the lookout for further guerrilla attacks. It will also provide good cover for you, to have so many coming and going. You'll go with Hugh and Amelia in an unmarked carriage," Ursula told me. Now she looked tired. She would be without us, also. It hadn't seemed quite real, when Amelia married and went off on her honeymoon. We knew she'd visit. Now the time of our girlhood seemed truly over. We would leave and Ursula would stay here, at our father's side.

No telling when, or if, we'd all three be together again.

I wasn't the only one thinking that, I felt sure.

I wanted to ask what she thought of Uorsin's blackmail. Or if she was used to his tactics.

She shook her head at me, wearily, as if she read my thoughts. "Don't worry, Andi. You'll learn that people behave oddly under extremes. All will come to rights."

I knew, though, that she had it backward. The extremes show how people truly are. I wouldn't forget that lesson.

I embraced her and Amelia joined us. Ursula tensed, then intertwined her arms with ours in our old three-way hug. We touched the tops of our heads together, staring at our toes. Amelia's silk rose slippers, my dusty riding boots, Ursula's gore-spattered steel-tips.

"Thank you, Ursula," I whispered into our little silence. "You probably deserved a brother, instead of me. Or a sister less . . . tainted."

"Don't say that," Ursula's voice hissed, ferocious. "You are our sister. You were right—what is in you is in us."

"Yes." Amelia's sweet voice smoothed over Ursula's, no less firm. "You are us and we are you. We always shall be."

Those traitorous tears welled up again, and I swallowed them down. I searched for words and found none. "Thank you," I offered again. It felt weak, but they squeezed me and we broke apart, ducking our faces to wipe our eyes.

Hugh, who'd been pretending to examine a balustrade, looked over to us. Somehow, even though the dead of night still hung over us, he gleamed with sunlight.

"Are you ready, my wife and my sister?"

Amelia and I nodded.

"Amelia and I shall load up our things, then. We'll appear to be making a judicious escape in the night." His usually jovial face carried a new sternness. "Andi—in half an hour's time, you'll join the servants loading the carriages. They'll be watching for you and will show you the hiding place. You'll have to carry some things, to look like one of them, in case we're watched."

I nodded, feeling a little impatient. Didn't he realize how practiced I was at disguise? At being invisible?

"That gives you time to select any of your things you want to bring. Ask the ladies you wish to accompany you to blend in with Amelia's ladies."

"There will be only Lady Mailloux—if she agrees to come."

Ursula flicked a glance at Lady Gaignor, then a knowing one at me. She nodded and gratitude filled me. Ursula understood what Fiona meant to me. She would also do what she could.

"You'll have to give Hugh your sword," Ursula reminded me. I sighed. Of course a servant wouldn't carry one. Not so practiced after all. I unstrapped it and, feeling oddly naked without it, handed it to Hugh, who received it with a grave nod. Yet again I wished I hadn't left my own dagger buried in Rayfe's heart. In his shoulder, that is. Why had I seen it buried in his chest? The image flashed through my mind, Rayfe dead in the snow, the center of a scarlet circle, eyes colorless and fixed on a sky they couldn't see.

My hand fluttered empty over the hip I'd normally strap it to. Hugh smiled in understanding. He snapped out his own dagger and handed it to me hilt first, sketching a bit of a courtly bow with it.

"Allow me to share my blade with you, sister Andi. It's not a pretty piece, but it has served me well for many years."

I took the dagger and slipped it out of its leather sheath while Amelia stood on tiptoe to kiss Hugh's cheek. It was a woodsman's tool, a working knife with a bone handle and a single-edged blade.

"Thank you, Hugh." Moved, I ducked my head and concentrated on threading my belt through the sheath.

He winked at me. "It's the least I can do for my favorite little sister."

Amelia elbowed him.

"What? She is younger than I am—by nearly a whole year. Ursula is my favorite older sister."

We laughed at his clowning, as he undoubtedly meant us to. Hugh's world was an enviably sunny place.

"See you in a little bit." Amelia worried at her rosy lower lip with her pearly teeth. Hugh ushered her off, and with a last nod to me, Ursula followed them.

"I'll help you collect your things?" Violet Gaignor asked me.

I shook my head, reality coming back to me with all its shadows. "Throw together whatever you think I'll need." None of it mattered to me, I realized. The gowns, the jewels, the pretty things. All of it seemed like a lie. None of it meant anything. Except the one thing I had from my mother, which I'd unexpectedly just remembered.

"Wait—" I grabbed Violet's arm as she nodded and turned to do my bidding. "The doll, with the black hair—do you know the one I mean?"

She frowned as she thought. "The one up on the shelf above your mirror, that ugly old thing?"

Unexpected relief undid a knot that had formed around my heart, dissolving a pain I hadn't realized was there until it left. "Yes. I want that."

I sounded crazy; I could tell by the carefully bland look on her face. "Perhaps, Princess, you should come look and see if there's anything else"—*more appropriate*, she didn't say out loud—"that you'd like to take with you."

"I have something else I have to do. Just the doll—and anything else you think right. I trust your judgment."

She nodded and curtsied to me, then bustled down the hallway. I turned to my sentries, not much time left.

"Would you escort me to Lady Zevondeth's chambers?"

I rarely exercised my royal powers of command. In my life up until then, I hadn't needed or cared to. It always felt vaguely unsavory to me. Now I wielded my meager authority like a weapon. The sentries didn't want to take me to Zevondeth, but they also dared not refuse me, despite my dubious status. Wondering if Dafne was even now cursing my name, I followed them to another wing of the castle, wasting another few precious minutes of my small window of time in the long walk.

Lady Zevondeth was just returning to her bed when her maid announced my arrival. She met me in her antechamber, wizened face creased in cranky lines. She didn't care for my summons, either.

"Princess Andi, what an unexpected honor to have you grace my private chambers—and at such an inconvenient time for you, I'm certain, what with all the carrying-on."

Her chambers practically dripped velvet. Small braziers of coals set in strategic spots, along with fires in two fireplaces, brought the room up to a high-summer daytime temperature. Her windows were covered over with tapestries. Likely sealed over, too, given the thick unmoving air, stale with old perfumes. Cloistered in this room, she considered the fighting, the suffering prisoners even now being dragged to the dungeons, the dead and dying being sorted and cast onto pyres or hospital beds, a bit of "carrying-on."

Unexpected fury consumed me and I nearly pulled my borrowed dagger on her.

"Oh, this is an exceedingly convenient time for me, Lady Zevondeth. I have questions for you."

"Might an old woman sit, then, and be comfortable?"

"Fine. This won't take long, and then you can tuck your frail bones back into bed."

"Speak, then, child—though I doubt I have any answers for the likes of you."

Ah, there her true nature peeked out. Took a teensy bit of pressure. Which questions to ask, though? So little time to find out everything I needed to know, most of which she wouldn't want to tell me.

"How did you come to be my mother's attendant?"

Surprise softened her face. "Someone told you that? Such ancient history. I hardly think it matters now."

"It matters to me. Tell me."

"You don't have as much power as you think you have, Princess. Full well I know what a precarious position you're in."

"Then you have nothing to lose." I didn't bother to wonder how she knew what only a few should.

She laughed at that, a sound like an old horse coughing. "You have no idea what I have to gain or lose. But"—she held up a crooked finger—"I am willing to be bought. Send your men to wait in the hallway."

They protested, of course, and another precious minute was lost while they shuffled out to wait with Lady Zevondeth's maid outside the door. Lady Zevondeth hobbled over to the chair by the fire and sat, raising an eyebrow, defying me to say anything. Waiting for my offer.

"What's your price? And how do I know what you'll tell me is worth it?"

"Oh, it's worth it. You do not hold what I want in high regard." She beckoned to me, holding out a hand that trembled with palsy. Uneasy, I went to her and laid my hand in hers. Her grip, stronger than I would have thought, held me while she picked up a slim silver knife from the marble-topped table beside her. She shushed me when I tried to pull back, and pricked my finger with the razor tip of the blade. My bright blood welled up. She caught it in a glass vial, letting my hand go and corking the little bottle. Gazing at it in satisfaction, she gave me a little smile while I sucked on my stinging finger. I imagined it turning into little birds and flying away.

"What will you do with it?"

"Does it matter? I thought you wanted other answers."

I did. I nodded.

"Salena had no manners when Uorsin wed her. No understanding of court politics. And she had that odd . . . feral quality. I had a school at that time—the best in Duranor—to teach all the refinements to noble young ladies." She sat up straighter in her fancy chair. "Yes, you didn't know that. As commanded by the old King of Duranor, I closed the school, sent my girls home, and taught your mother. I made a queen out of her—my finest creation. My masterpiece. And she let it all go."

I stared at her, unable to assemble my thoughts, and she inclined her head, regal, pulling an impassive mien over the hatred that had flashed so briefly, like a green shadow over her face.

"That answers the question you asked. Because you paid a high price for it—higher than you know now—I'll answer the questions you didn't know to ask. She would have honored that contract. It was her dearest hope to return with you to the Tala, to her own people. Uorsin knew it, too. We could all see it. Once she delivered Uorsin his third child, as required by the contract, she planned to take you and raise you among the Tala.

"She often said to me that if you were to marry a man of the Tala, she wanted you to grow up knowing their ways. She didn't want you to suffer as she did, lost among a foreign people. She had some other reason that you needed to grow up among the Tala. Something to do with the mark. She seemed to think something would harm you if you did not go to them."

"What?"

She squinched up her wrinkled face as if she smelled something bad. "Who knows? She made less and less sense as time went on. She should have known, though, that he'd take the opportunity to betray her wishes. She stopped him from having his greatest desire, so he took his revenge by denying hers. Toward the end, they had only hate for each other. The way he treated her . . ." Zevondeth shook her head, gazing at the fire.

"I think she would have taken you the day you were born, had she not owed Uorsin a third child. She should have gone before he destroyed her completely."

"And it took her another five years to quicken."

"She waited five years to quicken," Lady Zevondeth corrected me sharply. "Don't underestimate her as Uorsin did. He laid with her often, but her people believed that less than five years between babies weakens the mother and produces sickly children.

Even for you, she wouldn't jeopardize her third child's future. She was a demon on the subject. She always said you three were the whole reason for everything she'd done."

"But then she died of childbirth fever."

"So they say."

"Don't you know? You nursed her, I hear."

Lady Zevondeth looked weary. An old woman dwarfed by her velvet chair, canny eyes filmed with age.

"How and why does death take any of us? She had much to live for, but in the end, she failed to survive."

"You said he destroyed her."

She looked away, into the fire. "I'll deny it, should you repeat that, and you are the one marked for the Tala, carrying the taint of traitor to Uorsin's kingdom, not I."

The dismissal was clear and I was out of time—the sentries knocking on the door, calling me to go.

"Thank you," I said, though I'd paid for the information. Perhaps dearly, according to her hints. I nearly snatched up the little vial, the crimson of my blood gleaming in the firelight. It would tip the scales, though, something in me knew. Fair was fair. I turned to go.

"Andromeda," she called after me. I looked back, and she sat forward in her chair, a strange smile twisting her thin lips. "The bear never gives up what he believes is his. He kills to keep it and he's very good at killing. And he's always hungry. He's starving for the one thing he could never have. Beware of where his appetite reaches."

I pulled open the door and began running. So I would not be late, I told myself.

Even the clatter of my armored sentries jogging behind me didn't quite drown out Lady Zevondeth's coughing laughter.

7

From my nest among the trunks and bundles on top of Hugh and Amelia's carriage, I watched the fingernail crescent moon riding high in a sky turning from darkest night to the pure blue of dawn. I pressed my sore finger, still bleeding a little, against my thumb, savoring the bruised pain. It seemed fitting, somehow, that I should hurt, even in such a minor way.

Only you can stop all this.

Though I'd been awake all night, my mind wouldn't settle enough for me to sleep now, as the groomsmen tucking me into the baggage had advised. They'd made me a surprisingly comfortable spot amid the softer bags, padded with blankets, a thoughtfulness for my comfort that warmed me. The way they all wished me Glorianna's protection and vowed to protect me with their lives dug under my skin.

If my mother had lived, I would already be among the Tala. I tried to picture that girl and failed. I would have grown up Tala and perhaps their ways wouldn't seem so strange to me. Maybe they wouldn't have found *me* so strange. No one would have died protecting me, defending this honor I supposedly carried around with me like a precious jewel. Now, for the first time, I thought about turning myself over to Rayfe. Ending all of this, as he'd asked in my dream.

The implied warning, though—that bothered me. If my mother believed I might lose my mind if I married into the Tala, going to them full-grown—perhaps everyone was right that I needed to be saved from that. The thought fed my many fears. Salena had been nearly feral, Lady Zevondeth said. Did the Tala live like animals, roaming the Wild Lands, foraging for food and pillaging helpless villages?

If I hadn't met Rayfe, I might have believed that. Wild inside, yes, but with the veneer of a man, at least. He'd said something about where he lived, implying I might at least have a roof over my head. And marriage. Surely they wouldn't kill me. *Not until I produced children,* a voice whispered. Perhaps three for them, to repay the bargain. Blood for blood. I might get ten years, maybe a little more, according to their customs, before they asked for a death to balance Salena's death. Or was that Uorsin's thinking?

Ten years of Rayfe in my bed. Living a life where I would . . . what?

Toward the end, they had only hate for each other. It was impossible to imagine. My mother had always seemed so strong and powerful. How had Uorsin destroyed her? Would Rayfe do the same to me?

As for that, what of my father's threats? What were his plans for me? *He's starving for the one thing he could never have. Beware of where his appetite reaches.*

So many warnings and no sense of where I should turn, what I should do.

What's your plan? Dafne had asked me.

And here I still didn't have one. Just a command from my King, the earnest love in Amelia's eyes, promising to hide me and keep me safe, and Hugh's noble vows. I finally fell asleep to the rocking carriage, only vaguely wondering where I'd wake up.

We stopped for a late breakfast and for everyone to stretch

their legs. I climbed down from the carriage, and everyone pretty much ignored me. Amelia fluttered her fingers in my direction, but Hugh pulled her away to the satin quilts spread under an apple tree. I pulled my little cap down over my brow and went to help take food to the royals.

The other servants gave me thin-lipped or startled looks, but I shrugged and held out my hands to be filled. One of Amelia's maids handed me a glass teapot and a delicate little cup. I carried it to Amelia and set it beside her with a murmured "Milady," while I bowed deep.

"It's not funny, Andi," Amelia muttered under her breath. Hugh caught my eye and winked, patting Amelia's rose-clad knee.

Did I find this funny? I strolled through the camp, munching on an apple, feeling oddly free to be away from the castle and all those expectations. I liked being out in the air—all my fears and worries seemed less potent on such a lovely, sunny morning like this. On any normal day, I would have been cooped up in court, listening to tales of failed apple harvests instead of eating a piece of the fruit, counting the minutes until I could dash out to Fiona and go riding. No sense of lightness and freedom there. Inside me a fist of anger and despair festered for my father and his threats. I poked at it, last night's scene replaying in my mind, poisonous rage spilling into my blood.

Best not to think about that right now.

"Andi?"

Dafne Mailloux strolled up, decked out now in proper ladies' garb of a daffodil-yellow gown. It appeared we'd reversed roles, and I smiled at the thought. I ducked my head to her. "Milady Mailloux—how may I serve you?"

She wrinkled her nose at me. "I can't believe you're enjoying this."

"Thank you for coming with me."

"Thank you for saving the library."

"Yes, well—as to that—it's fairly temporary and contingent on my good behavior."

"I heard the gossip, that the King threatened to burn your horse on a pyre of those books."

Uorsin's voice did carry. "So much for my dramatic secret escape, then."

She dropped her voice and laid a hand on my arm. "Are you all right?"

"I still don't have a plan." I shrugged. "I'm being swept along."

"You'll know when to change that."

"Will I? I left my horse behind, Dafne. Just like that. And I can't decide which is worse—that I did or that what happens to Fiona matters more to me than all those people who died last night, whose names I don't even know." Tears were pricking my eyes, so I opened them very wide, keeping the betraying sorrow from showing.

"You're in a bit of shock, I think." Dafne held my gaze with reassuring steadiness. "You might give yourself more than two days to assimilate such a dramatic change in who you know yourself to be."

Her words struck me, like little barbed arrows burrowing into my flesh. Dafne gave me a last smile and went to sit with Amelia and her other ladies, bright and lovely blossoms in the shade of the tree. I walked in the other direction.

Overhead, a giant black raptor wheeled a gentle spiral in the clear air.

We stopped for the night at the Louson country manse of one of Uorsin's generals from the days of the Great War. He'd been richly rewarded with this fertile river valley. I blended with the servants. What had been long habit—reflexive, even—I now practiced in a more deliberate way. It wouldn't do for me to be seen here, and General Meanneres had been to court frequently and lengthily over the years. His attention, though, was all for Amelia—with almost insultingly scant notice for Hugh, who looked more than a little irritated at Meanneres snuffling kisses on Amelia's soft hand.

Remembering himself, or perhaps catching a glimpse of Hugh's mood, Meanneres asked after news of the strange attack at the castle, already being called the Assault of Ordnung, usually keeping his gaze on Hugh during the conversation and not on Amelia's gleaming white bosom. He relayed another tale, of convicts escaping from a prison nearby and wreaking havoc on the local farmers—chaos blamed on the Tala.

Meanneres never even saw me as I helped unhitch the horses and took them to the stables. I ate supper with the stable lads and lasses, too, a merry affair, as the servants from our retinue forgot who I was in the midst of pretending that I was just another servant for the benefit of the Louson folk. The servants of both households gathered around tables in the yard, enjoying the warm evening and exchanging tales. I tucked myself at the end of one bench and listened.

All any of them wanted to talk about was the Tala attack, though no one referenced them by that name.

"Did you see the demons with your own eyes?" asked one young stableboy, face alight with horrified excitement. "I heard they have teeth as long as my hand and black blood that's poison to good people."

"Glorianna protect us." The prayer murmured through the group.

One of our sentries allowed as how he'd been on the wall during the attack. "The night was quiet—all as usual. Then such noise!" He shook his head, as if to clear those shrieking howls from his memory. "The air was full of these giant crows. We couldn't see to loose our arrows, even, and when we did, we missed more often than not. The man next to me had his helm off, and one of those cursed birds went for his eyes . . ." He rubbed his own in sympathy.

"And the dogs," another sentry added, "they swam the moat and went for the throats of anyone in their way. All the time they're baying, just as hunting hounds after a fox. Calling and calling, like they expected some kind of answer."

I shivered remembering that lonely cry.

"And the demons?" urged the first stableboy.

"I dunno." Another soldier drained his mug before he continued. "I don't know what demons look like, but they captured one . . . man, I guess he was. Black hair as long as a woman's, and pale white skin. Whiter than the pampered breasts of Princess Amelia."

No one cast awkward looks in my direction at that. They'd forgotten my presence entirely. I let the stories roll over me. They exhausted the Assault at Ordnung pretty quickly, since it seemed very few people had seen much of anything and it hadn't lasted all that long, all told. They'd gone on to wilder and more gruesome tales from the distant past. I didn't know a lot about battles, but this one hardly seemed devastating. Rayfe was simply tweaking Uorsin's nose, the thought came to me. And he'd sent his people close enough to offer that urgent invitation to me, to provide distraction, if I'd been brave enough to take it.

If the sentry hadn't held me, in that wild and painful longing, I would have gone. I shivered at how close I'd come to disaster.

And yet—the thought whispered to me that I could go now. Walk off into the night. He'd find me, no doubt. That black bird—surely it was the same one—had followed us all day. Uorsin had underestimated Rayfe in thinking he wouldn't know I'd left Ordnung. *I have the taste of your blood now.* It seemed that something moved in the deep shadows, just beyond the stables, where the lamplight failed to penetrate. Nauseating fear chilled my gut, and yet I stood, strangely compelled, torn between the opposing forces of my terror and my longing.

"There you are," Lady Dulcinor hissed in my ear. "I'm sent to fetch you, Princess Andi. I've been standing here forever, looking and looking for you. I didn't dare ask any of them, because I promised to be discreet, of course. Still, I thought, surely I'll see the Princess immediately and it will be no trouble, but then I didn't see you and—"

"Yes, Lady." I bobbed and ducked my head. "I'll come serve you right away."

She gaped at me and I simply started walking, as if she'd scolded me to hurry. Moranu, I'd never done this sort of subterfuge before, either, but some things seemed intuitive. She scrambled after me.

"Where are we going?" I asked under my breath.

"Princess Amelia asks that you meet her in Glorianna's chapel. I'm sorry, Princess An—"

"It would be wise, I think, not to call me by name."

"Oh, but I would never wish to show you a lack of respect, Prin—"

"Maybe best not to talk at all, hmm?"

I found Glorianna's chapel easily enough, since they're always situated on the south side of any property, and almost always as pink as can be managed. If the property owners can't find a way to make the chapel pink, they plant pink roses or add stained glass or what have you. They're always lit from within, too, so at night like this the chapels are beacons of glowing pinkness.

Amelia met me as soon as I walked in the door, enveloping me in a crushing embrace of amethyst silk a shade deeper than her eyes.

"Oh, I hate this!" she exclaimed. "How are you holding up—is it awful?"

"No, darling." I hugged her back, seeing she was on the verge of tears. "It's fine. I'm fine. All is going well."

"I'm just so afraid. I keep thinking—what if the Tala attack us while we're on the road? Hugh says he and his men will fight them off, but I worry so. We won't reach Avonlidgh for days, even going at this pace. The tales people told at court dinner. You wouldn't believe it."

"I've heard stories, too. You know how people are, always wanting to top each other with something worse."

"It's not something to laugh at, Andi." Amelia clutched my shoulders, digging in with a fierce grip. "If something were to happen to you, I—"

"Nothing will happen. Don't fret so much. Look—I'm fine."

"You're *not* fine," she hissed. "Don't pretend for me that all of this isn't awful. I'm stronger than you and Ursula think. And I've arranged for a protection ceremony. There are three priests of Glorianna here and they'll do a High Protection, just for you. That way if there is any magic—or anything—you'll be safe."

I opened my mouth to protest. The last thing I wanted to do right now was spend the next several hours being purified by Glorianna's priests. The desperation in Amelia's face stopped me.

"Thank you, Amelia." I hugged her again and she relaxed fractionally. "Let's do that."

The priests waited for us at the altar, slender young men with bald heads and ornate robes in shades of mauve and rose. Consecrated to Glorianna as boys, they never knew a woman's touch—or a man's, for that matter—as their vows prohibited it. Stories abounded, though, of what Glorianna's priests got up to with one another, as part of her worship. Virginity could be a relative concept. Many noble families sent sons who seemed overly feminine as youths to Glorianna's temple. Whether this was to offer the boys an accepting home or to save the family from shame very much depended on the family.

If the former, the gambit seemed not terribly successful, because Glorianna's priests had a reputation for cattiness and cruelty that seemed at odds with the goddess's peaceful message. But then, I'd always enjoyed more the midwinter ceremony that was Moranu's, though Uorsin had declared these low holy days.

Maybe that was one reason I liked them, the quiet observances of the change of seasons. The way the full moon shone through Moranu's silvered window high in the ceiling, when we doused all the torches and toasted the turn of the year. Those were fun, informal parties, not like the elaborate rituals in spring and fall to observe Glorianna and her gracious descent and ascent.

A woven mat of pink roses covered the white marble. Rose-scented candles burned in every nook, loading the air with such heavy perfume that my nose stung with it. An enormous rosepaned circular window loomed behind the priests. The image sang through my brain of the bird crashing through the identical glass at Ordnung, how easily it had shattered. The slender priests seemed like pale flowers when I remembered the storm of fury in Rayfe's midnight-dark eyes.

The priests are a conduit for Glorianna's divine power, I reminded myself. The stories of the Tala drawing from the darker magics were just that, stories meant to frighten children. Surely the odd things I'd seen, those weirdly prescient dreams, all had some reasonable explanation.

Amelia made the circle of Glorianna in the air, and we knelt, her fingers interlaced with mine. We bowed our heads as the prayers washed over us. I'd never been so grungy for such a ceremony before, but the traditional bathing and perfuming seemed superfluous at this point—not to mention that we really had no time for it. Amelia's amethyst silk confection was more in keeping with it all. When we'd been girls, every spring we received special new dresses very much like that one for Glorianna's feast of planting.

My knees grew tired and my mind drifted on the waves of numbing prayer. I studied the patterns in the rose window so I wouldn't fall asleep. In the center, as with all of Glorianna's windows, rested an enormous blossom in full flower, so painstakingly re-created, the petals appeared to be velvet soft instead of cold glass. Shapes of petals and leaves radiated away from it, whirling in an unseen wind. Behind those lurked darker shapes, unseen shadows. Or was that a shadow from outside the chapel, moving just beyond the glass?

Then one of the priests stood before me, his soft brown hands holding a cut-crystal bowl filled with rose petals swimming in clear fluid. I closed my eyes and tipped back my head. He dabbed my face with the rose water, the scent cloying. I'd received Glorianna's benediction many times since my childhood. This particular concoction seemed amazingly pungent. For extra cleansing? The candles consumed all the air from the chapel until every breath I took burned. The restlessness shifted inside me, and I longed for the fresh, night air. Only a minute's difference and I might have overcome the fear and walked into the woods, instead of coming here to kneel, suffocating under this false perfume.

The other two priests flanked me, each taking a hand. Amelia moved off to the side, engaged in silent prayer before Glorianna's window. The priests held my hands up high and wide, while the third moved behind me, gently tugging my head back so I gazed at the ceiling, my back arched, his perfumed fingers on my temples. They chanted prayers I didn't know, naming demons, names I'd never heard, beseeching them to leave me. I forced myself to stay still under the ceremony, but it became near impossible.

That restlessness grew bigger, swallowing my heart and my patience. I wanted to snarl, to scream. But I held it all in for Amelia. For Ursula, too. I would be deserving of their love and trust, if only for these few hours. Someone pressed the cool rim of a goblet to my lips and I sipped gratefully, my throat parched. I gulped too much, though, and choked, the sweet rose water going down my breathing passage instead. Convulsing, I coughed up the fluid, wrenching my hands from the priests and bending over, desperate to breathe again.

The heaves shook me, my muscles clenching in waves of pain, tears squeezing out of my eyes.

When I could breathe again, I became aware of the silence. I looked up from my crouched position, blinking away tears, to see the four of them—the priests and Amelia, like an orchid amid roses—staring at me with identical expressions of horror.

"Glorianna refuses Her protection," one of the priests, the one with the soft brown hands, whispered. "I've never seen it so."

The other two priests circled their hearts in the prayer to Glorianna. Amelia knotted her white hands together, worry ravaging her beautiful face.

"I choked, is all," I told them. "With my head stretched back like that, I couldn't help it."

Amelia began to weep, silent tears silvering her cheeks. I

climbed to my feet. Some of the hysteria rumbled in my heart because I wanted to laugh at the absurdity of it all.

"It was an accident! I'll drink the potion." I seized the goblet, but the priest holding it wrapped his hands tightly around it and curled his lip at me.

"No," he snarled. "Glorianna refused you. You may not have it."

"Give it to me." I stared him down, tempted to kick his knee, so he'd drop like the weasel he seemed to be.

"No." His lips trembled and firmed, his rabbit gaze darting back and forth to the other priests, who stood back. Poised to run.

I leaned into him. "Do you dare ignore the command of a Princess of the Realm?"

He gulped. "Glorianna is above mortal kings and queens." It came out as a whine.

"Ah, but kings and queens are above mortal priests. Will Glorianna save you from the High King's wrath? Or mine?"

"Andi . . ."

I held up my hand to Amelia, to stop her plea. "No, Amelia. You thought of this ceremony and potion for me, out of the goodness of your heart. I will have it. Give it to me, Priest. Look—Glorianna's avatar commands it."

Granted, Amelia rarely seemed very commanding, but the threat worked. With a high-pitched subvocalized wail behind pressed lips, the priest yielded the goblet and scurried back to the others, their eyes huge in their soft, hairless faces. I raised the goblet to my lips, steeling my congealing stomach against the curdling sweet smell, and caught Amelia's gaze over the rim.

She looked as if she didn't recognize me.

It stabbed at me, the uncertainty in her shadowed eyes. The rose perfume stung my nose and the bones of my skull throbbed with it. Drink or no? It would be better if I did. She would be reassured. It would make everything right again.

I pressed my lips to the warm metal rim and tilted my head back, determined to drink it down.

Glass shrieked in a tumbling shatter of sound, followed by the high wails of the priests.

Time slowed to clockwork precision, so I impossibly saw it all, the enormous rose-glass window giving way, imploding inward like a pink, beating heart. Blackness at its center resolved into the snarling face of a giant black wolf, blue eyes like flames burning through the pink-riddled air of the close chapel.

The glass shredded around him, falling away as he leapt through the window, over the altar, and landed at my feet, fangs bared. The goblet fell from my nerveless fingers, spilling crimson fluid in an arc across the pale rugs.

I froze. As did the wolf.

A door slammed in the distance. Not daring to take my eyes off the wolf, I whispered, "Amelia?"

Silence. The priests had dragged her out and the soldiers would have swept her away to safety. Good. Not incidentally abandoning me, the one no one knew was here. Not so good.

The wolf glanced about, took a step to sniff at the spill of crimson potion, and growled. My heart hammered against my ribs, my still-uneasy stomach burning. I took a step back and his head snapped to follow my movement. I slid my borrowed dagger from the hilt at my hip. It felt off, the balance unfamiliar.

I took another step back and he followed, intent and predatory. I had nowhere to run to. Blood pounded in panicked thumps in my heart, flashing the image of that great wolf in the courtyard in Ordnung, jaws locked on the woman's throat. And she'd been a trained soldier. I had no hope of escaping a similar fate.

He advanced on me and a little whimper escaped me.

I didn't want to die.

With a cock of his head, the wolf settled his black fur and strode past me. I caught the scent of pine and musk. The wolf paced down the rose runner to the arched wooden doors, shut against the night and its dangers. He looked at me expectantly.

I didn't blame him for not wanting to linger in this place. And there was only one way out, for both of us, unless I wanted to climb through the window's shattered remnants.

My throat crawled acrid and a headache throbbed behind my eyes—from fear or the rose potion. I took a step or two toward the doors and the wolf, keeping the point of the blade between us. He sat back on his haunches, waiting, patient. I circled around him, keeping what distance I could. The wolf cocked his head in that same way, and I could have sworn he laughed at me.

I had to turn an awkward sideways to work the unfamiliar latch with one hand and have the dagger at the ready with the other. I risked a glance at the latch and something bumped my leg. I gasped, stumbling back. The wolf followed, pressing his head against my thigh like a cat. He looked up at me, at the knife, with interested intelligence. I pressed back against the doors and he pressed his muzzle against my leg, nuzzling me just as Fiona might, looking for apple slices or a scratch for that itchy spot between her ears.

Hesitant, ready to snatch my hand back, with a sense of unreality as in those dreams, I reached down and stroked the gray-black fur of his broad head. The wolf pushed forward so my fingers slid between his tufted ears. Obligingly I scratched. The fur felt both rough and soft, the skull under it as hard as rock. He shifted and the ropy muscles rippled under his black coat.

His eyes closed in utter wolfish bliss. Then, with a shake, he moved away and looked inquiringly at the doors again.

Feeling like I was in one of those dreams again, I unfastened the latch and pushed the doors open, half expecting a mob of soldiers rushing to my rescue.

Not yet.

The path stretched away, shadowed and empty through the eerily silent woods. In the distance the lights and sounds of people demarcated another world. Here the moon shone down, silvering the pink light spilling out of the chapel.

The wolf took several steps toward the deeper, darker forest, then looked at me. Clearly expecting me to follow.

"No," I whispered.

The wolf took another step. Looked at me.

"I can't." But, Moranu take me, I wanted to.

He blinked at me, a silver flash of eyeshine. With a bound he was off, black coat dissolving from sight. I lingered, trying to make out his shape or movement, my fingers still tingling from the feel of his fur, my mind turning over what I knew to be real.

"Rayfe?" I whispered, asking the question of the night and no one.

"Right here," he answered from behind me.

8

I didn't scream—though my already pounding heart nearly burst.

I spun around to find him standing there, that half smile twisting his lips. His hair spilled loose and his dark clothes blended with the shadows as surely as the wolf's hide had.

My frantic thoughts battered against one another. I wanted to ask if he was a dream or real. If he was the wolf or the raptor. Or both.

Shape-shifters and wizards.

"Those things don't matter, Andromeda. Not truly. You know that," Rayfe said, as if he'd read my mind.

He reached out and I stumbled back a few hasty steps. "Don't touch me. I'll scream and they'll capture you."

He held up empty palms in reassurance. "No, they won't. I'm not so easily taken. I'm here for you. We can be beyond their reach in a moment."

"I'm not so easily taken either."

He laughed, a dry sound, and rubbed his shoulder where I'd stabbed him. No knife protruded from his muscled arm. Of course it wouldn't. Those were dreams only. "Believe me—I know that."

"Are you . . . real?"

"Touch me and find out."

I shook my head. "I've had . . . dreams. You felt real in those, too."

"Dreams are just a different reality, Andromeda mine. Touch me. I'm just a man. One who wants to make you his queen. I would never hurt you." But a lean hunger infused his face, half-lit in the pink light.

"You hurt me in the meadow."

"A nip—and I'm sorry for it." He held my gaze, steady. "But I had to know. You had to know. Desperation drives many ill deeds. And I apologized for that before."

"That was a dream," I insisted, stubbornly, I know. But still.

"In point of fact, you hurt me."

"I won't apologize for that."

"No." He looked grimly amused. "I never imagined that you would. Touch me."

"Why?"

"So you'll know I'm only a man. That you can trust me."

"You are the last person I can trust."

"That's not true. Besides we have to start somewhere." He clasped his hands behind his back. "One touch."

Why I wanted to, I didn't know, but my fingers itched to do it, as if his presence pulled at me. I took a hesitant step forward, achingly aware of how alone we were. He watched me, intent and somber, much as the wolf had. I stepped close and he held very still. I reached up and touched his cheekbone, rough with evening stubble, his skin hot and smooth beneath.

His eyes gleamed, and, very slowly, he turned his head and pressed a kiss to my finger.

I jumped back as if burned, and pain flared between my eyes. That awful potion. I rubbed at the spot and Rayfe frowned.

"Do you have a headache?"

"It's nothing. A tiresome evening."

"You have to let me help you." Fiery determination rippled through him, and he nearly reached for me, then fisted his hands by his sides. "Come with me. Come to me now and put an end to this chase. You should have come to Annfwn long ago—I can only hope it's not too late."

My heart fluttered at the edge of panic. Or maybe I'd drunk a bit of his desperation.

"I have to do nothing!" I nearly shouted the words. "I won't betray my people. I won't hand myself over like a parcel of goods to be exported."

His jaw flexed in frustration. "Well, nothing is exactly what you are doing, Andromeda—and it's costing both of our peoples. I know you're afraid, but I do not have the luxury of your inaction. You belong to Annfwn."

"I am my own person."

"Are you, Princess? Are you sure about that?"

"No, actually, I'm not, because you appear in my dreams. When you attacked Ordnung . . . very strange things happened in my head. I feel like I can't trust my own thoughts."

He nodded, acknowledging the point, though he seemed angry and frustrated.

Shouts rang from the manse, and I glanced back, startled. "Soldiers. You must go."

I didn't question my impulse to have him run. To evade capture. I could imagine all too well what Uorsin would do to him. Execution would be kind.

He held out a hand. "Come with me. Let me help you. It will only get worse."

"Never."

"Always," he replied. That same vow.

And then the guards were upon us. No, charging past me and attacking Rayfe, who swung a great broad-bladed sword, blurring with speed, impossibly dodging them all. His face twisted in a fierce grimace as two men fell from one ferocious swing of his weapon. Other Tala poured out of the night woods, long black hair flying and blue eyes blazing. Swords met with shrieks, and hoarse shouts of pain shattered the peaceful night.

I'd thought I was rooted to the ground, in my horror, unable to decide which direction to go, but a guard picked me up easily enough, carrying me over his shoulder like the parcel of goods I'd sworn I wouldn't be.

Amelia had roused the entire manse. To rescue a servant girl. What little cover I'd had was well and truly destroyed.

I suppose I couldn't expect her, with her soft heart, to do otherwise. It's not like she could pull an Ursula and launch a stealthy one-woman rescue mission. Still, in the aftermath of the abrupt and unexpected battle, even Hugh shook his head.

"So much for secretly smuggling her to Avonlidgh," he sighed, dismissing the soldiers with a salute and sending his man to disburse the bystanders.

Amelia tipped her head at him, gorgeous curls sliding in the torchlight, fire over gold. "Would you prefer that I let her die there? Or be kidnapped?" Amelia's sweet voice chimed as softly as always, but the edge in it caught his attention.

"No, darling." Hugh slid an arm around her delicate waist and pulled her close. "Of course you couldn't. Just—next time come to me first."

"There wasn't time." She pulled away, took a step toward me, and faltered. "I thought you would be dead already, before I could get back to you. I thought you'd be torn limb from limb. That horrible wolf . . . and then the Tala attacked! Hugh, you said they wouldn't find us here."

"I was wrong." He looked grim, his gaze going to the wagon bringing back the wounded and dead from the forest. Through the trees, a pyre burned, committing the few fallen Tala to ashes.

We'd lost three soldiers for every one of theirs. Unpromising odds for our future.

"How did you escape the wolf, anyway?" Amelia demanded, then gasped, her hand going to her slim throat. "Is it still in the chapel? We must warn the priests!"

I tried to think fast, not easy with my skull tightening on my brain. "I managed to open the door and the wolf ran out."

"Ran out?"

"Yes." I didn't like the look in her eyes. Belatedly I remembered that my white shirt must be spattered with Glorianna's sweet wine, which I'd coughed up like a soldier regretting last night's overindulgence. I wanted to cross my arms over it "You know what they say—they're more afraid of us than we are of them."

Amelia laughed, high and hysterical.

Hugh cleared his throat. "It's late and we have much journeying to do tomorrow. Now that there's no need for secrecy, I'd like to increase our pace. And we won't stop at any more manses."

"You'll take us directly to Windroven?" Amelia's smile shone radiant with relief. The way she spoke of the place—something told me she wouldn't feel safe until we were there.

"Yes, my love. You'll feel much better when you're both inside Windroven's deep walls. The Tala will never reach us there."

He closed the space between him and Amelia, once again encircling her with his arm. She melted now, leaning against him and closing her eyes.

"I'm sorry," she whispered. "I wasn't meant for this. I don't understand anything."

"It's late," he murmured, pressing a kiss to her temple. "Go up to bed and rest. All will be better in the morning."

"But Andi . . ." She spoke this directly to him, not looking at me.

"She'll be safe now. You know I pledged this to you."

She nodded. "I know."

Hugh and I watched her go, then faced each other in that little ante-courtyard. He scrutinized me, even strong and noble Hugh showing uncertainty. I wished I could tell him the extraordinary story. Now it seemed just like another of those crazed dreams, when Rayfe showed me my dagger in his arm. Him, dead in the snow, sightless eyes staring as the snow turned scarlet. A castle rising out of a rocky hillside strewn with bodies, blood running down to a turbulent sea. I wanted to cover my eyes, the torches far too bright.

"Are you unharmed, then? Not covering for Amelia's sake?"

His question yanked me out of the strange fugue of images. No, I couldn't tell him. That I'd spoken to Rayfe and touched him.

"Yes. The wolf truly ran away."

"After crashing through the chapel window."

"Yes." Um. "Perhaps it was ill? Crazed with fever."

"And as you ran back, the Tala attacked you."

"Yes." I really didn't like lying, and now I seemed to be speaking one every time I opened my mouth.

"The captain of the guard said you were just standing there."

"I was afraid." It came out as a whisper, though that, at least, was true.

"That happens, even to experienced fighters." Hugh nodded at me, slow, considering. "I've vowed to protect you, Princess Andi. Not only for my beloved wife, but because I consider you a sister. You are family to me. All chance at secrecy is lost. I think you know our situation is more dire."

My lip stung where my teeth dug in, and I wrapped my arms tighter around myself.

"I think they knew all along where I was. They've been following."

Hugh scanned the night, pressing up against the edges of the lights, beyond the fancy stone balustrades. Then he nodded again, confirming something to himself.

"That was no ordinary wolf, then. Still—they die like any animal. I would say we should stay here, hunker down, and fight them off until they give up, but this pretty manse wouldn't last a day. I think only Windroven can withstand that sort of siege."

"A siege?" The word crashed through me, shattering my hopes for an outcome without many deaths and massive suffering.

Hugh glanced at me, his face uncharacteristically hard. "You expected anything else? The Tala have demanded you and no one else. Their attention—their attacks—follow you and only you. We cannot match them on the ground. Our only option is to lock you up where they cannot take you. Windroven is far enough from the Wild Lands that they will be cut off. We'll outlast them."

"There is another option." If I had just gone with Rayfe, the siege wouldn't have to happen. *I do not have the luxury of your inaction.*

I must have sounded bad, because Hugh sheathed his sword and took my hand in his before I could stop him. He went down on one knee. He had proposed to Amelia like this, with joy, while she smiled down at him. With me in this deserted courtyard, his mouth flattened with determination.

"I vow I will not fail you, sister of my bride. I will lay down my life before the Tala take you."

He dropped his forehead to my hand, then faltered, frowning at the dregs of Glorianna's potion between my knuckles.

I pulled my hand away. "Take that back."

He blinked at me.

"Take it back," I insisted. "I don't want your life. Protect me, yes. It's your duty. And mine. I have no death wish, no desire to be fodder for the Tala's demons. I won't betray my King and my kingdom. But . . ." I drew in a deep breath, tried to even out my rising voice. "I won't have anyone else die for me."

He shook his head, then climbed to his feet. "You can't command something like this, Andi."

"Neither can you," I snapped back.

"Fair enough." He grinned at me suddenly, taking me by surprise. "You're not who I thought you were, Princess Andromeda."

"Is anyone?"

"Most, yes. The coming days ought to be interesting." He sounded as if he was looking forward to it. Then he sauntered off, whistling, to join my sister in their marriage bed.

Leaving me to my own devices. And regrets.

True to Hugh's promise, a small group of us rode hard for Windroven.

Though the rest of the ladies would follow at a more leisurely pace, Hugh allowed Dafne to stick with us. In the predawn light, he'd assessed her and given approval. I suspected he knew asking Amelia to forgo all assistance would be asking too much. Dafne slid her glance to catch my eye and winked. She clearly thought so, too.

For her part, Amelia looked wan and subdued, not her usual effervescent self. She rode in the curtained carriage, clutching her rose pendant, violet-shadowed lids closed while her rosebud lips moved in silent prayer.

Because Hugh made me ride in the carriage, too, I had ample opportunity to observe this. She prayed for me, so I shouldn't feel irritated. But the argument with Hugh, that odd encounter with Rayfe, the sudden bloody fight, had left me out of sorts. I wanted to ride. Being out in the open wouldn't make me any more vulnerable than being within Rayfe's reach. He wasn't going to try to capture me against my will.

Only as a last resort, perhaps.

I caught myself short in midthought. Why had he changed tactics? He would clearly continue to fight this war, but he wouldn't force me.

No matter how I knew, it was clear to me that the danger truly threatened everyone but me.

But no, Hugh wouldn't budge. In his ever-charming way, he

insisted. Then Amelia wept. And I rode in the stuffy carriage, unable even to see the landscape of the adventure that had been thrust upon me.

Dafne glanced up from the book she read and raised an eyebrow at me.

"Is there anything I can do for you, Princess Andi? You seem . . . restless."

I narrowed my eyes at her and she smiled, all innocence. Amelia still prayed, oblivious.

"Yes, there is, Lady Mailloux. Why don't you read to us—to pass the time."

That gave her pause. Her gaze flicked to Amelia and back to me. "This tome is quite dry. I don't know that you'd be interested."

"Is that so? What is the topic, then?"

"It's a, ah, bestiary of sorts. A catalogue of animals."

Amelia's eyes flew open. "Wolves? Does it discuss those enormous black wolves?"

I grinned at Dafne. Never think Amelia isn't paying attention, for all her pretty flightiness.

"It does, Princess Amelia," Dafne replied carefully. "However, the text is archaic and not meant to entertain. I do not think you would find it amusing."

"Nonsense." Amelia turned coaxing. "We would love to hear you read it. I find wolves most interesting—especially black ones."

She sat back, wrapping her fingers around the pendant again, lids fluttering closed. Dafne looked at me in question, and I lifted my shoulders. What she read could hardly be worse than what Amelia had already witnessed. Besides, Amelia had always been good at getting her way.

Amelia opened her eyes and pinned Dafne with a violet glare. "Please read, Lady Mailloux."

Dafne sighed and flipped to find the section Amelia demanded. She wore white gloves, I now noticed, turning each page with her careful reverence. I wondered how many books she'd managed to bring.

"Black wolves, which are substantially larger than commonly observed gray wolves, derive primarily from the region north of the Crane Isthmus, west of the mountainous spine that defines the western boundary of the Kingdom of Avonlidgh, and south and west of the Kingdom of Branli, encompassing the land of Annfwn."

"You found it," I breathed.

"Annfwn?" Amelia broke in. "There is no such place."

Dafne nodded at me. "The older texts use that name for the Wild Lands. Sometimes interchangeably; sometimes the Wild Lands seem to be referred to as a sort of buffer zone. A no-man's land."

I smiled my gratitude. She hadn't forgotten my question.

"But if they're Wild Lands, how can they have a name? I thought no one lives there," Amelia pressed.

"The Tala live there," I pointed out.

"The Tala are not people."

"How do you know?"

"Andi! You've seen them—they're demons and animals. People don't do the things they've done."

Never mind the things our people had done. I sighed and repressed the impulse to respond.

"I thought you wanted to hear about the wolves."

She pressed her pretty lips together. "Yes. Yes, I do." Amelia sat back again and waved her hand at Dafne to proceed. Dafne, face carefully blank, cleared her throat and continued reading.

"The term 'black wolf' is likely a misnomer and appears only in nonscientific texts. It's thought that the pigmentation in these wolves is almost certainly a cinnamon form that appears black in most lights. As most reports insist that blue irises often co-occur, which is a nonmelanistic trait, this reinforces that the fur pigmentation cannot be a true black.

"It's long been commonly accepted that the Law of Geophysical Transposition explains the unusually large size of these wolves. However, the range of the common gray wolf overlaps the reported range of the black wolves, with the black reported to be far greater in height, girth, length, and mass. It should be noted that the gray wolf size does align with this law, with specimens in Elcinea much smaller than those found in the far Northern Wastes.

"This curious disparity leads many researchers to conclude that these two variations are, in fact, separate subspecies. However, physical examinations and necropsies have been performed on only the gray variety, so it has remained impossible to verify this theory."

"Why?" Amelia interrupted. "Why couldn't they examine the black wolves?"

Dafne raised her eyebrows. "Apparently one has never been caught."

My head swam and I realized I'd been holding my breath. The midnight-blue eyes. Really, I'd known it all along. In and out of dreams, he was the same.

"It was him, wasn't it?" Amelia's eyes glittered hard like amethysts in the weak light.

"Who?" I tried.

"Rayfe. I'm not a fool, Andi. Don't treat me like one."

"I don't know, but I think so."

"He shape-shifts. They all do, don't they?" She turned to Dafne on that one.

"No one knows for sure," Dafne replied, even and soft.

"Glorianna knows." Amelia nodded at me. "She appeared to me in my dreams last night. She says you're in grave danger, Andi."

"Are you sure that dream wasn't just a reflection of everything that happened last night? It's hardly news that I'm in danger."

"Don't condescend to me, Andi. I know a vision when I have one. Glorianna appeared to me—so radiantly lovely, surrounded by sunshine. She waved a sword and killed the black wolf, pinned it through the heart. She spoke to me then and said that if I was to save you, we must kill the wolf."

The words chilled me; the headache that had lingered since the night before blazed back. I saw the wolf stabbed through. With a sound like shifting sand, the wolf became Rayfe. I shook the image away and said the first flip thing that came to mind.

"I didn't know Glorianna carried a sword."

"Are you mocking me?"

I sighed. Dafne studiously examined her book, staying well out of it. I shouldn't have let my restlessness goad her into reading aloud.

"Amelia, I think you're overwrought. I think we all are."

Her lower lip trembled and her eyes filled with tears. She groped for my hand. "I can't lose you, too. Not having Mother was awful enough, but if you—"

I squeezed her hand. "Nothing will happen to me. See? I'm fine. And soon we'll reach Windroven and we'll all be safe. Hugh will see to it."

A smile glimmered through her weeping, wobbly but full of love. "He will, won't he? He promised."

"Yes. He promised me, too."

She sighed and leaned against my shoulder, happily drowsing now.

Dafne looked up from her reading finally and caught my eye with her somber cinnamon gaze.

Really, there was nothing more to say.

We arrived at Windroven in triumph.

An almost absurd amount of triumph, since we clearly hadn't won anything except escape. Still, Castle Windroven, perched as it was on the craggy side of the dead volcano, rearing dramatically against the blue early-autumn sky and silhouetted against the white-capped sea below, made a reassuring sight. No wonder Amelia felt safe here—nothing could make it up the steep hillsides without being seen.

They'd built the castle into the rock itself, carving away at the mountain, polishing the stones they pulled out and using those to build the walls and turrets. I remembered now Violet telling me about it, though she thought I wasn't listening. It looked almost as if the castle had grown from the mountain, stately and magnificent.

With a greasy turn of my stomach, I recognized it immediately from the vision that had flashed through my mind. Only without all the dead bodies.

All along the winding narrow road that led up to the fortress, people cheered, waving pennants in Avonlidgh's festive greens and purples. Musicians played, a hodgepodge of music that changed every few minutes as we left one group behind and passed another.

This was Amelia's element.

She wore her amethyst gown again, which draped glamorously over the pure white mare she rode. Her bright hair tumbled down her back and over her horse's flank. She laughed, a pure song of loveliness, while she handed candies to children and accepted posies in return.

Hugh rode beside her, the golden prince, handsome as the sun that beat down on us.

Maybe it was the heat on all that bare rock, but it seemed that shadows wavered around him, blurring and distorting his heroic outline. Or it could be that the last several sleepless nights in fortified, airless outposts had left me drained and exhausted. It seemed I felt worse every day, and I worried over it—and Rayfe's dire warnings.

I followed them on my borrowed horse, whose trot felt unbearably stilted after Fiona's smooth pacing. I missed her with an enduring ache. This place felt all wrong, too far from the forests, too full of people who celebrated too easily. I began to regret that

I hadn't brought more of my own things. Amelia had insisted I looked perfect in the rose-pink gown she'd lent me—which was far too tight around my waist and bosom, so I could barely breathe—but I felt silly and wrong.

I couldn't even quite be as invisible as usual, because the stories had preceded us.

People waved to me and shouted out encouragement and vows that I would be safe with them. Young men brandished weapons, promising death for any that might threaten me. I smiled and waved, imitating Amelia's gracious bearing, but when I looked at all those merry people, I kept imagining them dead, collapsed and bleeding out over the unforgiving mountain. The headache pounded through my temples.

It was a relief to reach the cool shadows of the massive arched gates. Hugh helped Amelia down with a grand flourish. Soldiers who ringed the turrets above tossed down more flowers, and the two of them waved to the gleeful cheering.

Stiff from my horse's unbalanced gait, I started to climb down, but she danced irritably away.

"Whoa, there!" A man's strong hand grabbed her halter and stopped her bad-mannered dancing. "Let me help you, Your Majesty Princess Andi. This is a spirited horse for such a lovely young lady."

I finished sliding down, resisting the urge to smack the mare between the ears. Or whoever was calling me "Your Majesty." Only Uorsin should be called that.

"No, she's poorly trained," I told the tall man, who handed the horse off to a passing lad without a glance. How I missed Fiona.

He swept me a bow, chestnut locks flopping down and back again, and grinned with perfect white teeth. "I shall make it my personal mission to secure a well-trained steed for you, Princess Andi. From my own stables, I assure Your Majesty."

"Princess Andi." Hugh stepped up to my side. "I see you've met Lord Einsly, governor of this region."

Einsly bowed again, if possible even more ostentatiously than before. "I am at the service of the daughter of the High King. Your Highness will be safe in our midst. We shall protect you like the most delicate of hothouse flowers, shield you as the most precious jewel in the treasury."

"Ah, thank you."

Where was Ursula's sharp tongue when I needed it? She'd know exactly what to say back to this guy. My head pounded.

"Princess," Dafne murmured at my elbow. She handed me a goblet of blessedly cold water and rolled her eyes.

"Moranu bless you, Lady Mailloux." I gulped the water, grateful for both it and the save.

"You appeal to Moranu, Your Highness?" A frown knit Einsly's high forehead. "I believe High King Uorsin outlawed such superstitious nonsense."

"My father," Amelia said sweetly, offering a graceful hand to Einsly, "is a wise and tolerant king. He allows his subjects much freedom, treating them not as children. My sister, Princess Andi, however, is a follower of Glorianna, as are we all, in our hearts. Pay no attention to her childhood phrases. See? She wears Glorianna's rose."

"So she does." Einsly looked tremendously pleased. "My household follows Glorianna in all ways." He waggled his eyebrows in what could only be called a leer. "She is the goddess of love, you know, Your Highness Princess Andi."

"How nice for her."

Undeterred, he plowed on. "As governor of this lovely corner of Avonlidgh, I will lead our gallant soldiers in all battles. I hope to prove myself to you, that I might be worthy of your hand."

Suddenly every other man wanted to marry me. It would be funny if I didn't feel so ill. The cold water sat heavy in my stomach and my teeth ached. Dafne took the goblet from my hand with a concerned look.

Hugh laid a hand on my back. "The sister of my wife is under

120 • Jeffe Kennedy

my protection in all ways while she is away from her father and King. This has been a difficult ordeal for her. I'm sure you understand, Einsly—I cannot allow her to be importuned."

"Oh! Oh, surely so." Einsly hurfled. "I just wanted to—"

"Of course. And now, I'm certain the ladies would prefer to rest and refresh themselves."

I clung to Hugh's proffered arm and followed along into the depths of the castle. In the distance, I thought I heard a wolf howl.

9

The cool cloth Dafne laid over my eyes felt better than any of Glorianna's benedictions. My stomach still roiled unhappily, but at least the pounding in my head receded.

"I can search out an herb woman, get you a headache cure." Dafne sounded worried.

"No—I got too hot is all. Some rest will see me better."

Her silence spoke volumes. I lifted a corner of the cloth and leaned up to see her standing an arm's length away, arms folded.

"Are you actually tapping your foot? And Amelia would warn you that your face will freeze that way and you'll look old before your time."

"Andi—you are a master of ducking and hiding, but you don't fool me. You're puke green. What's wrong with you?"

I felt puke green, actually. With a sigh, I collapsed back on the bed. "I don't know. I just need to rest. Please?"

Water splashed in a basin and the cloth left my eyes to be replaced with a colder one. "Ah, that helps."

"I'll let you rest, but I'm finding an herb woman."

"I'm fine."

"Then she'll agree and be on her way. Here."

She tucked something under my arm. Long, silky hair tickled my skin.

"What is that?"

"Your little doll. It's the only thing you brought. I thought it might make you feel better."

Oddly, it did. The dreadful wrenching in my stomach subsided and I fell into a cool and soothing sleep.

I surfaced to the scent of rosemary carried on steam. Another herb rode with it, one that reminded me of the gentle perfumes from Elcinea that traders and minstrels brought back, weaving tales of turquoise waters, warm coastal breezes, and flowers that bloomed only at night.

Mermaids danced in blue coral ballrooms . . .

"What is she singing?"

"Who knows? Wake up, Princess!" This voice had to belong to the herb woman I hadn't wanted.

"I'm awake." I reluctantly opened my eyes, but thankfully the light no longer stabbed in like knives. A woman with a young face but silver-white hair sat on my bedside. Her eyes were a striking aqua blue. Around her neck hung a finely wrought chain from which dangled Moranu's moon.

"How do you feel?" Dafne peered over the woman's shoulder.

"Much better, actually."

"Drink this." The herb woman handed me a goblet. I peered inside it. The potion was warm, and a black and bitter smell rose from it. The herb woman raised fine white eyebrows. "I won't lie to you—it will taste truly awful. But it will help you, I promise. It's better drunk warm."

"What's wrong with me?"

She glanced down and away. "It is something perhaps best discussed in private."

"I'll leave." Dafne gathered up a few things.

"Oh, no, Dafne, you don't have to—"

"Believe me, Princess. There are things I don't want to know. That I'm likely better off not knowing." She gave me a half smile. "Besides, I could use a nap myself."

She left, snapping the door closed. Balancing the goblet in my hand, I scooted myself up. They'd put me in a grand room. No doubt the suite Hugh had promised me, because windows ringed three sides of it. Somewhere far below, surf crashed against rocks.

"The potion is a combination of bitter herbs that work to counteract poison," the woman said.

"Poison? I've been poisoned?"

"In a manner of speaking. Tell me—is it true you encountered Rayfe of the Tala?"

That should not be common knowledge. Who was this woman?

"I'm a priestess of Moranu—the Tala are her children." She touched the moon at her throat, seeming to read my thoughts. "But then, you recognized that immediately. Your lady-in-waiting was right to come to me. If anyone can help you, I can."

"Help me with what?"

"His blood passed your lips, didn't it?" She nodded at my surprise. "I can see it, if no one else can. Now he comes to you in dreams, and perhaps when you are awake, yes?"

I didn't answer. She didn't need me to.

"You are Salena's daughter, more than the others. You bear the mark. Her blood in you is also his." She shrugged. "When you drank his blood, it started a change in you. I understand it can be painful. Especially outside of Annfwn. And, of course, you're old for it."

"I did not drink his blood," I replied, stung on several levels.

She smiled at my denial that admitted so much else. Careless of me.

"It doesn't take much, especially for someone like you. This potion will help."

I sniffed it. As bitter as Glorianna's had been sweet. That might actually be a good sign. "It will counteract his blood?"

"No."

"What, then?"

"It will make it easier for you to assimilate what the blood is doing to you."

"Then I don't want it."

She refused to take the goblet I thrust back at her. "Princess Andromeda," she said gently, the voice of someone practiced at giving bad news, "you have already started down a path you cannot retreat from. You must go forward. I offer you a way to make it less painful. That's all I can give you."

"How do I know you're telling me the truth?"

She shrugged. "How do you know anyone is? I suspect you have a talent for that."

"When I drank a potion in Glorianna's chapel, for the rite of protection—I couldn't."

"Not surprising. Your path does not align with those of Glorianna's followers."

"What does that mean?"

"It means what it means, Andromeda. You will find your own answers. Drink the potion or not—it matters not to me."

"What do you know of Annfwn?"

Her serene expression tightened. "I know there are many trapped outside the borders who would benefit by being allowed in. It's difficult for the Tala outside—and you are Tala. More with every passing night, whether you wish it or not."

The priestess smiled, stood, and began sliding paper packets into a leather bag.

"But your goblet—"

"A gift." She shouldered her bag. "Moranu blesses you, Andromeda. Remember that. Her chapel is always open to you. Find me there, should you think of some better questions."

She slipped out of the room before I realized I didn't know her name. Setting the silver goblet on a little table next to the bed, I clambered up, tangling my legs in the obnoxious pink gown. The movement made me a bit dizzy, pain pounding into the base of my neck. Not so much better, after all. I managed to stagger to the door and open it. Two surprised soldiers snapped to attention.

The long, curving hallway was empty in both directions.

Of course. Can't be mysterious without a disappearing act.

The goblet waited for me, still steaming. I could see now that the silver bore the imprints of Moranu's moon in all four phases, moving in endless cycles around the rim. I picked it up, wrapping my chilled fingers around the welcome warmth, eyeing the doll also sitting on the little table. Glass blue eyes somber amid a tumble of black hair.

Steeling myself against the bitterness, I drank down the potion in one long swallow.

Amelia just loved having me visit Windroven. She happily settled in as if this was the pleasure jaunt she'd imagined, seeming to forget for long spaces of time what had driven me here.

As soon as I emerged from my chamber, feeling much more myself, Amelia practically pounced on me and insisted on a full tour of the castle. She danced along, chattered, and showed me every nook, every pleasing feature. She did not seem to notice, however, how busily all the denizens worked.

Or how distracted by my dark thoughts I was.

Workers in lower rooms piled up bricks and mortar, to be used to seal accessible windows. Chains of brawny lads handed barrels of dried legumes down into the cavernous cellars. The spectacular views Amelia pointed out also showed soldiers streaming in from outlying villages to join those drilling below in the fields being harvested early. I half expected to see Ursula come striding around a corner in her fighting leathers, snapping out orders.

Hugh was preparing for siege, indeed.

I barely listened to my sister. Happily, she didn't need me to do more than make the occasional admiring sound. My headache had eased but my mind still roiled. The priestess's words kept going through my head. *A path you cannot retreat from.* Even Dafne had said when I first met her that I'd need to form a plan. So far I'd avoided that, letting events carry me along.

I do not have the luxury of your inaction.

Rayfe's taunting words rankled. I needed to make a decision. The dread building with every preparation for battle I witnessed spurred me to do something. Worse, I felt strange changes inside me. Sometimes it seemed my skin didn't fit right. My fingers would suddenly spasm, and I'd look down, expecting to see claws bursting forth. My spine ached, lengthening and then contracting. A fluttering sensation bubbled in my veins, and I imagined tiny black birds fledging inside me, their wings beating to break free.

The headache might be gone, but my body was changing. Shifting into something else.

When the rest of Amelia's ladies arrived, Amelia went to greet them and see them settled. I slipped away and sought out Hugh.

Wearing his jeweled armor, he held court near the still-open main gates, greeting a country lord, newly arrived with a ragtag group of rosy-cheeked workers from his estate, there to become soldiers. I could just see Ursula rolling her eyes at their inexperience. Hugh, though, asked after their skills and thanked them so graciously that they all seemed taller as they trotted off to join one of the drilling battalions.

Hugh immediately turned to me and took my elbow to lead me away from the entrance—and the tantalizing promise of freedom. "How do you fare, Sister? You are well?"

"Yes, Hugh, I'm fine. Nothing a little nap couldn't cure."

He frowned in concern. "I pushed you all too hard in getting here. I should have taken your more delicate constitutions into account."

I nearly burst out laughing at that. Delicate constitutions! A little black magic and shape-shifter blood transforming me into a monster only gives a girl a little indigestion.

"Really, Hugh, I'm fine. I'm grateful for the protection you've offered me—and that you got us here safely."

He beamed at me, so pleased to be the hero. I bit my lip, unsure how to phrase what I needed to say.

"I'm concerned, though, that—"

"You mustn't be," he broke in. "You must not fret or worry. I've made a promise to keep you safe, and I will. Look about you! Windroven can withstand a siege for years, if necessary, and—"

"Years!"

Hugh looked aghast at my outburst. I had nearly shrieked the word. Years of being confined to this castle, looking out the high windows at armies below and never leaving, never riding or feeling the grass on my skin. I felt like I had days until those thousands of birds pecking at the insides of my veins tore their way free, leaving me a dying, shredded mess.

"I'm sorry, Hugh, but I just can't . . . I can't see us living under siege for years, for all these people to ruin their crops and their lives for me. For me."

"You're wrong, Andi. It's not only about you. The Twelve Kingdoms are united against this enemy. The High King will triumph once again and drive this scourge from our lands. Besides, all we have to do is hold out until the King brings his forces behind the Tala. They'll be crushed between us."

"But I could stop this," I argued, my voice weak against his ringing tones of certainty. "This is foolishness, to risk so much, when I could stop it. Wouldn't that be the truly loyal thing for me to do? The one thing I could do for the kingdoms?"

"No. You three are the greatest treasures of the Twelve Kingdoms. We will never give you up to them."

A tumult of noise announced a wagon trundling through the gate, piled high with metal armor and bristling with bundles of weapons. It stopped me from responding to that absurd statement, and Hugh's eyes gleamed with excitement at the sight.

"You'll see, Sister. None shall defeat us!" He spun on his heel to survey the new weapons, and I caught his sleeve. Hugh turned back, burying his impatience with a comforting pat on my hand. "Go have tea with Amelia and relax. All will be well."

"Wait—where is Moranu's chapel? I'd like to pay a visit. With an escort, of course, and—"

Hugh had started shaking his head before I'd finished the second sentence.

"I can't let you do that, Andi. Even if it wasn't outside the walls. It doesn't look good for you to pay homage to anyone but Glorianna, especially with this current conflict."

"I'll go in secret. In disguise."

He shrugged me off. "It's outside the walls. It pains me to refuse you, but it's impossible."

"I could go now, before the siege begins."

"Ah—that's where you're not listening to me, Sister. The Tala have already arrived. The battle will engage by morning."

If nothing else, Hugh and his generals could predict the onset of battle.

I awoke with a start in darkness. For a moment, I couldn't be sure where I was. The muffled rhythm of surf reminded me, but the other roar had me confused. Then I remembered and sat up. The crash of arms and angry shouts tumbled outside, though I couldn't see it. When I'd returned to my chambers after a mind-numbingly long feast the night before, I'd found my own windows bricked over, with only small slits remaining to let in air. I supposed I didn't have to worry about Rayfe or his creatures visiting me now, though he hadn't appeared in my dreams since our encounter outside the chapel. A good thing, I reminded myself. Though it just indicated a new phase in his strategy. My trunks had arrived, thankfully, so I pulled on my practice leathers and affixed my borrowed dagger to my belt. Even if Hugh wouldn't let me fight, I'd be happier having better agility. My door guards trailed after me with grinning anticipation. They wanted to see the battle too. We climbed to the upper walls and found a viewing spot in the press with everyone else who lived in the castle, new and old.

The drawbridge was up, the gates of the castle down and barred. Spilling over the mountainside around the outside walls, like a patchwork gown, were Hugh's troops. Our defenders. No longer human looking, they formed phalanxes distinguished by flags and colors, Glorianna's pink predominant over Avonlidgh's purple and green. They guarded the narrow road, making ascent impossible.

Below that, the valley teemed with an encamped army in somber colors. More streamed in from the distant forests, which had been cut back to make the fertile fields of Windroven. Fields now stripped bare of everything their owners could carry into the castle and now bearing only the fruit of Rayfe's armies.

How could there be so many of them?

Perhaps their movement fooled me, for they constantly shifted, horses galloping about, manes and tails streaming along like the wild black hair of the Tala themselves. Where our troops stood in disciplined ranks, theirs tossed like an angry sea. The small ratlike creatures teemed over the ground like ants. Wolves as big as ponies wove in and out, circling the fields like a hunting pack surveying their trapped prey. Birds of all sizes, all black, clouded the skies, flocks changing direction in a flash of movement while enormous raptors soared high above.

I imagined the birds in my blood flapping their wings in the feral desire to join them, and my fingertips burned. Refusing to look, in case claws were indeed sprouting, I scanned the assembled enemy, trying to count but somehow unable to focus on any group long enough, like clouds that dissipated if I stared too hard.

"Who knew there are so many of the Tala? I thought they were a wild and scattered people." I said it to myself, but one of my guards answered.

"Black magic, Princess. 'Tis said they multiply overnight, like insects."

"Aye. And if you cut one down, two more grow in its place," the other guard added.

"You don't really believe that, do you?" I turned my back on the unsettling sight below and assessed the two brawny men. They exchanged sidelong glances, edging slightly away from me.

They were afraid of me. Just another creepy insect.

"Andi! Andi, over here!"

I followed Amelia's voice, not caring if the guards kept up with me or not. Of course they would. They'd give their lives to protect me, a woman they couldn't quite look in the eye, for the odd dread curling in their guts. All for a chance to prove their mettle in battle. For the glory.

Amelia and her ladies were perched in a makeshift grandstand. Dressed in daffodil yellow, her hair flowing loose down her back, Amelia looked like rosy morning. Her ladies were all in pastels, too. Dafne sat with them, dressed like me in fighting leathers. She raised a sardonic brow at me but shifted aside so Amelia could scoot past to embrace me.

"Hugh said you were exhausted, so we let you lie in. The battle hasn't started yet, so you haven't missed a thing. Why are you dressed like that? It's not like Ursula will show up to make us practice." She wrinkled her pretty nose, seized my hand, and pulled me to the seat next to her. "I begged Hugh to let us watch. I'm never sitting in a dark, closed-up safe room again where I can't see what's happening! He says it's safe here for now, though we might have to go in later. Something about catapults. Anyway, I'm sure it will all be over soon. Did you see all of those horrible creatures? So dreadful!"

Amelia talked when she was nervous. She wasn't as carefree as she liked to appear, but I knew her well. She clutched my hand

and chattered about Hugh, his generals, how brave they all were, and how she'd arranged for a lovely midmorning snack for us.

The sun rose higher and beat down on us. Still nothing happened.

Servants erected a striped silk awning over our heads. Still nothing. Even Amelia grew bored and huffed about the delay.

The crowd on the parapets thinned as people went off to do necessary chores. Several of Amelia's ladies begged off, citing fatigue and a desire to work on sewing. Dafne moved to sit next to me while Amelia flirted with one of Hugh's courtiers, one of her favorite pastimes.

"Now everyone discovers what siege is really like," Dafne murmured.

"You've been through one?"

She nodded, face carefully blank. "My family's castle, when I was young. Weeks of boredom punctuated by stark terror."

"I admit, I thought more would happen today."

"You're right to dress in leathers—you never know when things *will* happen. Right now they have no reason to engage. Avonlidgh's local forces are all within the bounds of Windroven, and it will be days or weeks before others can be mobilized. Patience is their weapon."

"And what is ours?"

She flicked a glance at me. "Fortitude."

Midafternoon, something did happen. A stir ran through the field below, surrounding a streaming white pennant. Two horsemen made their way through the teeming army and halted at the bottom of the road leading up to Windroven. They waited.

After a bit, we could make out Hugh's glittering form, riding down the mountain on a palomino stallion. Einsly rode beside and a little behind him, carrying the flag of Avonlidgh. He glanced up and saluted us. Hugh kept focused on the men below.

The four met, a wide circle cleared around them.

They were far enough away now that I couldn't make out faces, but surely the lean man on the black horse was Rayfe. His hair would be tied back for battle, so no wonder I could see no sign of it beneath his helm. Not like Hugh, in his bareheaded and confident glory.

At one point, Rayfe offered a package to Hugh, something wrapped in a dark silk with fluttering ends. He and Einsly unwrapped and examined it, then Hugh dropped it on the ground.

After a time, Hugh and Einsly spun their horses about and left Rayfe and his man in a cloud of dust. Rayfe dismounted, picked the thing up off the ground, brushed it off, and held it, looking up toward where I stood—though surely he couldn't pick me out in the crowd from that distance. A fleeting headache pulsed behind my eyes. He seemed to nod at me, and tucked the package in his pocket. Then he and his man were swallowed up in the crowd on the field, white pennant folded away. Hugh and Einsly took their time winding up the road, stopping to visit with various lords and generals. Encouraging the troops, most likely.

With an impatient sigh, I stood. Amelia glanced up, gave me a little shrug, and returned to listening to some story about a nine-day fox hunt. Dafne went with me down to the main gates to wait for Hugh's arrival.

He came through a smaller door, so narrow he had to turn sideways to pass through. Einsly must have stayed in one of the outer courtyards, with the horses. Hugh's glance flicked over us. He seemed resigned but unsurprised to see me there.

"What did he say?" I asked without preamble. Wound in my own way, I couldn't bear to take time with polite greetings.

Hugh seemed to understand, though he looked pained. He took my hand in both of his, stripping off the chain-mail gloves to do it.

"Just what you'd expect, Andi. Rayfe renewed his demands. Exactly the same. Made threats. Nothing has changed."

I wanted to ask him how Rayfe had looked. If he seemed angry. Or . . . something about him. A message for me. Anything. Hugh's face revealed nothing of what he'd thought of the man. Maybe men didn't think that way.

Hugh sighed. "He's promised not to attack, if that makes you feel better. He seems confident he can wait us out. So that's where it stands."

"I see." I waited. Hugh said nothing more. "What did he give you?"

"Give me?"

"That you threw on the ground."

"Ah, nothing of importance."

"But—"

"Let it go, Andi." He kissed my hand and dropped it. Suddenly he no longer looked like the cocky, handsome boy who'd walked into our court. Under the blazing confidence, he looked drawn, with shadows under his eyes.

He looked angry. And afraid.

10

The other thing I learned about sieges is that it's impossible to maintain a high state of alert for very long. And that sooner or later, people get tired of the waiting and have to do something.

That's when it gets ugly.

The first night, we barely slept, waiting for the attack to come. I lay restlessly in my stuffy room, listening to the guards calling out their positions and status. A series of shouts brought me bolt upright, pulse pounding, dagger in hand. The all clears that followed spoke to my brain but not my heart, which insisted on believing only the alert, not the stand-down.

When I managed to sleep, I dreamed of him. This one, though, was more truly a concoction of my own mind. A dreadful one.

Rayfe stood in that acid-green meadow, wolfhounds milling around him while a wind I couldn't feel tugged at his black cloak and hair. He held out a hand to me. The black silk package rested in his palm, the wrapping fluttering in the same way.

"I can't," I whispered.

He only smiled at me. Tempting my curiosity. The restless pacing in my heart accelerated.

I took a step toward him, and his smile widened, pleasure

lighting his midnight eyes. But before I could take another, Fiona screamed behind me. I spun and there she was, tethered to a pole atop a blazing pile of books, writhing while the flames ate at her crackling flesh, while she cried for me. I tried to reach her, to save her, but my feet wouldn't work. They crumbled off my ankles, turning into scales and feathers as I walked, so I left a bloody black trail in my wake. With every step, more of me fell away, becoming other. Fiona screamed and I echoed her terror.

I sat bolt upright before I knew I was awake.

Not difficult to interpret that one.

We repeated our new siege rituals for the next few days, dutifully assembling on the parapets to watch nothing at all. Amelia's ladies began to bring their various sewing and tapestry projects with them. Dafne brought her books. Every morning, nothing happened. Every afternoon, Rayfe and his man rode up under the parley flag and offered Hugh the package. Every time, Hugh tossed it away and refused to speak to me of it.

Every day, I felt more strange to myself.

After a time, we stopped holding vigil. Amelia declared it more comfortable in her usual chambers. Dafne stayed in her makeshift library. She was deep into some sort of research, and her thoughts tended to drift off in midconversation. I didn't have anything to say anyway, so I let her be.

My blood and muscles restless, I paced the parapets, alone but for all the silent guards keeping their endless alert.

I discovered that it's possible to be both bored and on edge. You wouldn't think so, but they become one state of being. One that eats away at your peace of mind. I looked forward to the one moment every day when something changed, when Rayfe rode forward, when he searched me out on the parapets.

I dreaded the dream that recurred every night.

One midday—hours yet from the one interesting event I could count on—on one of my circles around the tops of the castle walls, I spotted Rayfe's now familiar form riding from the edge of his encampment into the forest. I knew him by the headache flashing behind my eyes, if nothing else. Holding up a hand to shield against the sun, I watched, fascinated, but he did not reemerge. The sentries had grown used to my rambles, barely paying attention to me as I made my way up and down, from tower to tower, along walkways wide and narrow, so I had to tug the sleeve of one to get his attention. I pointed.

"That road that leads into the forest—where does it go?"

He shrugged. "Nowhere."

"You all are in the habit of maintaining roads that lead nowhere at all?" I asked drily.

"He means, *Princess*"—another guard threw the first a reprimanding look—"it leads only to a series of villages, an old chapel few visit. Nothing of interest, he means."

"Moranu's chapel?"

He scratched his scalp under the metal helm. "Aye. Seems my granny went there from time to time, Princess. Of course, the people of Avonlidgh are loyal to the High King and have forsaken Moranu's worship now."

I thanked him and stood there studying that road I could never go down. No more than I could go to Rayfe and put an end to all this, no matter how the birds in my blood sang piteously for it. From this point, the castle wall fell straight down, a dizzying sweep to bare rock below. That would be one way out, it occurred to me. I could fling myself over the edge before the guards could move. I'd be dead before I felt it.

Then everyone could just go home.

Annfwn needs you.

A chill wind swept over me, from a different direction than usual, promising of long nights and winter snows. I shivered at it.

"Weather's turning," one sentry commented.

"Aye," another grunted. "See the forest? Leaves are starting to change."

"We'll see how long the Tala stay camped through one of our Mornai storms."

"What's a Mornai storm?" I asked.

"Storm off the ocean, Princess," my talkative sentry explained. "Water-heavy clouds blow in and hit the cold winds you all send down from the north. Snow like you wouldn't believe."

"Those Tala will be buried alive by it." A guard chuckled in glee.

"No, son." The guard squinted at the sky. "Our forces won't wait for that. They can't afford to. I hear King Erich's troops have rounded up the escaped prisoners and the Mohrayans have done the same. Reinforcements are coming in from Aerron and Duranor to join with King Uorsin's and King Erich's armies at Castle Avonlidgh. This stalemate will end. Mark my words."

I looked down at the rocks below and thought about endings.

Among the dreams of poor burning Fiona, the image of Rayfe dead in the snow, the slopes of Windroven covered with dead bodies, and the constant, sliding sensation of my body coming apart, I often thought I might be losing my mind. I felt like I had the pieces to a puzzle in my hands, but I couldn't fit them together. Every time I tried, an edge fell off and shattered on the floor.

That night, though, the dream changed. It wasn't the acid-green meadow, or any of the others, to my relief.

This time I walked along a road through a dark forest—familiar, yet one I'd never seen. To confirm my suspicions, I looked over my shoulder. In the distance, across fertile farmlands, stood Castle Windroven, pennants flying in the coastal breezes. I could pick out the spot where I'd stood, watching Rayfe travel this very road.

Unerringly I followed his path, where the road branched into smaller trails, hemmed in by trees so huge I wouldn't be able to wrap my arms around them. But I wasn't in this dream to look at trees. My feet took me down the trail until a clearing opened up at Moranu's chapel.

It was built of the shell-encrusted volcanic stones from the seashore, much like Windroven, but the forest had gone far to make its mark, covering the charming garrets with ivy and moss. Dark where Glorianna's chapels were bright, the chapel had Moranu's moons arching in progression over the humble door, inlaid with now tarnished silver.

Rayfe waited there, of course.

Though I halted at the edge of the clearing, I was much closer to him than in the usual dreams. His blue eyes intent on me, he nodded, showing me the package but not holding it out. He opened the door and went into the chapel, glancing back over his shoulder, reminding me of the wolf leading me out of Glorianna's pink candy chapel.

Uneasy, I glanced into the shadows, waiting for the apparition of Fiona to appear. But all stayed quiet, except for a soft soughing of wind through the upper branches. Unlike on the path, I had a choice now about whether to follow Rayfe into the shadowed interior. A choice he'd very deliberately handed me.

I probably shouldn't have, but I simply couldn't stand it any longer. I had to make a decision, even if it was the wrong one.

I took a step. Then another. And another.

A feeling of clean liberation poured through me. *Follow your path to the end.* By Moranu, I would.

Inside the chapel, round windows ringed the ceiling. The moon shone through one, a gleaming opal in a sky the color of Rayfe's eyes.

He waited by the stone altar. When I finally looked at him, his face was carved in somber lines, almost sad. He knelt and moved a stone at the foot of the altar. After placing the package in the hollow, he fitted the stone back in place.

Abruptly, he stood and strode toward me, cloak flaring with the movement. I tried to step back but hit up against a stone bench. He started to pass me, paused, turned a bit. Had his eyes been so darkly blue in waking life? He raised a hand, framing my cheek with it. Not touching, yet I could feel him. I couldn't breathe. His lips moved without sound, saying something I couldn't hear.

He smiled, an affectionate curve that seemed out of character for his stern mouth. He mouthed the words again and left.

Come to me.

In the morning, the mood of the castle had shifted.

I felt it even before I went down to breakfast, like a storm approaching. Amelia's violet gaze caught mine as soon as I walked in the room, and she held out a hand to me. Bad news?

"What's happened?"

"Several battalions disappeared during the night," she whispered to me.

"Left?"

"No. Their gear, tents, everything is all lying there, but the people are gone. Hugh has taken troops to investigate."

"He must think they're dead, then. Or taken prisoner."

"Well, it *is* a war, Andi. That's what happens."

I didn't have to reply to that because Hugh and his men returned just then, to a loud commotion in the courtyard. Amelia and I, along with all the ladies already at breakfast, rushed to the open balcony that overlooked the inner courtyard. Hugh and Einsly shouted at each other, while Hugh's page stood nearby, arms loaded with black scarves that dangled silver coins.

By the time we ran down the curving stairs, Einsly had departed, along with a goodly portion of the men. Hugh caught sight of us and sent his page in the other direction, taking the scarves with him.

Glad I wore my fighting leathers, I put on a burst of speed and chased the boy down, seizing him by his scrawny arm. He blanched, cringing away from me, fawn-brown eyes wide.

"Andi!" Hugh barked behind me. "Leave it be!"

Beyond listening, I yanked one of the scarves from the page. The coin attached shone prettily, a wolf carved on one side, on the other, three words: *Come to me.*

I dropped it as if burned, my fingertips alive with a sharp ache.

Hugh's hand fell on my shoulder, squeezing warmly. "Princess Andi—Sister—this is not for you to see."

"It's clearly a message to me. Who else should see it?"

"He seeks to manipulate you. To turn your emotions."

It was working. I felt like crying. Like falling to my knees in the dusty courtyard and keening out my grief and fear. Hugh seemed to see this, watching me with troubled eyes.

"These were in place of the missing soldiers?"

He hesitated. Nodded.

"Prisoners, then. And I am the ransom. Exchange me for them and this ends."

"No." The noble line of Hugh's jaw firmed. "Einsly has already left to organize a rescue mission. Enough of this waiting. Enough of these games. Rayfe wants a war, by Glorianna, he shall have one."

"But—"

He'd already turned, gone to Amelia, and swept her up in a fervent embrace. Hugh kissed her and Amelia clung to him, passion shimmering in the air around them. Feeling unaccountably old and ugly, I had to look away. The silver coin at my feet winked up at me. Taunting.

Hugh's page darted in, snatched up the scarf, and dashed off.

Hugh released Amelia and paused a moment, cupping her cheek and whispering something to her. It speared me—how the movement recalled my dream. Amelia's face shone with love, all rose and gold, though. Not at all like my own moment, in Moranu's nighttime chapel, with dark Rayfe and the swirling portents all around.

But then, I was never meant for Amelia's life. Nor she for mine.

That day marked the true beginning of the battles.

The rescue mission returned, bloodied and unsuccessful, having lost six men and women to the Tala. No one would tell me how many Tala had died. The rumors of monsters and wizardry amplified, tales of people disappearing into thin air warring with stories of dragons and wolves becoming panthers and then eagles.

Shouts and screams in the night spoke of more confrontations. Sometimes the Tala snatched more prisoners, leaving those taunting coins in the place of living people. More often, Hugh's people attacked, driving potential raiding parties back. No one seemed to be able to find the ones who'd disappeared, nor ever saw them being taken.

The mystery chewed on us all. More and more, the people of the castle whispered of black magic and cast fearful glances or angry glares in my direction. The place reeked of rose water.

I no longer dreamed, instead falling into a deep sleep that felt endless. Each morning I crawled out of bed, groggy, bogged down with inaction, my skin crawling over my bones like the birds that circled Windroven in untiring spirals. When I was allowed up on the parapets, I spent most of my time studying the way to Moranu's chapel. It might as well be in far Noredna. I couldn't get there.

I paced my gloomy rooms, going from one blockaded window to the next. If I leaned my eye up against the narrow slits, I could see slices of the action below. The day had blown in cold, with freezing rain, and I'd been forbidden to walk the castle walls, for fear I'd slip and fall to my death. I hadn't pointed out that more than a few people would rejoice to see that happen.

The nasty weather didn't stop the fighting. The two forces clashed against each other, charging forward, falling back. Sometimes a swarm of black creatures would seem to surge over a battalion like a wave from the ocean, and when it receded, all the soldiers would be gone, washed clean from the earth. Not all disappeared. From my vantage point, I could see the wounded carried into the courtyard, to be taken below for healing or to be mercifully killed. None were Tala. Hugh refused to take prisoners.

Others muttered that the wizards could not be captured.

I turned my back on the sight, clenching my teeth to keep from screaming. The doll my mother gave me sat by the bed, staring at me with glassy, accusing eyes. I felt I knew what she would advise me. What she herself had done.

Annfwn needs you, it whispered.

Each passing moment drilled Rayfe's words through my skull, echoed by the shrieking birds in my veins.

Come to me.

Come to me.

Come to me.

Finally, I no longer harbored any doubt that I would. That I must. The only question that remained was, How?

I found Dafne in the set of rooms Hugh had indulgently given her. I say "indulgently" because the interconnected suite was larger than even Amelia's. The rooms weren't in a desirable part of Windroven, though, so none of the other ladies were likely to complain. Here the castle ate deep into the rock of the old volcano. Windows weren't even a possibility. She'd set up shelves and tables, organizing the tomes according to her own arcane system.

"It's warm," I said, surprised. I looked about for the woodstove, like she'd had back at Ordnung, but didn't see or smell one.

Dafne didn't look up from the tome spread on the table. She spoke to the pages she bent over. "It's from the ground. The volcano may be defunct, but the warm rivers that used to fuel it still run below."

"Oh." Another thing I didn't know much about. I could just picture Ursula shaking her head at me. With a pang, I missed her, suddenly and fiercely. Always I'd thought Amelia was closer to me, but these days forced together showed how little Amelia and I bore in common, when I couldn't ride off on Fiona and leave her to her gossip, flirtations, and love poetry. "I'd, um, love to hear more about that."

Dafne glanced up at me now, tucking her hair behind her ear. "No, you wouldn't. What is it you do want to know?"

Now that it had come to the point of asking out loud, I couldn't quite bring myself to do it. What if she laughed in my face? Or worse, told Hugh I'd completely lost my mind, which I likely had. I circled the room, examining the shelves. I glimpsed more in the next room.

"You can't possibly have brought this many books with you."

"No—it turns out Avonlidgh packed many away. Windroven happened to be a convenient place to keep them. Far from the High King's displeasure."

"Anything good?"

"All knowledge is worth having."

I wound my fingers together. "Anything about . . . shape-shifting?"

She narrowed her eyes. "You're still wondering whether that wolf in the chapel was Rayfe in another form?"

I laughed at that. I wondered a lot of things, but that wasn't one of them. That I knew.

"I'm wondering how I learn to do it."

Silence fell between us. I couldn't bear her considering gaze and fiddled with a little book lying on the edge of the table. Love poetry. Of course.

"You think that kind of thing is in a book?"

"Well, I don't know, do I!" I snapped at her. She didn't blanch but regarded me with that scholarly calm. "But how else am I to learn? How else can I get out of this fortress and put an end to this stupid war?"

"If you go to Rayfe, it won't end the war, just this particular battle."

"That's enough for me. You asked me what my plan was? This is my plan."

"To what? Learn to shape-shift into a bird and fly over the walls?"

"You make it sound silly, but after everything we've seen, I know it's there. It's in me, somewhere." I clutched the leather vest over my heart, leaning over the table to persuade her. "I can feel it, more every day, my mother's blood, like an animal clawing to get out."

"Fascinating." Now she regarded me like one of her books.

"Don't act like you didn't know this. You knew to get Moranu's priestess here to help me. How did you know that?"

She sighed. "Why don't you sit down, Princess?"

I slammed my hands on the table. "Don't 'princess' me! How did you know?"

"Sit, Andi." Dafne pointed at a chair. "Stay."

I glared at her, then yanked out the chair and plopped myself in it. "Fine. Happy now?"

"Yes." She sat down opposite me, folded her hands, and propped her chin on them. "Tell me your plan."

"I already did."

"In rational detail."

"I fly over the walls, meet up with Rayfe. He sends the prisoners back. And I—I guess I marry him and go back to his castle or his tree house in the wild forests of Annfwn or whatever. Happily ever after."

At least until I'd popped out some replacement babies. *Blood pawn.* Ursula had thrown that phrase out. Now I wondered if she hadn't been uncannily accurate.

"You left out the part where the combined armies of the Twelve Kingdoms dog your heels, laying waste to everything in their path, to rescue you. Rayfe and his people have made an effort to minimize bloodshed and damage."

"How can you say that?"

"Open your eyes, Andi." She held up a palm, as if showing me evidence. "Have they burned the fields? Set fire to the forests? Hurled rocks to break down the walls? I've been on the receiving end of Uorsin's battle strategy. Believe me—he would not be so patient."

"But—"

"You read the histories of Uorsin's campaign to become High King. He is not a man to give up what he believes belongs to him."

"But if he thinks I betrayed him—" Tears caught in my throat, choking me. Screams, the smell of charring flesh. So many people were dying, and yet I couldn't bear to think of that happening to Fiona.

"You must convince Hugh that you're making a sacrifice. He must be forced into a binding alliance. There's no other path."

"He won't. He keeps citing his honor. His word to me and to Uorsin."

She stared me down. "You have to give Rayfe enough leverage."

"Leverage?"

"What is the one thing Hugh values above his word?"

"Nothing. The man is as noble as the day is long. He lives and dies by his word. Nothing matters to him more than that . . ."

I trailed off. There was one thing.

Amelia.

I stared at Dafne, aghast. "How can you suggest such a thing?"

"I'm not suggesting anything. I'm offering you possibilities."

"I couldn't put Amelia in danger."

"She wouldn't have to be in actual danger. She only has to appear to be."

"I can't do that. It would be true treason."

"No one would have to know. No one but you."

"And Rayfe."

She nodded at me. "Yes. He would have to know your plan."

Come to me.

"Which leads me back to flying over the castle walls."

"Shape-shifting is not in any of the books, Andi. Not our books, anyway."

"I know how to make contact with him, with no one else knowing, if I can just get there." I held my breath, but she seemed unsurprised by my confession. "But I have to get outside the walls."

"Did you say you wanted to know more about volcanoes and how they work?" Dafne raised her brows at my confusion. "The warm currents."

"I'm contemplating betraying my beloved sister to blackmail her husband into selling me into marital slavery so I can betray my father and King's commands, and now you want to tell me how volcanoes work?"

"Yes, I do. See, it's easier to build a castle like this into a volcanic mountain because it's not solid rock."

"Dafne, this is all fascinating, but—"

"It's not solid rock," she repeated. "It's riddled with caves and tunnels. That's how the warm air gets in here. Through natural passages in the mountain."

Passages. Tunnels.

"Do you already know the way out?"

"Yes." She stood and pulled a scroll from the shelf. She spread it over the table. "I love a builder who keeps careful plans."

"Why doesn't anyone else know about this tunnel?"

"I imagine someone did, once. It's right here." She traced the route with her fingertips.

"And it's been sitting here in storage."

She raised her eyebrows, giving me a pointed look. "This is why it's perilous to ignore a librarian."

11

In the end, it proved surprisingly easy to escape Windroven. That's another thing about sieges—everyone gets so focused on keeping the enemy out that it never occurs to them that someone might try to leave.

I left just after midnight, after the sentries changed over and had settled again. I pleaded fear and expressed a need to sleep in my sister's chambers, with all the other ladies. My guards didn't give it a second thought. They certainly didn't notice when I slipped out the other door to her suites.

We'd figured on an hour for me to walk to the chapel, half that to leave a message for Rayfe, and twice that to get back, since I'd have to be more stealthy on the way back in. That would see me safely inside well before dawn.

Dafne waited for me with clothes and supplies. She showed me the path again on the plans and offered to point the way. Or go with me. We'd had this argument already and I'd told her no. In case I didn't make it back, I needed her here, to spin whatever story she could. She also didn't need to be more involved than absolutely necessary, in case this went very, very wrong.

The tunnel wasn't all that long. Tight in spots, but I'd clambered over enough rocks in my time not to have too much difficulty. It emerged into a cave. I had the borrowed dagger out, in case any beasts made a home there. But it was a craggy and narrow space, with a sharp floor.

I made my way outside and took a moment to get my bearings. And to enjoy being outside those crushing walls.

I swear the air tasted sweeter than it ever had before. The stars glowed bright, twinkling in merry welcome. I looked for where I thought Moranu's chapel should be and saw the place—under the waxing moon that hung low in the sky, shining through the scudding clouds like a beacon.

So be it.

It should have been more difficult to pass through the denuded farmlands and the successive rings of sentries, then the surrounding ranks of Tala. The half-moon shed some light, but the night lay dark and heavy. Torches blazed on the main castle approach, where even now I could hear the clatter and shouts of conflict. Above me, the guards on the parapet gazed out over the landscape, watching for an attack to approach, not one woman leaving.

I might not be able to shape-shift, but I've had a lot of practice at not being noticed. I drew heavily on that skill now.

The real test would be getting back again.

It felt like one of the dreams, really. I wondered if I'd know the difference. The dreams felt real and this seemed so unreal, animal shapes melting into the night as I made my way to the edge of the forest, weaving through the giant dark trees. Just to test that it wasn't a dream, I stopped and wrapped my arms around one. The bark scraped my cheek and the leaves tossed far overhead in the stormy night. The trunk, though, never moved. Enviable, that— how trees might bow in some ways to the blasts and gales of the world but stayed firm and strong in all other ways.

Soothed, I continued easily intersecting with the road and following it down path after path.

Moranu's chapel waited for me, hardly more than a cottage in the woods. Hair prickled on the back of my neck as I searched the looming shadows. I more than half expected to see Rayfe there, waiting on the doorstep. But he would be off with his people, storming the castle. Or looking for me in dreams.

Nevertheless, I sidled around the edge of the clearing first, before approaching the door. I held my breath as I turned the handle, hoping against hope that it wasn't locked. I'd ring the bell if I had to, if my priestess had barricaded herself in, safe from enemy rampages.

But the handle turned silently under my hand, the door opening inward to the darkened chapel. The moon had obligingly risen high enough to shine through one of the round windows, shedding a bit of light. Enough for me to find the altar and kneel down where Rayfe had. The stone scraped my fingers. Clouds occluded the moon again, dropping me into utter darkness, leaving me to feel my way along the cracks.

There. The stone wriggled, moved a bit, then came loose. I felt inside and a small package wrapped in silk met my seeking fingers.

I pulled it out in wonder.

Real. All of it was real.

Holding the package up to the faint light, I unwrapped it with a frisson of anticipation. What had Rayfe been trying so hard to give me?

The scarf fell away to reveal a wooden box with a hinged lid. Some design inlaid the top, but I couldn't make it out. Inside rested my dagger, blackened with dried blood. His blood. A message in that, as he would know never to leave a blade uncleaned.

I lifted it out and set it on the stone floor next to me. I knew there must be something else.

A leather pouch rested in the bottom of the box. I set the box down, putting the dagger back inside, and unknotted the tie. Silver caught the light, and something with a dark sparkle. I held it up to the windows.

A ring. Chased runes shadowed the sides, with a stone set in, cabochon-style.

"My vow to you."

I cursed on a half shriek, bobbling the ring. Tucking it into my palm, I stood and whirled around in one movement, my back to the altar.

A chuckle came from Rayfe's dark shape near the doorway. Yes, very funny.

"You frightened me." My heart pounded in my throat, choking me, but I managed to get the words past it. I could slide the borrowed dagger at my hip out of its sheath. Too bad I'd left mine on the floor, though the edge was undoubtedly dulled, sullied by his blood all this time. It would do in a pinch. Still, I'd come to negotiate.

"I apologize, Andromeda. My pleasure at seeing you finally here outpaced my sense."

He stepped toward me, still a sinister black silhouette in his cloak, and I deeply regretted being trapped against the altar.

"Shouldn't you be off, oh, laying siege to the castle?" The stone on the ring burned into my palm.

"Why should I be when the treasure I seek is right here?" Relentlessly he moved closer.

"But you didn't know I'd be here tonight."

"I hoped. You know I've been waiting."

He stopped. Close to me. So close that, though I was on the raised dais of the altar, I still had to tip my chin back to see his face. Not that it did any good in the deep shadows.

"How have you been?" he asked. "I've worried about you."

"I'm fine," I lied.

He raised a hand and stroked my cheek with one black-gloved finger.

"Don't," I whispered.

"Do I frighten you still?"

Yes. "No. You make me angry."

"And yet, you've come to me as I asked, to give yourself to me."

"I haven't."

"No?" He growled the word and I shivered. What had I been thinking? Wordlessly, I handed him the scroll I'd prepared. He took it and a stray gleam of moonlight showed that he raised a hawklike eyebrow at me.

Thankfully he stepped away, unrolling the parchment. A small blue light appeared near his shoulder, illuminating the sharp planes of his face. He heard my breath of surprise, because he glanced at me with a half smile. "A minor magic. I'll teach you this and much more, my Andromeda."

It was on the tip of my tongue to tell him I wasn't his anything, but I realized that wasn't true. If all went according to the plans I myself had made, I would be handing myself over to him. Presumably after that I would be his, to do with as he liked. *Blood pawn.* The thought filled me with a kind of dreadful anticipation. An image of Hugh kissing Amelia with such tenderness flew through my mind while I studied Rayfe's sharp profile, highlighted in silver blue. I shivered again. No golden prince he.

"Are you chilled?" he asked, still reading.

"It's a stormy night."

"It is. And you have no cloak."

"I thought it would draw attention and perhaps hamper my movements. Secrecy is very important—as you can see."

"Wise."

He rolled up the scroll and tucked it into an inside pocket, his magic light winking out. Then he unfastened his heavy black cloak and swung it around me, long fingers tying it at my throat. His warmth and scent enveloped me, too, and I couldn't meet his eyes.

"So this is your plan."

I nodded.

"Clever," he mused. "Have you no affection for your sister, then?"

"I have tremendous affection for her. You must swear to me that no harm will come to her."

"Must I?"

"Or the deal is off."

"You could simply come with me now. That would also put an end to this battling—without jeopardizing your sister."

"It can't happen that way."

He grinned at me, wolfish. "Do you think to test me?"

I put the point of my borrowed dagger against his heart. "I'm serious. My father wouldn't rest. He'd come after you."

"Do you think I care about that?" His tone whipped out and I flinched.

"You should. If you care about the land and the people. He doesn't."

"You are all I want. Annfwn needs you. Everything else is secondary, at best."

"You keep saying that. Why does Annfwn need me?" I ground out.

"That is an old and complicated story. Trust that we do. And that I admire your desire to save the lives of my people."

"My people, too," I shot back.

"In truth, they are all your people, aren't they?" He fingered my braid where it hung over the cloak. "Put the dagger away, my part-blood."

"That's an ugly thing to call me." I shot a glance up into his shadowed face.

"I don't mean it as such."

I didn't know what to say in reply, so I stared at the center of his chest, the blade gleaming silver against his dark vest.

"Why are you willing to come to me, if I frighten you so?" he finally asked, in a surprisingly gentle voice.

"I already told you. I explained it all in that letter." Except the part about the strange changes in me. I superstitiously hadn't wanted to put that into words.

"Only because you feel trapped into this course of action, then?"

"You are the one who accused me of indulging in inaction. What other reason could I have?"

"None, I suppose." He sighed, and there might have been disappointment in it. "Put your dagger away and give me the ring, please."

I hesitated.

"Believe me, you won't get the drop on me so easily again. And the blade is at the wrong angle—you'd only get it stuck in a rib."

"It would hurt, though." I tried to sneer at him. He regarded me somberly, eyes dark.

"Yes, but my heart would be in no danger. The ring, Andromeda."

I put the knife back in its sheath—what else could I do?—and opened my palm. He took the ring from me and brought it to his lips.

"I hadn't dared hope that I might be able to do this for the first time myself. Your other hand, please."

Mesmerized, I gave him my hand and watched him slide the ring onto my finger.

"My vow to you, Andromeda. I accept your plan. No harm will come to your sister."

And to me? The dark stone glittered in the moonlight, my hand white against his fine black gloves.

"I can't wear it—they'll see."

"For now. Then, keep it hidden, until our wedding."

Our wedding. I knew that. Still the word blew through me like a hard fall.

"And to seal our pact—a kiss." His voice echoed rough with hunger.

Did he kiss you?

"What?"

"You heard me."

"What will it do?"

"Do?"

I cleared my throat and made myself look at him, his lips, just a hand's length away. "It binds me to you somehow, doesn't it?"

He smiled, a flash of true amusement. "Not in the way you mean."

"Does it have to be now? Can't it be . . . later?"

"No. I think not. I've given you my vow; now I require yours. A kiss, Andromeda."

"Everyone calls me Andi." I wanted to sound strong, but my voice came out nervous.

He lifted his hands and cupped my face, coaxing me to look into his eyes, black in the darkness.

"I'm not everyone else. My kiss."

With a sense of fatality, I nodded and steeled myself. I would have to give him much more than this. He sighed out a long breath, as if he'd been holding it, and dropped his head, angling a bit. Unable to bear it, I closed my eyes.

His lips brushed over mine, warm and soft. Just a whisper of a kiss. He pulled back and I opened my eyes, surprised. He flashed a grin at me, then wrapped his arms around me and pulled me in tight against his hard body. His mouth captured mine again, lips feeding on mine, coaxing and pulling, until I opened up and his tongue swept mine, hot, arousing.

Fire blazed through me. That animal something that had been pacing through my heart, clawing at my veins, swelled up and rose to meet him. I kissed him back, ferocious, starving.

I clung to him, rising on my toes to better reach him, to press my body against his, my fingers tangling in the black silk of his hair while his hands plunged under the cloak to roam my body.

He hummed, low in his throat, a pleased male animal. The sound wrenched me back to reality. I pulled back but he held me tight.

Dropping my weight, I fixed my palms on his chest and pushed, with more strength than I ever remembered having, sending him staggering back an arm's length, a surprised and delighted laugh escaping him.

"It's not funny," I hissed. "And be quiet—what if we're discovered?"

"Then I take you with me now and we begin our wedding night that much sooner."

"Absolutely not! You have no idea what Uorsin—"

"I've lived my life under the threat of Uorsin and his fearsome retaliation. Annfwn has paid a dear price for his obsession. I won't do it any longer. It's time to balance the scales."

"That's easy enough for you, but you don't know the price I'd pay!" My voice broke and I turned away, scrabbling at the ties of his cloak. "Here. Take your cloak and go. You promised to abide by my plan."

"What price?" Rayfe's voice came soft in my ear as he laid gentle hands on my shoulders. "Tell me."

"Small in the grand scheme," I tossed over my shoulder, moving out from under those warm and possessive hands. "Something that's important only to me."

"Yes?"

"Meaning I don't expect it to matter to you." I dropped his cloak on the floor, since he wouldn't take it, and picked up the wooden box, the wrapping, and my dagger. "You should have cleaned this blade. It might be ruined."

"You might have need of my blood yet."

"What do you think I'll do with it?"

"You don't need to do anything—just keep it. If you feel . . . strange, it will help you. Don't clean it until we're together."

Together.

"And what happens then?" I asked quietly.

"Do you need another demonstration?" He sounded amused again. And hungry. Heat flooded me at his words, despite it all.

"I think I understand the ravishing part." I kept my tone dry. "What about after that?"

"What price, Andromeda?"

I didn't answer. My throat closed on the words.

Rayfe stepped over his cloak. Slid one arm around my waist

and lifted my chin with a gloved finger. He kissed me, tenderly, then seemed to search my eyes. I wondered if he could see any more of my expression than I could of his. An odd courtship, where we forever fumbled around in the dark, not really knowing each other at all.

"Though it may not seem like it to you"—he cupped my cheek—"I regret that it's had to be this way with us. If there is a pain I can spare you, I will. Tell me what he holds over you."

"Will you let me go?"

"No." His voice hardened. "I cannot do that. Let me do something I can."

"You can't." Oddly, the way he held me felt comforting. The arms of the enemy. "It's only my horse. He'll kill my horse if he thinks I went to you willingly."

"Ah."

"See? Not important. Not when people are dying."

"The horse you rode the day we met—I remember. She has gorgeous lines."

I nodded and pulled away yet again. "On that note, I must go back."

"I'll escort you."

"No, no, no! I can't be seen with you."

"Oh, Andromeda," he chuckled, sweeping his cloak off the floor. "No one will see me. And this way, you can guide me to the tunnel entrance, so I'll be certain to find it."

I tripped on that. "You won't . . ." I couldn't finish the thought.

"Storm the castle? Lay waste to Windroven? If I wanted to do that, I would have done it by now."

Something about the ferocious certainty in his voice made me shiver.

"Why haven't you, then?" I whispered.

"You know the answer to that. For the same reason I've agreed to your plan."

"Which is the reason you didn't just kidnap me that night at Louson."

He tipped his head in acknowledgment.

"Annfwn needs you, yes—but we need you willing, Andromeda."

"What for?"

"As I said before, it's a long tale, and some of it I cannot tell you until I am certain of your loyalty. Suffice it to say that without you, my land and my people will be lost."

"Uorsin said you can't go back in, once you've come out."

A shade of surprise crossed his face, but he acknowledged it with a nod. "We've never been entirely certain how much Salena confided in him. There's some truth to that, but it's not the whole story. Still, yes, many Tala will not be able to return to Annfwn if you do not come with us."

"Quite the incentive to fight."

That feral grin flashed. "Indeed. You could call us desperate."

"It makes me wonder at the incentive for them to leave, then."

"Even more powerful."

"I don't understand how I can help them return—I know nothing of magic or any of this."

"You will," he replied with firm confidence. "You'll learn." The way he said it made me think he'd said those words before, convincing others besides me.

"I hope you're right. That this—all of this—hasn't been for nothing."

"It won't be." His voice resonated with fierce determination. "It can't be."

On the dark walk back to the castle, while I slipped between checkpoints and made my silent way, from time to time I glimpsed the wolf pacing me. Guarding me all the way.

12

~

Just after breakfast, I took Amelia's hand and lied to her.

I commenced the biggest acting job of my life by picking at my breakfast and casting nervous glances about the room. It helped that I hadn't slept all night. Once I'd made it back to my rooms—after answering Dafne's questions, changing back into my night-clothes, finding my drowsy guards, and telling them I *had* to sleep in my own bed after all—the first glimmers of dawn were breaking along the horizon.

I put my eye to the space in the bricked-up window, wondering if I'd see his wolf shape among the many, running black on black between the encamped armies. Instead I heard a howl. Vital. Triumphant.

Shivering, I drew back and climbed under my covers. Not sleepy, I lit the lamp and examined Rayfe's ring. The dark stone turned out to be a ruby. Such a deep red that it looked black unless I tilted it to the light exactly right. Moons and other symbols I didn't recognize chased each other around the outside. On the inner circle, words had been inscribed into the silver. I'd thought to ask Dafne if she knew the language, but I had hidden the ring from her at the last moment.

I didn't tell her Rayfe had shown. In the flesh.

Both kinds.

I don't think I feared what she would say. The whole thing had felt . . . intimate. I wanted to keep the experience close for now, where I could examine it in the silence of my heart. The way he'd touched me. The kiss.

How I'd responded.

The animal he'd further awakened in me had prowled through my blood while the castle came awake, keeping me from feeling the least bit drowsy. That and the terrible anxiety over what the morning would bring.

Amelia, always so sensitive to my moods, stopped me in the hall, as I knew she would, asking after my health.

I bit my lip. "I'm so afraid, Amelia." I poured all my fear, terrible dreams and worry for the future into it. Really, it wasn't a lie at all.

Her violet eyes darkened with concern, her clear brow furrowed as she held on to my hands.

"You mustn't be frightened, Andi. We're safe here. That horrible man can't breach these walls. Come and sit with my ladies today. That prowling around the parapets can't be good for your peace of mind."

"I can't! I can't sit there wondering if . . ." I trailed off, looking nervously down the hallway.

"If what?" she asked me gently. Soothing me. It got easier and easier to feel genuinely awful.

"If there's really a tunnel under the castle," I whispered.

"Oh, Andi!"

Frantic, I hushed her.

"I've heard rumors. What if he gets in? What if he gets into the castle and takes me and—"

She bent her head to mine, lowering her voice to match my hushed whispers. "There's not. Hugh would know."

"*I* have to know. I can't bear not knowing!"

"We'll ask, then."

"No! I'm so embarrassed to be so afraid, Amelia. Please don't tell. Please, please, please."

Amelia's eyes welled with sympathetic tears. "Don't be embarrassed, Sweetie. Anyone in your place would be afraid. Of course you need to know. Let's go look."

"Oh, no—I don't want to make you do that."

"It'll be fun. An adventure! Remember how you used to look under the bed for me, to check for monsters? This is just like that. We'll look, you'll see there's no tunnel, and then we'll have a lovely, relaxing day. Yes?"

Not trusting my voice, I pressed my lips together and nodded.

We made our way down to the depths of the castle. Alight with the game, Amelia willingly scooted down back hallways and ducked around corners to avoid servants. At one point, a page boy fetching supplies from the cellar nearly stumbled upon us. We crouched behind a wine barrel, Amelia pressing a finger to her lips, eyes dancing with merry excitement, waiting for him to leave.

Once he did, nearly stepping on Amelia's gown on his way out, we both burst into giggles. Mine might have been more hysterical, punched out by the anxiety in my chest threatening to stop my heart.

"See? This is so fun!" Amelia squeezed my hand. "Like when we were kids. I've missed those days."

"Thank you for doing this for me." I meant it. Hopefully she'd never know how much I meant it.

"Let's go back upstairs and have some wine, then!"

"But we haven't checked all the corners yet." I let the worry creep into my voice.

"Then we'll look in every one until you're happy."

I had to nudge her into seeing the place—the too-dark crack between shelves that had come ajar. Because I had moved them last night.

Curious, Amelia took a few steps. Hesitated.

"This is most odd. Perhaps we should tell Hugh."

"Oh, but he's so busy. It's probably just a little cave. Let's explore. You don't want the game to end yet, do you?"

"I don't know, Andi . . ."

"Please? It's really taking my mind off everything."

"Okay, then." She smiled at me. "Whatever makes you happy."

By the time she realized the light in the tunnel wasn't only from the lamp she carried, but from daylight, Rayfe's men had seized us.

Screaming and fighting came easily.

All that nervous energy boiled up and I scratched and clawed as if my life depended on it. My legs tangled in the court gown I'd worn, as did my sister's in hers. I carried no dagger, since I knew she wouldn't.

They dragged us out into the light, hands clamped over our mouths, iron grips inescapable. The men were a blur of dark hair and hushed commands.

They threw Amelia onto Rayfe's lap, where he sat on a huge horse, her gorgeous red-gold hair tumbling over his shoulder as he clamped her to him, easily holding her, muffling her shrieks. Making sure she saw me.

"The other is the one we want," he ordered the man holding me in a fierce whisper. "Don't let her escape!"

With that, I put on a burst of strength, biting down on the hand over my mouth and stomping on the arch of the man's foot. He dropped with a curse and I ran back for the tunnel mouth.

"Run, Andi!" Amelia screamed behind me. Shouts rang out from the castle walls above.

"Leave her!" Rayfe ordered. "Retreat!"

Just inside the tunnel, I looked back to see them riding away. A few arrows plunged into the ground around them, threatening nothing. Everyone had seen the bright flag of Amelia's hair. An arm of Tala quickly swallowed them up.

I drew up my skirt and ran to perform the next scene in the greatest acting job ever attempted.

Liar.

Traitor.

The ugly words pummeled through my brain as I climbed through the cellars, Amelia's terrified face emblazoned there.

Hugh and his men found me before I'd gotten far. Enraged, his face distorted with emotion, Hugh seized my arms in a bruising grip.

"What happened?" he shouted in my face.

Sobbing, out of breath, I gasped for words. He shook me.

"Tell me!"

"A tunnel," I choked. "That way. Seal it. Oh, for the love of Moranu, they took her."

Hugh released me and my legs gave way. I lay there in a crumpled heap, crying out my guilt and fear. *Liar. Traitor. Please, Moranu, let this work.* Dimly I heard the men race off to find the tunnel.

Someone grabbed my arm and dragged me to my feet. Einsly.

"Gently," Hugh ordered him. "Look, she's been hurt." Hugh pulled me from Einsly's grip and enfolded me in his arms. For a moment I clung to him, the golden prince. Whose heart I'd ripped out and tossed to the enemy.

"Tell me what happened, Andi. No one blames you."

I sobbed out the story. How it was all my fault, how Amelia had sought to soothe my fears. And now . . .

"Who told you these rumors?" Einsly demanded.

Blankly I stared at him. I hadn't thought up a story for that.

"Servants," I stammered. "One of the maids said her gran talked about it. She was afraid."

"The one time a maid has useful gossip and they don't tell the men who can actually do something about it," Einsly griped, glaring at me.

"Come, you're hurt," Hugh told me. "Let's get you upstairs." Ever courteous to me, he quaked under the fear and grief. "Your dress is torn—did they?"

Surprised, I looked down. My bodice had torn open, showing a fair amount of bosom. Shaken, I pulled the ragged edges together.

"Did they . . . harm you?" Hugh could barely speak the words.

"Oh, no. No, Hugh. Nothing like that. I'm sure they won't harm Amelia, either." I struggled to find the right words, to ease at least this dread for him. "They know who she is. She's too valuable to . . . harm."

"I will rescue her," he vowed. "I won't rest until she's safe with me again."

"Whatever it takes?" I stopped him. "Swear?"

"I so swear, to Glorianna and above." Hugh's summer-blue eyes glowed with certainty.

Hopefully Rayfe would send the parley soon.

He did. By the time we'd made it up to the main court room, everyone was abuzz with the word that a messenger had ridden up to the castle under the white flag.

"Go to your chambers," Hugh ordered me upon hearing the news. "You do not need to suffer through this."

"She's my sister." I firmed my jaw. "I won't cower in my rooms while she suffers."

"Very well, then." Hugh snatched up a goblet of wine and drank it down. I wanted to tell him it would be all right. I hoped it would be. I took a step and Dafne stopped me.

"Your shawl, Princess." She draped it over my shoulders, artfully arranging it to cover my bosom, giving me a stern look. Right. Don't blow it now. Abruptly my frenzied energy bled away. My legs felt weak and exhausted. My head swam. "Have a seat, Princess. Gather yourself."

I tried.

In silence, we waited for the messenger. At any rate, Hugh, Dafne, and I were silent. The courtiers whispered among themselves and one of Amelia's ladies wailed dramatically in the background, her voice echoing down the hall in an eerie whine that reminded me of the howling I'd heard the first night the Tala attacked. I clenched my jaw against it.

Einsly and a few of his men escorted the messenger in, looking like they'd prefer to cut him into little pieces. He held himself with arrogant confidence, as if he didn't notice their presence. His short dark hair glinted here and there with highlights as red as a fox's coat; his sharp blue eyes swept the court and fastened on me with intense curiosity. And perhaps dislike.

He gave me a little nod, however, and bowed to Hugh with mocking courtesy.

"Prince Hugh of Avonlidgh, I am Terin of the Tala. I am here to propose a trade. Your lovely wife, the Princess Amelia, for your sister-in-law and our kin, the Princess Andromeda."

This should have been a surprise to no one. Nevertheless, a shocked murmur ran through the assembly. I wanted to hiss with impatience.

Hugh, looking unutterably weary, leaned his head on his hand and rubbed his eyes.

"I'm sure I need not point out," Terin continued, "that this is simply a renewal of our previous request, one supported by a previous treaty, one that predates most of your births, entered into by High King Uorsin himself. My liege, Rayfe of the Tala, simply wishes to see the terms of that agreement sealed. He proposes to wed the Princess Andromeda in full sight of both our peoples at high noon. Then we shall cease all hostilities and return to our lives."

Hugh had sat up straight at this. "Noon of this day. Good Glorianna—that's absurd."

"Princess Amelia—who is in excellent health, I assure you—may stand up for her sister, then return with you to Windroven, and we will decamp immediately after. We feel this is a most reasonable offer."

"Now, see here—"

"Prince Hugh," I interrupted.

His head whipped around to me, shocked.

"Brother." I gentled my voice. "We must agree. We have no choice."

"You would wed the enemy?" He sounded horrified.

"To save my sister and my people?" I stood. "Yes. I will do my duty as my birth dictates. You, Prince Hugh, should understand that my own honor compels me."

Terin tilted his head, surveying me, then flicked his gaze back to Hugh, who still stared at me, face flushed. I gave him a little smile. Hugh did not deserve the pain I'd put him through.

"You've kept your word to me and to the High King," I told him. "You've done everything to win this. Now we are defeated—through no fault of yours—by a wily enemy. It's time to pay the price."

"Let me kill him, liege!" Einsly called out. "We'll send his head back to Rayfe, and—"

"And he will send Amelia's head back to us!" I shouted him down. "I refuse to be the agent of my sister's death."

"Andi," Hugh pleaded, "I can't break my word."

"You don't have to. I might point out that, as Princess of the Realm, I outrank all of you." I turned to Terin. "In place of High King Uorsin and his heir, Princess Ursula, I accept your terms. We shall meet at noon."

"You must be wed by a priest of Glorianna, and they might not agree," Hugh inserted. "They take days to prepare for a wedding."

"Then the Moranu priestess shall marry us. Ask one of Danu's to be there, as well." I turned to Terin. "Have the Tala any other spiritual followings that should be represented?"

He cocked his head at me, studying me with sparkling eyes. "We shall see to it, Princess Andromeda. Provide your acolytes of Glorianna and Danu, if you wish. We shall see that Moranu seals this wedding."

"Fine." I drew myself up, putting on imperious Ursula airs, scanning the pale and horrified faces of these courtiers I didn't know. "I offer my gratitude to the people of Windroven and greater Avonlidgh for their protection and their sacrifices on my behalf. Today shall see the end of your suffering, and I'm glad of it."

My voice unexpectedly broke and Dafne put a hand on my arm.

"I am glad of it," I repeated, looking at Hugh as I said it.

With that, I left the room and prepared to marry.

This was not Amelia's wedding. With only a small space of time to prepare, there would be no glamour or elaborate lace. It wouldn't be right, anyway, for a battlefield ceremony, for me to wear fancy satin slippers on ground still soaked with blood.

Amelia's ladies rallied brilliantly, dragging out a gown of silver cloth Amelia had put aside because it was a rare color that did not flatter her peach and gold complexion. They rattled on, setting to altering it for me, amid thanks and tears for my sacrifice. They wouldn't pet me so nicely if they knew how I'd betrayed their lady.

My guilt worsened as they found hot water for me to bathe in, gently washing and drying my hair, brushing it until it gleamed. They left it unbound so it streamed nearly to the backs of my knees. I kept thinking about the plan to decamp and ride off following the ceremony, how impractical my outfit and hair would be if I had to travel any distance.

Then again, that would likely be the least of my worries.

I tried not to fret about it, what would happen next. Rayfe wouldn't harm me. But he would take from me what Uorsin had taken from my mother. I might become like her, forever gazing out the window at the homeland I'd lost, babies wrested from my loins at my husband's will. Perhaps they'd assign someone to me, to teach me whatever their manners might be.

And yet, when Rayfe had spoken—in his cagey way—about why Annfwn needed me, he hadn't mentioned babies. They clearly had plenty of shape-shifters. Maybe it was something else about my blood. Salena's blood, mixed with Uorsin's.

I deliberately did not think about how Uorsin and Ursula would receive this news.

Dafne arrived as the ladies finished every bit of buffing and polishing they could think of. She stopped, eyes wide. "Princess Andi—you look phenomenally beautiful!"

"You don't have to sound so surprised," I grumbled.

She winked at me, and some of the anxiety dissolved in my chest. "They've set up a platform at the base of the road and draped it with silk. It looks quite nice."

"Oh, good. I'd hate to marry my blackmailer on bare wood."

The other ladies gasped, but Dafne laughed. "Sorry I'm late— but I've packed all your things. This is for you." She handed me a little blue velvet box.

I held it, tears pricked the edges of my eyes, and I blinked them back. All I needed was for the ladies to have to fix the paint on my eyes. "I wish you could come with me."

"I wish it, too, with all my heart. But outsiders are never allowed into Annfwn. You can ask, but I'm sure that's what King Rayfe will say." She held my eyes, a solemn promise. "Open your gift."

Inside lay a necklace of silver with a full moon pendant. It would perfectly match Rayfe's ring. Dafne slipped the rose of Glorianna off my neck, remarking that the gold clashed with my dress. She fastened the necklace with Moranu's moon in its place and smiled. "Much better, don't you think?"

And then it was time to go already.

I fussed with my mother's doll, taking Rayfe's ring from the hiding spot and tucking it into my bosom. One of the ladies promised to pack up my few remaining things and send them down. They kissed me good-bye, weeping. Their sympathy warmed something in me, and I thanked them for their care.

Hugh met me in the main inner courtyard, resplendent in gold and white, jewels flashing. A full set of cavalry, all on white horses, waited to precede us, Terin neatly pocketed in the center on a giant roan.

Hugh took my hands, blue eyes somber. "You don't have to do this, Andi. We can still find a way."

I squeezed his hands, my heart cramping with guilt. And a tinge of impatience. Why couldn't he see that the time for the noble gesture was over?

"I've already given *my* word, remember? This is the only way. No turning back now. I imagine I am far from the only or last princess—or prince, for that matter—to wed for peace."

"No." He tried to smile, but it didn't reach his eyes. "But I would have wished for better than that . . . beast of a man for you."

The way he spat the words took me aback. Fear I thought I'd set aside stirred, prickled in my gut, as I remembered the ravenous way Rayfe had kissed me. The wolf in him. The black raptor, too? How my mother had faded to nothing and died. "You don't think he'll hurt me, do you?"

His face creased with concern. "He won't kill you, no, but he will—" Hugh stopped himself, shook his head. "It's not my place to speak of these things. Has Amelia talked to you of the . . . ways between a man and a woman?"

I smiled to cover the laugh. Or between a man and a man or a woman and a woman, I wanted to remind him. Avonlidgh seemed a simpler place than Mohraya, one where the bawdier songs were never sung, apparently.

"I know something of it. I will be fine. Don't fret for me."

"If he isn't gentle with you—"

"Hugh." Impulsively I stood on tiptoe and kissed his cheek. "Don't think on it. I'm no cringing flower. Noon approaches and we must retrieve Amelia."

Over his shoulder, I caught a fleeting sneer on Terin's face. He might be the one I'd seen at Rayfe's right hand all those days they rode to parley. I ignored the contempt he clearly harbored for me, though it made me feel a little tired inside. Oddly, despite Hugh's fears, I found I trusted Rayfe to keep his word, that he meant it at least when he spoke of me as valuable to him and Annfwn. One doesn't destroy what's of value.

Still, I wouldn't feel right until Amelia was back in Hugh's arms and the Tala headed back to the Wild Lands and beyond.

Never mind that I'd go into exile with them.

Hugh helped me onto a white palfrey draped in the High King's crimson. I sat uncomfortably sidesaddle, rearranging my streaming hair, glad that it would be a short ride to the bottom of the hill. After that, I promised myself, I'd ride astride even if I had to hike up my skirt and do it bareback. Dafne smirked, clearly reading my thoughts. A note of normal life amid all this drama and playacting.

After this, I'd be totally alone.

13

This descent was the shadow side of our arrival.

No cheering crowds lined the route. Instead troops, weary of the weeks of siege, wearing their losses hard, stood at somber attention, saluting me as we passed. The bright morning had surrendered to another stormy day, and the wind off the ocean carried a new bite, tumbling ominous black clouds overhead. Between the defeated and grieving faces of the people who stood vigil and the oppressive feel of a looming storm, I had trouble shaking the feeling I rode to my own funeral.

At least I no longer saw an overlay of blood and bodies on the rocky slopes. A possible future averted, then, if I accepted that these visions were real.

It seemed I had no other choice.

The wooden platform stood out at the bottom of the hill, where the road widened and branched, leading out to farmland and forest. The attempt to make it seem festive had the opposite effect. The chill winds tugged at the scarves, ripping one away and sending it tumbling through the assembled soldiers. The pink-clad priest of Glorianna huddled miserably in one corner of the platform, looking pitifully out of place.

And there was Rayfe. Waiting for me.

He stood out in any crowd. He wore his long black hair loose, and the wind tore at it, whipping it like a pennant, a contrast to the deep bloodred of his garments. His face looked fierce, eyes hooded and fastened on me.

Next to him, a weeping Amelia was held upright by several Tala guards, two blades at her throat.

Hugh hissed out a furious breath and kicked his horse into a gallop for the last short distance, his horse shouldering past our armed escort that surrounded Terin. So much for ceremony. I urged my palfrey after him.

By the time I rode up, Hugh had already swung down and charged up the platform steps—only to be stopped by spears. A cry went up from the escort, several pulling swords.

"Stop it! All of you, stand down!" I shouted. Judging by the array of astonished faces, I'd surprised more than myself. "Prince Hugh—would you help me down, please?"

He flashed a furious red look over his shoulder at me and gestured to Amelia. "Surely this is not necessary! What beast treats a Princess in such a way?"

"Simply a guarantee, my enemy," Rayfe growled, eyes never leaving my face. "In case any of you think to renege."

"Renege!" Hugh pushed his white-velvet-clad chest into the spear points while Amelia wailed for him. "How dare you impugn my honor!"

I blew out my frustration and struggled with the stupid saddle. I would never strap myself to one of these contraptions again. To my surprise, Terin appeared at my knee to help me down, hastily followed by his erstwhile guards. No contempt for the moment, just that foxy sardonic expression. "Allow me to escort you, Princess."

He didn't waste time, but lifted me down and led me immediately to Hugh's side. I put a hand on Hugh's arm. When he ignored me, I tugged sharply on him, then ducked under the spears. A hissed order from Rayfe had the spears dropping. Hugh started to surge forward, the spear tips pushing hard on his chest.

"Think!" I urged him quietly. "A few minutes more and she's safe."

Hugh's eyes were wild. "We can't trust him."

"We already are. Hugh! Don't turn this into a bloodbath. Please."

"Princess Andromeda?" The white-haired priestess of Moranu now stood at the top of the steps. "Are you ready?" Her aqua eyes surveyed Hugh with grave understanding.

"Yes." I slipped my arm through Hugh's. "Prince Hugh?"

A bit of sanity crept back into his expression and he nodded, covering my hand with his. I saw Rayfe take note of it, dark-blue eyes glittering. Dafne hastened up, adjusting my dress and hair. Like it mattered how I looked.

Hugh led me up the steps with a semblance of dignity and, with a show of deep loathing, placed my hand in Rayfe's outstretched one. Rayfe bowed deeply and kissed the back of my hand with great ceremony. Behind me, the spears dropped again, fencing Hugh from me.

"Princess Andromeda. It is a pleasure to see you in person once again. Welcome to the Tala."

I couldn't find my voice all of a sudden. I had no words, with my heart choking my throat. Now that I'd accomplished the insurmountable, the reality of what I planned to do hit me hard. The tattered silk scarves snapped in the wind. I stared into Rayfe's feral gaze, unable to reply.

"Let us begin the ceremony, then," Rayfe declared.

"I would have my sister stand up for me," I whispered, the best I could manage at that moment. But Amelia heard me.

"I won't," she cried out. "I won't have you do it, Andi."

She was only a few arms' lengths away from me, her tear-ravaged face distorted, her usual beauty shredded by her trials.

"I'm so sorry for what you've been through, Ami." More sorry than she could possibly know.

"It's not your fault, Andi. It's him. Don't marry him—he's a horrible beast." She dissolved into tears and I glanced up at Rayfe, who watched me with that impassive gaze that covered so much.

"Have you been harmed?" I asked her, holding Rayfe's eyes. One corner of his mouth twisted at my accusation and he subtly shook his head.

Amelia simply wept.

"Ami—I have to know. Did anyone hurt you? Did *he*?" I held out the challenge. My line in the sand.

She lifted a tearstained face, lips wobbly. "No. Not in that way," she whimpered.

"In any way at all?"

"Yes!" Amelia flung at me. "He means to take my heart from my breast and leave me forever only half of what I am. I won't stand for it, Andi!"

It pained me, though I understood her reasoning. Amelia had never been without spine; she just chose her battles differently than most.

"I will stand up for you, Princess." Dafne stood by my side. Terin stepped to Rayfe's right hand, which surprised me not at all.

Rayfe nodded at someone off to the side, who stepped forward with a bundle in her hands. He took it from her. "A wedding gift for you, Andromeda."

He shook out the cloak, deep red, but lined with sparkling white fur. He draped it over my shoulders, lifting the long fall of my hair to stream down the back of it. The warmth engulfed me, easing some of my fear. Which made no sense, since it was he who frightened me, not the cold.

"I suspected you might not have a cloak with you." He said it gravely, but his eyes reminded me of those moments alone. Last night and an age ago.

"Thank you. It comes as a comfort to me that you wish me warm."

"I wish far more than that for you, my wife, but this will do for a start."

"I'm not your wife yet."

"Then we shall remedy that immediately."

The priestess of Moranu, whose name I still didn't know, the miserable-looking bald priest of Glorianna, and another woman draped in deep blue, who must be one of Danu's, all stepped forward.

One by one, they intoned their blessings, while Rayfe held my hand and two silent armies surrounded us. And while my sister wept as if her heart were breaking. Once the three finished, all offering me the blessings of their goddesses, they fell back and a man stepped into their place. He wore no festive garments but rather was clad in furs. His dark hair fell in knotted ropes around his shoulders, braided with bits of colorful rags and beads. He smelled musky and wild. He carried a large blade and wore a textured silver disc that could only be the full moon.

I must have drawn back slightly, because Rayfe squeezed my hand in a fierce grip. Startled, I glanced up at him.

"This is our way," he said softly. "It is now your way. Moranu has many faces."

I couldn't swallow the cold spit in my throat. Would I be sacrificed after all? Wed before my people and then cut down? It would be easy for Rayfe to do it, to kill us all. And I'd engineered it for him.

"Never fear, my Andromeda." His stern face urged me to agree, even as he held my hand captive.

Managing to swallow finally, I nodded.

Amelia's wild sobbing increased in pitch and Hugh shouted as the feral priest stepped close, knife held before him like a candle. Dafne took my other hand, echoing Terin taking Rayfe's on the right. The priest chanted, words I couldn't understand, to a deep, throbbing rhythm.

He lowered the blade to the underside of Rayfe's wrist and sliced, opening a crimson well. I steeled myself and managed not to jerk back when he sliced my wrist also, Dafne squeezing my fingers in sympathy. I half expected thousands of tiny black birds to fly out, but only my blood welled up, bright red and ordinary. The priest took our two hands and held them apart, demanded something unintelligible of the sky, turned my wrist over, and put it on top of Rayfe's. I hissed at the painful sting and the surge of . . . something like fire where our blood mingled. Dancing and ducking, the priest wound strips of dark red silk around our joined arms, binding us close together.

Dafne dropped my hand and Terin stepped back. Rayfe adjusted the angle of his arm, interlacing his fingers with mine, bringing us nearly breast to breast. He stared down at me, inscrutable, while his wild priest danced and leapt a circle around us.

"This is one way of keeping a bride from running off," I muttered.

His stern lips twitched, but he didn't comment.

The priest stopped his wild gyrations. Said something expectant.

"The ring," Rayfe whispered.

Oh. Three curses.

"Please tell me you have it."

"Yes."

He raised an eyebrow.

"I have to get it out. Shield me so no one can see."

"Where is this hiding spot?"

"My bosom. Don't look." The glorious cloak covered my movements as I slid my unbound hand up and reached under the tight neckline. It must have shifted around with all the activity—I was hampered by being one-handed and by the lightning flowing through my blood. The bodice was too tight for it to have fallen out, though. I just needed to get to it. Rayfe watched my search with great interest.

"Would you like me to help?" That amusement rolled through his voice.

"No," I hissed.

"I'd be pleased to."

"No doubt." Oddly, I wanted to laugh back at the glint in his eyes. Perhaps it was simply the relief of having it finally done with, but I felt lighter, some of the awful tension and fear in me uncoiling. I pressed the ring into his free hand. "Here."

He took it from me, held it up to the sky, then kissed it, as he had before. Then he slid it on my finger again, on the hand joined to his.

"No ring for you?" I asked.

"I would be delighted to accept such a token from you, Andromeda. I hadn't anticipated that you would be ready to offer one yet." A subtle tension rode through him, a kind of heat.

"I don't have one," I confessed, feeling like I'd forgotten my sister's natal day. Sure enough, a flash of something passed over his face, quickly covered.

" 'Tis not important."

While we talked, the priest had begun chanting again, picking up the pace and pitch of it. Rayfe slid his free arm around my waist, pulling me close. Uncertain, I laid my palm on his chest. Hugh in the background, protested loudly.

"This is not how my people do things," I told him.

A fierce hunger transformed his face. "You belong to my people now, to our people, Andromeda. Never forget that." His mouth descended on mine, possessive, consuming. Despite my enormous audience, the heat swept through me again, pushing aside all thought, setting the blood birds into frenzied flight.

When he let me go, the air suddenly chill on my wet lips, the look he gave me, the look of a man who had succeeded in a wild gambit and triumphed against all odds, left me shaken.

The feral priest said something loud and final even as Rayfe said, "It is done."

A roar went up from the Tala, thunderous, woven with animal calls—howls, caws, and the full-throated roars of big cats. On the Windroven side, only the wind keened over the landscape.

Rayfe tossed an order over his shoulder at Terin. The guards around us dissolved away, as if by magic.

"Prince Hugh." Rayfe tucked me against his side, our bound arms between us. "I greet you as a brother now."

Indignant, Hugh opened his mouth to protest, then looked at me and stopped. With a gasping sob, Amelia flung herself across the platform to him. He gathered her against him, murmuring soothing words and kissing the top of her fair hair.

"I regret any unhappiness the Princess Amelia may have suffered."

Hugh looked at me again. "You may have forced my hand with this low deed, but I hold you accountable. We of the Twelve Kingdoms do not treat our wives as beasts of bondage."

Rayfe smiled, a wolfish grin. "I am as tied to her as she to me. On that note . . ." He put out a hand and Terin placed a scroll in it. He handed it to me. "Andromeda—I ask a gift from you on this our wedding day, to celebrate our alliance."

I couldn't open the scroll one-handed. He helpfully held one end with his free hand, so I could read. Oh, Uorsin would *not* like this. I handed it to Hugh. Amelia still wept against his chest, refusing to look at me.

"A list of Tala prisoners held by the High King at Ordnung, along with a list of prisons in the Twelve Kingdoms suspected of holding Tala prisoners," I explained. "Rayfe is asking—"

"*You*, my queen, are asking," Rayfe inserted, a hint of a growl in his voice.

I searched his face, anger burning warm in me. "Am I to do as I'm told, then?" I would have yanked away but, obviously, could not.

"This is not an order," he told me softly. "I request it, as a gift. How can we celebrate a true alliance—something so many have suffered for—if our people are held prisoner?"

I sighed out a long breath. He had a point. Uorsin's rage would know no bounds as it was.

"Are you sure this is even correct—Tala in all these prisons? I've never heard of such a thing."

"There are many things you have been ignorant of before this—isn't that true?" he replied in an even tone, holding my gaze.

I sighed for the truth of it.

"Prince Hugh." I thought about the wording. "Please see that my father receives this list with my message. I send him, and Princess Ursula, my loving regard and everlasting fealty. I ask that they not mourn the sacrifice I've made for the peace of the kingdoms, but rather, to celebrate the promise of continuing peace, that they release these prisoners. If necessary, the freed captives can be escorted via armed guard and we will arrange to take custody of them. I will look forward to continuing communications with my family and hope to visit soon."

I didn't look at Rayfe. I didn't have to—his body spoke of his annoyance. Hugh nodded somberly.

"Now I shall keep the rest of our bargain." Rayfe raised his voice. "We decamp immediately."

With a cumulative shout of acknowledgment, the Tala pulled back and began preparations. At the far edges, some troops already streamed away, walking, trotting, and riding over the horizon. Birds arrowed off in vees and on their own. Some remained, keeping a watchful eye from above. It seemed some smaller creatures almost melted into the ground. Rayfe nodded at Hugh.

"Those prisoners we took have already been returned to you, yes?"

"Yes." Hugh thinned his lips.

"Shall we depart?" Rayfe inquired formally.

Abruptly, I felt at a loss. This was it. I looked around for Dafne. Right there, by my side.

"I like him," Dafne said in my ear, taking my free hand.

"What?"

"You heard me. Rayfe. I like him. He's good for you."

I sputtered at that. "How can you possibly say that? You've barely met him."

She shrugged. "With some people, it doesn't take long to have their measure."

"I'm really going to miss you." I searched for more words.

"We'll see each other again, I'm sure. Take care of yourself, Princess. Stop looking like an abandoned puppy. Oh, and enjoy tonight." With a salacious grin, a wink, and a curtsy that barely skirted the correct form, she left.

"Amelia?" Hugh spoke against her hair. "Andi is saying good-bye."

"No!" she cried against his chest.

"Ami." I put a hand on her shaking shoulder, Rayfe obligingly going with me. "Don't cry. This is just like when you married Hugh and went off to Windroven. We'll see each other again soon."

"It's *not* like that!" She tossed her hair back to give me a tearful look, then blanched to see Rayfe so close. "You're wed to that—that *beast* and it's all my fault!"

My heart tore. "It's not. It's not your fault, baby sister."

She simply buried her face again. Hugh shrugged, uncomfortable. "She's distraught."

"Yes." I stroked her hair. Sighed. "She is. Take her back to Windroven. Take care of her."

He nodded, grave. "I always will."

"I know." *And I used it against you.*

"Rayfe of the Tala." Hugh lifted his chin. "I charge you with the same. Take care of Princess Andi. If she comes to the least harm, a moment's distress, I shall hold you personally responsible."

"No more than I hold myself so," Rayfe responded in kind, then squeezed my hand. "Shall we?"

Rayfe led me away, to the large black stallion I'd seen from the towers, waiting saddled and bridled. Several grooms waited to assist us and I soon discovered why. With much effort, they managed to help us onto the horse, still tied together. I would have said it couldn't be done, but I ended up sideways on Rayfe's lap, perched on his muscular thigh. They untied my cloak briefly and he lifted his arm over my head, snugging me up against his chest. It meant I had to cross my own arm tightly across my breasts, but it wasn't uncomfortable. The grooms retied my cloak, rearranging it around me with Rayfe's arm inside.

"It would be far easier to simply untie us now."

He shook his head, looking out over the decamping army. "Not yet."

"You know, in the Twelve Kingdoms, the men don't have to tie up their brides to keep them from running off."

"Don't they? Perhaps the women are more biddable there."

I opened my mouth to retort but couldn't come up with a good answer. "How long, then?"

"The ties must remain until our marriage bed."

"Wait—when will that be?"

He glanced down, amusement sparking through the dark blue of his eyes. "Anxious, my sweet?"

"I'm thinking more of the inconvenience in the interim," I answered drily.

"Soon," he answered my question. "Once I'm certain all are on their way, there is a place we can be together. Once I'm buried inside you, we can undo the wrappings."

His words reawakened that heat, and I felt my cheeks burning. He chuckled. "I hadn't thought you'd be shy."

I hadn't thought so, either.

He cuddled me closer, a warm hand on my thigh, nuzzling the small hairs at my temple. "You smell delicious. I like the feel of you on my lap. Kiss me."

"No." I refused to look at him. "No one can think that I'm eager for you."

"And are you? Eager for me?"

I didn't answer.

"There was a kingdom once, conquered by a mighty warrior. To cement his triumph, he married their queen, in a public ceremony before all her people. Then he stripped her and consummated the marriage while all watched, so that they would know her defeat as theirs. After that, he kept her alive, but as a collared slave who knelt next to his throne. Thus the people were daily reminded of their own servitude and his mastery of them all."

He fell silent. A troop of horsemen, wild looking, with streaming hair, rode past and saluted us with cocky grins.

"I have never heard this story," I finally replied.

"The kingdom was far on the other side of the Onyx Ocean. And it happened long ago. It's not surprising your minstrels wouldn't know it."

"But yours do?"

"Ours know different things. Annfwn has been . . . insular, if you will."

I turned that over in my mind, tying it together with the hints about border crossings and lack thereof.

"Why would you tell me such a story now?"

He cupped my cheek in his free hand and tilted my face up so I'd look into his eyes. His fingers were chilly against my hot skin. Bits of ice swirled in the air now, and the ocean roiled under a freezing fog.

"There are brutal men in the world. I am capable of a great deal, but I am no brute. I tell you this story so you'll recognize the difference. However, you are mine now, and I will have everyone know it."

"I thought we agreed to be bound to each other. I'm not a horse you purchased."

"True enough," he agreed easily. "I am also yours. You are welcome to kiss me also, if you wish."

His lips curved in a tempting, taunting smile. It bothered me that I wanted to. That, despite it all, I was apparently eager for him, my woman's center burning to be touched.

"I don't wish to."

"I think you are lying."

"What happened to her?"

"Who?"

"The queen, the one who became a slave to her enemy."

He frowned thoughtfully, his thumb caressing my cheekbone. "I don't know. I don't think the stories ever said."

Of course they didn't.

"I should point out that you have not defeated Uorsin."

"Not yet."

"You'd be foolish to try. You might be many things, but I don't believe you are a fool."

"I have what Annfwn needed, what Uorsin hoped to deny us. I've won this round." He seemed about to say something more and stopped himself. He dropped his hand from my cheek and tucked the luxurious cloak around me to seal off the drafts. "It grows cold. Soon we'll be able to leave."

The game, it seemed, would not end here. Just as I was on my own journey, we were moving into the next phase of history, written or no.

14

At last, the final ragged edges of the Tala army had retreated from the vast plain and the armies of Windroven had withdrawn inside or returned to their homes and stations.

Dafne rode off with Hugh's retinue early on, so they could settle Amelia, turning to give me a last wave. Rayfe finally had seen enough and wheeled his horse around, and we set off at an easy canter into the forested hills. We rode in silence. Though I remained pressed against him, he felt far away now, deep in his thoughts. It was better than the alternative.

As we climbed, the trees broke the wind and the ice crystals became fat snowflakes. The ground disappeared under the fall of white, all sound but ours muffled.

Unfortunately the call of nature pressed hard upon me and the jogging of the horse made every moment more excruciating.

Finally I had to break our tacit truce, with the most banal of requests.

"I have the same need," he replied. "I apologize. Usually the bride and groom go directly to the marriage bed, so this is normally not an issue. We are nearly there, however, if you can hold out. I fear that if we dismount it will be too difficult to mount again."

"You could just cut the bonds now," I pointed out. "That's the simple answer."

"No, the ceremony must be completed."

"It's not like anyone is going to know. I won't tell."

He was studying my face, but I kept looking out at the falling snow.

"Are you so casual of blood magic, then, that you would play with the truth of it as easily as you lie about your desire for me?"

Ouch. I floundered, embarrassed that he saw so much. But for what? I had nothing to be ashamed of. I was out of my depth as much as if Ursula had thrown me in with her best swordsman. No wonder I kept misstepping. I simply needed to master new skills.

"I have little experience with either," I replied, "and all with you on both counts. How should I know where to draw the line between what is real and what is not?"

He laughed, looped the reins around a peg on the saddle, and cupped my cheek, urging me to look at him. I caught my breath at the hunger in his face.

"Trust me, my queen, all of this is very real." His mouth descended on mine, surprisingly hot, lips moving over mine with a tender ferocity that made my head swim. The flames in my groin roared to life, burning me with relentless need. The lightning in my blood, made of claws and beaks and fangs, tore at me with renewed urgency. Before him, no man had kissed me, so I'd wondered if perhaps I would respond this way to any kiss, any desiring touch. Or maybe just to someone else with Tala blood.

Somehow I didn't think so.

His hand moved into my hair, winding it around his fingers as he continued to kiss me. The horse slowed to a walk, following the narrow path through the woods. I sank into the red velvet heat that Rayfe spun around me, letting him shower kisses over my cheeks and closed eyes, then return to my mouth to feed on it like a hummingbird visiting a flower over and over.

I could almost believe in his desire for me.

"And we're here." His voice penetrated my fog, rough and amused. "Were you sufficiently distracted?"

I flushed—again, still—and realized we'd halted at a cabin. Lights glowed within and spicy woodsmoke promised a warming fire. We managed to slide off the horse without too much trouble and Rayfe led me into the trees, soft snow sinking around my ankles. Such a good thing I hadn't worn those satin slippers.

"It's best to do this out here," he explained, "since the indoor privy would be more difficult to manage."

He guided me behind a tree and turned away as best he could while I squatted in the snow. I kicked more snow over my stain, then waited, trying not to listen while he accomplished his business. *Such is the crashing intimacy of marriage,* I thought. In some ways I could see the wisdom of this method. Like jumping into the cold lake instead of easing in, toe by toe. We were intertwined with each other now. Slow or fast, the sting is the same. I was no longer only myself.

The physical ties just demonstrated it.

We cleaned our hands in the snow and took care of the horse together. It was an odd companionship, finding the ways to work together to accomplish these small tasks. Once his stallion was tucked in the stall in back, happily munching hay, I was grateful to get out of the chill.

Rayfe undid the knots at my throat, his handsome face intent as he plucked at the cords with fingers clumsy from the cold.

"It seems you spend a lot of time either putting cloaks on me or taking them off again."

He slanted me a wicked grin. "Any time you need assistance removing your clothes, I am delighted to provide it, my lady."

"Just as long as you're willing to help me dress again. There are no servants here?"

He shook his head, shrugging out of his own cloak. "For at least tonight, it was best that it be just the two of us. But here, we have wine, some meats, cheeses, fruits, if you're hungry. I realized

I have no idea what you like to eat, so I asked for as many things as I could think of."

I surveyed the groaning bounty of the little table, the elaborate bed tucked in the corner, its covers invitingly turned back while candles blazed in every nook. "How did you assemble all this so fast?"

"I've had nigh on four seven-days to prepare this place for us."

"You couldn't have known how the siege would end."

"Oh, but I did." He drew me close, weaving his fingers with mine, free arm going around me to rub up and down my back under the long fall of my hair. The touch warmed and alarmed me, as did the implacable certainty in his face. "I knew I would win you or die trying."

I searched his fierce visage, wondering what drove him so hard. He wasn't Hugh, to sacrifice all for true love or a noble ideal. "Why did you want me so much?"

"Isn't it enough for you to know that I do?"

"I don't know. I don't think so." I bit my lip, uncertain.

"Let me do that for you," he murmured, brushing my lips with his, then tugging on my lower lip with his teeth. I gasped at the surge of desire. "If you're not hungry, perhaps we should complete our marriage?"

"I'm not hungry," I whispered.

"I can't tell you how glad I am to hear that, Andromeda."

"Mostly I'd like to have the use of my arm again."

"Is that all it is?" He trailed hot, hungry lips over my cheek and nipped under the corner of my jaw. The tender skin there sparked at the touch, the sensation arrowing through my body to my groin. He nibbled down my throat, licking here and there, spreading that melted feeling through me.

Then he was tugging me toward the fireplace and the white fur rug in front of it. He sat me in a chair and began working the laces of my boot, his shining black head bent over the task. Soon he'd have all my clothes off and would be inside me. No going back. I scanned the room, not really looking for escape. Just to settle myself. The fire blazed with welcome warmth and the fur looked soft.

"What has white fur that's this big?"

Rayfe glanced up, dark-blue eyes glinting. "To the north are great white bears. Lethal hunters."

More stories come to life. He slipped the boots off my feet and smiled that wicked half smile at me. "I wouldn't lie to you, Andromeda." He stood, urging me to my feet, and swept his free hand over my hair. "Would you help me with my boots?"

I understood the hesitation in his voice when I knelt at his feet to pick one-handed at the wet knots. Though he'd performed the same service for me, I felt oddly subservient. The image of the long-ago foreign queen slipped through my mind, forever kneeling at the throne of her conqueror while her people glared at her with accusation and pity.

"I wonder what you're thinking about," Rayfe mused. "Not about the bears of the north, I think."

"Perhaps I am. Or about lethal hunters in general."

"Is that how you see me?"

I looked up to see that he'd leaned forward, tails of hair that escaped from the knot at his nape falling around his sharp cheekbones.

"Trying to choose the right words?" He sounded amused and I remembered Ursula teasing me the same way, standing in the exercise yard a lifetime ago. I could see the echoes and layers around him, just as I'd seen around her that day.

"I see the wolf in you. And the raptor. I see—" him dead in the snow, surrounded by a circle of crimson blood. I willed the image away.

"What do you see?" he urged, curiously intent.

I shrugged, abruptly self-conscious. "Dreams and visions. It's of no matter."

"Visions were one of Salena's gifts. If they are yours, too, you'll have to learn to wield this ability."

I stared at his boots, the black scuffed and worn. "What about shape-changing?"

"That, too. Have you ever?"

"No." I shook my head, confirming it to myself. "But I *feel* . . ."

"Most learn as children," he told me in a gentle tone. "And even for the most experienced, it's far more difficult to accomplish away from Annfwn. I'll teach you that, too."

"But not tonight. My mind and heart can only stretch so far, so fast."

He slipped his fingers under my chin and raised it, brushing my lips with a kiss so sweet my heart turned over in my chest.

"No. Not tonight," he murmured.

Flustered, I slipped the loosened boots off his feet. The sight of his long, slender feet, almost elegant toes, struck me. Had I ever seen a man's feet? They looked oddly vulnerable, attached to this man who unsettled me so.

"Come sit on my lap," he invited in a gravelly tone. I settled myself on his muscular thighs, in the same position we'd ridden in for hours. No cloaks divided us this time. It seemed like I could feel his hot skin burning through his clothes. Not giving me time to settle, he captured my mouth with his again, kissing me long and deep.

I let the warm tide take me over. Rayfe's hand roamed my body, stroking me like one might a cat. I could imagine myself purring, while he plumbed the depths of my mouth, learned the contours of my hips and waist. Then his hot hand slid up my calf, smoothing the skin up to my thigh. The longing intensified, my woman's center growing heavy, burning.

When he stood us up again, I murmured a protest, swaying a bit on my feet.

"This will go far better with fewer clothes." He spoke in my ear, tugging on my earlobe with his teeth. I blinked my eyes clear and saw he held a small silver knife. "This is a lovely gown—will you grieve to see it ruined?"

I shook my head, bemused. "It was Amelia's. But will I have anything else to put on?"

He flashed that wicked grin. "If I had my way, no. But yes, I have clothes for you, for when we ride out again. Hold still."

Deftly, he slipped the little blade under the cuff of my sleeve and worked it upwards. The fragile silk peeled away like a butterfly wing, leaving my arm bare. He cut through the shoulder and the fabric fell down, the bosom of the dress loosening, the fire suddenly warm on my skin. Reflexively, I put a hand up to stop it from falling off. Then realized how silly that was. Rayfe watched me with gentle patience, and I knew then he'd let this take as long as I needed it to.

But, in the end, I would be naked in front of him.

With a sigh, I let the dress go. It slithered off me like a snake's skin, leaving me bare and vulnerable. I busied myself with stepping out of it. Couldn't stand it anymore and looked at him.

Rayfe reached out and brushed my long hair back over my shoulders, then took his time surveying me, his hooded eyes roaming from my toes up my naked body to my face and down again. My mouth dry, it was my turn to wonder what he saw when he looked at me. Not the most beautiful woman in the Twelve Kingdoms. That was certain.

I fixed my eyes at a point over his shoulder. "I'm sorry I'm not Amelia."

"Why would you say such a thing?"

"It's just—it must be disappointing not to get the beautiful daughter. Especially now that you've seen her."

He stroked a hand over the crown of my head, trailed it over my cheek and down my throat. He paused to trace my collarbone, then cupped my breast. I gasped at the sensation. When his thumb brushed my nipple, my knees weakened. Rayfe stroked it again, blue eyes blazing into mine.

"You are far more beautiful than any woman I've ever known, Andromeda."

"That's kind, but I know it's not true. A thousand poets can tell you otherwise."

He shook his head, giving me that mysterious half smile. "They didn't see you. They didn't know you like I do. The woman behind those storm-gray eyes that see so clearly."

"You don't know me at all," I protested weakly, because the things he was doing to my breast made it impossible to think.

"Oh, but I do. I know you better than you know yourself."

I gazed at him, bemused. Aroused. I didn't know how to assimilate that.

"Would you like my clothes on or off?" he inquired, just as he'd asked if I was hungry.

"I have a choice?"

"Some gentlewomen of the Twelve Kingdoms prefer not to be offended by the sight of a man's body, so I'm told. It can be done that way."

"You didn't offer me the choice to keep my clothes on."

That wolfish grin. "No, I didn't."

I lifted my chin. "Off, then."

Gravely, but with eyes sparking, he presented me with the hilt of the silver blade. "As my lady wishes."

"Turn your head."

Without hesitation, he did so. As if I'd never used a blade against him. I severed the tie that held his hair back so it spilled loose around him. Like in my dreams. I followed his method, starting at the cuff of his dark red sleeve and slicing up. The cloth parted, revealing the strong muscles of his forearm and upper arm. His shoulder gleamed in the firelight, with gorgeous masculine lines. The impulse to bite it seized me. I resisted.

It moved me in a way I hadn't anticipated, to cut his garments away and see him revealed before me. I forgot my own nakedness as I discovered his chest—whole and unscarred—his flat belly with fine black hairs arrowing down to where his manhood would be. I set the blade in the waistband of his pants.

"Those can be removed without cutting." His voice was rough, his face alight with desire.

I widened my eyes. "But you could have had me by lifting my skirts and yet my dress was totally ruined. Fair's fair."

He laughed and wound his fingers in my hair. "Hurry, then."

In full agreement, I sliced the trousers, peeling them off him and tossing the little blade aside. His thighs were long and leanly muscled. His manhood. Oh.

"Touch me, my queen."

He groaned when I did, tipping his head back, stern face clenched in a look of near pain. I had meant to caress his throat and chest, explore the lines of his belly, but that upthrusting manhood had drawn my unthinking first attempt. To most rewarding results.

I wrapped my fingers tighter around him and stroked, watching the pleasure reverberate through his body. The hunter, tamed. He clamped his hand around my wrist, stopping me. He kissed me like a starving man, pulling me against him. The shock of flesh on flesh astounded me. It felt like coming home.

"My turn," he growled, pulling my hand off him and setting it on his shoulder. I stroked the velvety skin there, absorbed in the musky smell and feel of him. Then convulsed when he plunged a hand between my legs.

The enormous pleasure shook me and I clung to him, winding his hair around my hand to anchor me. He caressed me, sliding through my slippery folds. I had never imagined a man's touch could feel so much different than my own.

"So hot, so ready." He groaned the words between kisses. "Can it be now? I fear I can't wait."

"Yes. Oh, yes." In that moment, I wanted nothing more.

He laid me on my back on the white rug, bracing himself over me and settling between my spread thighs. His hair fell around us, a black curtain gilded by firelight. He fitted his manhood against my core, nudging me open. I moaned at the feeling.

He kissed me, slow and tender, and dropped his forehead against mine. "This may hurt."

"I ride a lot of horses," I whispered.

He smiled at that, then sobered. "This is the first way. With this, I make you mine, Andromeda, my queen."

He thrust into me, a long clean stroke of the blade, and I cried out as if mortally wounded. But no wound ever spun such delirious pleasure. My body welcomed him in, wrapped around him, and shimmered with a golden glow.

I waited for the next, but he didn't move.

I clutched his hip with my free hand, frantic for more.

"Are you all right?" he asked through clenched teeth.

"Yes. Now, Moranu take you, move!"

He laughed, wild and delighted. Then drew back and plunged in again. I cried out my thankfulness, nails digging into his hip, urging him deeper, harder. His skin grew slick against mine, heightening the sensation each place we touched. I wrapped my legs around his waist as we flew higher, lightning sparking between us. The fire filled my blood, building to an impossible tension. I sank my teeth into his shoulder and he shouted out, convulsing against me. Still he drove on, increasing his pace until the blood burned red under my eyelids.

With a broken cry, I clung to him while the storm raged through me, washing the fire away with cooling rain, cleansing, releasing. Lowering me gently down again to the real world, where Rayfe lay draped over me, buried inside me, the taste of him in my mouth.

15

~~

Whatever I had expected—from Amelia's letters, from the songs and stories—it hadn't been this. It occurred to me that it would be different every time, each coming together a magical intertwinement. And this moment was so infused with Rayfe, this man buried between my thighs, that I couldn't imagine it any other way.

He levered himself up and brushed the hair out of my face. Then he snagged the little knife I'd tossed aside and severed the ties binding our wrists together. I stretched my arm, relieved to have it free again. His lips twisted in that half smile.

"That goes"—he tossed the silk away—"this remains." He stroked himself inside me and I arched my back at the deep pleasure.

"That will make it even more difficult to get around," I gasped.

He chuckled, then withdrew from me, leaving me oddly empty. My whole life I'd spent not filled, yet now it felt wrong for him to go. As if I already craved him. He walked to the kitchen, his masculine backside a stirring sight. He moved sinuously, long muscles flexing, his body made of hard lines, so unlike mine, and disappeared around the corner.

I held my wrist up to the light to examine the wound from the priest's knife.

The skin looked as always. I couldn't possibly have the wrong arm—the red ridges and bumps from the tight bindings remained and my fingers prickled still with the returning movement. But there was no cut, no scab, only a fine white scar, as if ages healed.

"Believe me now?" Bringing back a cloth and a pan of warm water, Rayfe knelt beside me. His manhood lay long and heavy against his thigh, no longer upthrust. He'd cleaned himself of our fluids and now reached out with a damp cloth.

"I can do it myself." I took the cloth from him and turned away slightly, conscious of his eyes on me, wiping hastily between my thighs and ignoring the slight burn. I scrubbed a bit at the pink-tinged stain on the white fur, too. "Sorry about this. White was probably a bad choice."

"Your blood is precious to me. I'm happy to have that souvenir of this night."

"So you can hang it on the castle walls as proof of my virgin status?"

He laughed and took the cooling cloth from me. "And you call us the barbaric people. Lay back." I hesitated and he took another cloth, dipping it in the warm water and holding it up. "Please." I did as he asked, feeling more vulnerable now. Though he'd seen me already, without the haze of desire I became acutely aware of my nakedness, especially as he stroked the cloth over my skin, examining every inch in the bright firelight.

"The Tala care little for such things." He drew my arms up over my head, laving the undersides. "Truly I'm relieved that your first time caused so little pain. I'd heard stories otherwise."

"Oh, yes, believe me, I had, too."

"Your sisters?"

"Amelia, yes. Not Ursula." I started giggling at the memory. "But you should have seen this letter Amelia wrote to us after her wedding night. Oh! The pain. Oh! The glory. And Hugh! The kindest, gentlest, most noble man ever, but Oh! The rivers of blood!"

Rayfe's amused eyes crinkled at the corners. "Amelia is a pretty girl, but a bit dramatic, it seems."

"Yes." I felt a stab of guilt at agreeing. "Though she's not false. I believe she truly feels every bit of what she expresses."

He trailed the cloth over my belly, intent on his task. "You know I was most careful with her, don't you?"

I didn't answer immediately, and his eyes flicked up to meet my gaze, all laughter gone.

"Yes," I told him. "I have to believe that. All the guilt is mine."

"No. I will share in your burden. I forced you into making a choice."

"Why did you?" I whispered. "Won't you tell me now?"

He raised an eyebrow, trailing the cloth over my breasts and tweaking my nipples so they crinkled and popped up. My breath caught at the bright sparking that lit the heat in my belly once more. *This is the first way*, he'd said. Clearly he proposed to do more. "Why, to have you at my mercy, exactly like this."

His dark head bent over me and he dropped light kisses on my nipples, then took them one by one into his mouth and suckled them. I burrowed my fingers into his silky hair, not sure if I wanted to pull him closer or push him away. The sensation of his mouth on my breasts undid me. I unraveled, all thoughts melting away, my woman's core heating in a flash.

With a pleased sound, he left my breasts and trailed his mouth down my belly, which fluttered and trembled under his soft kisses. He was between my legs again, raising my knees and running long fingers over my hips and down to the tender skin at the juncture of my thighs and body.

He dipped those clever fingers into my weeping woman's core, and I cried out. He watched me, dark-blue eyes burning with renewed hunger. Kneeling between my splayed thighs, black hair spilling around him, he looked like the wolf now, and I realized he could see my most intimate folds in the bright firelight. His manhood, at full life again, pointed to the truth of it.

And yet, I was helpless to close my thighs to him. I wanted him to keep touching me that way, especially when he slid a finger inside my slick passage, slowly, seeking. I writhed under his hands and didn't care.

"Not too sore?" This wasn't the polite inquiry. His voice was a growl, and I felt a surge of gladness that I was not the only one feeling consumed by need.

"No," I gasped. "Please." I waited, expecting him to plunge into me again.

"Turn over."

I didn't understand.

"Turn over, sweet. Onto your hands and knees, then." He urged me into the position he described, arranging my hair over my shoulder so one side of my neck was exposed, and running his hands along my flanks. He covered me from behind, pressing against my upraised bottom and reaching beneath to gather my hanging breasts in his hands like so much ripe fruit.

I moaned, then pitched against him when he slid a hand down my belly and into my hot sex. He positioned his manhood against my woman's mouth. My body strained, vibrating with anticipation and need.

"This is the second way," he growled in my ear. Then his teeth sank into the ribbon of muscle at my neck and he plunged into me, spearing me with unspeakable pleasure from two directions that somehow met in the center and shattered me.

This way was for the animal nature, then. He pounded into me, feral, ferocious, and I screamed out my pleasure, unable to get enough of his hands on my breasts, in my sex, his manhood spearing me and filling me to the core.

I bucked under him, a wild mare, and he responded in kind, wrapping a fist in my streaming hair and arching my head back, fastening his mouth on mine in a kiss that poured through me like the melted rocks in the volcano.

This time I came apart first, while he sucked the cries from my lips. Then he seized my hips in both hands and held me still while he plunged in and out of me, finishing with a hoarse shout that echoed in my mind like a wolf's howl.

He collapsed onto his side, taking me with him as he slipped out of me, my hips snugged up against his, arms wrapped around my breasts and belly, his breath hot on the back of my neck.

I blinked blearily at the fire, near emptied out. Sweat soaked and limp muscled, I might as well have been at sword practice for hours, the way I felt.

Finally I found words. "How many ways are there?"

Rayfe chuckled, sounding as spent as I felt, pressing a warm kiss to the nape of my neck, lingering there. I shivered and my breasts tightened. How could my body possibly want more?

"I'm not sure anyone has put a number to them," he murmured. "You'll have to keep count. But the two are all that are needed, by our customs."

I turned over his hand, the one that had been bound to mine. Only a fine white scar on his tanned skin also. Up and down his forearms, though, were other scars, little starbursts and divots, as if something had taken bites out of him. "Your customs are remarkable."

"You have no idea." He started to lever himself up.

"No, let me." I gathered up the used cloths and carried the bowl of now cool water to the little kitchen area. A kettle of warm water stood over a low flame. I poured the dirty water out and refreshed it, then took the opportunity to clean myself in private.

I needed a moment, to gather myself again. In such a short space of time I'd transformed from, if not who I'd always been, then much closer to that person than this naked, sweat-soaked woman by the fire who let a man cover her like a stallion mounts a mare. Some part of me whispered that I should regret it. I couldn't imagine noble Hugh taking the lovely Amelia in such an . . . earthy way.

And yet, I didn't feel bad at all. My body still sang with Rayfe's touch.

I wanted more.

This time, though, would be mine. I would make the third way. Probably not at all what Dafne had in mind when she suggested I'd need to make my own plan, but it was a start.

Rayfe lay on his side, head propped on one arm, long legs stretched out, watching me walk up to him with languorous eyes. He held out a hand to me and I let him draw me down next to him. I set the bowl down and bent over him, to give him the kiss he urged me toward. I liked this angle, kissing him from above. He stroked my hair back from my cheek.

"Thank you for this."

"The water? You fetched it last time." I started to reach for the cloths, but he stopped me, sliding his warm hand behind my neck and drawing me in for another lingering kiss.

"The way we came together—what I put you through. Not every woman would have come to me so sweetly." He traced my cheekbone. "In truth, I didn't dare hope we'd find this kind of passion together. Especially when I courted you so badly."

"Lie back." He obeyed, stretching himself before me like the banquet on the table. I wondered at it myself as I washed him, learning the golden lines and shadows of his lean form in the firelight. How much of what I'd done had been driven by this desire for him? Perhaps Uorsin had the right of it and I'd been a lightskirt traitor in my heart all along. Daughter of my mother, longing for her other blood, fatally attracted and compelled by it.

"I'm sorry I said anything," Rayfe murmured. "Now I've made you sad."

I shook my head, my hair slithering over my shoulders, tickling my skin. "Just thoughtful."

"You can speak to me of your thoughts."

He had his head pillowed on his hands, showing his dark-furred armpits. A memory struck me and I reached for his left arm. He obliged, letting me look at his shoulder. A scar like a starburst marred the muscle, puckered in the center, with white lines radiating out. The real scar. The dagger buried in his chest hadn't been true. Only a fragment of a nightmare. Or a vision.

"I dreamed you came to me, with my dagger still here"—I traced the deep scar—"and you asked me to pull it out."

He simply regarded me with somber eyes, waiting. I couldn't tell him about the other vision.

"Why did you let me stab you?"

His teeth flashed in a smile. "Believe me, Andromeda, I would have stopped you had I realized what a fierce wildcat I had cornered. My first mistake was underestimating you. I shall not do so again."

"Were there other mistakes?"

Lingering pain crossed his face. "I perhaps overestimated you, as well."

"How so?" I felt a pang at that, that I'd failed to rise to some sort of standard.

"No, no." He wound his fingers in a lock of my hair that trailed over his chest and tugged me down to kiss him. Light and sweet. "Don't look so stricken. I simply thought that once you understood, once you knew who you were, you would come to me."

"I still don't understand," I whispered, searching his face.

"I know. You will. I promise. Tomorrow, we'll ride out. Once we are near the border, we will both know more. After that I'll begin to teach you what you should have always known. For now, perhaps we'd best sleep."

"I haven't finished cleaning you."

He started to take the cloth from my hand. "I can finish—"

"No." I held it out of his reach. "It's my turn. Now, lay back."

I liked taking him by surprise. He gave me that half smile, then popped a kiss on my nipple before stretching out again. I gasped at the little shock and laughed. So many sides to this man that I hadn't expected.

Warming and wetting a new cloth, I set to my plan in earnest, stroking the hard planes of his body with the cloth, following with little nips, licks, and kisses, as he'd done to me. He stirred under me, slight tremors, the occasional hum and sighed breath. I responded to his pleasure, too, my core warming and melting yet again.

His manhood had been relaxed, heavy against his thigh, but now it stirred, lengthening, then darkening. By the time I picked it up to wipe it clean, it twitched in my hand, almost like a live thing. The skin, especially over the head, was surprisingly soft, velvety. An odd contrast in an otherwise hard man.

"Andromeda," he growled, "you're killing me."

"Am I?" I answered, all innocence. "I'll stop, then." I laid his manhood down. With him on his back, it now pointed up his belly. I'd wondered if it would still stand straight up. Apparently I'd have to help with that.

He started to sit up.

"No. Lay back. It's my turn to ride you."

Bemused, he did as I said. "Then mount me already. I can't take more of your teasing."

"No?" I straddled him, bending over him on all fours and nipping at his wiry man's nipples, delighted when he groaned. "I think you could."

"I've created a monster."

I tossed my hair over my shoulders and grinned at him. "You have no idea."

I had to rise on my knees and hold his manhood up, to guide it to the right spot. He braced my thighs with his hands, avidly watching. He hadn't said this wouldn't work, so I persisted, though the angle seemed wrong.

Rayfe closed his eyes with a pained look. "Lean forward a little—ah, yes. Just there."

Slowly, I seated myself on him until I rode him like a horse. The fullness stretched me more this way, with almost unbearable intensity. His fierce gaze locked with mine.

"Well, my queen? Take me, then."

I did. I clutched his muscled chest, digging in my nails, and found my rhythm, working him while he bucked under me. His face transformed with pleasure that looked like a dying man's agony. The waves of spearing delight echoed through me, arching my back. He claimed my breasts, thumbing the nipples, and I cried out, a cry that abruptly became a shattering scream as the climax took me by surprise, and Rayfe seized my hips, working me up and down his shaft until he convulsed and I draped myself over him, like a blanket.

I woke in the bright light of a snow-filled morning, in the fluffy white bed. The events of the afternoon and evening before rushed back, flooding me with hot embarrassment. And desire, yet again.

I've created a monster. Apparently so.

I vaguely recalled waking to him stroking my hair and murmuring my name, then urging me to bed, where we'd be warmer as the fire died. I'd been perfectly comfortable, on my bed of him, but I let him tuck me under the blankets and wrap himself around me. It seems I slept that way all night, because now I felt stiff and sore in all sorts of unaccustomed places.

The covers next to me were pushed back, but there was no sign of Rayfe.

Which was just as well, because it gave me time to assimilate what had happened. I stretched, long and lazily. I felt replete in a way that was difficult to put a finger on, as if I'd been hungry all my life for some food that I'd finally been fed. That restless animal in my heart purred now, my blood surging quietly. I felt quite deliciously used.

And, oh, Moranu, what would Ursula and Amelia think if I told them? Here they were likely worrying themselves sick over my dreadful fate at Rayfe's hands, and I'd not only enjoyed his hands—I'd begged for more. Hugh, thinking I wouldn't be treated gently. He'd been spot-on. Rayfe hadn't treated me like china— and I'd loved it.

The cabin door opened with a whuff and sparkle of snow. I sat up fast, clutching the covers to my naked breasts. Rayfe latched the door behind him and raised an eyebrow at me. He'd tied his hair back again and wore his black leathers, snow melting on his dark wool cloak.

"At last, she awakes."

"I didn't sleep much the night before last—it must have caught up with me. You should have awakened me."

"I was coming in to do just that. We have a great deal of ground to cover today." He strode briskly across the room and began packing food into saddlebags. Perhaps I'd missed breakfast. He glanced at me, looking surprised I was still in bed. "We should really get going."

"Well, then. You promised me clothes?" The shredded silver gown lay tossed on the floor nearby, a sullied reminder of how willingly I'd gone to him.

"I left them in the washroom, next to the privy. There's water there, too, so you can wash, if you like. If it's grown too cold, I can warm it again."

"I know how to warm water." My reply had a bit more snap than I'd intended. I busied myself with extracting a sheet to wrap myself with, struggling out of the high, soft bed. Then Rayfe was next to me, taking my hand to help me down.

"You weren't shy with me last night." He studied me. "What's wrong—are you sore?"

"No." I pulled my hand back so I could hold up the sheet. "It's different in the bright light of morning, okay? And I never did eat yesterday, so I'm hungry. I'd like to have a cup of tea." I stopped my fretful litany. Somehow I'd gone from feeling deliciously lazy to cranky. Had I hoped for Hugh-variety protestations of affection? "Just—give me a few minutes and I'll be ready."

Gratefully, I closed the washroom door between us. The water was too cool, but no way would I go back out there to warm it up now. I dropped the sheet and wiped myself down as quickly as possible, teeth chattering. At least the chill made it easier not to think about Rayfe's touch as he'd washed me. The soap smelled of a flower I didn't know, reminding me that I'd be riding farther away from my own realm, into a place I wouldn't understand, married to a man still a stranger to me. I yanked on my fighting leathers, sending a silent thank-you to Dafne for thinking of them.

He'd left a wooden brush for me, made with bristles from some animal. I grimaced at myself in the mirror, pulling the brush through the snarls and tangles. Nothing like loose hair in a windstorm plus rolling around on the floor. I pulled the mass over my shoulder to work the underside and saw the imprint of his teeth in my neck, crimson dark, edged with blue bruising. Bastard.

Briskly I braided my hair, tying it off. I had no pins, though, so I left it dangling in a long tail down my back.

I packed my things together. There. I was ready to ride out. If he thought I was the sort of princess to linger over her toilette, he was mistaken.

I bundled up the sheet, grabbed my bag, and headed back into the cabin. Rayfe sat at the little kitchen table, with an array of food set out and a steaming pot of tea. When he saw me, he poured it into a cup and patted the bench.

"I'm an idiot. Please forgive me." He propped his chin on folded hands. "Come sit. Drink your tea."

Part of me wanted to refuse, stubbornly insist that we leave right away since he was in such an all-fired hurry. But the gesture softened me. And I really wanted that tea.

I sat and sipped it, cradling the cup in my chilled fingers. Rayfe watched me, appearing all patience now. "Are you always grumpy when you wake up?"

"I don't know," I muttered into my tea. "I'm not usually around anyone when I wake up."

He smiled at that, a rueful twist of his lips. "And I'm usually around men."

"You bit me," I told him, tilting my head so he could see.

"Are you asking me to apologize?"

Was I? I didn't know what I wanted.

Solemnly he unfastened his leathers, peeling them back to show me the long, furrowed scratches in his chest, some so deep they'd bled. "You marked me, too."

Blood rushed to my cheeks. I studied my tea. "I'm so sorry."

"No, that's not what I meant." Rayfe pulled the cup from my grasp and set it on the table, wrapping his fingers around mine, dark-blue eyes somber, holding my gaze. Our knees bumped under the table. "The morning after is always difficult. You and I—we still have much to learn about each other and little time to do it in. I apologize for being clumsy with you."

I found myself smiling. "But not for anything else?"

He didn't smile back, but that feral light gleamed in his eyes. "What passed between us last night, Andromeda, is a memory I will hold close until my dying breath. I regret not one whit of it and I won't pretend to. No matter what else happens, being with you was an unexpected gift."

"You make it sound like your dying breath is around the corner."

His eyes flicked away. "Enjoy your tea. Eat something. It will be a long day."

"What aren't you telling me?"

He shrugged, leaning back in his chair, deliberately nonchalant, but he still wouldn't look at me. I sighed and began carving up an apple with a little silver paring knife. It might have been the same one we'd used last night. The fruit tasted bright and sweet, and I chewed it as I watched him try to avoid my gaze. The patience was a sham; that was clear now. His anxiety to leave leaked out of his pores. I took a pastry. Poured some more tea. Sipped slowly.

He glanced out the window. Tried to relax.

"Is Hugh looking for us?"

He frowned. "Of course his troops are running patrols. Making it seem like they don't search for you while they do. Hugh does not concern me."

I didn't roll my eyes at his arrogance. "Then, what? You might as well tell me now, because if it's something more than Avonlidgh coming after us, I'm likely to find out sooner or later."

He dropped the chair onto all four legs again and scrubbed his face with his hands. "I don't suppose I could persuade you just to ride out with me and we can discuss it once we're closer to the border?"

"No. Especially not now. Tell me."

He dropped his hands and glared at me. "You're a stubborn woman."

"Yes. I would have warned you ahead of time, but I figured that much was obvious. Tell me."

He laced his fingers together, jaw tense. "Your sister, Uorsin's heir, leads an army to relieve the siege at Windroven. They apparently left several days ago and her scouts should reach the area soon. If we wish to avoid a confrontation, we must leave."

The blood drained out of me. If I'd just waited a few more days, I wouldn't have had to marry Rayfe. He observed my reaction with grim satisfaction. He wasn't surprised.

"So we ride out immediately," he informed me. "It's imperative we cross into Annfwn as soon as possible."

Was he more concerned that I'd be rescued or that I'd make a run for it?

"I made a vow to you, Rayfe. We're bound together. I do have my own sense of honor." Never mind that it had turned out to be remarkably flexible lately.

"Be sure to remember that, for I won't let you go. No matter what regrets you may harbor." His eyes flicked to the bruising on my neck and met mine in bold, sensual challenge. Even annoyed with him, I responded, my breasts tightening.

"How did you hear this?"

"My men await us outside. They brought the news."

Ah, a troop of however many soldiers impatiently waiting in the cold for him to roust his ravished bride from her lazy lie-in.

"Well." I drank down my tea. "Let's go, then."

16

⚇

They'd brought an extra horse for me, so at least I didn't have to ride on Rayfe's lap. This turned out to be a comfort to my confused heart, but not to my well-used body. My sore nether tissues bounced against the unfamiliar saddle, a painful reminder of how I'd passed the night. The mare, a docile short-legged thing who preferred to bury her nose in the next horse's tail, spoke volumes about how they regarded me: pampered foreign princess.

Rayfe, of course, rode far ahead, deep in conversation with his men. They kept me buried in the center, well protected. Or guarded. On my shorter steed, all I could see around me were soldiers. I'd simply moved from one kind of prison to another, it seemed.

Terin reined up beside me, giving me his ironic half bow. "How fares my lady this morning?" he inquired, all politeness, though his eyes flicked to the bite mark on my neck, the glance followed by a sly grin. The fur collar of my cloak didn't quite cover it. I'd nearly rearranged my hair so it wouldn't show, but Moranu take me if I'd have all those men wait while I fussed with my hair.

And I'd done what I needed to do. Never mind that I liked it. I refused to be ashamed.

So I gave Terin my best steely-Ursula look, not easy when I had to look up to do it. "I'm quite well. Though I fear this child's learning-pony will have difficulty keeping up with the pace my lord husband plans to set."

Terin raised his eyebrows at me in mock concern. "Well, we couldn't have our foreign princess tumbling off her mount in an untidy heap, could we?"

"Why don't you like me, Terin?"

"I neither like nor dislike you, my lady." His gaze fastened again on the bite mark. "You belong to my liege; therefore, you have my loyalty. I don't believe I'm required to form an opinion about you."

"And yet, you have."

He shrugged, an echo of Rayfe's.

"Are you Rayfe's brother?"

Terin tipped his head back, observing a circling hawk overhead. "A distant cousin, but you'll find most Tala can find mutual ancestors somewhere in the tree. In truth, you and I are more closely related than I am to Rayfe."

He'd startled me with that and he knew it, with his sly smile. Of course I would have relatives among the Tala. How had this not occurred to me?

"At any rate, Princess"—he managed to make the honorific sound like a joke—"I came to inform you that your things have been sent ahead and await you at Annfwn."

"How thoughtful of you."

He cocked a head at me. "In the meanwhile, you might find yourself lacking in the usual comforts."

I was silent, refusing to rise to his bait.

"Well, then," he finally huffed. "My message is delivered. Good day."

"Good day, Cousin."

He glanced back, wily eyes sharp, considering. "Uncle. Ex-uncle, truly. Make of that what you will."

I remember my mother's hair had red in it. Dark red, like dying embers. In some lights her hair looked black, but when she let me brush it for her, by the fire at night, all the reds came out. Like Terin's. Was he her brother? But why "ex"?

We rode hard through the day, keeping to the back roads, winding through the hills. Clouds gathered in the afternoon, promising more snow, yet we pressed on. I fingered my dark braid from time to time, seeing all the auburn in it now. *Salena's stamp.*

Rayfe stayed clear of me, and besides Terin's odd visit—I didn't believe for a moment he'd stopped only to discuss my luggage—no one else spoke to me. The soldiers sometimes spoke among themselves in a language I didn't know. Not the common language of the Twelve Kingdoms. Of course, Uorsin had decreed the language of Duranor—and thus Mohraya—the official common language only after the Great War. The Tala sequestered away in Annfwn would not have been subject to such a decree.

The light faded and fat snowflakes began to fall. Tiredness crept in around the edges of my vision. Even though I'd slept longer than Rayfe, it hadn't been enough to catch up. Still, I wouldn't complain, no matter what.

We rode on. And ever on. Hours into the night.

I'd never spent much time out at night. Princesses were usually expected to be tucked up inside the castle by twilight. So, other than gazing out my window, and my sojourn to Moranu's chapel to sell out my people, I didn't have much experience with the dark. That night I'd been preoccupied with my mission and my guilt. Now boredom led me to pay more attention.

I could see better than I'd thought I could. As I had on that night, too. On the rare occasions I caught a glimpse of something besides the flanks of the horses around me, I could clearly make out my surroundings. The overcast sky hid the moon, but the branches overhead stood in stark relief anyway. The men's faces were shadows and shades of gray. They felt the press of the pace also, their profiles growing severe with exhaustion.

Finally, sometime in the small hours, at the bottom of a steep and winding road, we came upon a cabin. Lights shone from it and I dared hope we might stop to rest. We did. One of my guards swung down and without a word offered a hand to help me off my horse. At every other stop, I'd dismounted on my own. This time the stiffness was enough that I accepted the hand, creaking down like an old lady might.

"Thank you," I told him, and he smiled at me, a surprisingly cheerful grin.

He took my little horse and I let him, content to be served this time. Rayfe and Terin stood deep in conversation on the threshold of the house.

". . . cannot afford to have our people pinned against the border if she fails . . ." Terin's angry words floated on the air. They fell silent as I walked up. I tamped down my surging irritation.

"You'll find your things upstairs," Rayfe told me. "That room is yours. Go ahead and sleep as long as you like. I'll wake you—in plenty of time to eat before we leave." His lips twitched with amusement.

"Thank you." *Here's me, grateful for the smallest crumbs anyone tosses my way.* They waited, clearly unwilling to resume their conversation until I left. I moved past them into the house and they bowed to me. A narrow stairway led to a second floor, and I started up. Turned back. "Am I the enemy?" I asked Rayfe, giving him a hard stare.

Terin looked away, possibly muffling a laugh. Rayfe blinked at me.

"That's what I thought." The bloodred ring he'd given me

gleamed on the hand I rested on the plain wooden banister. "I've had occasion to train horses. They become what you expect them to be. You might keep that in mind, my king."

I continued up the stairs, stripped off my clothes—I still had no night things and I hardly cared at that point—and fell gratefully into a deep sleep. Rayfe could go hang himself, for all I cared.

Cold morning light touched my face and I stirred, my heart thumping to think I'd overslept again, but Rayfe, warm and naked, cuddled me close again, murmuring soothing noises. I fell back asleep, obscurely comforted by the touch of his skin, trying to remember why I'd been angry at him.

When I woke again, the light slanted toward afternoon. I'd thought my mother had been calling my name, down haunting memories, but no, it was Rayfe. He leaned over me on one elbow, stroking my cheek and calling me Andromeda, the way he turned the syllables sounding like her. His black hair spilled around him and his skin gleamed golden in the light, shining with a masculine beauty all his own. He murmured my name once more and lowered lips to mine in a slow, burning kiss.

It flowed through me, gold as the afternoon sunshine, and I dampened for him, desire spiraling sticky and sweet. He drew back the down covers and caressed my breast, brushing the already peaked nipple with his thumb. I groaned, arching my back to fit myself better into his roughened palm. A swordsman's hand.

He broke our kiss, trailing firm lips down my throat. The sharp stubble from his sleep pricked the soft skin there, sparking through me. Taking my nipple in his mouth, he sucked on it, hard, so sharply it nearly hurt, fanning the little sparks into flames that burst into fires throughout my body, like campsites of an invading army. He moved to my other breast, laving the nipple, then sucking and nipping on it, holding my rib cage in his large hands. I wound my fingers in his trailing hair, so silky, and held him there, whimpering my pleasure.

With a wicked smile, he pulled his hair from my grip and continued down my fluttering belly, spreading my thighs and positioning himself between them. I thought he'd kneel up now and plunge into me as before, and I braced for the brilliant flash of that penetration. But he slipped lower, nuzzling my furry mound and kissing the sensitive hollows that flanked my womanhood.

Tension rode me, though I was uncertain why. Then his tongue touched my inner folds and lightning struck. I cried out at the shock of it. Then again at the unbearable intensity of the pleasure. As he'd done to my nipples, he sucked on the pearl of my womanhood, then nipped at it, holding my thighs spread wide, though my hips threatened to leap from the bed.

In a roaring rush, the climax took me and I cried out a long call of pleasure. As I rode the wave of it, Rayfe climbed up my body, sliding into the hot glove of my sheath and thrusting, urging the wave onward. His skin stroked mine and I gloried in it. He wove his fingers through mine, pressing the backs of my hands against the bed, while he kissed me, long and deep, and I wrapped my legs around his hips, savoring the fading of the fire.

I opened my eyes to find him staring at me, the deep blue intent and serious. Wary.

"No, Andromeda, you are not the enemy." He kissed me again, then withdrew from my body and my bed. He fetched a washbasin and cloths, apologizing that the water, again, was too cold. I cleaned myself, feeling awkward now, while he dressed in his fighting leathers with quick efficiency. Outside, the sun declined into late afternoon.

"Do we ride out, then?" I asked.

He looked over his shoulder at me, some of that dark suspicion still in his gaze, despite his words. "Yes. We cannot afford to be caught out with such a small company. You must understand this."

"I *do*." I took a deep breath. "I only ask because you've left it until so late in the day."

"From now on we ride at night. The darkness is a friend to the Tala."

I climbed out of the bed and began brushing my hair, standing naked in the center of the room. His eyes stayed on me, hunger warming them again. "You might have said," I informed him mildly.

Surprised, he met my eyes again. "What's that?"

Totally lost his train of thought, then. Useful to know.

"I'm not a child or an idiot, Rayfe. You assure me I'm not a prisoner. You could tell me your plan instead of expecting me to obediently trot along." I began yanking on my clothes.

"You are angry again."

"Still!" I snapped.

"You weren't angry a moment ago." He pointed at the empty and disheveled bed, as if it had somehow turned on him.

I sighed. "That appears to be different. You said we don't know each other well. For some reason, that part works."

He strode over to me and took my upper arms in his grasp, searching my face. With a hint of urgency, he kissed me, and my body hummed to life again. Oh, yes—this part certainly worked. His lips twisted in that half smile. "The animals in us know. Perhaps we just have to find a way for our minds to know, as well."

"Is that how the shape-shifting works—the animal inside somehow comes out?"

"Once we reach Annfwn, I will teach you. Just, please, bear with me until then."

His tone carried a note of apology, and I sighed, nodding my agreement.

"Come downstairs when you're ready. I asked them to have a meal and hot tea waiting." He cupped my cheek and kissed me softly, leaving me then to finish preparing. It occurred to me that already we had come to know each other, the little habits. He paid attention to what I liked, and I imagined many men would not.

Small things, then, could say a great deal.

As promised, tea awaited me, though the room was empty. Also an apple and another pastry like the one I'd eaten yesterday sat on a plate. The man had his moments, whatever his high-handed ways.

I ate quickly, certain they all waited outside for me, and left the dishes for whatever invisible denizens manned this house, pocketing an extra apple for the ride. Yesterday's stops had been few and far between, with only a hard jerky to chew on. I walked out into the late-afternoon light, to find my sturdy little mare, saddled and ready, my stalwart guard nearly encircling her.

Biting back a sigh, I readied to mount her, dreading her brittle stride.

Rayfe's hand appeared under my elbow, helping me up the half a length it took to be astride her.

"I understand you're not fond of this mare." He raised an eyebrow at me. His amused look. I searched out Terin, who grinned at me, a baring of the teeth more than anything.

"Rayfe—she's all of, what, eight hands high? I'd put a ten-year-old on her. An inexperienced one."

"So you feel insulted by this choice?"

I sighed. I'd asked him to explain, and I needed to try to do likewise. I put a gloved hand on his arm, and he started at my touch, as if he hadn't expected it. "I know you don't know me, but riding is something I love—something I'm good at. And here I'm riding through country I've never seen and it's on a horse with a miserable stride and I'm surrounded by guards so that I cannot *see* anything at all, and—" *And I feel so very alone.* I stopped myself because the pitch of my voice had risen and I was suddenly perilously close to tears. I turned my face away, blinking furiously. Not what I'd wanted him to see at all.

"I understand now." He took my gloved hand in his. "Come."

I obeyed, if only so I wouldn't cry. Rayfe led me to his big horse, bade me wait while he mounted, then held down a hand for me. "Can you reach?" he asked.

Now, this stirrup was much higher, but Moranu take me if I begged for help. I took his hand, put my booted foot atop his, and vaulted up. He caught me and laughed, a free and delighted sound that seemed most him. The men looked away while he kissed me, except for Terin, who watched with a dark and disapproving gaze.

"I should have known you'd need to see," Rayfe told me, brushing a strand of hair out of my eyes. "Are you comfortable astride? Then let's be off."

He'd put it well. I did need to see. The restless tension of the day before bled away as we rode, harder and faster than before, without me burdening the short-legged mare. I was far too diplomatic to point this out, however. Though we rode through darkening forests, I thrilled to the changes in the trees, the road uncoiling before us.

At one point, perhaps near midnight, we topped a hill to find a valley spread before us. The moon had risen, waxing more than half-full. Silver light illuminated the valley, rolling in fertile meadows, green and untouched by the snow we'd left behind. Beyond, another ocean tossed at a distant shoreline. I caught my breath at the grandeur of it.

"You can see clearly?" Rayfe whispered in my ear.

I nodded, too awestruck to speak.

"Cat's eyes." He sounded approving. "See off there, where the craggy peaks go down to the ocean?"

"Yes," I breathed.

"On the other side of those is Annfwn. Once there, we are safe. Or more safe. Things will be better."

"What is this valley, then?"

"You don't know?"

"How should I?"

"This is Mohraya. Behind those hills, just beyond, lies Ordnung."

I stilled. I hadn't known. Ursula would have, what with studying the maps. In all my journeys, I must have traveled a large circle, coming up, around, and behind the very piece of the country I'd always called home.

"You asked to know." Rayfe sounded strained, and I twisted in the saddle to see his face, knocking my knee against the sword he'd strapped to the saddle. He looked wary, tense. I cupped his cheek with my gloved hand and urged him down to kiss me. He obliged, and I kissed him long and deep, the way he liked.

"Thank you," I murmured against his lips. "It is good to know." I turned again and studied the mountains, rearing against the silver sky. On the other side was an acid-green meadow I'd ridden into, not knowing how my life would change. "It looks so different from this side."

"Everything always looks different from the other side," he agreed, nudging the stallion so that the company moved on.

I looked to see his expression, his sword knocking my knee again.

"I'm sorry—I need to have it there, in case I must draw it."

"I know," I reassured him. How many times had Ursula told me to do the same? "Wait—why wasn't it there when we rode to the cabin, that first night?"

"As you might recall"—Rayfe's tone was dry—"there was a woman tied to my sword arm. The weapon would have availed me little."

"Then you weren't concerned about attack."

"I posted guards, to hedge my bets. But that's part of it, for the man." He chose his words carefully. "To give up his defenses, his strength, to risk attack."

"I see." And I did—now. I hadn't thought what it would be like for him to be bound to me. Hugh and his men could well have followed and slaughtered him while I was a dead weight on his arm. I wondered how close they'd been.

"Could you have . . . shifted, like that?"

"No. Not in such close contact with you."

I hadn't thought of Rayfe as saddled with me. With all his relentless pursuit, the triumph of his obtaining me as his prize, it hadn't occurred to me that a foreign princess might not be his first choice in mates. Clearly some other reason drove him. The "Annfwn needs you" thing. He wasn't Hugh, to have fallen in love at first sight. No, from what he'd said, he was relieved that we at least could bed each other in a satisfying way. In addition to his other agenda.

"Rayfe?" I asked him quietly.

"Yes, my Andromeda?" His voice was pitched low to match mine.

"Was there another for you? One you might have wished to wed, if not for . . . whatever this thing is that demands it be me?"

"No, my queen, it has always been you."

"How could that be? How could you want a woman you'd never met?"

"None of us have met before we actually meet; isn't that so?" He threaded his arm up under my cloak, to wrap around my waist and hold me close.

"Which doesn't answer the question."

I felt him shrug. "I saw you in the meadow and I knew."

"You didn't—you thought I was Amelia."

He chuckled and pressed a kiss against my ear. "I didn't know which daughter you were, but I knew *you*."

"The animal in you recognized me. My blood."

"Yes."

"The wolf?"

His body tensed. "This is not the place to speak of such things."

"I didn't know you, in the meadow."

He sighed and I realized I'd hurt him. "I know, Andromeda. I also know that you still don't. I hope that will change."

I had to ask. "And if it doesn't? I have no wolf to know yours."

"You have more than you know—you just fight it still. And we will speak of this later. Not inside Mohraya."

I bit down on the rest of my questions, on the restless pacing in my heart that had started up again as we talked. Finally I had to say, "You've invested a great deal in something that may not be so."

"You have no idea, my queen." He barely spoke the words aloud. "You have no idea."

17

We descended into the sleeping valley—warmer here—skirting the settlements whose names I likely should have known but did not. I could see why he'd timed it this way: everyone slept during these small, dark hours. Rayfe murmured these things to me, when I wondered that he didn't worry about the farm animals sending up alarms. Very few animals are truly nocturnal, he said. Most are about in the crepuscular edges of night and day. Bats returned to their roosts. Even the cats had ceased chasing mice, resting for the dawn hours.

All was still but for us, now riding at dangerous speed through harvested fields and fallow meadows, then creeping with quiet stealth past a sleeping house.

He kept glancing back, over his shoulder to the east, where the approaching dawn hadn't lightened the sky. It looked like full night to me, but he pushed us to go faster. Then a single bird sent out a quiet whistle, and, as if a minstrel had signaled for all to join in, a tree full of songbirds burst into a chorus. In the distance, a cock crowed, and Rayfe cursed, a harsh growl in comparison.

We kicked into a flat-out run.

Rayfe stretched over me and we leaned together over the horse's neck, his mane lashing us.

"It's not even light yet!" I gritted out.

"The birds know," he shouted against the wind in my ear. "And even your people follow that."

Sure enough, lights began to flicker on in a few of the farmsteads. The far hills loomed near, but a disquieting amount of cultivated land still lay between us and them. Terin pulled beside us, pointing to the road. Rayfe shook his head and Terin made a complex gesture back. Rayfe cursed again, then nodded, and Terin galloped that way. We followed.

I didn't have to ask what it had been about. The road would be faster than taking the horses over the hummocks and pits of the fields. We would also be in the open. They were betting on speed now.

The attack came as we rounded a bend. Hoarse shouts from Rayfe's forward scouts warned us in time for him to wheel about and plunge us into a copse of trees. To my astonishment, the men around us suddenly melted away. No, that was a trick of the light. They disappeared and became something else.

Here a hawk burst from the saddle. There three wolfhounds leapt from their mounts and charged down the road. The horses themselves became the ratlike beings I'd seen back at Ordnung, swarming after the larger beasts. Behind me a bear roared a challenge but stayed close on our heels. Watching them shift from one being to another gave me a spinning sense of falling, as if I'd lost contact with all reality. Though I saw it happen, I couldn't quite make sense of it.

"Moranu!" I gasped.

"Surely this is not a surprise to you." Rayfe's voice was tight, nearly angry, as we plunged through the bracken. I clenched my knees tight to keep to the saddle.

"It's one thing"—I lost the words when the stallion leapt over a log—"to have an idea. Another to see it."

"Get used to it, my queen." He punched the words at me and I didn't reply. Even if I could have. His arm gripped my waist so tightly I could barely breathe, much less speak. I wondered if he thought I'd scream. Then I wondered why it hadn't occurred to me to do so.

The clash of swords, an angry howl, human shouts, echoed down from the road. Rayfe took us away in a direct perpendicular, but ahead the trees thinned again, opening into yet another field. He turned us, staying inside the wooded border, going too fast through narrow openings and deep bracken. Faster than I would have gone, but then, apparently the horse was smarter than I'd known.

"Let me talk to them," I told him when a tangle of fallen trees forced us to slow.

He growled, like the wolf. If he hadn't still felt like a man pressed against my back, I would have wondered what form he wore.

"I mean it, Rayfe. I can tell them of the treaty. They must not know that we are in alliance now. If I tell them to desist, they will."

"You think to escape me."

I gasped at the injustice of his accusation. "I came to you willingly!"

He snarled in my ear, plunging on now that we'd escaped the fallen trees. "You came to me to stop the bloodshed, as I knew you would. Don't think to sway me with your sweet and reasoned words."

"Yes. I wanted to stop the bloodshed," I gritted out, the saddle pounding at my tender inner tissues, which the man accusing me of wishing to betray him had so thoroughly pleasured and plundered. "I want to stop it now. Uorsin and Ursula simply have not yet received the news or—"

"They know, all right."

"What?"

He changed course again, back into the deeper shadows. A crow flew ahead of us, I now saw, flitting from tree to tree. Marking our path. The clatter of combat echoed behind and to the left. Soon we would reach the road again. I would lose my chance to explain.

"What do you mean they know?"

"Uorsin received our missive and denied your request for the release of the Tala prisoners. He declared his intent to burn one alive each day until you are returned to him. We are as at war as ever."

The news hit me like a cold fist in my throat. My father, my King, had made me foresworn. Oath breaker. And Fiona—she was likely already dead. Her beautiful alabaster coat turned to charcoal. Though I rarely prayed, I sent a fervent wish to Moranu to give a thought for the mare, perhaps take Fiona under her wing. Surely a goddess needed a good horse.

I didn't weep for her. Perhaps I'd run out of tears. Or the frozen tightness in my throat that wouldn't let me breathe, wouldn't let me think, stopped everything else. Numb, I simply clung to the saddle, baggage to be transported over the border. If it worked.

. . . *cannot afford to have our people pinned against the border if she fails* . . .

An overwhelming urge to break away from Rayfe seized me. In that moment, I wanted nothing more than to run to my people— ones who didn't nauseously become something *else*—and beg them to rescue me, to take me home. There, no one expected anything of me, except that I disappear. My many failures to distinguish myself mattered to none.

Rayfe said nothing more, but his viselike hold on me suggested he knew the direction of my thoughts. The speed of our travel prohibited conversation, especially as we reached the road again.

One by one, the men caught up with us, riding the horses that I knew now weren't truly horses. A couple remained as wolfhounds, loping easily alongside. They must have lost their mounts. Terin arrived last, glancing at me with a hard stare, then holding up three fingers, then five, to Rayfe. Three men lost, I guessed, and five of the ratlike creatures.

The rising sun glittered in the turning leaves now, rust and gold against a brightening blue sky. Our party blew past a farmer towing a cartload of vegetables to market, the only astonished witness to my passing out of Mohraya and into the land of nightmares.

I think, when you're a child and you see maps, you get this idea that there will be something to show the boundaries. Oh, you realize there won't be a big black or red line on the ground, but you imagine things will look different, like passing from one room into the next. Here is the place of one kind of people. Here is the place of another. As you grow older, you know that going from one place to another doesn't give you any particular feeling. There is no actual barrier.

This is not true of Annfwn.

We'd long since turned off the road again—not long after the farmer—and moved through denser forests and wilderness, deeply shadowed enough that the growing day did little to illuminate it. Eventually we came to a craggy path that wound up the mountain range Rayfe had pointed out to me half a day and ages ago. Had I felt like I understood him at that moment? I could hardly recall it now.

This hardly seemed the way into another kingdom, but I knew Ursula would appreciate the strategic value. No one could bring armed forces in here very quickly. On either side of the path—hardly more than a goat trail in places, which forced us to go single file—the rocks rose steep and sharply tumbled. Snow pooled in deep fissures. With every hour that passed, the air grew thinner and colder.

My eyes grew gritty from unshed tears and being awake too

long. More, I dreaded the trial to come. I had no idea what I was doing. All I had were Rayfe's vague guarantees that I possessed some sort of innate magic—which had never seen fit to present itself to me in all my life—and the unsettling changes in the way I felt. I seemed doomed to fail.

What would become of me then?

We came to a place where the path widened enough for three to ride abreast, flanked by enormous boulders. An icy wind roared through the narrow opening.

"Odfell's Pass." Rayfe broke our hours of silence. "We're nearly there."

The path abruptly dropped after that, and we rounded a bend. I lost my breath at the sight.

Waiting in the cold, wrapped in layers of furs, were thousands of Tala, all in human form. They stretched into the forest and down the ravines on either side. Countless sets of fierce blue eyes focused on me, their expectation strong in the air. They ranged along the border, which seemed to sparkle in the air.

My blood sang with it, a low hum of recognition. Even if I didn't have that, or the abrupt line where the crowded people ended and open land began, the other side made it clear. Where we stood in frozen, high-mountain early winter, the land beyond appeared to be in the bloom of late summer.

Verdant trees spread enormous leaves to the setting sun. The forest floor, velvety moss studded with jewel-like blossoms, became a great meadow, waving with tall emerald grasses.

"You can see it?" Rayfe asked in my ear, squeezing my waist when I nodded. "She can see!" he shouted, relief and triumph in his voice. The Tala cheered, a cautious rumble of approval.

"Simply seeing isn't enough." Terin pulled up beside us, looking grim. "No more delay. We have to know if this reckless plan was worth it."

"We will, Terin," Rayfe growled at him. "Give her a thrice-damned moment to adjust."

"We are out of moments," Terin snapped. "Look, King! Your

people are trapped outside their homeland. Fix what you've done."

Just then, a flock of black starling birds with blue eyes arrowed through the shimmering wall and passed through with no trouble. A few soldiers tried the wall, pressing their hands against it, to no avail.

"It's not working." Terin sounded bleak now. "We are doomed."

"Just—" Rayfe ground his jaw, the sound cracking in my ear. "Back off, Terin. That's an order." Urging the stallion forward, he shot us up to where the trail ended at the wall, halted, and handed me down to the ground, then jumped down beside me. Absurdly, I clung to him for reassurance, though he had brought me to this moment.

"Give us some room." Rayfe's tension carried and the pressing crowd backed off. He cupped my face in his gloved hands, dark-blue eyes intent. "This is in you, Andromeda. Just follow your instincts. Trust in that."

"I don't understand what I'm supposed to do. Why is it important that I can see through the barrier?"

"To people who can't pass through, the wall reflects this side. It looks like more of the same to them."

"So seeing is important, but not necessarily enough."

"Yes. Some can see but not pass—it depends on their blood, their parentage."

"Why can the birds fly through, but the people are trapped outside?"

"Animals can always pass. The people you see are Tala who cannot fully shape-shift, for whatever reason. They cannot cross without help. Your help."

"Have you ever shape-shifted, Princess?" Terin, calling out from a short distance away.

"You know full well she hasn't," Rayfe answered for me, eyes not leaving my face. "Ignore him. You and I know you have the mark. We saw it together, remember? Trust in that."

"What do I do?" The birds in my blood came back full force,

singing with the hum of the barrier, pricking me with their hopes and demands like the many desperate eyes focused on me.

"First, just walk across."

"To make sure I can."

"To demonstrate that you can." His thumbs caressed my cheekbones. "I believe in you."

It didn't help to hear that. Of course he believed in me—he'd asked all these warriors to leave Annfwn, to fight the armies of the Twelve Kingdoms for me, with the guarantee that I'd bring them back in. What would they do if I failed?

I'd never performed well under pressure, and this . . .

I wished profoundly that I'd never gone to the meadow. That I'd stayed inside my circumscribed boundaries, stayed invisible Andi, the space between my sisters.

I pulled on that old self, shrouding myself in that comforting sense of invisibility. Unseen, I walked up to the shimmering curtain, enticing summer just beyond. *I'm not really here*, I told it. *Don't mind me.*

And I stepped through.

It was like passing through a curtain—one made of sparks that zinged invisibly along my skin. The wind stopped and I was in Annfwn.

Every drop of my mother's blood in me knew it.

For maybe the first time in my entire life, I felt right in my flesh.

I looked back to see all the people outside in the winter, like the starving pauper children that crowded around Ordnung's walls until the guards drove them off again. Rayfe alone smiled at me, hope and belief shining from him.

He stepped through, a bold stride, and signaled to the other Tala. Terin rode up to the barrier, a rime of fear under his anger. He must be one who couldn't shift, I realized. With a grimace, he urged his horse through at a speed that would surely knock him from the saddle, should the barrier be solid to him. But he passed, with a hoarse shout of joy.

After that, others followed.

Rayfe stood by my side, watching his army reenter their homeland. He could have come through in his animal form at any time, but he'd waited, walking through in human form, as all these warriors must.

They came through, all along the wall, like ghosts emerging from another world, shouting their excitement and saluting me with yells and fists pumping in the balmy air.

But others did not.

They remained outside, defeat and despair on their faces. Staring in, they silently implored me to help them. After a time, fully two-thirds of them lingered, still trapped outside.

"What do I do now?" I asked aloud, not really expecting an answer.

But Rayfe did answer. "Salena could . . . communicate with the barrier. I hoped it would be enough to have you inside—and look, it is for some. There must be something more. Can you ask it to let the others in somehow?"

A derisive snort came from behind me. I didn't have to look to know it was my faithful ex-uncle, anxiously awaiting my failure.

And fail I did. Whatever in me allowed the people to pass through didn't respond to all of my beseeching. While the sun slid lower in the sky, I did everything I could think of to "talk" to the barrier. Though my blood hummed to its presence, and even though I could move back and forth, from summer to winter and to summer again, nothing I tried let me bring the rest of the warriors through.

Finally, Rayfe put a stop to it. I protested, but he pointed to the falling darkness, stepped through on his own, and sent them away.

"Where will they go?" I asked him, rubbing my arms, though I'd long since doffed my furred cape and could hardly be cold.

He slanted me an opaque look. "They'll find places. The Tala are survivors. Many of the people you saw here have been outside Annfwn since Salena left. A few more days—or months or even years—won't matter that much. They can wait for you to learn the way."

"But they came now because—"

"There's always hope. More so now than ever. But you're tired. Let's go to the campsite."

In truth, Rayfe seemed to be the weary one. Though he'd glossed it over for my sake, it showed in the lines of his face how much it bothered him to send those people away. They had been hoping, and though they still seemed strange and alien to me, their disappointment cut me.

But maybe I could still help them.

I walked with Rayfe down a forest path, the others having gone ahead while I worked at the barrier. We rounded a bend, and before us lay a crystal-blue lake, practically at our feet, almost entirely fenced by a wall of tall, dark trees, straight as spears.

A shout from farther down the lake rang across the water. Rayfe squinted, then a look of profound relief and . . . joy? . . . crossed his face, like the sun breaking through clouds. He grasped my upper arms, squeezing them, and grinned at me.

"Perfect timing. I have a surprise for you."

A group of Tala men picked their way along the shadowed shore, now screened by trees, now breaking out of the shadow. A flash of white in their midst threw me off. Then the breeze shifted, and *she* whinnied at my scent.

If grief clamps down and stops breath, then joy is like the beast breaking free, shattering ribs and exploding the heart. I couldn't breathe, couldn't gasp out Fiona's name. All I seemed able to do was clutch my hands over my mouth, to hold what in I don't know. But suddenly I was laughing and sobbing and Rayfe was leading my horse to me and watching me with such hopeful yearning, my already laboring heart nearly broke.

With a glad cry, I wrapped my arms around Fiona's neck, while she nuzzled at my hair. The silky white coat, her familiar scent, all of it centered me again, and I had something of who I'd always been.

"She is a beautiful creature," Rayfe observed. "It would have been beyond a shame for her to have been so carelessly destroyed."

I dashed my tears away—Moranu, Rayfe must think me a silly maid to weep so often—and tried to smile, but my wobbly lips wouldn't hold the shape. "How . . . why? But *how*—?"

"The night you told me about her. I sent some men for her. I couldn't let you suffer such a loss when we're asking so much of you."

The wary hope in his eyes moved me. He didn't have to want me happy. We both knew this. I unwound my fingers from Fiona's white mane and laid my hands on Rayfe's chest.

"Thank you," I whispered, mindful of the men who ringed us. "This is the greatest gift anyone has ever given me."

I stood on tiptoe, slid a hand behind his neck, and kissed him with all the emotion that surged through me. I couldn't separate all the joy, relief, and love swirling around in my blood from the desire that fired at his response, the way his big hands tightened on my waist, and how he deepened the kiss, urgent, fierce with unnamable longing.

I drew back and held his face in my hands, the way he touched me.

"Thank you," I said again, firmly, like an oath.

He wrapped long fingers around my wrists, holding me there, then turning his face to press a kiss into each of my palms. "I wish you happy, Andromeda. Remember it. Despite all the rest, I want that for you."

I would remember that.

Reading my father's letter only drove the point home. I bathed in the cold lake and took the time to run my hands over every inch of Fiona's crystal-clear hide, to reassure myself that she was unharmed. Then I sat a private distance away while Fiona searched out the tender water plants at the lake's edge.

He demanded my return, accused me of treachery, yet again. More, he named Annfwn as his by right and threatened to take it by force. His hatred of Rayfe and the Tala oozed from every line. The man who wrote this wasn't the wise king he pretended to be. But then, nothing seemed to be what I had always believed. I wondered if Derodotur had watched him write this missive, his serene face impassive, if he'd seen the cracks running beneath the surface.

No wonder Rayfe hadn't wanted to show it to me until he knew Fiona's fate. I wondered how he would have broken the news to me if they'd been unable to retrieve her.

Not one word after my well-being.

"He's insane," I remarked, hearing the footstep behind me.

"Like father, like daughter?" Terin quipped.

He stood just inside the tree line, head cocked saucily, eyes glittering.

"Has everyone read my personal business?"

"You have no personal business, Princess." Terin circled around behind me. I refused to crane my neck to watch him, so I gazed at Fiona instead and twisted the silver ring on my finger, with the bloodred stone. "Everything that involves you is a matter of national security, which means it concerns me."

"I didn't ask for any of this. You can hardly consider me a spy."

"I didn't ask for it either," he snapped back, "and yet here you are. Everything you touch becomes distorted beyond recognition."

He finally stalked around into my peripheral vision.

"You mean Rayfe."

"He wants what cannot be had. He gives you what he should not. All to chase after a pipe dream."

"What is the dream?"

Terin grinned, foxy and canny. "Oh, no, it's his to tell you."

"Is that why you hate me so?"

"Do I hate you? Hmm." He pretended to ponder the question, squinting at the sun and tapping his chin with dirt-stained fingers. I wondered what he'd been digging at. "How would you feel about the child of the woman who drove your brother to suicide?"

I stiffened. "I've never heard such a story."

"Ah, so sweet Salena dishonored his memory as well. Alas for that. History is written by the victors, by the callous survivors and the murderers. And by their vicious progeny."

"I was a child when she died. She could hardly have told such a horrible tale to someone so young."

"She wouldn't have cared about that. You were a means to an end for her. If she'd truly seen you as her daughter, she would have taught you something."

"My mother loved me." I remembered the sound of her voice, singing to me. The way she let me brush her hair. Her face when she gave me the doll.

"Salena loved no one."

"Why would you say such a thing?"

"You didn't know her," Terin snarled. "You were a sniveling brat when she died, and she was nothing more than a weeping teat to you. She was incapable of love or she never would have—"

"Terin." Rayfe, voice pitched low, even, and with unmistakable command, cut through the man's rant. "Enough. Begone."

Terin snapped his mouth shut with an audible click. Then he clicked his heels and saluted me in a mockery of some of the Avonlidgh customs. The man disappeared and a large red fox blinked cinnamon eyes at me, then dashed into the forest.

Rayfe sighed and lowered himself to sit next to me.

"If Terin can shape-shift, why did he wait for me to open the barrier and cross as a man?" I asked.

"Shifting outside of Annfwn is tenfold more difficult. Not all Tala can manage it."

"Do you all become one particular animal?"

Rayfe chuckled, shaking his head and drawing up his knees to dangle his hands between them, casual and relaxed.

"I heard pretty much everything Terin said to you. You hold the letter from your father filled with poison—and you want to ask about the shape-shifting?"

"Well, I have ten thousand questions, but that seems like a fair place to start. And I don't care to talk about my father or my mother just now."

He studied the glimmering lake. "Are you not tired?"

"I think I'm so exhausted I've passed into this state where I can't even feel the need for sleep."

"And your mind is busy." He reached over and took my hand, holding it between his to study the ring he'd given me. "Supposedly, our ability to shift is limited only by our imaginations, or so I was taught. Unfortunately, some of our imaginations seem to be quite limited. Most of us have a favored form—an instinctive one, if you will. The more time we spend as that animal, the more it . . . leaks over into our human forms, the more it becomes instinctive to become that one thing and the more difficult to become something else. Most Tala have one form only. A few can do more. The magic lives within all of us to greater or lesser degrees."

"So you become animals other than a wolf?"

He glanced sideways at me, with that half smile, and rubbed my fingers. "A rather large black falcon."

"Not fond of stained glass, are you?"

"Not when you are on the other side, no."

"I never saw my mother shape-shift."

"No. You wouldn't have. Uorsin would have insisted upon that, I'm sure."

"Why would she agree to such rules?"

He sighed, turning my hand over and lacing his fingers with mine. "I don't know all of it. I never met Salena. She was born to another family—one of our oldest, the purest blood. Really, her family—your family—is the stuff of legends among our people."

"But you said I look like her."

"I saw her once," he admitted, voice soft. "When she was

queen of the Tala and I was but a boy. Her hair dragged on the ground, it was so long then, like a cape. She radiated Tala magic like a lily redolent with sweet perfume."

"Why did she do it?"

"Abandon Annfwn and wed Uorsin? Some say ambition. Some say the simple powers of Annfwn were not enough for her and she longed for more. Others say she did it for love."

I studied his profile, in bright relief in the glittering light from the lake. "That's not what you think."

He looked at me, raised an eyebrow. "I have reason to believe otherwise."

"The reasons you've engaged in this entire enterprise. Bringing me here."

Rayfe held my gaze, solemn. "You do have the look of her."

"But I am not her."

"No—you're more. I think you are what Salena left Annfwn to get."

"A child who benefited her not at all? Who she didn't live to see more than a few scant years?"

"Salena didn't want you for herself. Make no mistake—Terin is a bitter fool. I'm sure she loved you all, the daughters of her heart that she sacrificed so much to have."

"To gain what?"

"Everything. Not for herself, but for her people, for all the people of Annfwn. To carry on her family's legacy."

My heart quaked. I could barely voice the words. "Rayfe—I'm not that."

His eyes blazed, fiercely dark blue.

"Oh, Andromeda. You will be."

Mute, I shook my head.

"You want proof?" He tapped the scroll in my other hand. "Uorsin knows it, too."

"Your men who brought Fiona—they're the prisoners you asked to have released from Ordnung."

"It's difficult to keep shape-shifters imprisoned. There's always a friend who's mastered the knack of changing into a smaller shape, even outside the borders."

"Then why go through the motions of having me ask for their release?" I found I dreaded his answer. Feared that I already knew what it would be.

He nodded, confirming my thought. "You believed Uorsin would honor the treaty you made. I needed to find out if that was the case."

"No, you wanted me to find out for myself that he wouldn't."

He stared out over the water again, as if he saw something beyond it. Opened his mouth to say something, stopped. Sighed. "Yes."

I turned that over in my mind. Rayfe didn't wish to cause me pain—I believed that. He'd gone to great efforts to prove it. My mother's great plan that she hadn't bothered to clue us in on. Perhaps she'd died too soon, before we were old enough to understand. The empty place she'd left behind pained me even more now. Amplified by the loss of my father in almost as profound a way.

Though it was clear he'd never really seen me as a daughter, only as a tool. Or Salena's triumph over him.

Which was what Rayfe had surely wanted me to see. The lines had already been drawn in the sand, before I was even born. All of this had forced me to choose between conflicting loyalties. Was I a traitor to one just because I chose another?

No.

I was still both.

Then it occurred to me that perhaps my mother had tried to tell me. The doll she'd given me waited for me in Annfwn. Perhaps it contained answers. Maybe it would show me how to open the barrier for the other Tala.

"My mother chose him for a reason."

Rayfe glanced at me, perhaps surprised at the direction of my thoughts. I liked catching him off guard, when he wasn't quite so . . . flinty. I wound my fingers in a lock of his hair and tugged him to me for a kiss. He hummed in pleasure. Definitely not what he'd expected from me.

"He wasn't High King when she met him. I think she put him on the throne as part of whatever deal they made. She picked him for some other reason."

"Which was?"

"I think I need to find out. Where to next?"

He smiled, warm and full of anticipation. "Tomorrow you get to see the heart of Annfwn."

18

We camped by the lake that night, the Tala men celebrating their reunion and mourning those lost in battle. They broke out a dark-red wine I'd never tasted before and shared it around.

It didn't take much of that before all the missed sleep caught up to me and swept me under. Rayfe tucked me into a roll of fur blankets and curled up at my back. For the first time in my life, I slept under the stars instead of a roof. The animal in my heart uncurled and relaxed at the freedom of it. I fell asleep wondering what kind of animal she was, what I could become.

In the morning, Rayfe asked me to leave my hair loose and I saw no reason not to indulge him. When I brushed it out, it shone from being washed in the cold lake water. The long swing of it felt right somehow as I mounted Fiona. They hadn't brought her saddle or bridle, so I rode her bareback, as I'd often done in my more carefree youth. That felt right, too.

Thus I rode into the heart of Annfwn, on my own horse, at Rayfe's right hand, followed by a triumphant troop of long-haired shape-shifting barbarians.

It was so much better than riding into Windroven.

How a place can feel familiar without being so, I don't know. Perhaps I felt my mother's memories drifting through my mind, but Annfwn unfolded before me like a cherished childhood fantasy.

From the lake, we'd ridden up another ridge, then wound our way down. Huge trees, gnarled with age and fat from the moist, gentle air, towered around us. There seemed to be no roads, only trails, winding around wind-carved rounded boulders tumbled like a giant cat had knocked them about and trotted off, soon to return. I became aware that the regular birdcalls and rustlings in the canopy represented a complicated line of defense. If I tipped my head back and observed the dense canopy above, small animal shadows flitted about.

Rayfe caught me looking and grinned, wicked and wolfish. Delight spread through me, though I couldn't say why.

Then we broke out of the dense woods and I saw the city.

This was not Ordnung or Windroven. This was something altogether *other*.

Altogether beautiful.

A white cliff rose, startlingly high, riddled with caves and various openings. Here and there, larger arches were filled with fanciful structures carved from the same stone, with balconies and towers, some swooping out at seemingly impossible angles. Window openings were lined with jewel tones of lapis, ruby, and emerald that glittered in the sun. Stone pathways wound up and around, bordered by low walls draped with vines and flowers. Giant trees rose from the valley floor, multilevel dwellings built in and around the massive limbs. Bridges of rope and wood connected them to the cliff homes. At the base of the cliff, paths dived under and into shadowed recesses.

The air swirled around me fragrant and warm, filled with salt moisture from a turquoise sea in the distance.

"Welcome home, Andromeda," Rayfe murmured.

"How is it all so warm?" I marveled. "How is it even here?"

"Haven't you heard?" He grinned at me, black hair shining in the sun. "Magic."

I had seen too much to disbelieve him. We rode through a meadow of lush grass—acid green, I noticed, and tall with it—past orchards of trees laden with fruit. The path beneath our horses' hooves gradually changed from dirt to pink to white, lined with crushed seashells. The cliff city towered above us, level upon unimaginable level, stretching off into the distance, shimmering against the blue sky. Farther down, a white-sand beach brought the gentle sea nearly to the base of the dwellings, and I imagined what it might be like to change into a fish.

"How many Tala are there?"

Rayfe shrugged. "Difficult to say. Annfwn is quite large and they come and go. Some prefer to live above, where it's cooler, others down below. Some as far as the northern ice. There are groups who dwell in the deep forests, keeping to the canopies."

"Depending on their primary animal."

"Indeed."

"So how does a wolf come to prefer a cliff dwelling?"

"Ah, but the wolf is only one part of me. I'm also the falcon—that form came first to me, though the wolf can be more useful. And one makes sacrifices."

"To be king."

"To protect my people."

"I can see why now." I surveyed the incredible beauty and bounty of the place. No one starved here—I felt sure of it. "This is a rare jewel. I confess I can understand why Uorsin wants to lay claim to it."

"He never saw it." Rayfe caught my gaze with his intense blue eyes. "Salena led him away before he could. All he knows are stories he was told."

"No wonder she missed it so," I commented softly.

"Did she?"

"Yes. She used to sit in her window and look westward. She lived here, didn't she—in this cliffside city?"

"I've asked that her rooms be prepared for you, unless that would be too painful."

"I would like that. It's thoughtful of you. But I—"

I stopped myself, unsure of what I'd been about to say. I wanted to be in her rooms, yes, maybe to find something of her.

But I did not want rooms that Rayfe did not also sleep in.

Last night had not been the time or place for lovemaking. I knew that. Still, it made me uneasy, thinking of taking Salena's place here and reenacting a mirror of her marriage with a foreign man. Had she felt this passion for Uorsin at first? Only to have it crushed under the pressure of becoming someone else, forever helpmeet to fulfill some fate? It mattered not whether Rayfe and I took separate chambers. Ours would never be a marriage based on love. It would always be political first. There was nothing wrong with that. I followed in noble footsteps that way. I'd be lucky if a silly fantasy of love was all I had to sacrifice.

In ten years' time, I might be the one gazing out my window, looking to the east and the people I'd turned my back on.

"What?" Rayfe raised dark, winged eyebrows at me.

I shook my head and looked away so he wouldn't see the damp emotion in my eyes.

"You asked me to be honest with you, Andromeda," Rayfe reminded me in a soft voice that nevertheless held the hint of a growl.

"I fear I'll be uncomfortable living on a cliff face—don't people fall off?"

He eyed me, and I knew I hadn't fooled him for a moment, but, thankfully, he let it go.

"It goes deeper than it looks," he explained as we rode closer, a polite tour guide, "so the young children can be kept away from the edges. And there is rarely a drop-off without some sort of barrier, if only as a reminder."

The Tala, it seemed, were not given to overt demonstrations. No fervent or cheering crowds lined the polished stone paths. People acknowledged Rayfe in various ways, with no standard bow or salute. They glanced at me with curiosity. Some gave me more penetrating looks than others, and I wondered if they remembered Salena.

Most of the folk went about their business, airing out bedding or hanging laundry. A woman worked a pottery wheel in a small courtyard, surrounded by pale pink urns. Down one lane, a marketplace bustled under a curving cave wall, bright silks draping stalls filled with glittering items and wafting the scents of cooking food, making my stomach growl. A trio of little girls with raven-black hair dashed by, giggling and trailing ribbons. I realized these were the first female Tala I'd yet seen.

"Do your women not go to war?" I asked.

Rayfe glanced at me and raised a brow. "Tala women don't leave Annfwn, as a rule."

"Too busy cooking and making pots?"

He frowned and tipped his head at a group of women coming down the road carrying stacks of scrolls and arguing with enthusiastic animation. "That is one of our legal teams, so no."

"Then why?"

"It's too dangerous." He held up a hand. "No—before you start—they're not prevented. But a woman can be forcibly impregnated, and the risk of being unable to return is very high. We dare not allow Tala children to grow up outside Annfwn. For their sakes."

"But Salena left."

"Exactly," Terin inserted. "And look what happened."

"Men cast seed," I pointed out.

Rayfe's gaze darkened. "Men do not make full Tala children. Though they are strongly discouraged from doing so"—he raised his voice and the soldiers around us grinned—"should a Tala male bed a non-Tala female, the child will never shift."

"You're not concerned about those children being out in the greater world?"

He cast a sideways glance at me, his profile sharp. "We do not . . . worry about them as much."

"Why?" I pressed. "From what you say, I carry this trait and I was just fine growing up out there. My sisters, too."

"Were you, niece?" Terin sneered from behind us. "Are you sure?"

"What does that mean?" I twisted on Fiona's back to see his expression. His foxy eyes simply glittered with what looked like anger.

"This is not the place to discuss such things," Rayfe said quietly, but with the force of command.

I concentrated on the sights and sounds of Annfwn, willing to drop the subject in this very public venue. Still I flicked a look at Rayfe to let him know this conversation wasn't over. This couldn't be all about recovering Tala progeny, because Rayfe hadn't tried to take Ursula and Amelia, too. But then, perhaps that's what he meant about me carrying the mark. They might not have the shape-shifter blood. It seemed to be important for whatever more Rayfe wanted from me, and I might be one of those who just couldn't shift, which would mean he had gambled a great deal to recover nothing.

Not just Rayfe, but Salena, too.

I also thought uneasily of the vial of blood I'd left behind, which Lady Zevondeth had been so eager to obtain. What did she plan to do with it?

We rode higher, past the market levels and into what looked like residential districts. More excitement greeted the return of the erstwhile prisoners and warriors, who were one by one swept away by mobs of family. Their horses disappeared, becoming the ratlike creatures. Or sometimes birds who flew up to the towers to sing brilliant songs. Our stalwart escort similarly bled away at various intersections, until only Terin shadowed our heels. We entered more stately neighborhoods now, high up and with spectacular inlaid mosaics and hanging gardens. It was quieter here, serene, with endless views of the turquoise sea.

"I thought it best not to make fanfare of your arrival," Rayfe told me quietly. "Most of the fighters returned last night with the news of our marriage. Everyone knows they will meet you later, so there was no need to trumpet it about."

"Obviously, not everyone is thrilled about it," Terin commented.

"Also," Rayfe continued, as if Terin hadn't spoken, "it occurred to me that you don't really enjoy being the center of attention. I thought a cheering crowd might annoy you more than please you."

I gave him a grateful smile, remembering the headaches at Windroven, the horrible premonitions. I felt at peace, I realized, as unlikely as that seemed. None of those visions had come true. Perhaps none would.

"Terin," Rayfe tossed over his shoulder, "I'm sure you would like to enjoy your own homecoming. Take yourself off, then."

"My lord, I—"

"No, I wouldn't think of keeping you a moment longer. Till later."

I didn't look back, but Terin's displeased grumble and rapid hoofbeats signaled his departure.

"Are there truly many here who will hate my presence?" I tried to sound casual and clearly failed, because Rayfe reached out to wind his long fingers with mine.

"These have been extreme times for the Tala. People react in different ways. There will always be some who see only Uorsin the Annihilator when they look at you. Others will see only Salena. Like any place, we have our political factions, agitating for this path or that one. Over time, they will learn to know you for yourself, and you will know their agendas, too."

"And you—what do you see?"

He kissed my fingers and released my hand. "I see my queen." Something else lurked below the words, but I didn't ask to know what he wasn't saying this time. In a place so lovely, I didn't think I could bear to hear that here, too, I was something uncanny and unnatural. No matter which world I lived in, I would always carry half of the other.

We'd stopped at a place where the lane we followed swung out in a wide arc, bordered by a low stone wall dripping with intense blue flowers. The sea spread before us from this angle, echoing the color of the tiny blossoms. On the inside, a pearly wall rose, with a massive gate of wrought iron set in, flanked by glass lanterns and more of the blue flower vine. Within, a fountain splashed in an intimate courtyard.

Servants rushed up to take Fiona when I dismounted, chattering greetings in the lyrical Tala tongue. Apprehensive, I looked to Rayfe, who was similarly handing over the stallion's reins. "Do I need to tell them that she's, um, a real horse?"

Rayfe threw back his head and laughed. "No. They can tell the difference. Dyson here is a 'real' horse, also. Besides, all the animals are truly themselves, no matter what else they can turn into."

"I'm still learning the ropes," I muttered.

"I know." He slipped an easy arm around my waist and led me into the courtyard. He, too, was more relaxed in this place, I realized, that edge of tension gone, like a sharp blade now sheathed. "After you begin your lessons, you'll be able to see, also."

"When will that be?"

"This evening. Dusk is always the best time for a beginner. We'll bathe, rest, I'll show you the house, and—"

"Eat?" I inserted hopefully, my stomach still growling from the delicious marketplace scents.

"We'll do that first." He grinned. "I'm coming to understand that keeping you fed is the key to your heart."

I didn't answer that, not wanting to be argumentative. Food was important to me lately only because I hadn't been getting regular meals. And I knew perfectly well Rayfe wasn't interested in winning my heart. Besides, I seriously doubted the way to it was lunch.

Even the fabulous lunch that waited for us in the courtyard.

Several people gathered near a long table draped with white flowing cloths, sparkling with crystal and silver, and laden with a bounty of exotic foods that glistened in the sun. They all bowed or curtsied with grave courtesy, and I followed Rayfe's lead in returning the gesture.

Rayfe took my hand and led me forward. "Mother, may I present my wife and our new queen, Andromeda."

Panic seized my stomach and I fought the urge to smooth back my hair. The tall woman raised winged eyebrows that matched Rayfe's, then studied me with hawklike dark-blue eyes. I should have seen the resemblance immediately, even with her black hair twisted in complex braids. I had no idea how to address her. I wanted to stomp on Rayfe's instep for his careless failure to warn me.

"Welcome home, Salena's daughter." She hadn't liked Rayfe's introduction. As mother of the king, wasn't she queen? The woman's eyes rested on my throat, and I wondered if the bruise showed after all. "Has my son treated you as he should?"

The question seemed to carry layers of meaning, and I floundered, searching for the right answer. Amelia would flutter her lashes and be charming. Ursula would call the question and seek the upper hand.

"Rayfe and I are still learning how to treat each other," I answered. "All of this has not been easy for either of us, I think."

A half smile quirked her lips, and I thought that might be approval warming her eyes. She flicked a glance at Rayfe.

"I can see how you knew her immediately. She is very like Salena. Trinor?" A young man came forward with a tray of sparkling glasses containing a golden liquid with tiny bubbles rising. She took two glasses, pressed one into my hand, and gave Rayfe the other. The other men and women came forward with polite smiles and raised glasses, following the dark-haired lady's lead.

"To my son, my king, and his bride," she intoned, as if giving a blessing.

"To the safety and prosperity of Annfwn and all the Tala," Rayfe replied gravely.

We sipped from the glasses and the liquid burst on my tongue, icy cold and sparkling. Rayfe's mother—I wished I knew what to call her—asked us all to sit, and plates were passed. She sat at the head of the table, Rayfe at her right hand and I at her left. Rayfe stretched out long legs under the table and caught my ankles between them, giving me a little squeeze and a smile. I raised an eyebrow at him. We would talk later.

I was introduced to the others—names only, no titles or relationships, so I still wasn't sure who everyone was—then heaped my plate, plowing into the delicious food with enthusiasm and ignoring Rayfe's amused smile. I listened while Rayfe talked with his mother in low tones and the others conversed among themselves, making the polite court conversation that must be universal.

"How do you like Annfwn, Princess Andromeda?" asked the cool brunette, Payla, who sat opposite me.

"This cliff city is amazing. I've never read even a whisper about it. It's so well hidden, I didn't see it until we came out of the forest and around that last bend."

"You did not blindfold Andromeda?" Rayfe's mother looked aghast.

He caught my gaze with sober dark-blue eyes. "No, Mother. She is Tala and asked to be treated as such. Our queen should not be treated like a foreigner or a hostage."

"Do you *know* she's truly one of us, then?" Payla inquired, looking at me with sharp light-blue eyes. "She looks . . . vague."

"We've been busy," Rayfe replied, "and I thought it unwise to discuss any of our secrets outside of Annfwn's veil."

"Still—" she continued, but the man beside her put a hand on her arm.

"We will know soon enough," Rayfe's mother put in, her voice mild while she sipped the sparkling wine, but her dark gaze pinned the brunette to her chair. "I did not invite you to my new daughter's welcoming, Payla, to stir doubts in her heart."

Payla flushed, ducked her head to me "My apologies—I did not mean . . ."

"More wine?" Trinor put in with a dazzling smile, refilling my glass. "If the lovely Andromeda has been tormented with Rayfe's dour company these last days, I'm sure she needs plenty of wine, food, and pleasant conversation. Tell me, lady, did he remember to feed you, or did he expect you to gnaw on jerky like his wolfhounds?"

A laugh burst out of me at that, and Rayfe flashed the man a sour look.

"How did you know?" I sipped the deliciously cold wine and exchanged grins with young Trinor.

"We weren't exactly on a pleasure excursion," Rayfe growled, but he handed me a platter of pastries, as if to make up for it. "And she hasn't starved on the journey here."

"There, there, darling." Rayfe's mother patted his hand and winked at me. "I'm sure you at least fed her breakfast after your overnight stops."

I focused on breaking open the pastry I'd chosen, relishing the warm aroma of almonds that wafted up, but the giggles started breaking free by the time Rayfe's mother mentioned breakfast. I tried to hold them back, but they exploded in an unladylike snort. I looked up to see Rayfe watching me with that eyebrow raised. Trinor fell back, belly laughing, and Payla pressed fingers to her lips to keep from laughing along.

"I'm sorry," I gasped between laughs, "I don't know what's come over me."

"The wine." Rayfe held up his glass to the sun. "It promotes frivolity." He drank it down, grinned, and held it out to Trinor for a refill, clapping him on the shoulder. "It's good to see you laugh."

He stood with his full glass, sparkling-blue gaze on mine. "To my new and lasting queen, Andromeda." He threw the title out like a challenge. "May our marriage be full of laughter, sunny afternoons, and many, many good meals."

19

Rayfe's mother sent him off after we finished the delightful lunch, declaring that he had things to take care of and that she would settle her new daughter in.

I confess, it warmed me in a way I had never expected, that she called me "daughter," as if I'd been unexpectedly un-orphaned. Rayfe's mother led me to the rooms he'd spoken of. They were on the topmost floor, which made me smile, with windows that looked out in three directions, over sea and forest, and wide seats tucked into the nooks beneath to allow one to sit and look. None faced east, I realized. Ordnung was literally behind me, with mountain ranges between.

"These were Salena's rooms." Rayfe's mother stood in the center of the sitting chamber, surveying it. A ghost of something crossed her face.

"Did you know my mother?"

She gave me her sharp look. "Not many people did."

"So Rayfe told me."

"Did he, now?" She folded her arms, strolled around the rooms. "I had her things—the few she left behind—put here and there. In case you wanted to see them. Anything you don't wish to keep, simply set outside your doors and it will be taken away."

"Thank you." There were books on the shelves and small objects that bore further scrutiny. They didn't look like the sorts of things she'd left behind at Ordnung, but it seemed, the more I learned about her, that she hadn't been the same person by that time.

"I did know her." Rayfe's mother sighed, blowing out a long breath and staring out at the sea. "I miss her still. When news of her death came, I—" She shook her head. "It's been nearly twenty years, more than that, since I last saw her, and I still feel the ache of her absence."

"Me, too," I whispered.

She glanced at me and held out a long-fingered hand, Rayfe's gesture. "Forgive me. Of course you must miss her far more."

She pulled me down onto the window seat, tucked her feet under her, and leaned an elbow on the ledge, looking out.

"She was my friend." She nodded at me, as if she expected me to be surprised. "We grew up in neighboring households, much farther down the coast from here. You know how it is—we were the same age and lived nearly in each other's laps, so we became best friends."

I did not know how that was, but I didn't like to tell her that my childhood in Ordnung had been lacking in any way. They already seemed to think me profoundly scarred somehow. Why I felt defensive about that, I didn't know.

"Later, when people questioned what Salena did, well, I didn't. But no one else knew her secret sorrows."

"Sorrows?" I echoed.

Rayfe's mother glanced at me, a vertical line between her hawk-wing eyebrows. "You have to understand. Salena was the best of us. Beautiful, smart, witty, full of the ancient magic."

"You make her sound like a paragon."

"Do I?" She wrinkled her nose and laughed. "Well, she was

also impatient, impossibly stubborn, and arrogant enough to decide that she knew best how to single-handedly save the Tala and
Annfwn." She waved her graceful hands in swirling arcs, an-
nouncing the feat like a court minstrel might. "But"—she leaned
forward—"her greatest flaw was her pride. That's what kept her
from telling anyone what happened to her first child."

"First child?" Ursula? Oh, no. Another. I struggled to keep up.

"No one knows this, and I'm asking you to keep your mother's
secret."

I nodded, biting my lip to keep the questions back.

"After she became queen and later married Tosin and all was
well for a while—"

"I'm sorry," I interrupted, "who was Tosin?"

"Terin's twin brother. He didn't tell you?" She tapped her fingers on the window ledge in irritation. "Of course he didn't. And
Rayfe is likely being his cagey self. But you're Salena's daughter,
and if she'd lived, she would have told you all of this. So, I'm going
to. It's what she would have wanted. I can do that much for her.

"Terin and Tosin were of another of our oldest families—not
as old as Salena's and yours, but very strong, pure blood. Salena
won the right to be queen, as is our custom, and elevated Tosin to
king. All seemed well. Then, so far as anyone knows, Tosin killed
himself one dark night. Terin took off wandering in his grief and
Salena left Annfwn to wed Uorsin instead."

"Leaving Annfwn without a ruler."

She inclined her head as if I'd scored a point. "Worse, even,
but I'll get to that. So a tournament was held, to select the best."

"And Rayfe won."

"Yes." She propped her chin on her hand. "He wouldn't be
dissuaded from trying—and he was only fourteen at the time. He
was always such a serious child, so determined, driven." She
shook her head. "Well, I'm sure you've noticed these things about
him. Salena envied me him and it distanced us. That I had my first
child so easily." With a finger that trembled slightly, she wiped

away a tear. "It grieved me, but I understood that she couldn't look on my fine boy without feeling pain. And her responsibilities kept her busy."

"Her child . . . died?"

She nodded, closing her eyes at the memory. "It happens. More and more, some say, since we've stayed within the boundaries of Annfwn for so long. The babies are born twisted or weak. Or die in the womb."

"I've seen this—only with horses." The deformed foals that had to be put down still haunted me. "We had a royal breeder who tried to line breed too closely. After he was dismissed, the Master of Stables had to bring in studs from far away, to strengthen the stock again."

She nodded, her face somber.

"That's why she went to Uorsin."

"I think so. I think she had two reasons. After the babe died and Tosin killed himself, Salena was nearly out of her mind with grief. She confided in me that she'd had terrible visions of the future. And they all pivoted around this part-blood from Elcinea."

"Part-blood?"

"Many Tala believe we are the direct descendants of Moranu—that it is her blood that allows us to perform magic and that connects us so profoundly with our animal brethren. But our differences have long made us . . . uncomfortable for the mossbacks to be around. Then, the magic granted Annfwn great bounties. We were attacked, over and over again, decimating our people. Finally, one of our queens—your ancestress—created the barrier."

"Which keeps people out, protecting Annfwn and the Tala."

"Yes, with the unfortunate consequence of also sealing us in, so the magic intensifies—we sometimes get odd backlashes from it—and we interbreed too much, so our children fail. And once we go out, we can't necessarily come back in."

"But we did yesterday. Some of us."

"Once you crossed over, yes?"

"Yes."

"When the queen is in residence, she can somehow interact with the barrier and change how it behaves. It's a closely guarded secret and Salena would never say how that worked. Whether Tala can cross on their own seems to have to do with how much of a pureblood they are. It's obviously not something we can experiment with much. Clearly some of it is affected by you simply being inside. The barrier knows you.

"But what is crucial is that Annfwn needs a queen who can talk to the old magic, if we're not to die in here, like insects trapped in a corked bottle. Salena believed that she needed a child by someone outside Annfwn to be the next queen."

"But wouldn't breeding with an outsider just dilute her blood?"

Rayfe's mother raised her eyebrows at me and I remembered she'd called Uorsin a part-blood.

"My father is part Tala?" The concept rocked me. I wondered if he knew. No, of course he didn't.

She was nodding. "So Salena saw in her visions. He was descended from Tala who'd had a political falling out, long before the barrier went up. They fled to Elcinea and quickly lost their magic and became as any other mossbacks."

The way she used the word, with a hint of contempt, though I'm sure she didn't consciously intend it, conveyed the image clearly—people so stolid and unchanging that moss grew on them as if they were rocks.

"But wouldn't the bloodline have gotten weaker over time?"

"Not necessarily. Tala are drawn to one another in the outside world, I understand, like a kind of deep, irresistible attraction." She smiled then, as the blush heated my cheeks. "Ah, yes—you felt it with my son. That's all to the good. You two will have enough to face together. You deserve to at least enjoy each other."

Her words echoed Rayfe's; recalling the circumstances under which he'd said them did not help my blushing. Thankfully she let it alone.

"So, over generations, your father's family found one another again and produced Uorsin—a man of sufficiently intense blood to long for Annfwn. Which brought him to Salena's attention."

"Because he could father viable children for her. But why not bring him here?"

"Ah." She looked grave. "She foresaw terrible things if she did. That was what she confided in me, that no matter what path he followed, he would become the tyrant he is today."

"I'm not sure it's fair to call the High King a tyrant." I felt stung enough by that to defend him. "He brought lasting peace to the Twelve Kingdoms."

"As Salena channeled him to do. She had that arrogance, as I said, to believe she knew best. Making him High King, she insisted, was the least destructive option. And she would breed a new queen for Annfwn."

"Or three."

"She said one of you would have the mark—enough of the magic in her blood to work the barrier." Her lips quirked as she studied me. "We'd hoped to meet Salena's daughters long before this. She'd be so proud of you."

A rush of emotion made my heart stutter. I hadn't known how much I needed to hear that, to feel a connection. I blinked back the sudden tears, for once not minding them.

Rayfe's mother smiled. "I'll let you settle in and take some time to mull all of that over. I took the liberty of providing a range of clothing. You didn't bring much."

"I left in rather a hurry."

"I can just imagine. I'd apologize for my son's tactics, but I'm so very happy to have you among us, to have you as part of my family." She squeezed my hand and turned to go.

"Um, my lady?"

She raised an eyebrow at me.

"What should I call you?"

"Garland," she told me. "My name is Garland."

A little piece fell into place with a snap. The name I'd given the pony, not the doll. I smiled at her, wanting her to see the truth in my eyes. "I've heard your name. She never forgot you."

Now her eyes glistened with unshed tears. "I'd like for that to be true."

Rayfe found me sometime later, in the little library room, with the doll my mother gave me laid out on the carved wooden desk.

"Planning to perform surgery?" he asked, brushing my shoulder with light fingers. He'd changed out of his leathers and wore loose white pants and a flowing blue silk shirt that brought out the glints in his eyes. His hair was tied back in a casual knot and his feet were bare. He seemed like a totally different man. Something that put me at a loss. I knew how to handle Rayfe my sometime enemy, not this relaxed man with the charming smile.

"You look different."

"And you look just the same," he replied. "I thought you might have bathed and changed by now."

I'd lost track of time, frankly. The sun lowered over the sea outside the windows. I frowned at it. "I am thinking about surgery. My mother gave me this doll and I'm wondering if she left a message in it for me. Something about how to talk to the barrier and let those other people through."

"They'll be all right, you know. You don't have to solve everything in the first day."

"I know." But the burden weighed on me. I had never wanted to be responsible for other people this way. Hadn't I told Ursula that countless times? "But if there's something to the doll, I'd like to find out."

Rayfe smoothed a hand over my hair, a comforting gesture, and examined the doll with curiosity. "It's not a very pretty thing, is it?"

I chuckled at his careful wording. "No. Still, I hate to damage it."

"But you think there's a reason to?"

"Well, it's not at all something you give a child to play with. I think she made it."

Bracing a hand on the table, he bent over it, sniffing. "Yes, she used hair from one of her animal forms, and—look." He turned over one of the paw-like hands and tapped the sharp tips of the meshed fingers. "Claws."

"What does it mean?"

He shook his head. "I've never seen anything like it. Could be that it is a message of some sort."

The doll lay there, glassy eyes staring at the high ceiling. It did smell kind of funny. "I need answers."

"Come." Rayfe held a hand down to me. "I have answers for you. Change into something comfortable. I'd like to be up top by sundown."

"Up top?"

That wolfish grin slanted across his face. "Yes. The training grounds."

It seemed to me that anyplace referred to as the "training grounds" would call for leathers, not the silky sweep of a dress Rayfe pointed me to. My closet here apparently contained little else. Great for walking on the beach maybe, but not so much for scaling cliffs, if "up top" meant what I thought it did.

"What about shoes?" I fretted.

"I'm barefooted," Rayfe pointed out.

"Yes, well, you're used to it."

"Fewer clothes are better when you're learning to shift."

"I saw the soldiers shift with their clothes on. They were dressed when they came back, too."

"It's an acquired skill and not easily won. The horses lost everything not part of their bodies, did you notice?"

I hadn't. Had I? I tried to picture it.

"We're hard on tack around here, so we don't use much to begin with. The staymachs are innately magical, but their intelligence is more animal. We can suggest the forms they take, but not much more than that."

254 • Jeffe Kennedy

"I can just imagine."

"Best to take off your jewelry, too."

"Even my—your—ring?"

His lips twitched with amusement. "Worried you'll forget who your husband is?"

I wrinkled my nose at him, snatched up the peachy silk, and flounced into the little dressing room with my best Amelia-style hair toss.

I wiped myself down and put on the dress. It skimmed my bare skin like a cloud, perfect for the warm, moist air, really. I felt nearly naked, though. And nervous. I brushed my hair out, to soothe myself. Then set the pendant Dafne had given me and Rayfe's ring in a little dish. When I emerged, Rayfe took my hand, lacing his fingers with mine with a half smile.

"Now you truly look like a woman of the Tala."

"Yes, well, you can dress up a pig as a horse, too—that doesn't mean you can ride her."

He raised an eyebrow at me but didn't comment. Improbably, we climbed up the stairs to leave the house, instead of going down. I'd have to break my habit of thinking I needed to come and go by the front courtyard. My rooms weren't on the highest level of the house after all, and several hallways led out into pathways that became roads. It was as if, at the edges, the place became community property again.

"Not much security," I commented. It felt odd to walk hand in hand with him like young lovers.

"No," Rayfe mused. "Nothing like what you're used to. Really there's not much call for it. We respect each other's territories."

"And you rely on the barrier to ward off outside enemies."

He glanced sideways at me, some kind of foreboding darkening his visage. "That has long been the way, yes."

"Ursula would say that doesn't give you much defensive depth."

"And what would you say?"

I shrugged. "I'm not the soldier or the strategist—what do I know?"

"More than you think, I suspect."

We walked along a narrow winding path now, that switch-backed up the cliff. The stones felt smooth and polished by many footsteps. No dwellings here. Brushy plants, touched here and there with salt from the sea breezes, clung to the dirt with envi-able tenacity. Somehow I didn't think I'd have this ability they all looked for in me. That my mother had sacrificed herself to get. Everything had been much simpler when I could just get on Fiona's back and ride, ride, ride.

"There's no reason to be nervous," Rayfe told me in a quiet voice. He met my gaze when I looked up at him. "Trust me."

Oh, yeah. Trust the guy who blackmailed you into marriage, changes into various large animals, and glibly promises you can do the same. Funny thing was, I found that I did. When he studied me with that deep-blue gaze, it seemed he saw me more clearly than anyone ever had. With him I was Andromeda, not the mid-dle sister. Not invisible.

Unfortunately, it seemed visibility came with a price.

The training grounds turned out to be a stone-lined ring dug into the flat top of the cliff, circled with wind-twisted scrubby trees that laced together, forming an impenetrable fence.

"I kind of thought there'd be a view up here."

"What we can't see, can't see us. This place is for privacy."

We entered the ring and Rayfe moved a hinged gate into place, closing the wall. A sharp sea breeze tugged at the silky dress I wore and I shivered a little. The sun had nearly set, casting long shadows.

"Look there."

I followed the line of Rayfe's finger. The moon, round and pink-gold, rose over the arena wall, glowing impossibly large in the shimmering blue evening sky, impossibly lovely.

"Not quite full, but close enough."

"Enough for what?" I murmured, feeling spellbound. Rayfe pressed against my back and wrapped his arms around me. The heat of his body burned through the light silks we wore.

"We draw our magic from the moon." He kissed my temple. "From Moranu. You've always known this, just . . ."

"Without really knowing."

"Yes."

"I feel it," I whispered. "I feel something." Something like the desire Rayfe woke in me poured sweet and hot through my blood. It seemed the moon sang. Promises and passion.

"Yes," Rayfe repeated, his voice rough.

I turned in his arms and his mouth caught mine, feral and devouring. His manhood thrust against my belly, hard and insistent, and I dampened immediately, suddenly famished for his touch. I wondered if he'd make love to me right there on the stones. I hoped he would. Pressing the palms of my hands against his muscled chest, I returned his kisses with my own hunger laced into them.

"Hold that thought," he murmured into my mouth. "Keep that feeling."

His blazing blue eyes drilled into mine. Deliberately, he bit down on his lower lip, dark blood welling up. I gasped a little and he shushed me.

"Trust me. This will help."

I flinched a little, but he held me steady for the next kiss, the hot taste of his blood filling my mouth along with the desire that flared hotter and higher, consuming me. The beast in my heart roared in delight. Wanting to burst free.

"Let her go," Rayfe told me, slipping the dress off my shoulders so I stood naked, following it with his hot hands, caressing my skin. I purred under his touch, feeding off it. "Let her go," he insisted.

His words kept pricking me. I didn't want to talk. I just wanted him to touch me, to fill me. I needed to devour him.

"Andromeda—focus." Rayfe cupped my face in his hands while I tore at his clothes. "That hunger, that need—let her go."

"I want you," I cried against his mouth, and he laughed, kissing me.

"You'll have me, I promise. As much as you like. Later. Concentrate. Relax. Let her go."

"I don't know what to do."

"You don't have to do anything. All your life you've restrained her. Tucked her inside. Let her go."

He caressed the tips of my breasts, and I moaned, his blood still in my mouth, in my veins. I writhed against him, losing my fear in the moment, in the building tension. He slipped a hand between my legs and I exploded.

"Now, my love. Now, Andromeda!"

I came apart as she broke free, leaping up and out of my heart.

The world changed, shifting to shades of gray, layered and sharp. The stone arena looked both larger, with taller walls, and at the same time, more scalable. Hunger rode me. I needed to hunt. I could leap up on that wall, quite easily. My muscles bunched, full of power.

"No, Andromeda. Stay here, please."

The man stood there, smelling delicious. Like blood. I wanted to devour him.

I stalked toward him.

Rayfe.

I knew him. Something popped and I found myself naked and crouched on the stones, Rayfe grinning like a madman. He seized me by the arms and lifted me to my feet, running his hands over my skin and raining kisses on my upturned face.

"Perfect. Just perfect. I knew you could do it. That you weren't too old." He clasped my head in his large hands and kissed me with fierce joy. "I knew it!"

"Too old?" I repeated faintly. The bones of my skull seemed to vibrate. Panic shimmered in my stomach. They'd said that before.

"Oh," he brushed off, "a long-standing debate. A lot of non-sense, obviously."

"So . . . I did it? I shifted?" I felt . . . odd. Like I didn't quite fit in my skin.

"Yes, you surely did." He beamed with pride, stroking my hair back from my face. "You turned into a large cat—as I suspected you might—and held the shape for a good several minutes. Well done, indeed!"

"I didn't mean to shift back, though." Not much control at all, it seemed.

"You were surprised when you recognized me through your cat eyes. That's the most difficult part to control. When you start thinking like a person too much, it pops you back out into human form. We'll work on that."

"That's why you kissed me—to get me thinking more like an animal."

"Yes. And it worked. I told them it would work." He clasped me to him, his mouth feeding down my throat. Instead of plea-sure, I felt . . . irritated. "Now let's do it again."

"Maybe not tonight." I still felt unsteady in my skin. The beast's bloodlust ran hot in me. Somehow I didn't think that was right. I hesitated to ask Rayfe. Maybe I didn't want to know how wrong it was. My blood—my part-blood—wasn't good enough, I feared. The headache that had assaulted me at Windroven clung to the back of my skull.

"You need a lot of practice. Try it again, while the feeling is still fresh in your mind."

I tried.

It didn't work.

What had felt like a releasing, the first time, eluded me like a word I couldn't quite recall. Now that I knew Rayfe's technique, my mind kept drifting away from the pleasure of his touch to other thoughts. How did my body know to become something else? More important: how did it know how to get back?

And Rayfe, arousing me in such a skillful way. I didn't want it. Not like this. Not like the intimacy was a tool to get me to become this thing he wanted me to be.

That maybe I couldn't be.

I tried to let go, but the surging of the beast frightened me and I found myself grabbing at my own familiar form again. How could my skin grow fur and lose it in an instant? What if I couldn't get my human shape back again? I blew out a breath and let it go, trying to sink into Rayfe's kiss. But the sick drop in my stomach lurched me back into reality.

"You're thinking too much," Rayfe muttered.

I wrenched myself from his embrace, biting my tongue on the twenty-seven things I wanted to say to him, and snatched up my dress. Sliding it back on over my head, I took in and released a deep breath. The moon shone smaller and higher now, lighting the sharp planes of Rayfe's face with bright silver. How could I explain my queasy fear? I searched his face. What in Moranu was wrong with me? I'd walked into this knowing that I was only a means to an end for him, that I followed in my mother's footsteps in wedding myself to the enemy.

My mother's plan.

"I have questions."

He folded his arms and shook his head. "No. No questions. This is about instinct, not thoughts."

I clenched my jaw. "Tell me about being too old."

"You're not too old. You shape-shifted just now—that proves it."

"But normally, the Tala learn younger. As children, right?" I saw the truth of it in his face. "That's why my mother wanted the one of us with the mark of that ability sent back here as a child, so she could learn. That's what she was afraid of."

He scrubbed a hand over his face. Sighed. Then tipped back his head and stared at the round moon. "She should have taught you herself. That's what should have happened. Even outside Annfwn she was strong enough to shift—she should have given you her blood and showed you how to manage your beast. Think back— are you sure you never did?"

"Never. None of us even knew she could."

"That's not possible."

"I don't think you're the person to spout off about what's possible."

The anger he'd tried to tuck inside roiled through him, the wolf gleaming in his eyes. He gripped me by the shoulders, fierce, fingers digging into my flesh.

"You don't understand. She would have known you needed to shift—why wouldn't she have taught you?" He finished on a shout.

"She died!" I shouted back. "She died giving birth to Amelia and she didn't have time! *You* have to understand, these . . . abilities are anathema in the Twelve Kingdoms. They call you demons and worse. He never would have let her teach us black magic like this."

He let go of me in a burst of frustration, clenching his fists by his sides. "I could rend Uorsin limb from limb for fouling your mind like this. For betraying the treaty. For putting you at risk like this."

"What risk?" I scoffed. "Politics and religion."

"Oh, he knew," Rayfe sneered. "He knew from being with Salena. She had to shift or she would have lost her mind. She knew you would be weak and prone to illness if you didn't learn. She had to tell him that."

I stared at him in horror.

"She did," I finally whispered.

"What?"

"She did lose her mind. I understand now." And I had always been weak, hadn't I? Growing sicklier every year, though I hadn't liked to think of it.

"Wait, how do you know—what do you mean?" He tried to

take my arm, but I shook him off. Turned my back and walked away.

"You need to practice," he called after me.

"No more tonight. I have something to do."

"You can't give up. Andromeda. You have to learn—"

I fixed him with a steely glare, feeling the cat rise in me, a match to his wolf. Nothing invisible about her. I stalked back to him. Did he flinch a little at the look in my eye? Good.

"You don't tell me, Rayfe." My voice stayed smooth and even. "King. Husband. I don't know who you thought you married, but I am not your tool, to wield as you please. I am Uorsin's daughter as much as my mother's. I decide for me. Not you."

"So you're just giving up?" He challenged me, matching my anger.

"I'm not giving up. And it's not about you. You're right—my mother should have taught me. This is between me and her. I have to go."

I spun on my heel and walked away without a backward glance.

20

My grand exit failed in the execution. I couldn't work the latch on the gate and had to wait while Rayfe maneuvered it for me. I stared stonily off into the darkness, while he did so without a word, then followed behind as I picked out the trail. Everything looked brighter and more defined than before, shading with the gray scale of the cat's vision.

I would never again be who I was before.

At a loss to explain my rage, I let my thoughts run free. The memories bubbled up now, blurred by time and childish incomprehension. But the way my mother had stared endlessly out the window, her eyes empty. I'd brushed her hair because it had always been snarled and only Ursula and I could touch her.

Ursula—had she seen the madness, known all along?

That look in her eyes when she made me burn Rayfe's feather. She had known enough to suspect me of madness, too. Salena's stamp. No wonder I made people's skin crawl. A sudden sob escaped me and I stumbled over a rock.

"Andromeda."

"No," I choked out.

Rayfe caught my arm. "Stop. Talk to me."

"I don't know who I am!" I shouted at him. I clenched my fist and thumped my breastbone. "This beast crawls around inside of me, wanting to rend and tear. I am apparently defective, either from birth or the accident of my mother's death. I'm supposed to take over this barrier that's so thrice-damned important for people who don't even want me here. And now I'm afraid I'm evil or mad or both, and I don't know how to save myself from this!"

His hard, angry gaze softened. He drew me into his embrace and held me gently, like a child. The sympathy broke me and I wept, hot tears soaking the silk over his chest, the sobs wrenching out of me like so many pounds of flesh. All this time, I'd mostly managed to hold the tears in, but now they poured out of me, beyond my control. Rayfe sank to the ground and pulled me onto his lap, cradling me there and making soft, soothing sounds until I cried out all the anger and grief.

When the storm passed, embarrassment found me. So much for being the dignified princess, emissary of my people and proudly following in my mother's footsteps.

"Done?" Rayfe asked quietly.

I nodded against his chest and tried to move. His arms tightened around me.

"I didn't think," he said, leaning his cheek against my hair. "I've been around this all my life, so I didn't think through what it would be like for you. Salena was—she was so bright, so beautiful, and you seem so like her."

"I'm sorry to disappoint you." I wanted it to sound dry, but it came out pitiful.

"Is that what you think?" He sighed, the muscles of his chest moving under my cheek. He smelled of man and something dark, spicy. Even now the warmth curled through me for him. "I shouldn't be surprised."

"I know you wanted me because you thought I could be this . . . thing that you want me to be. Salena's legacy or what have you. But

264 • Jeffe Kennedy

you have to know, Rayfe. I'm just the middle daughter of a broken
and lonely woman. The rejected child of a brutal man. A traitor to
my sisters, who loved me."

He made a wordless sound of protest, lifting my chin so he
could gaze into my face. The bright moon shimmered in the
depthless silver of his eyes.

"Never say that again, my Andromeda. Never think I'm disap-
pointed. You are far more than I hoped to imagine." His lips
brushed mine, then again. He deepened the kiss, and I returned it
as I couldn't before, the bloodlust singing through me. In this way
I could devour him. "As for the beast. Trust me. I know how to
handle her. I know how it feels. Take it out on me. I want you to."

I couldn't have stopped it if I'd wanted to. I turned to straddle
his lap, digging my nails into his muscled chest through the silk,
now tearing it away in my haste to touch his skin. He growled in
response, shredding my dress in an easy movement, hands roving
over me in a desperate hunger that echoed mine. His manhood
thrust against my belly, hot and eager.

I pushed Rayfe back and he lay before me, spread out like a
banquet. All mine. I bit and licked my way down his hard warrior's body, relishing each shudder and moan I wrung from him.

Remembering how he'd put his mouth on me, I took him in
my hands, stroking the surging length of him. Such soft skin over
hot, blood-filled flesh. I kissed the tip and he flexed like a wild
thing in my hands, making me laugh softly with the power.

"Andromeda . . . ," Rayfe whispered on a growl, "you torture me."

"Good," I answered, swirling my tongue over the tip of him.
"You could stand a bit of torture."

With that I drew him into my mouth and he wound his hands
in my hair. I played with him, now sucking lightly, now licking
with little nips. Whenever it seemed he might lose his seed, I
backed off, enjoying the shadowed flex of his abdomen as the
pleasure wrung through him.

"Enough!" he finally shouted to the sky. "I concede—you've conquered me, my queen." He tugged my hair, urging me up his body to capture my mouth with his. Our skin slid together, nearly sparking in the moonlight.

He rolled me under him and slid inside me in one movement.

I cried out as he speared me, the sensation nearly unbearable. He plunged in again, stroking the pleasure through me, melting away the tense and dark feelings. I dissolved into it, barely hearing his hoarse cry of completion as I stared at the full moon over his shoulder.

It seemed she smiled at me.

We lay there, connected, skin damp with the moist air. Something surged through me, a vast and intense affection for this man who'd become my husband and my lover. Who saw me. Whose skin did not crawl at my strangeness. Because it was in him, too. I kissed his shoulder, overwhelmed. He raised his head, staring into my eyes. Wordless, he kissed me, deep and tender. Pulling out of my body, he tucked me against him, so we lay in the grass, gazing up at the moon.

"I became King of the Tala when I was but fourteen—did you know that?"

I nodded against his shoulder and he picked up a long lock of my hair, idly winding it around his finger. "Your mother told me."

"After Tosin died and Salena . . . left us, things fell apart. The magic wasn't working right without her to guide it. My mother, she grieved for months. Everyone did. The weather became unpredictable. The staymachs sometimes turned into distorted forms and had to be put down. Someone had to fix things. No one thought I could win, but I *did*."

Grim satisfaction echoed in his voice, but I saw the boy he'd been. Tall and skinny with it. Not yet grown into this hardened man.

"They all thought Salena would return. That she'd only gone to distract Uorsin. Or she'd get with child and bring it back. Surely it would be impossible for her to stay away. Then the wars unfolded, she summoned more and more of our warriors to battle, and it became clear that she was using her magic—the magic of Annfwn—to help him."

"How? How can the magic of a place go with a person?"

I felt the tension in his muscles, the hesitation that tightened his body while he considered his words.

"There's a ceremony, when you're made ruler in truth, that connects . . . one to the heart of Annfwn."

"And the barrier."

"An extension of the heart, yes."

"That's why no one calls me queen, except you—I'd wondered."

His arm clenched, holding me almost painfully close. "You will. You have to. It's meant."

"You don't need me—you've done it. You said so."

"No." He sighed, long years of grief and fear seeming to stream from him. I tilted my head up to look at him, but he stared fixedly at the sky. "I could stop the worst of the troubles, but I'm not enough. You don't know what it was like."

"Tell me."

He laughed, a soft sound with a bitter edge. "Piece by piece, we cobbled things together. And we waited."

"For Salena to return."

"For something. Because I wasn't enough. I could feel the magic leaking away in some places, turning in on itself in others. So many of our people found themselves trapped outside, unable to return. It all looks more or less like it should, but Annfwn is unstable. I couldn't do it alone. We needed Salena's daughter." He rose on his elbow, stroking the hair away from my face. "The treaty promised us Salena's daughter, so I figured that was Salena's answer for us. They all thought she left without a backward glance, but I believed. Twenty years I waited for that, my salvation." His face creased with contempt for his idealistic youth. "Hoping they'd never find out what a fraud I am."

I made an inarticulate sound of protest and he pressed fingers against my lips to stop me.

"You say you're a tool to me? I can't deny it. All these years I've thought of this woman and all the things she'd bring to me, to Annfwn. A means to an end, yes. You're right to doubt my motives. They are the worst kind."

I nodded and moved his hand, disappointment darkening my heart. Foolish, silly girl. "I understand. I always understood that."

A wild impatience broke the lines the old griefs had carved into his face. He laced his fingers with mine and pressed our joined hands against my heart and spoke all in a rush.

"No—you haven't thought this through. You didn't have to marry me. It wouldn't have been easy, but you could have come here and claimed your rightful place as queen without me. I planned to offer that. I would have helped—it didn't have to mean civil war.

"And then I met you and all that fell away. You are . . . yourself. This thing I waited for—I had no idea who you would be to me. That you would be like my mirror self, this canny, stubborn woman who makes me laugh, who stands up to me. I don't know how to tell you who I see when I look at you."

I reached up with my free hand and traced the high line of his cheekbone.

"It's enough that you do."

His lids lowered, shadowing his eyes. "I'd like to think that it was more than duty to you. That maybe you weren't entirely unwilling. In another world, perhaps I could have courted you, won your heart. I know it's too late for that, but if there's a way to make that up, I will."

I bit my lip against the words, then let them go. "If I were Amelia, I'd make you work for it, write me poetry and bring me flowers, but in truth, Rayfe, this is all so new to me. I don't know what I feel, except that I'm all jumbled up with it. I don't know what's in my heart. But I wouldn't change this. And I'm trying."

268 • Jeffe Kennedy

He took my hands in each of his and drew me up. "It's enough that you do."

I smoothed my palms over his muscled chest, fast becoming familiar to me. I kissed his skin, just over his heart, inhaling the masculine fragrance of him. Mine, my dark and fierce husband.

"Tell me what I have to do. It takes shape-shifting, doesn't it?"

He searched my face. Even I heard the dread in my voice. "No, we can go home. We'll wait until you're ready."

"Why do you think I can somehow do this thing that you've been working on for so long? What are you doing wrong that I can do right?"

He scrubbed his fingers over his scalp. "I don't know." He ground out the words. "That's just it. I hope you can."

"So all of this"—I swept my hands as if to encompass the last several months of suffering, death, and betrayal—"is all a wild gamble on your part?"

Rayfe regarded me steadily, like the wolf had, like the falcon had. "Yes. Call me a fool, but yes."

"But no pressure, right?" My laugh still had a hysterical edge, and he smoothed a hand over my cheek.

"No pressure. We'll find a way. For tonight, we'll go back. Rest."

The relief of reprieve washed over me like gentle rain. He picked up the shreds of my erstwhile dress, trying to position them over me strategically. A scarf-like piece he draped over my shoulder to cover one breast slid off while the knot he attempted to tie around my waist came undone. I started to giggle.

"Hold still," he ordered and switched to putting his clothes on me, which I'd apparently torn even worse than he had mine.

I tried to be still, but the slippery silk refused to cooperate. He cursed, and a laugh burst out of me. He looked up with a wry twist to his lips.

"This won't work, will it?"

I shook my head, pressing fingers to my lips to keep the giggles in.

"Do you laugh at me, my queen?" He mock growled, standing and pulling me into his arms.

I kept my face very serious, but my lips trembled with the effort. "Never, my king."

He frowned at me. "Yes, I can see how long 'never' will last. Wait here and I'll go fetch you another dress."

"Wait." I touched his arm, making the decision as I said it. The stakes were bigger than me and my fears. "Bring the doll, too, would you?"

He stilled. "Are you sure?"

"Yes. This isn't only about me and Mother. You're part of it, too. And I have this feeling that time is running out."

"Thank you." He said it as solemnly as a pledge, then kissed the back of my hand in as courtly a gesture as Hugh might have managed.

I waited for him in the bright, moonlit night. From where I stood, on this high point before the path started to wind down, the silvered sea spread out below. The night caressed my naked skin, moist and warm and gentle. Oddly, it felt natural and right. I stretched, replete and a little sore from our nearly violent lovemaking, my palms up to the moon. I thought of the moon pendant Dafne had given me. I missed her with a sudden pang, wishing I could ask her advice.

Though I knew she would tell me to follow my own instincts.

Which meant the cat inside. And whatever other shapes lurked within. They would all be me, right? Not demons, like Glorianna's priests shrieked. Only the priests, I realized. Glorianna herself had never rejected me or shown me ill favor. And Moranu was her sister, as was Danu. Other faces of the same light, as Ursula, Amelia, and I had common blood but different faces.

None of us was the good and right daughter. We were all just ourselves.

My hearing sharper than before, I knew Rayfe approached long before I saw him, even imagined I smelled him on the warm breeze, along with a hint of jasmine from the low bushes he pushed through.

"Ah, look—a beautiful, naked woman waiting for me."

"But no naked man for me." He'd put on a new set of loose trousers and a shirt.

"That can be easily remedied." He kissed me, weighing my breast in his palm. Tempting, but I stepped back.

"No, I'm determined."

I shimmied into the gown he'd brought me, this one a sheer white that dipped so low it barely covered my nipples, which showed through the fabric anyway. I raised my eyebrows and Rayfe gave me his wolfish grin.

"I figured since no one would see you up close anyway . . ."

"Ha to that."

He handed me the doll, wrapped up in black silk.

"It seemed wrong to carry it around unprotected." His brow creased as I cradled it in my arms. "It has a very strange feel to it."

"Yes, I feel it, too. Let's find out what it is."

This time I took his hand as we retraced our steps back to the arena. Rayfe was right—the doll almost seemed to vibrate in my arms. I realized that, as much as I'd examined it, I'd rarely held it. It wasn't a thing that asked to be cuddled. Not of the light and happy world. A vision of my mother, heavy bellied, flashed through my head. She sat in her window, the moon hanging low while she sewed the doll and sang to it.

> Under the waves, deep under the sea
> Sands dissolve the cicatrix of thee.
> Cobalt crabs pluck at deep-frozen lies
> Eating the corpses of what she denies.

I started and Rayfe glanced down at the doll. "What's wrong?"

"Nothing. A memory. Or something." Unborn babies didn't remember seeing their mothers. Somehow I knew it was me in her round belly, not Amelia this time.

"If you have the visions like Salena was said to . . ."

"Said to?"

He shrugged, but a strain of tension ran through him.

"You're hoping that I can."

We'd reached the arena and he dropped my hand to move the stone again, speaking over his shoulder. "I won't lie to you. Yes, it was something I thought about. One of the many things I hope for."

"Rayfe." I tugged at his silky tail of hair to stop the diatribe. "It's okay. Remember, we have an understanding now."

He turned and slipped a hand behind my neck, kissing me with sudden fierceness, the doll crushed between us. He broke the kiss as fast as he'd launched it.

"I know. I just . . ." He faltered. "I'm not a gentle man, Andromeda. You need to know that. Even as I recognize that none of this is your responsibility, I know in my heart that I'd lock you up to keep you from walking away like Salena did."

I stared at him, my heart in my throat. Emotions chased across his face, determination, desire, self-loathing.

"I don't believe you."

"You don't know what I'm capable of."

"Well, I know what I'm capable of, and you need not worry that you'd imprison me, because I would never let you."

He stared at me, surprised. A ghost of relief ran over him. A startled smile flashed through it. "You're right."

"I know."

I turned to walk into the arena, and Rayfe cuffed my arm in a strong grip, stopping me. "What you said before, about how the beast feels. I know what you mean. The wolf can be . . ."

"Wild."

"Yes."

I took a deep breath. "Okay. I want to try something. Hopefully I'm right about this."

For the second time, I laid the doll out and pillowed her on the pile of black silk wrappings. Feeling a sense of ritual, I set her in the exact center of the arena, the moon like a spotlight overhead.

Rayfe stood back, his tangled black hair shadowing his face. For the moment, the wolfish hunger in his gaze didn't bother me. Or perhaps I recognized it for the same in my own heart.

I knelt on the hard stones, held my breath, and, using my dagger, the one Ursula had given me after our mother died, now clean of Rayfe's blood, I made a small cut in the worn fabric. It gave with a little sigh of age and continued to split, laying itself open under the sharp edge.

I confess I'd half expected a scream of pain.

At first I couldn't make out the mass of dark fiber inside. Hesitant, I touched it, both brittle and silky.

"She stuffed it with her own hair," Rayfe breathed over my shoulder. I started, not having noticed that he'd moved up behind me. "I've heard of this kind of magic. I had no idea that Salena was powerful enough for this."

Feeling ridiculously unsettled, I stroked the stuff again, hoping it wouldn't shatter into dust, and then probed deeper into the doll's guts.

Then my fingers brushed cool glass.

"What?" Rayfe asked at my gasp, laying a hand on my shoulder, ready to yank me back to safety, I realized.

"Something. It's okay."

I drew out the vial. The upper part seemed to be dipped in wax, layers and layers of it by the feel, but the bottom was clear and showed fluid within, silver-black in the moonlight. Using the dagger edge—and with a silent apology to Ursula, who'd skin me for using a weapon as a tool—I scraped the hardened wax from the top, then set to worrying the cork out. My blade slipped, biting my finger. I hissed, sucking the stinging tip, the salt taste of my own blood filling my mouth.

"Let me—"

"No! I have to open this!"

"I'm offering to help," Rayfe said in a mild tone, crouching next to me. He slid the vial from my hands and picked up the dropped dagger. "Do you know what you're doing here?"

I didn't reply.

His clever fingers worked the cork with deft ease. "Tell me what you're thinking."

"I think . . . I think it's her blood. This is how she's giving it to me. How she left it for me, just in case. Though how it would be not rotten, I don't know."

"I've heard it can be done," Rayfe mused. "That our blood, if freely given and immediately sealed, will stay fresh. I've never seen it done, but we are warned from early youth to never give our blood to anyone, for any reason."

My stomach went cold.

"What would happen if someone—one of you—did?" I asked carefully. I didn't fool Rayfe for a moment. His gaze flew to mine, sharp with concern.

"Why? Did you give your blood to someone?"

Moranu, why had I given Lady Zevondeth that blood? Would she even know what to do with it, whatever that might be?

He took my silence for assent and shook his head. "I don't know. But I'd be wary of that person. Is this blood back at Ordnung?"

"Yes." That is, if Lady Zevondeth still was. Somehow I doubted she'd ever stir from her overheated chambers.

"I'll get it back, then."

"You can't just waltz into Ordnung, Rayfe!"

"You don't say." He grinned at me, but stern resolve was carried under the words. "Besides, a waltz is too circular. I prefer a more direct approach."

With a sigh, the cork gave way. Rayfe sniffed the bottle.

"It's blood, in truth." He handed it to me with a flourish.

I held it clasped in my palm, the glass warm from his hands. He watched me, calm, expectant.

"Do you think I should?"

"Now you wonder?" He held up a hand to silence my protest. "I think there's a reason you thought to do this. And Salena was nothing if not a clever and driven woman who took the long view. She knew you'd need this.

"Tell me this. Did she have reason to believe, even long ago, that Uorsin wouldn't honor the treaty and send you home?"

I coughed out a laugh.

His lips twisted in the half smile. "I believe you have your answer."

"Well, then." I toasted him with the vial. "To Salena. May she have found peace and happiness, wherever she might be."

I resolved to choke it down, no matter how it tasted, but it tasted like nothing. A bit like saltwater, maybe, with a metallic glint. Perhaps it would be nothing. My eyes closed against Rayfe's discerning gaze, I waited, letting it slide into my stomach.

Nothing.

Nothing.

And then the night exploded into bright light.

21

The arena lit up like daylight.

But I hadn't changed form. I looked down at my body, just to be sure. The sheer white gown fluttered around me. But the doll was gone. No Rayfe either. The boundaries of the stone arena faded into mist.

Not a good sign at all.

Hopefully this wasn't death. Ursula would have plenty to say to me if I'd blithely drunk down a poison and killed myself. It would reflect badly on Rayfe and the Tala, come to think of it, if Uorsin thought I'd died at their hands.

"You're not dead."

I spun around and a woman stood there. Dark-red hair cascaded around her, and my own gray eyes gazed back at me.

"Mother?"

She smiled, soft and sad. "An echo of her, yes. I am more of a message. A letter, if you will, that only you, my darling Andromeda, can read. A bit more than that. This is a little piece of myself that I carved away and left behind. It wasn't easy."

I choked on the disappointment. Such a new hope, that I

might be able to talk to her, know her a little, to be so quickly dashed.

"You did well to find the vial I left for you. I hope your sisters found theirs, as well."

I shook my head. "I don't think so."

"You must help them find their own vials. There are things they need to know."

"That might not be easy—I'm not sure if I'll see them again."

"Then you are in Annfwn." She sighed and closed her eyes as if in prayer. "I am so thankful. I worried for you, most of all."

"Because Annfwn needs me?"

That same anger I'd felt before leaked through my voice. If she'd been mad, I couldn't blame her for taking her own life, if that's what Zevondeth had been hinting at. And yet, in doing so, she'd abandoned us. Leaving behind a little spell, saying it had been difficult.

"No, it does. Make no mistake. But because you were always the one who felt the most deeply."

"That's not true. Amelia is the drama queen and Ursula is forever chiding me for not caring enough."

She smiled then, a ghost of love that hammered home. I remembered her like this. The sweet smile and how she'd brush my hair from my forehead and call me her moon daughter.

"You distance yourself because you feel so much. It's a tool, this armor of uncaring, but don't let it isolate you. I don't regret my choices, Andromeda. I want you to know that. I did what I did to protect Annfwn and to pass my own mother's blood on to the world. But, my moon daughter, never marry a man who doesn't love you."

"Is that why you killed yourself?" I threw out as a challenge, past the dreadful fear that she'd done exactly that.

"Is that what you believed happened to me?" Dreadful sorrow crossed her face. "I would never have. Once Amelia was born, I planned to take all of you to Annfwn. You must look elsewhere for the cause of my death."

"Are you saying you were murdered?" I whispered it, unwilling to speak aloud who might have done such a thing. Who alone would have had the power to do it?

She shook her head ruefully. "Whatever happened occurred after I made this message. I can point no fingers."

"Did you love Uorsin?" I blurted out.

She tipped her head. "No. Never. He was handsome and powerful, attractive like a wild stallion. With him I forgot my old sorrows, and that was something I needed. But that's not why I married him—it was never for me. I won't tell you not to love your father, Andromeda, but be wary of him. I urge that."

"This is what you wanted to tell me?"

"Only if you asked. I hoped that, perhaps, he would mellow with age and you would never have cause to question why I did what I did."

"I've met Garland."

"Ah. Would you tell her something for me? Tell her I thought of her every day, that I kept the seashell—she will know what you mean. Most important: tell her I wish her son the very best, that he lives up to his early promise. I hope she had many more and my greatest regret was that our children did not grow up together."

I pictured growing up with Rayfe as a kind of big brother and thought perhaps it had been just as well.

"I have three gifts for you, my moon daughter, child of my ancestors." She drew close and I realized I was slightly taller than she. She placed a ghostly hand over my heart, a cool shiver running through me at the touch. "Follow me."

In my mind, she appeared as herself. Then she became a graceful mare, then a cat, then a sleek falcon, then a fish, like the ones over the bed, flicking from one to the next. With each change, I understood how she did it and how it fed into the magic of the land itself. My blood thrummed with awareness. Such a simple thing, really.

"Trust the animal within. That is the first and that is the heart."

Now, still in my mind—though wasn't this all in my mind?—she led me to a pool in a deep forest. The moon, dead overhead, shone down, making the glassy surface into a mirror. In it, scenes, both that I'd experienced and that I'd imagined, played out. I saw the slopes of Windroven covered in blood and corpses, as I'd imagined that day we rode in, something that never happened.

Another scene appeared, a valley that looked familiar, with tilled fields between two high mountain ranges, but it seemed wrong. Wrong, I realized, because soldiers filled the roads. They streamed over the mountain pass, pouring into the gentle summer of Annfwn, flashing with metal, bristling with weapons. At their fore, Ursula and Hugh silently conferred, clearly planning to attack Annfwn.

"Trust in the visions—they will guide you. That is the second."

Then we stood again in the misty arena, one step back toward the world of the living. I thought I saw a little girl, maybe five, ducking behind her ethereal skirts.

"Your invisibility. That's a real thing. Remember that what was made invisible can be made visible at will.

"Good-bye, Andromeda. Know that I love you, that part of me is always with you."

"Wait!" I cried out, trying to seize her, my hand, as insubstantial as she, passing through her. "Please don't go."

"I must. I already have." She smiled, and love warmed her gaze. "One more, then. Trust in love—and in those who love you. You have always had mine. Know that I'm proud of you, my moon daughter."

I awoke in Rayfe's arms, something that felt surprisingly natural. Or perhaps that was just in contrast to the world-shaking strangeness I'd experienced.

He had my head pillowed in his lap and curled an arm around my waist. The moon had dropped significantly lower in the sky.

"Welcome back," he said, soft, as if not to startle me.

I blinked at him, disoriented. "Was I out for a long time?"

He cocked an eye at the moon. "Just shy of three hours."

"Whoa." I sat up, his hand supporting the small of my back. "I didn't expect that."

"You mean, you had expectations?" Rayfe's voice was dry, and I looked over my shoulder at him. "You blithely drink down something decades old of unknown provenance and you had, what? A pretty clear plan for what would occur?"

"You have a point," I agreed weakly. I twisted around and slid my hands into his hair. I kissed him then, long and deep, showing him how I felt, even if I couldn't quite say it. *Never marry a man who doesn't love you.* He wrapped his long fingers around my wrists and gave me that wry half smile.

"What was that for?"

"For not getting in my way. For letting me try it."

"You were right. It's not my place to tell you." His face was serious in the moonlight. "This is your legacy. I brought you into this. The game is yours now."

"Our legacy." I slid my hands down and laced my fingers with his. "I was always a part of this. I just didn't know it. And so are you."

"I am honored to have such a worthy partner by my side for the battles ahead."

"Moranu!" I jumped up, appalled that I'd forgotten. That I hadn't said something immediately.

"What?" He stood in a fluid movement, tossing his hair back over his shoulder and scanning the walls.

"A vision. Oh, Rayfe—I saw—"

My throat closed on it. My sister. My sister's husband, who tried so hard to protect me. Uorsin's armies advancing. I searched Rayfe's face, the dark shadows in the sharp planes of it. What would he do if I told him they thought to bring an army to Annfwn? Salena had sacrificed her life to guide Uorsin away. What lengths would Rayfe go to in protecting this precious place? The image of him, dead in the snow, a spreading circle of crimson bleeding out around him, chilled my stomach and sickened me.

"Tell me, Andromeda." Rayfe studied me, keen eyed as the falcon. I remembered that first time he came into my bedchamber and asked me to pull the blade from his heart. *Only you can do this.*

This wasn't about loyalty. I could see that now. My father commanded loyalty at the point of a sword. Maybe at the cost of my mother's life. Ursula and Amelia—they hadn't seen what I'd seen. Loyalty is blind. Judgment is clear-eyed.

"My father plans to attack Annfwn. Even now, Ursula is amassing an army, below the pass." I closed my mouth over the rest.

"I know."

I gaped at him. "You know? What do you mean, you know?"

"Did you think Ursula's troops would pursue us only to the border and then go home?" Irritation creased his brow and his hand passed over one hip, reaching for the sword he wasn't wearing, I realized.

"Yes. I thought that, once I was safely here, then perhaps she—"

"But this isn't her war, is it, Andromeda? She's not making the calls."

"I need to meet with them. Go meet with Uorsin and convince him—"

He went deadly still. "I thought you promised that you wouldn't leave."

"I'm not!" An image of a tiny Amelia stamping her foot jumped to mind. I resisted the impulse. "But I have to stop him. Turn him back!"

"Like Salena did?" He growled the accusation. "Would you sacrifice yourself and go with him, serve him as she did, help him keep his grip on his ill-gotten empire? Leave Annfwn to waste away?"

"How did she do such a thing? By calling in the Tala soldiers? And he seems to have held the Twelve Kingdoms together just fine since she died."

"Has he? Look around you, Andromeda! His grip crumbles by the year, by the month and day. Your people are starving and it grows worse every year. Surely even in your ivory tower you heard about the unrest, the new castles and fortifications."

I felt a little weak. "Ursula always said I didn't pay enough attention to politics."

"Hey." Rayfe brushed the hair off my forehead. "It's not politics you didn't pay attention to. You believed in them and trusted that they protected you. That Uorsin holds the Twelve Kingdoms in peace, love, and harmony, enjoying Glorianna's grand benedictions. Isn't that what they always told you?"

I swallowed against the dryness in my throat. It was true.

"You and I did not start this war." Rayfe stared over my shoulder, at his own vision, perhaps. "I have always known that Uorsin would come again to Annfwn. Once he knew such a jewel existed, he could never let it go."

"And now he has an excuse to come here."

"No. He doesn't. I'll make sure he knows that."

"Rayfe." I wrapped my fingers in the silk of his shirt. "I can't be the reason for war, for all those deaths. Again. Still. I won't be that. I want to go to him now, talk to him. Whatever it takes."

He pulled me close, kissing me with surprising hunger. "I loved that first about you—this nobility you have. So unlike him."

I stared at him, my heart pounding, unable to process what he was telling me.

"However." He frowned at me. "You may not leave Annfwn. We need you here. And we have the barrier to keep him out."

"But the army—"

He shook his head. "It's nearly dawn. We must sleep for a bit. Then we'll discuss strategy later."

"Rayfe—they are on the other side of the pass. They could be here in hours."

"No, my queen, you're mistaken."

"I *saw* them!"

"Did you? And how do you know what you saw is happening at this moment and not in the future?"

Oh.

"I have scouts watching. Ursula is camped back in the small valley, but Hugh is still amassing his troops and supplies. The generals gather at Ordnung. We have time yet."

"So I only saw what might happen?" I seized on this. I could stop it. He wouldn't be dead in the snow. I wouldn't let it occur.

"I don't know—this is not a common gift. Have you had visions that did not come true?"

I thought of Windroven, the rocky slopes covered in blood and bodies. That hadn't come to pass. Never like that.

"Would you really have slaughtered everyone defending Windroven to get to me?"

"Is that what you saw?"

I shivered. "Yes."

He shrugged a shoulder, not meeting my gaze. "Then I likely would have. I warned you that I am capable of a great deal. Especially when it comes to you. And Annfwn."

"And to Uorsin," I whispered.

His jaw clenched. "Yes."

I bent to gather up the doll, gently wrapping her in the silk again.

"I understand if that's not something you can stomach about me." His voice and face were completely neutral. No sign of the young man in him who had felt so alone. Still, I somehow knew he was in there. I took his hand.

"I'm learning that there are many shades of gray in life. Mine has always been the middle path, neither here nor there. You're part of that, Rayfe. I think you always will be. Just promise me that, when the time to fight comes, you'll tell me."

"I will make sure you know," he promised, and distracted me with a kiss.

22

For once, I awoke before he did.

Not surprising, because I think he paced for much of what remained of the night and into some of the morning. I fell asleep the moment my head hit the pillow. I barely saw anything of the bedchamber Rayfe led me to, the one between our suites of sitting rooms, accessed by both, that we would share. From time to time, I surfaced from deep sleep to see his silhouette by the window, gazing out into the early dark or the pearly dawn.

"Rayfe?" I asked once, fighting past the cobwebs of slumber.

He turned and shushed me, brushing the hair from my forehead and urging me back to sleep. Which really took no urging. When he finally came to bed, curling his body around mine under the light sheet, I sighed and murmured, "Good," and he kissed the back of my neck.

So when I awoke in late morning, I lay still, so as not to bother him. He snored a bit, something that amused me, from this remote and cool man. A man who only seemed cool and remote on the surface, I was learning. I savored this intimacy with him, the parts only I could see.

Now I noticed the enormous four-poster bed, carved from

polished stone. The ceiling, inlaid with a mosaic tile, arched over-head. In the design, fish swam in aqua water, brilliantly colored and exotic, like nothing I'd ever seen. I wondered if the artist had shifted into a fish, to see such creatures. As I watched, the tiles seemed to swirl and change, showing another underwater scene. More magic. I could have watched it for hours.

Unfortunately, I had to answer the urgent call of nature, so I slowly extricated myself from Rayfe's embrace. He grunted, reaching for me, found the pillow instead, and subsided back into sleep, long black strands of his hair snarled over his face, so much softer in repose.

My heart sighed.

In the dressing room, I brushed out my hair and sang softly to myself.

Under the waves, under the sea,
The currents carry your heart to me.

Not really a love song, with the ominous lines about scars and corpses, but somehow it felt like one. Appropriate for Rayfe and me, a thought that made me smile. And then I realized that envy of Amelia that I'd carried for so long had somehow faded away. She and Hugh belonged in their world, of true love, adulation, poetry, and crowds tossing roses. I'd found my own place.

Today would be for strategy. And for meeting more people—taking my role in this place. I poked through the closet of flowing dresses, looking for something more . . . queenly. I chose one of ruby red because it made me feel powerful.

When I emerged, Rayfe was sitting up in bed, bare chested and heart-stoppingly seductive. He raked the tangled hair back from his face and assessed me.

"Don't you look fresh and lovely this morning. And—dressed up?"

"Too much? I thought there might be court. Or courtlike things. Do you do court here?"

He grinned at me. "Yes. We do courtlike things here. I think the dress is perfect. And you left your hair down."

Self-consciously I smoothed a hand over the long fall. "Too informal? Should I put it up? Normally I would, but I don't have anyone here to help me with it. I could braid it, though, and—"

"Andromeda." He climbed out of the big bed and stalked toward me, gloriously naked and male. "Relax. You look perfect. They will love you."

He lifted my chin and gave me a brief kiss, then moved past to his own rooms.

"That's not true," I felt compelled to remind him. "Many of your people are not happy that I'm here, a foreign princess foisted upon them. Who maybe is not capable of being queen in truth."

He glanced back over his shoulder. "*Our* people. And remember—you are not foisted upon them. You are Salena's gift to them. One she destroyed herself to give. Keep that in mind."

Those words helped. Though, as the day wore on, I had to remind myself more and more often.

"Court," as I suspected, looked nothing like Ordnung's throne room. No looming throne dominated the room, no fastidiously dressed ladies hovered. Instead, all public meetings took place in an open-air pavilion that overlooked the sea. Comfortable benches and small sitting areas were scattered throughout. Rayfe led me to a pair of chairs behind a desk piled high with various scrolls and papers.

Terin, who had been sitting there, stood as we approached and scowled at me. "You missed the morning sessions."

"We were busy." Rayfe stared him down. "Is there a problem?"

Terin gestured at the piles. "I've answered all the queries after those who are yet unable to come home. What remains is only all the business of Annfwn that you've let slide all this time that you've pursued your . . . quest." His foxy eyes slid to me and away again.

"Good day, Uncle," I said. "I'm feeling quite well. And yourself?"

He flicked his gaze to me, now looking me up and down. "Good day to you, Salena's daughter. Do you think to fill her shoes along with her rooms?"

"I hope to one day become someone she would have been proud of, yes."

Grudgingly he nodded, but he turned to showing Rayfe which knotty problems he'd been able to work through and which he'd set aside for consideration. They conferred, Terin nodding to various waiting groups and summarizing their petitions.

"Later this afternoon," Rayfe told him finally, "we'll meet in the inside rooms, to discuss next steps. I know everyone just arrived home, but I'll need all the higher officers."

Terin glanced at me, raising his eyebrows.

"Andromeda will join us."

"If she doesn't tear us apart," Terin muttered, before striding away.

"Pay him no mind. Now, let's deal with some of these issues."

In truth, he dealt with the issues while I watched—especially since many of the petitioners spoke only the liquid Tala language and only a few were presented in the common tongue used by the Twelve Kingdoms. One of Terin's lieutenants, whom I recognized from the journey, stood by my elbow and translated quietly. Thoughtful of Rayfe, but the multisided conversations were not always easy to follow, regardless.

With a mental sigh, I moved *learn the language* up my list. Right after *learn to shape-shift, rescue the Tala stranded outside the barrier, plug into Annfwn's magic somehow, figure out how to use the visions to good purpose,* and, oh, *stop the greatest warrior in recorded history with the might of Twelve Kingdoms behind him from making Annfwn into the thirteenth.*

All in good time. Rapidly vanishing time. And yet, here we sat, dispensing with what amounted to gripes.

Most of the problems that ascended to Uorsin's attention had involved property disputes and political alliances. Here, those problems seemed to be entirely absent. Most of the thorny problems seemed to do with lineage and, sadly, family arguments. Many of the issues seemed like the sort of thing Ursula or even the lower courts would have decided in the Twelve Kingdoms. But I could see many had waited for Rayfe's particular input.

It seemed beneath him, but I grew to understand.

I watched him handle the problems with the same even-handed wisdom he used with me. He thought differently than I did, but then, I hadn't contemplated these questions much.

On a project involving the carving out of new quarters, apparently quite a ways down the beach, so far down that the proposed residents brought up the distance frequently in their complaints, Rayfe turned to me. I confess I'd fallen into a bit of a dream, contemplating Terin's animosity mixed with how to stop Uorsin, what the barrier might be made of and wondering where I might find Fiona and if she would like running on the sand. The mosaic over my bed came to mind, with all those brilliant fish. If I swam, would I see them? More likely I'd drown.

"In the Twelve Kingdoms," Rayfe asked, "are the property taxes prorated for distance from the population centers?"

He raised an eyebrow at me, and I knew he'd realized I wasn't paying attention. A gleam of challenge also glimmered in his deep-blue eyes. It was on the tip of my tongue to tell him I had no idea, that I'd never paid attention to such things, but I held the remark back.

The Tala making the petition were a small family group of several males and two females, representing a much larger group that hoped to create another set of cliff dwellings. A large-eyed little girl clung to the hand of one of the men, peering at me with that odd combination of admiration and trepidation I remembered feeling for the glamorous court ladies. I smiled at her and she hid her face against the man's leg. The adults studied me with frank curiosity—and a hint of wariness.

Our people.

"Each of the Twelve Kingdoms has its own tax structure." I turned back to Rayfe, calling up memories of court petitions from the lesser kings. "And each then tithes, quite heavily, to the High King." Bitter complaints in the back hallways over that, despite the bowing and scraping before Uorsin. "In most of the kingdoms, the rural folk bear the brunt of taxation, though they often provide it in the form of food or other supplies for the population centers." If they had food, I realized, remembering some of the more specific arguments and Rayfe's caustic comment about people starving in the Twelve Kingdoms.

The petitioners watched me closely, clearly not understanding my words. They flicked anxious gazes to Rayfe, waiting to hear what this foreign queen had said. It occurred to me that a fine method of governing might be to do the opposite of what Uorsin did.

"But I don't think this system works very well."

"No?" Rayfe's face was solemn, but amused interest lightened his eyes.

"Well, that system is in place to sustain an empire. That's not the situation here, is it?"

"True. What, then, do you suggest would be an equitable structure?"

How should I know that? Surely there were people who understood this sort of thing better. Like those very sharp women I'd seen when I arrived, a legal team, Rayfe had called them. "Turn the question over to one of your judicial groups?"

He gave me a little nod and turned to the family, speaking in their language. "So be it. We will send the matter to the judicial group for consideration. Until then, you may continue with your efforts—abiding by Tala building principles, please—at the old level of taxation."

With relieved smiles and gratitude, even directed toward me, the group left and we had a moment alone.

"Your Wild Lands are not nearly so wild as I was led to believe."

"You know far more of Twelve Kingdoms law than you led me to believe."

I flashed a smile at him. "I didn't know that stuff was in my head."

"There's a great deal in your lovely head that you haven't been using, I believe."

I felt my smile fade. Back to this. "I don't know if that's true, Rayfe. I'm not Salena."

"No," he countered, "you're more."

And then another group of petitioners was before us.

Rayfe cut off the hearings by midafternoon, promising the remaining groups overnight lodging in the capital city. It seemed the Tala used "Annfwn" to refer to both this cliff city and the overall kingdom. Dafne would have pronounced it imprecise. The more I picked up, though, the greater the sense of hugely rambling territory formed in my mind.

"Just how big is Annfwn?" I asked Rayfe as he escorted me to a small table on the terrace set with a late lunch. We had the little balcony to ourselves, in a perfect spot in the sun, overlooking the water. People ambled by on the roads set a distance away, looking at us and whispering to one another. A public appearance, then.

Rayfe poured some golden wine into a lovely glass for me, then for himself. "Nobody really knows. We don't perform detailed censuses. No need to count and quantify every citizen." He raised an eyebrow at me, waiting to see if I would rise to his jibe about the ways of the Twelve Kingdoms.

"How big is your army?"

"Didn't you ask me this before?"

"Yes, and as you no doubt recall, you gave me a vague answer."

He shrugged, sitting back and sipping the wine. "Why is it important to you to know?"

I tamped down the impatience. "*Why?* Uorsin is bringing the might of the Twelve Kingdoms down on your heads, and instead of planning, you've been listening to petitions on taxes all afternoon, and here we sit, eating lunch and drinking wine in the sun and—"

"*Our* heads. And I might point out that you are neither eating nor drinking. Here I've gone to such lengths to keep my promise to see you properly fed and you don't even notice."

How he could tease me at this moment, I didn't know, but I set my jaw and dug into what turned out to be a most succulent fish. Rayfe leaned forward and laid his hand over mine, where it rested on the table.

"This is not wasted time, Andromeda. The people need to see you. They need to know you care about their daily troubles. And they need to see us enjoying the treasures of Annfwn. Seeing their king happy will set them at ease. Seeing their queen will give them hope."

He picked up my hand and kissed it. My heart melted at the affection in his deep-blue gaze, and I thought I heard a chorus of sighs. I followed the sound to a nearby balcony that overlooked ours. A trio of young girls hung over the edge, watching us with avid interest. When they saw me look, they burst into giggles and scurried off, talking to each other rapidly.

"Life goes on. The Tala love to enjoy life, more than anything else. I want you to know what it is I'm asking you to help save." Rayfe released my hand and nudged my wineglass toward me. "Relax, my queen. Enjoy."

I did, after all. Rayfe told me entertaining stories, recounting the histories of some of the petitioners we'd heard earlier. More than once he made me laugh, drawing approving smiles from the passersby. I began to see his point. This was not solemn Ordnung, where power and might ruled. This was Annfwn, a warm land of pleasure, magic, and loveliness.

Wherever that vision of Rayfe was, it held snow. Therefore, it could not be Annfwn. All I had to do was keep him from leaving. And keep Uorsin out.

How hard could it be?

23

I, of course, had never attended a war strategy session before. As I sat at Rayfe's side and listened to the debates on troops, defenses, and guerrilla tactics, I fervently wished Ursula could be here to take my place.

It turned out the others shared my impatience to make plans, however. They proposed various strategies—including storming Ordnung again—some sliding suspicious looks in my direction. Rayfe let them spin through their ideas, sitting back and watching. The ideas grew grander and, to my ear, more and more unlikely. When Terin suggested letting Uorsin's army assemble and then surrounding and slaughtering them like rabid sheep—his exact words—I finally stepped in.

"Unless the Tala have a far larger army than I've been led to believe"—I flicked a glance at Rayfe, who watched me with the same equanimity he'd given everyone else—"we cannot withstand a direct conflict with Uorsin's forces."

"*We*, Princess?" Terin hmm'd with fake surprise. "Have you so easily traded sides then?"

"Do you question my loyalty, Uncle?"

"I do, yes." Terin stood and set pointed fingertips on the table, addressing them all. "I would say your loyalty is, at best, not yet tested and, at worst, deeply questionable, given how easily you forsook your family and kingdom for, what? A good rogering? What happens when the next sexy man comes along?"

"Terin," Rayfe growled. I laid a hand on his forearm, the muscles twitching under my touch. He looked surprised but gave me a slight nod. I stood also.

"You say, Uncle"—I used the title deliberately, again—"that my loyalty has not been tested. I would put forth that none of you has faced a test of loyalty such as I have." I surveyed the group around the table, the older generals, the young angry captains, the platinum-haired woman I recognized from the law group who assessed me with keen blue eyes, a priest of Moranu. "I venture that none of you knows what it's like to be born of two enemies, to wed who you were told was a worse enemy, to make a real choice to be loyal to what seems right.

"Have I forsaken my loyalty to my father and my King? Yes. Yes, I have."

They shifted, not meeting my gaze. Except for Rayfe. With his hair pulled tightly back, his face looked all fierce planes and angles, but his eyes held something softer and I wondered if he was remembering last night.

"I don't know what loyalty means to you, but I don't believe it's blind. It's not something you offer and never reconsider. Loyalty, like love, is based on trust and belief. I will always be loyal to my homeland and to the people who live there. There is good and bad, true, but they are worthy of my belief. Rayfe, my husband, has proven himself worthy of my belief. Outside of bed, as well."

Several of the men chuckled at that, and a glimmer of approval lit the woman's eyes. The priest studied me, as if he looked right through me.

"Uorsin means to attack a kingdom that has never done him wrong. He has committed crimes against his people and my family."

"Can you prove these crimes?" The woman from the law council spoke up, her gaze a shrewd challenge.

"In a court of law? I don't know. But in my own heart, where I decide—" I realized I'd clenched my fists and slammed them on the table. In slow consideration, I unfolded them, Rayfe's ring gleaming on my finger. "In my own heart and mind, where I decide my loyalty, Uorsin has lost it. Rayfe has won."

Suddenly weary, I sat. Rayfe's fingers twined with mine under the table.

"A fine speech." Terin hadn't moved. "But what of your sisters, the noble Prince Hugh, whom you so admire—will you turn your back on them so easily? Would you sacrifice them to preserve Annfwn?"

"I don't know." I could give nothing but that honest answer. "If you could have Salena back, with a healthy child, your niece on the throne, would you wish Rayfe away?"

His face flooded with ruby rage. "Don't you dare question my loyalty. I would never take any action that—"

"But you might feel it, wouldn't you, Uncle? Isn't that what you're asking me—to imagine how I might feel if something terrible happened?" I shook my head at him, slow and measured. "No. I refuse to play that game. I am here. I've declared my intention to support Rayfe and protect Annfwn at all costs—for my sake and to honor my mother, who sacrificed her own happiness. As you know better than most, Uncle."

Terin gazed at me, fulminating.

The priest spoke, asking me a question in the Tala language. His tone was gentle, but the challenge in it unmistakable. I glanced helplessly at Rayfe, but the woman from the law council translated.

"Is she even truly one of us? Can she shift, can she speak to the heart, or is her blood too weak?"

"You know full well we do not demand any such thing for citizenship." Rayfe's words cut like a cold blade. The priest understood his words, I could see.

"And you know full well that many of us think we should."

Terin's jaw worked as he spoke. "We have too many part-bloods—that is why the magic grows unstable."

"It's true, though," said the judicial woman, "that our queens must be able to speak to the heart."

The priest spoke to her in Tala and she replied to him in the common language, casting a sideways glance at me.

"Yes, if she cannot shift, she will be of no real help to Annfwn. Not as queen."

"She can shift—I've seen it myself," Rayfe inserted.

"Excellent!" The woman beamed at me. "Then if Princess Andromeda would simply demonstrate for us, we can settle this question and proceed with making her queen in truth."

Two dozen pairs of eyes fixed on me, intent. I forced myself not to quail.

"I would not subject her to such indignity."

"She can't perform on command?" Triumph, tinged with something else—disappointment?—radiated from Terin. "Or perhaps you're not speaking the full truth, King?"

"Are you calling my honor into question?"

"No—your judgment. You wouldn't be the first to be swayed by a pretty face and a comely figure."

Rayfe stood, the wolf growl coming out in his voice. "First you accuse my queen of poor choices for love of my bed; now you question my honor for want of hers?"

"I would put forth," one of the older generals inserted, "that this is not the subject of our meeting, but rather time-sensitive strategy planning."

"This is about strategy," Rayfe replied with strained patience. "Andromeda is key to our defenses."

The general huffed. "Ridiculous. We have you. Have had you lo these many years and all is fine. Salena's time is over. There's no reason a king can't do what our queens have. We don't need this child, pretty though she may be."

Rayfe opened his mouth, black guilt shadowing his face. And I knew he meant to confess his supposed failures to them.

I stood, again laying a hand on Rayfe's arm. "It's all right. Please excuse me, my husband and king. It seems as if the discussions might go more smoothly without my presence. You can stick to the very important subject at hand."

He looked up at me, the harsh lines around his lips softening as he searched my gaze. "You need not go. This is your rightful place."

"Yes," I agreed. "But I have something important to do."

He picked up my hand and kissed it. "I shall fill you in on everything discussed when we meet later, my queen."

In truth, Terin's words ate at me. What would I do if it came down to saving my sisters or Annfwn? I could only hope to Moranu I wouldn't be asked to make such a choice. And it seemed I'd have to prove I could shift. Do it reliably. *Then* find this heart and somehow talk it into doing what I wanted. If I could connect to this magic, maybe all of it would be moot. I could bring the exiled home, keep Uorsin out and Rayfe intact.

I only had to voluntarily turn my skin inside out.

I nearly went to find Fiona, to take that ride on the beach I'd been yearning for. A big part of me wanted to. But that was the old me, riding off instead of tending to things. And now I recognized that much of that urge had been me, looking for a way to Annfwn. I sympathized with all those part-bloods stranded outside in a way that the others couldn't. They didn't know how it felt, to have Annfwn calling and not heed the answer.

Even Uorsin, though he'd given up the dream of following his blood to his ancient homeland, had built his seat as close as he could get.

I made my way up the cliffside, looking for the stone arena. I figured, if you can find your way out of the hills by following the water downwards, then I could find the cliff top by following the roads upwards.

Really, I should have gone back to the house to change clothes, but I wasn't sure exactly which road to take. With a sudden rush of gratitude, I realized Rayfe had left me to my own devices. No attendants, no escort. A subtle vote of confidence that meant more to me than any vows.

I made my way, taking any road or path with an incline. Surely over time I'd build better leg muscles for this. Instead of weaker, I now grew stronger every day. Soon I'd be downright athletic. Here and there people seemed to recognize me, offering polite nods. Mostly they didn't, and for the first time in my life, I was just another woman, walking along, tending to her business. Even my coloring blended with the Tala.

I loved the feeling.

Eventually I saw a young boy bringing a herd of little black-and-white goats down a winding path. The afternoon was declining into evening, so I thought he must be bringing them down from daytime pasture. Sure enough, I soon found the low wall that bordered the plateau and a gate carved with roses.

The arena, though, was filled with children. I heard their voices as I approached, like in the practice yard when the youngest ones came to first swing their blades, raucous and filled with uninhibited joy. I leaned my folded arms on the low stone gate and watched.

A man in soft brown clothes lined up the children, as if to kick a ball in a game. He made them all settle and wait, then yelled what sounded like "Go!" The first child stepped forward and—*snap*—changed into a rabbit and went bounding off, running a rapid circle around the arena, to the back of the line, and popped back into his human shape, slapping hands with his buddies.

One after another they did this, skipping, cantering, and flying about, transforming as easily as the moon rises and sets.

So simple for them.

Some of the children tried on different forms, challenging one another to be a different animal each time. A couple complained to the teacher that the lack of water meant they couldn't be fish.

They all seemed to be using the common tongue, more city children, then, than the rural ones.

"You shouldn't be watching us," a high voice accused. "It's against the rules, you know."

What had been a songbird lighting on the wall next to me was now a little girl with black ringlets.

"Thalia!" The teacher strode over, lifted her, and set her down. "This is Queen Andromeda, and she may do as she wishes."

The girl's rosebud mouth formed an astonished O and she bobbed a curtsy. "My apologies, Queen Anderom . . ."

"Andi," I told her. "Princess Andi is fine. And I've only just arrived, so I don't know all the rules yet. My apologies to you."

"That's okay," she confided. "I don't mind if you watch. Look!" With that, she burst into songbird shape again and flew in giddy circles, singing. The teacher laughed and sent her back to play with the other kids.

"I am sorry," I told him. "Rayfe mentioned this was meant to be a private place. I'll move along."

"No need, my lady," he replied with an easy smile and a light bow. "I'm Zyr. We're cousins, actually. The family is greatly looking forward to meeting you. When things settle down a bit."

Zyr. I recognized that name. "Were you a prisoner at Ordnung till recently?"

He winced. "I did have that pleasure."

"I'm so sorry."

"Why would you apologize?" He looked genuinely puzzled. "I don't recall you turning the key in the lock."

"Yes, but my father—"

"Is a different person."

"Well, and you were all there for me."

"No, we were there for us, for Annfwn. People don't really do things they don't want to do, Queen Andi." He winked at me. "I suspect you have an exaggerated sense of responsibility. No wonder you and Rayfe have hit it off so well."

He laughed, delighted at my blush, and offered me a hand, clasping mine in both of his. "We are so happy for you both. Welcome home, Andromeda. May you flourish here."

Zyr clapped his hands three times, and the teeming circus of animals resolved back into a group of rosy-cheeked and grinning children. "We'll be on our way and you can have the arena."

"Oh, no—I didn't mean for . . ."

I trailed off in the face of his easy grin. He shrugged one shoulder. "They've done well today. Never hurts to have an extra hour's free time, just to play." He rolled the stone away and the kids took off, running down the hill with whoops, not unlike the little goats going home. "Besides, you likely have practicing to do."

"I don't—" I chewed my lip. "I don't really know what I'm doing."

"You saw the kids." Zyr tugged a lock of my hair, the irreverent cousin I'd never known to miss. "Do what comes naturally."

He tucked his hands in his pockets and strolled down the hillside, whistling like Thalia's little songbird.

I walked myself to the center of the arena. The moon hadn't risen yet and the sun still shone warm and golden on the sea. That hadn't mattered to the children, though. Nor had their clothes. Still, to be safe, I set my ring and necklace to the side.

That could have been me. It could have been all three of us, growing up here in this lovely, magical place, playing games and shifting from one creature to the next. Amelia would have loved it. Even Ursula, with her love of contests, would have excelled at this. Surely they had the possibility of this gift as much as I? I might have the mark that supposedly meant I could talk to this heart, but other Tala couldn't and they could still shift. Given the right circumstances—and our mother's blood—perhaps they, too, could learn. I could teach them so they could know the joy of it.

Joy. Not fear.

Fun.

Do what comes naturally.

Enjoy, Rayfe had said, flashing that devastating smile.

So I did. I thought of riding Fiona, the wind streaming through my hair, the pounding of her muscles that I knew as well as my own.

And I was her. My great heart pumped and I took off, playing like the children, racing as fast as I could around the perimeter of the arena, my sharp hooves clattering on the stone. I returned to my spot and let myself resolve back into shape. The red dress looked only a little tattered.

I did it.

The pleasure of the discovery boiled through me, and I wrapped my arms around myself, throwing my head back to laugh. This was my mother's gift. The gift of my people.

And I knew she was proud of me.

24

I found my way back to the house fairly easily from this direction, still giddy with success. I'd managed to become the horse and the big cat several times. The predator's mind still shook me a bit, but I was becoming more used to it. Perhaps tomorrow, I could take Fiona to the beach and run with her.

My suite of rooms stood empty, as did our shared bedroom. I hesitated before the closed door leading to Rayfe's rooms, uncertain of the protocol. Did I knock? Maybe he wasn't even back yet. And my news would keep. In some ways, I liked keeping it to myself for a little while longer. My secret joy.

A tray of food and wine had been left for me by some thoughtful person, so I took it out on my balcony and sat with my bare feet propped up on the balustrade and watched the last of the light fade from the sky. I had lost my slippers during one of the shifts—oops—so I was glad to have retrieved my jewelry from its safe spot. The tropical night caressed my skin and the wine was delicious. The Tala really had a point with this "enjoying life" stuff.

"Andromeda?"

"Out here, Garland!"

My welcoming smile faded in the face of her grim expression. I set my feet and my wineglass down. "What's wrong?"

"Rayfe sent a message. Hugh's troops have entered the valley and joined with Ursula's. He's riding out with a guerrilla force to stop them from reaching the entrance to the pass."

The blood fell out of my head and I saw him, lying in the snow, the blood radiating out in a scarlet halo, his dark-blue eyes glassy and sightless. Like a familiar aching tooth, it stabbed at me, and I let the pain in, let it fade away again.

My private nightmare had arrived.

While I recovered myself, I noticed the way Garland wrung her hands. She wasn't worried for Rayfe. Garland was afraid of what I would do.

"Why worry about the entrance to the pass? Let the barrier stop them."

She looked more ashen, if possible. "Part-bloods have been streaming in all day. The barrier has fallen."

"What? Why?"

"We think—it could be because you're inside and the heart hasn't received further instructions. But it might hear you at any time, so Rayfe wants you safe here."

"Did he leave any particular instructions for me?" I asked, trying to sound calm, but my emotions frayed beneath it.

"He asked that you remain here, to guard the city."

"Should I embroider something, perhaps? Make him a sigil to wear into glorious battle? Or maybe I should just stand on the balcony and yell at the heart to put the barrier back up."

"Andromeda." Her blue eyes glinted like Rayfe's when she became angry. "What if you went out and couldn't get back in? All of our sacrifices would be for naught."

"Salena left," I pointed out. "And you're all still here."

"But Salena—"

"She gave me a message for you."

That set her aback. Her face hardened. "I don't appreciate you taking advantage of my confidences by—"

I shook my head, the hair slapping around my face. Frustrated, I yanked it back, weaving it into a single braid down my back. I already knew what I would do.

"I found a—a kind of spell. A message she left for me. I talked to her, Garland."

"Even Salena didn't know how to do that."

"Then she learned." *And where did she learn that?* I wondered. "She asked me to tell you she thought of you every day. She kept some seashell."

Garland paled. "You know about the seashell?"

I finished my braid and went to the dressing room to find something to tie it off with. "No. I never saw it. She said you would know what she meant."

"I do."

"She said she wished your son the best. Wished him to live up to his early promise, which we can all see he has. She hoped you had more children and regretted we didn't all grow up together. Though, seeing as how things worked out, that might have been for the best."

I surveyed the closet for something to ride in and wondered where in the name of Moranu my fighting leathers had gone to. A little halting sound caught my attention, and I saw Garland had tears streaming down her face.

"Oh, Garland, I'm sorry. That was thoughtless." My anger at Rayfe's high-handedness had blinded me. Like Uorsin storming through Ordnung in a rage. *Better watch that in yourself.* I stepped toward her and she held up a hand to stop me, turned toward the mirror to clean up her face.

"It was long ago. Funny how these old sorrows seal over and you're fine until something breaks them open—and you feel it fresh all over again. You're right, Andromeda." She started rifling through the drawers. "It's good you and Rayfe did not grow up together. Meant, perhaps, even if Salena didn't foresee it. Or maybe she did."

She handed me a stack of neatly folded leather—all black. "I didn't think you'd need these so soon, but here."

I examined the leathers, modeled after my others, but new and matching Rayfe's. I raised questioning brows at Garland. She shrugged.

"Salena left for a reason. You are who you are—as much a child of that one as this. Who am I to stand in the way of that?"

I tossed the leathers down and hugged her. "Thank you," I whispered in her ear. "Your blessing means a great deal."

"Just—please, be careful." She mock-frowned at me. "I've only barely gotten to know you. I'd like to know more. And no matter what you think, we need you. More, we want you here."

"Thank you." I smiled at her, my lips feeling trembly. Some warrior I was making. "Now, do you have any idea how I can get the barrier back up? How do I communicate with it?"

A line appeared between her brows. "If Salena went to lengths to leave you a message, didn't she say? I always understood it to be a secret passed from mother to daughter."

"Of course she didn't say—that would have been too easy." My frustration came out in the bitter tone. Feeling this pressure did not help. I flopped on the bed and took a deep breath, letting the swimming fish in the mosaic above soothe me. What was I missing?

"Knowing my people—and our queens—it would not be easy. Likely there's a series of tests involved. Maybe there's a clue in something she said?"

Trust the animal within. That is the first and that is the heart. She had mentioned the heart then. Right after she showed me the animals.

And the fish.

Staring up at the image above, I felt the first stirrings of triumph.

Thank you, Mother.

Garland showed me the path to the beach, with raised eyebrows at the request, but no comment. We wended down and down and down, until my booted heels sank in the soft sand of the shimmering beach, impossibly white under the round moon. The song—the one that first propelled me to the fateful meeting with Rayfe—ran into my head.

Under the waves, under the water
All the days of his life he sought her.
Mermaids danced in blue coral ballrooms
While she watched from the dark of the sea.

I should have known all along. I wondered who watched from the dark of the sea. I supposed I was about to find out.

"You can leave your things here, if you wish," Garland told me. "I'll wait for you."

I eyed the water dubiously, having never learned to swim. "Should I strip down and swim? I don't want to be a fish onshore, right?"

She laughed. "Unless you're already good at changing size, too, that might be a good idea. A you-sized fish would be difficult to push into the water."

Not willing to risk my weapons or new leathers—especially if it meant more delays in getting to Rayfe's side—I stripped down while Garland politely averted her eyes. I braced myself, tiptoeing into the water, but this was no bracing mountain lake. This sea welcomed me like a warm bath.

Okay, big test, Andi. I tried to focus on that sense of joy and play. If only I had more time. But we were out of time. Rayfe, dead in the snow, the crimson blood . . . *Stop it.*

"It might be too soon," Garland said, quiet, without censure. "You don't have to try this yet."

She didn't know what I saw for her son. I wondered how she'd withstand the loss of him, too. It would not happen. I could not let it happen.

"I can do this." I said it as much for myself as for her.

Then I did. I felt my blood swim, as if tiny guppies were traveling through my veins like the birds before, and my skin change.

I gasped for breath, flopping against the sand as a wave retreated. I hadn't been deep enough, and I was too big, stranded above the surf. Then Garland waded in and shoved at me while another wave swamped over—and sweet water filled my gills. I plunged into the returning waves.

And entered, for the first time, the foreign undersea world.

I perceived it with my whole body, it seemed. Not seeing it so much as feeling the infinite shades of seaweed forests, the millions of coral creatures and swarms of other fish, gliding by. All in scintillating, variegated detail. I could feel the barrier reef farther out and tasted the cold winter sea battering at the other side of it. Not that way.

Knowing no other direction, I swam down.

I passed wonders I'd never guessed at. The unknown artist who'd made the mosaic over my marriage bed had surely been here. I wondered if it had been Salena herself, though no one mentioned art as one of her talents. Colors were the same and not. Cobalt became a smell, orange a sound like a bell. Magic shimmered through it all, as if I passed through it in condensed form.

I swam deeper.

The waters cooled and darkened. *Deep, frozen waters.* I felt like I couldn't breathe as well, my gills straining. Fear sickened me as the water pressed hard, crushing me in its fist. But that image of Rayfe, of Uorsin's army pouring over Annfwn, drove me on.

Likely there's a series of tests involved.

A large shadow, outlined in pinpoint phosphorescence, drifted past with ponderous ease. Adjusting my shape, I became that and breathed easier. And went deeper.

Finally, below me, a glow shimmered. It smelled of emerald and sounded like sugared berries. I headed for it and the pressure around me lessened. Warmed water surged through my gills. A golden wall held in the glow. I bumped my fishy nose against it and it gave slightly.

I pushed more. It sizzled like snowflakes on hot skin and I remembered Rayfe kissing me as the snow fell around us on our wedding day. Such a short time to grow to love so much.

I threw myself into the barrier, wriggling through it, feeling the sticky mucus of its song strip away my fish body until I popped through, once again my human self, into a bubble of warm air with nothing inside but a simple chair.

No one waited for me.

I'd hoped there might be some sort of guidance at this point, but apparently I was on my own. Yet another test. So be it, then.

Outside the barrier, the water looked opaque, no longer teeming with all my fish self had perceived. No moonlight made its way down this deep.

I shivered, realizing I was the one watching from the dark of the sea.

Spinning around, I went to the chair and sat. It was made of something pink and polished smooth, cupping my naked behind with surprising comfort. My palms rested naturally on the arms. I let my head fall back and I stared up at the deep black water surrounding me. My mother had sat here, and my ancestresses before her. What had they done?

Then I saw them. What I hadn't before.

Thousands of crabs crawled over the outside of the globe, the gold light catching the deep blue of their shells. They crowded in, watching me. Waiting.

Listening.

Understanding at last, I spoke to them. There, in the heart of Annfwn's magic.

I rode Fiona out of the city, through the dark before dawn, while Moranu's moon dropped behind me, lighting my way.

Rayfe's long dagger lay across the saddle before me, while my own sat at my hip. I'd tied the fur cloak Rayfe had given me on our wedding day to the back of the saddle. No doubt the winter chill of Mohraya would bite that much more now.

"This is beginning to feel like a thing for me," I remarked to Fiona, and she twitched her ears back at me. I paused a moment before entering the grassy meadow, for a last look at the lovely sea with the white-sand beach so bright in the moonlight, the dark waters quiet, giving no hint of the world that flourished beneath. I wondered if I'd ever see it again. Forever in my mother's footsteps, here I might also be leaving Annfwn forever, if that's what it took to keep Uorsin out.

I thought I'd reestablished the barrier, the outer echo of the dome beneath the sea that the crabs so diligently maintained. But I wouldn't know for sure until I got there.

A thrice-damned way to test something so important.

"At least we got to see it, eh, Fiona? And we'll tell them all it was full of untamed forests and wild beasts. Demons and black magic."

I knew the tree spies saw me when I entered the woods and started up the pass. They kindly let me know, I felt sure, so loud were their chains of calls, echoing through the treetops. It took me all night, but I finally arrived at Rayfe's camp at the lake right at daybreak. He was waiting for me, face stark in the harsh light of the rising sun.

My heart quailed, but my resolve didn't. At least he wasn't dead in the snow. Yet. He held up a hand to help me down, and I took it. He held on, pulling me very close to his armored chest, staring into my eyes without saying a thing.

"I figured out how to shift," I told him, just as I'd been planning to last night when I came back to our rooms, so full of giddy joy. And he'd already been riding out to meet my family in battle. It came out sounding like an accusation.

A half smile lit his grim expression. "I never doubted you would."

"I know. And yet you broke your promise to me."

His smiled faded. "I know. I don't know what to say to you."

"You can apologize."

"But I'm not sorry," he explained. "I wish you'd stayed in Annfwn. This can't turn out well."

"It's my story, too. Including the tragic ending."

He cupped my face with his hands. "Does our ending have to be tragic? I could have been happy, knowing you were in Annfwn, caring for our people, enjoying your life. That you would maybe someday find your way to being queen and hold the land safe for me."

"How would that have happened with the barrier down?"

He blanched. "Who told you?" Then he clenched his jaw. "My mother. Of course."

"She only told me what you should have."

"As if you needed more pressure!" he shot back. "I'd put you through enough. Learning to shift is amazing, but it's not enough. You have to find the heart, and I don't know where to tell you to begin to look. You'd think Salena would have mentioned *that* in her message."

"She did." I held up my hands and showed him the raw wounds where the crabs had tasted of my flesh, my blood. "It just took me a while to understand."

In horror, he stroked a shaking finger over my skin, then stared into my eyes. "What happened—where did you get these wounds?"

"Family secret." I grinned at him, profoundly feeling that sense of connection to my mother and the women before her. As if I'd finally come home. "But I found the heart and I restored the barrier. I hope."

His dark-blue eyes lit with fierce joy, his shoulders straightening as if a great burden had been lifted from them.

"You did it," he breathed. "I always knew it."

"I don't know how this ends." I closed down the image of him, bleeding out in the snow. It would not happen. "I know that it should be with us together. My mother didn't make the choices she did so I could hide away in paradise. Besides, I have to test the barrier. I have to go with you." *Just in case.*

"What shall I do with you, Andromeda, with all your insane and fierce certainty?"

"You could love me." I offered it softly, with a wisp of delicate hope.

"I do, my queen. I love you beyond need or reason." He kissed me then, pulling me in tight and slanting his hot mouth over mine, tasting of man and sleep and desire.

"I love you, too." I grinned at him. "Now, where is breakfast?"

25

The battle—that final battle at Odfell's Pass—took place the following morning. You all know what the minstrels tell of that day. What actually occurred is somewhat different, which should come as no surprise to any of you by now.

History is written by the victors, yes. But whoever tells their version to the most people has an advantage also.

We spent the day waiting, as I've learned soldiers spend most of their time doing. More and more Tala men joined us through the day, but the force still seemed pitifully small to me. No one else seemed to be coming through from the other side, which heartened me that the barrier might be working. Though I warned them that I hadn't mastered the ways of the heart yet and they might not be able to come back through, they went when Rayfe sent them into winter again, in small groups, to hide themselves along the route. It moved me, their willingness to trust in the magic and to defend Annfwn.

And I fretted, wishing I'd had more time to study the wall. Rayfe wouldn't let me go near it yet, not without the bulk of his force going with us.

Terin thought Ursula and Hugh would wait for Uorsin's massive armies to arrive, and Rayfe agreed to abide by his judgment.

I knew he was wrong. Ursula is one of the finest strategists I've seen. She would see immediately that no one would be dragging the massed armies of the Twelve Kingdoms up the narrow pass. She had her Hawks. With Hugh's picked men and her highly trained crew, she'd know they could take on at least three times their number, if not more.

More, she would want to please our father.

She would think to rescue me and bring me back to Ordnung in triumph. She had no idea Uorsin wanted Annfwn far more than he wanted me—unless he thought I'd be his ticket in. Had that been his plan all along, or had he simply wanted to best Salena in the end?

That didn't matter now. What did was that Ursula would lead her Hawks up the pass to rescue me and Hugh would join her. Between his reckless bravery and her keen mind, they could make it at least to the barrier.

Which would hopefully hold.

"I want you to let me parley with Ursula," I told Rayfe.

This time he listened. "No good can come of it." But he sounded less certain.

"I'm asking you to trust me."

He smiled and lifted my hand, kissing the back, and then my wounded palm. He opened his mouth to say something I never got to hear.

At that moment, word came of battle.

The wolfhound scout raced into our camp, snapped into human form, gasped out the message, and left as fast as he'd arrived. It galvanized them all. The quiet camp broke into a blizzard of activity, men becoming horses, wolves, panthers, and raptors, others in human shape still, weapons flashing.

As we neared the barrier—where it should be—the effects of its fall became apparent. Winter had poured in, freezing the grasses and flowers several lengths in. Fortunately, it looked to have been like a slow leak and not a bubble popping. I shivered, thinking of what could have happened, had it been that way, then I realized cold air still flowed in. An actual snowflake kissed my nose. The cold sting of it sent dread roiling through my gut. I grabbed Rayfe's arm and he looked down at me, initially annoyed at the interruption, then his sharp gaze softened with concern. He caressed my cheek with a gloved finger.

"Don't worry."

"The wall isn't right yet. It's still leaking."

"Can you work on it from here, now that you know?"

"Maybe. I'll try."

"You stay here and do that, then." He fastened his cloak, and with the snowy pass behind him, he looked like he had in my visions.

"Don't go. Please. I'm begging you not to go."

"Andromeda, my love. I have to. I can't send them to fight without me."

I wanted to kick him. Him and his exaggerated sense of responsibility.

I knew then there was no stopping this. The arousal in his gaze was for the fight as much as anything. This was also him. The relaxed man enjoying the wine and the tropical breeze. The fierce warrior spoiling to take out his enemies.

I'll understand if you can't stomach this side of me.

I stood on tiptoe and wound my arms behind his neck, kissing him with all the hopeful longing that swirled inside me.

"Then I'm going with you. No." I held up a hand to stop his words. "If you try to stop me, I'll just follow again. Better to keep me with you."

Instead of arguing, he kissed me, holding me tightly. "You are always with me, Andromeda, whether you know it or not."

Terin cleared his throat behind us. Rayfe squeezed my waist and gave me a little scoot toward Fiona. The moon was nowhere to be seen, but I sent a fierce prayer to Moranu to safeguard him.

We rode fast, galloping at a precarious pace to the bend Terin had picked to make an initial stand. I remembered the spot from the ride up, the huge boulders, the narrow opening.

Hugh and Ursula were ascending with a point formation, well shielded with spears and swords. They'd been taking out the Tala along the way with poisoned arrows—man and animal alike. I tried not to picture their broken bodies littering the pretty forested path. Instead, riding at Rayfe's left side, I concentrated on seeing him live through the day.

The snow grew deeper as we descended, making the way treacherous and slick. The cold ate its way into my bones, my blood already thinned by Annfwn's gentle warmth. The sight of the snow piling ever higher into drifts ate into my hopefulness. I wished I hadn't so carelessly referred to tragic endings.

I couldn't bear to think of what would become of me. I knew one thing: I would not spend the rest of my life sitting next to an empty chair.

When we passed through the barrier, in my mind, the crabs scuttled, using my blood magic to reinforce the shield. I wanted it to be as strong as possible, keeping the world out. For now. It crackled like a live thing against my skin, and I fancied I smelled emerald and heard sugared berries.

We heard them coming. The clatter of metal, the hoarse cries of pain and death, harsh sounds in the snow-muffled woods. Rayfe spread the troops around us, many shifting to take positions in the high rocks and tall trees. He positioned himself in the center of the trail, just this side of the densest guard, and tucked me behind him.

We waited.

Snow fell on Rayfe's hair, turning the black to ash. I held his long dagger in my hand, my fingers growing numb, my heart icing over with resolve.

The crashing approach grew louder, a cacophony that shredded my nerves, until I wanted to shriek at them to stop.

They did.

At this spot, they would have to come nearly single file around the corner. A narrow passage bristling with the spears and swords of the Tala holding it.

Silence fell, more deafening than the noise.

Rayfe rode forward. I followed. No one stopped me.

"Turn back," Rayfe commanded in a shout. I couldn't see past his wide cloaked shoulders. "Though I count you as family now, you trespass uninvited here."

"I demand the return of my sister, Princess Andi." Ursula's voice sliced through the cold air like the taste of metal. "Or I seek revenge, if you cannot show me she is well."

"Queen Andromeda is more than well. She flourishes. More than she did in that mossback tomb you call Ordnung." Rayfe bit out the retort with surprising venom.

"Brave words from a kidnapper, blackmailer, and demon." Hugh's voice carried over the angry mutters of the men.

Oh, for Moranu's sake. Squeezing Fiona with my knees, I urged her past Rayfe's stallion, shouldering him aside. She's a strong and wily little mare.

There, on the other side of the weapon-lined gauntlet, was Ursula. I caught my breath at the sight of her. The weeks had worn the last of any girlishness from her cheeks. Her steely eyes, full of worry, looked luminous in her carved face, her auburn hair pulled ruthlessly back—or cut short—under her helmet. She looked like the statue of Danu come to life. Like a goddess of vengeance.

"Here I am, Ursula. Prince Hugh. As you can see—I'm fine."

Relief flooded Ursula's face, and my heart cramped to see how she'd suffered. She'd truly feared for me.

"I do flourish here." I tried to let her see my sincerity through the lacing of weapons separating us. "I'm happy." I laid a hand over Rayfe's, fisted on his thigh. "I love him."

Ursula's gaze flicked to Rayfe, scorn whittling the softer emotions from her face. "You're not in love, Andi. You've been brainwashed. Not even Amelia would say something so foolish."

Hugh stiffened at that, and I wondered at Ursula's carelessness. Seething tension made her shoulders into high, sharp lines—I could see it from this distance—and her horse shifted restively beneath her.

"Believe me or not. It's nevertheless true. And you have no business attacking my home and my people."

Both of their faces blanked at that, she and Hugh seemingly unable to understand what I'd said to them. Rayfe loosened his fist slightly, just enough to squeeze the tips of my fingers.

"Andi." Hugh gave me his best, most charming smile, as if to coax a child forward with a sweet. "Your home is here, on this side of the pass. Come home with us and we shall sort this all out."

"If I do, will Uorsin withdraw his armies? Leave the Wild Lands and Annfwn in peace forever?"

Rayfe's fingers crushed mine at that, but I didn't wince. I spoke to Ursula and her alone. She met my gaze with a steady, steely glare, one I'd seen many times in the practice yard. This time, I wouldn't back down from it. A subtle flick of her eyes, a bit down, a hint of shame. Oh, she knew what Uorsin wanted. What he'd always wanted.

Everything.

"We will establish a military presence on the pass." She said it steadily, as if this wasn't a declaration of war, speaking only to Rayfe. She'd dismissed me from the conversation. "I will accompany you into Annfwn to see for myself how my sister fares."

"Impossible," Rayfe returned. "Outsiders are not permitted. Andromeda speaks highly of you, Princess Ursula. But I wonder what kind of fool believes I'd allow you to hold this pass."

Her fine lips twitched at that—amusement or irritation, I wasn't sure.

"You and the Tala have no choice, Rayfe. We are family now. Your father-in-law expects concessions—and his due as your High King. In return you'll receive the full protection of the Twelve Kingdoms."

"Ursula! You cannot expect—" The words burst out of me, and she cut me off with a slashing gesture.

"You stay out of this, Andi. Your loyalty is already suspect, and since when do you care about politics? Either you come home with us or we come into Annfwn. Clearly you cannot take care of yourself, so I intend to do it for you."

My cheeks blazed hot in the freezing air. The snow falling harder now, the chill moving from my bones to my blood. I never imagined she thought so little of me.

Hugh nudged his horse forward, holding up his hands, palm out, in peaceful nobility even as all the weapons pricked toward him, like an enraged porcupine.

"Amelia sends her love, Andi. Your rooms await at Windroven. She bids me tell you she's with child and begs you to attend her at this time."

The news thudded into my heart like a second arrow. Amelia having a baby. A child who would carry Tala blood. Salena's blood. I risked a glance at Rayfe to find him watching me. With a barely perceptible nod, he told me we would have to address that. Yet another reason to survive this day.

"You must give Amelia my regrets. I cannot come to her at this time." I watched Hugh's face crease with incredulity. "I have responsibilities here—especially during this time of unrest."

"After all we did for you?" Hugh's face flushed to a dangerous red. "After I sacrificed my people for you, to protect you from this . . . *demon*?" He drew his sword, and it was like a harp string plucked hard and discordant. The tension ratcheted up, and time began to slip through my fingers like so much seawater.

"Stand down, Hugh!" Ursula ordered, a steel-edged shout that didn't make the least impact on him.

"I won't return to my beloved Amelia to tell her that not only is her sister wed to an oath breaker, but she has turned her back on Glorianna, her family, and her homeland! I'll die first!"

Every moment is etched like shards of ice in my mind. The wild glint in Hugh's noble blue eyes, the way his golden hair caught even the dim light. The bloodred flash of the rubies on his mirror-bright armor as he lunged forward, sword aimed at Rayfe's unprotected breast.

Just as I had seen.

Only you can save me.

Fiona, smooth as silk beneath me, like an extension of myself, responded to my thought. She lunged forward, placing me between the point of Hugh's sword and Rayfe. I heard him scream, part raptor cry, part wolf howl, a man pushed to the farthest edge of reason.

I'll never forget the sound.

Or Ursula, with her perfect skill and speed, pivoting like a dancer on horseback and slicing Hugh's throat from ear to ear.

Her blade stopped his forward momentum as it bit into his spine, yanking him back off the horse and into the snow. His astonished blue eyes, as blue as the summer sky he'd never see again, stared sightlessly upwards, while the snow stained crimson in an ever-widening circle.

26

Ursula and I fell off our horses and onto our knees into the deep snow. Between us, we bracketed Hugh. She plunged her bare hands into his rent throat, as if to hold his lifeblood in by sheer force of will. Tears ran down her face, unheeded.

I held his hand as the last bit of brilliance left his face.

Dimly I became aware that fighting had begun and abruptly ended. I couldn't think about that. It seemed all I could do to track the slowing thud of my heart, to gaze on Hugh's lifeless face and grasp that he was dead.

Hugh was dead and Rayfe lived.

And I was frozen inside.

Ursula finally pulled her hands from Hugh's cooling flesh and wrung them together, the blood sticky and covering her to the wrists, like dull red gloves. Her gray eyes lacked all steel; instead they were haunted, ghostlike, the shadows of her skull ringing them in a wide circle of dread.

"What do I do?" she whispered. "Andi—I don't know what to do."

Rayfe dropped down beside me on one knee, his arm around my shoulders. "He was a good man. This is a dark day for us all."

"Not the least of which is that it means all-out war." I kept my voice as low as hers. Images of the days ahead flicked through my mind. Battles and the ravages of internal strife. Avonlidgh turning on Mohraya. Erich gutted at Uorsin's feet and Windroven dismantled. Amelia, weeping over a stillborn child.

No. This could not come to pass.

"You'll tell her I did it," I told Ursula. Yes. That felt right.

She gaped at me, her lips moving without sound. Rayfe squeezed my shoulder, one fierce spasm, but said nothing.

"I can't tell her that. This is my fault."

"You did it to protect me, Ursula." I took her hands in mine, Hugh's blood sticky and cold, as cold as the despair in her eyes. "This was my fault, too. We need you. The Twelve Kingdoms need you. We cannot afford civil war."

"Erich—he will want revenge."

"A revenge he cannot seek. He won't be able to reach me in Annfwn."

"And Amelia. She will believe you killed her one true love."

The thought stabbed through me, the twin arrows of my sisters shredding my heart. "She already believes I betrayed her."

In truth, this seemed fair punishment to me, that Amelia would know I'd deliberately hurt her, even though she'd blame me for the wrong thing. The penance fit my crime.

"How can you be sure it will work?" Ursula turned the thought over. "Passes can be taken. You are not safe just because you're over a meaningless border."

"Not meaningless, Ursula. Come see." I glanced back at her over my shoulder. "Bring a witness or two."

Rayfe raised a black, winged eyebrow at me but followed my wishes. My heart warmed at that, more than if he'd offered me a bouquet of hothouse flowers.

Ursula followed me with the same perfect trust, three of her key troop leaders following. I stepped past the veil, hoping I could, speaking to the crabs.

Pray Moranu this worked.

"Cross this meaningless border, Ursula."

With a wry twist of her lips, clearly humoring me, she stepped forward. And was stopped.

Wonder and shock twisted the faces of Ursula and her Hawks. Rayfe's hand landed on my shoulder in a fierce grip that shouted of his feelings more than any words could.

"You cannot, unless I allow it," I told my older sister. Hopefully I'd get that much control over it, to let in who we wanted to.

She looked at me then, as if seeing me for the first time.

I pushed my advantage. "Ursula—to protect me, you cannot let Uorsin pursue his plans. You must say that you were defeated. You could not take the pass. No one can."

She studied me, the lost look transforming slowly back into her usual keen stare.

"Without magic involved, I could have taken the pass. And held it." Her pride stiffened her slumped shoulders.

"No, you couldn't," Rayfe and I said on the same breath. A little laugh escaped me, and I looked up at him, at the half smile lifting his lips for me.

Ursula looked back and forth between us. "Perhaps you two are suited."

She stood, scrubbing the blood off on her thighs, looking back down the trail at Hugh's corpse, regret and grief lining her face.

"I suppose my penance shall be taking him back to her. Giving her the news myself."

"Help her, Ursula. Don't let her lose the baby."

She raised an eyebrow. "That was a lie, Andi. Hugh thought it might persuade you if you were too deeply"—she glanced at Rayfe—"enthralled."

I thought of the vision. There were two now. Amelia holding a golden-haired child, overlaying the shadowed bed where she wept for Hugh as the child died. And another, over a dead child. I swayed on my feet and Rayfe steadied me.

"No. There's a child. And she'll carry our mother's blood—the mark of the Tala—as I do. Make sure Amelia and her daughter survive this, Ursula. I'm trusting you to do that."

She tipped her head a bit, as if seeing me from a different angle would help her understand who I'd become. "Why do I think there's something more?"

"There is. The child should be with me, so I can teach her as we should have been taught. Send her to me."

Ursula barked out a laugh, and she shook her head. "I can't see that ever happening, Andi."

"I can."

Something in my certainty stopped her.

"And me?" Her face turned as grave as stone. "Do you still see me as a wise monarch, the murderer of my sister's husband?"

I stepped out from Rayfe's sheltering arm and took her hands again. I looked deep into her haunted gaze, past that.

"Yes." *Maybe.* "Find the doll our mother gave you. Help Amelia. And don't trust Uorsin."

She started to sneer. Stopped. Searched my face.

"What do you know, Andi?"

I opened my mouth to tell her and realized she would never believe me. Not until she learned for herself.

"Take Hugh to Amelia and remember what I've told you."

I squeezed her hands and started to let go. She grabbed me, embracing me in a fierce hug.

"Find the doll. Tell Amelia to find her doll."

"Dolls, Andi—really?"

"Yes. It's important."

"I wondered why you wanted to take that thing with you," she mused, a vertical line between her brows as she thought. "There won't be one for Amelia. Salena never had time to make one, the way she died in childbirth."

I shook my head, slow and measured, so the truth would sink in. "She didn't. Ask Zevondeth."

She nodded, slowly, not understanding. Not yet. She would, eventually, and a little piece of my shredded heart broke off for her, knowing that I'd consigned her to sorrowful discoveries.

"Done, then." Ursula gave it the force of a vow. Hesitated.

"I'll miss you," she whispered. "I won't be able to bear it if we never see each other again."

"Come back. I'll let you in. Only you. Annfwn could be yours, too. It's your birthright also."

She shook her head, duty replacing all else. "If you are our mother's daughter, I am our father's. My place is at his side."

"If you ever change your mind, Ursula, you know where to find me."

And with that, the Hawks shouldered Hugh's corpse, carrying him shoulder high in a mark of honor. Hawks were loyal only to Ursula and so would serve as witnesses to carry her version of this day into the greater world.

They escorted Ursula down the pass and away from me. Until, between the falling snow and deepening shadows, I could no longer see her.

"Shall we go home?" Rayfe finally asked.

I turned to find them all ringing me, watching with solemn concern.

As one, the men, led by Terin, sank to their knees in the snow and saluted me.

"My queen." Terin lifted his bowed head. "I know you loved him. Your sacrifice for us is great."

"Loved him? Hugh?"

I looked up at Rayfe, searching his gaze. He nodded at me. "It's all right. I understand. I never minded that you wished to be with him. It's my bed you slept in."

"No. You don't understand." I looked from Rayfe to Terin. "I never loved Hugh."

"I saw you kiss him, my queen"—Terin spoke the words without accusation, only grief—"at Windroven."

"Ah." I remembered the moment now. How I'd kissed Hugh's cheek for all I'd put him through, even as anticipation for Rayfe warmed my blood. "No. That wasn't love. That was good-bye, to everything I thought I was. That I thought I wanted."

I took Rayfe's hand. "I'm where I belong. There's nothing I wish for more."

I smiled at him, feeling my lips crack with the movement. The grief would never leave me, but perhaps I could yet find joy in Annfwn. I could enjoy my life. And find ways to make reparations to my sisters.

I stood on my tiptoes and kissed him. "Yes. Please. Take me home."

Keep reading for a special sneak peek of

The Twelve Kingdoms:
The Tears of the Rose

Available December 2014!

1

When they brought Hugh's empty body home to me, I didn't weep.

A princess never lets her people see her cry.

Father expected that much, of even me.

It wasn't even that difficult. My grief, my rage, they bloomed large in my heart, too huge to escape through such a small channel as a tear duct. All that he had been, so glorious, so handsome, full of life and love . . . gone.

The procession climbed the winding road to Windroven, lined by Hugh's people, all dressed in the ashy gray of mourning. The folk of Avonlidgh don't call out with their mourning. No, they observe it with silence, stolid as their remote and rocky coastline. Fittingly, however, the wind wailed instead. It tore at my griseous cloak with pinching fingers and snapped my hair painfully against my skin.

When we first received the news, I'd tried to cut it off, the long tresses Hugh had loved so much. But my ladies stopped me, saying I'd regret it later.

They didn't understand that I had room for only one regret. It edged out everything else. I couldn't understand how anyone could imagine that any other thing mattered or would ever matter again.

Hugh was gone.

Even though the words circled my mind in an endless cruel march, I couldn't quite believe it.

The members of the procession struggled against the ferocious wind, full of bits of biting ice off the churning ocean, my sister and her elite squad, Ursula's Hawks. They carried the pallet at shoulder height, despite the added effort, a gesture of highest regard. Not enough regard to have prevented his death, however. As they passed, the people and soldiers of Avonlidgh fell in behind, a drab parade in their wake.

Not so long ago, before winter set in, Hugh and I had ridden up that hill, bringing my other sister, Andi, with us. We'd given her protection, the shelter of our home. Sacrificed the armies of Avonlidgh to save her—and failed.

Hugh had gone to rescue her and died for it.

I loved Andi with all my heart—and I worried for her, married to that demon Tala king and exiled to his backwater country beyond the Wild Lands. Hugh's death was all their fault. And mine, for being so stupidly captured by the Tala. A sour ball of frozen guilt and hate choked me, the gorge rising every morning.

That channel wasn't big enough, either, so it just grew inside me, monstrous and vile.

They reached the top and Ursula's steely gaze found mine. The eldest and heir to the High Throne of the Twelve Kingdoms, she looked more gaunt than ever. In the past, some might have called her passably attractive, in her hard-edged way, but not at this moment. Her normally clear gray eyes clouded dark with defeat and her thin lips pursed tight with exhaustion.

She dismounted, saying nothing, gesturing for her Hawks to lay Hugh's shrouded body at my feet. They hadn't had the appropriate cloth to work with—we'd fix that—so they'd wrapped him in his cloak. I'd thought my heart had already died, but it clenched at the sight of the sigil I'd embroidered for him. Still, it could all be a lie.

Couldn't it?

"Show me." My voice croaked out, and Ursula, the brave one, she who never flinches, blanched ever so slightly. The she dropped to one knee and did the honors herself, touching the fabric tenderly with bare fingers the color of ice. The frozen wool resisted, then tore with a sigh that could have been a man's dying breath. One of my ladies broke into hysterical sobs that quickly faded as someone led her away.

I wanted to say it wasn't him. Surely this lifeless *thing* couldn't be my golden prince. When he first strode into the audience chamber at Castle Ordnung, he'd won everyone's hearts in an instant. We all fell in love with him, with the way the sun walked with him, radiant and perfect.

The light had abandoned him now.

There was nothing left to say good-bye to. Just a frozen husk.

Ursula stared at him, too, hands folded over her armored knee. The sour taste of guilt and metallic shame filled the air. Of course she felt it, too. Ursula never failed. Especially not in such a spectacular way. I saved out some of my hate for her. If she'd arrived in time to stop the siege, if she'd taken Odfell's Pass as was meant, Hugh would still be alive.

"Tell me what happened." I spoke to her only, where she still knelt by Hugh's pallid corpse, even his sunny blond locks sapped of color.

King Erich, who'd stood in silence behind me this whole time, stirred. A gnarled oak tree coming to life and moving its creaking limbs. "Perhaps we should go inside and—"

"No," I interrupted him. Someone gasped in shock, but I was beyond caring. "I want her to say it out loud, now. So everyone can hear. And bear witness."

Ursula measured me with her eyes. Maybe seeing someone besides her flirty, flighty baby sister for the first time.

"We attempted to take Odfell's Pass. King Rayfe and his Tala armies stopped us. Hugh fell in the battle." Her voice choked on the words, the burnt smell of lies floating up from them.

"Was Andi there?" I demanded to know.

Ursula hesitated—so, so unlike her—and inclined her head.

"Why didn't you bring her back with you, then?"

"We could not," Ursula answered, in a voice devoid of emotion.

"So the mission failed?" Old Erich sounded weary. He'd traveled to Windroven in the dead of winter to keep vigil for his fallen heir. Now all Avonlidgh had was me. Having the most beautiful woman in the Twelve Kingdoms for your son's wife sounds just great, until you realize she's the one who will be making the decisions when you're dead. Who wanted a girl who cared only about pretty dresses and picnics running a kingdom, after all?

Yes, I knew what they were thinking. The stink of their doubt filled the castle.

And soon I wouldn't even be beautiful, my one claim to importance. With every day, that famed beauty flaked away, dying on the surface of my skin and sloughing off like moss deprived of water. I felt it and didn't care. *Let it wither and die with everything else.*

"Princess Andromeda elected to honor her marriage to Rayfe and her commitment to the Tala," Ursula was telling Erich. "The pass cannot be taken by force. There is a magical barrier that cannot be breached. We tried and failed. It's over."

"I've heard such ridiculous rumors for decades." Erich's exhausted tone held a world of regret, possibly larger than mine. "You should not believe everything you're told, Princess. Especially by such tricksters as the Tala."

"I witnessed it myself," she replied.

"I highly doubt High King Uorsin will be so convinced."

"I will convince him," Ursula answered. "I shall go to Ordnung next and confess—"

"How did he die?" My voice cut through their conversation like a rusty knife.

Ursula rose. Met my eyes. So stoic. So steady.

"He fell in the battle at Odfell's Pass."

Her words smoldered, stinking of a lie. How I was so certain, I didn't know, but I was.

"Whose hand wielded the blade?"

Erich laid a hand on my shoulder. "Princess Amelia, in the heat of battle it is rarely easy to know—"

"*She* knows." I hissed it at her. "Don't you? Tell me what you're not saying."

Ursula's shoulders dropped, her hand finding the hilt of her sword, fingers wrapping around it for comfort.

"Hugh went for Rayfe and Andi stepped between them. She asked me to give you her confession: that he died at her hands."

A murmur ran through the erstwhile silent crowd, growing larger the farther it rippled away. I closed my eyes, listening to it spread. This. This was what I'd known. The burning ball in my gut turned, wanting to rise again. Andi. How could she?

"She offers you her grief and great sorrow. One day, when you're ready to hear it, she will offer you her apology. She knows well that it is nothing you will accept now."

"This is true then?" Erich's voice was ashen, weakened by the shock.

"It was never intended," came Ursula's reply, "but yes. In his zeal, Hugh thought to slay the King of the Tala. He died a brave and noble death."

I felt the sneer twisting my lips and opened my eyes to gaze down at the rotting shell of my true love. "There is no such thing as a brave and noble death."

"No." Ursula spoke the quiet agreement. "I erred in saying so."

"Yes." I swallowed, my mouth filling with the saliva that presaged vomit. I couldn't be ill in front of my people.

"She asked me to give you three other messages—in private."

"I don't want to hear them!" The world darkened at the edges. Ursula frowned at me. "Ami—are you all right?"

The childhood endearment nearly broke me open. I couldn't do this.

"I have to lie down." I fumbled to stay on my feet, and my hand found Dafne, solid and steady by my side. I leaned on her before I remembered that she had been Andi's friend first. Before Andi had betrayed me so foully.

"Shh," she soothed me, though I hadn't said anything to her. She wound an arm around my waist. "Let's get you inside. I'm sure it's not as bad as it sounds. Your sister loves you. They both do. Princess Ursula—would you care to accompany us?"

"I don't want her to—"

"Now, now. Save your energy, Princess." Dafne sounded all concerned, but I knew they were worried about offending Ursula. As if anything touched her hardened heart.

But I was beyond protesting, and my ladies swept me along, a sea of soft hands and gray silk skirts. As if my stomach knew we'd entered my chambers, it heaved in earnest just as I reached for the washbowl. Lady Dulcinor held my hair away from my face and I emptied myself into the basin. My eyes watered from the vicious spasms, but still I did not weep.

"How long has she been ill like this?" Ursula was talking to Dafne in lowered tones, and I couldn't make out the librarian's reply.

I lost the rest of their conversation in the rustle of silk and comforting murmurs of the other ladies as they swept me away from my sick and eased me onto the glorious bed I'd shared with Hugh for such a brief marriage. As I stared up at the fanciful draperies of lace and ribbon, his teasing words came back to me. *A beautiful princess bed for the most beautiful princess of all.*

Our story was not supposed to end this way.

Ursula sat on the bed beside me and I let her sinking weight draw my eyelids closed. I didn't resist when she took my hand, though hers was still cold as melting ice. I felt nothing.

"Ami—"

"Don't call me that." My voice was dull, but she heard me.

"Let me help you, Amelia. I want to be here for you."

"I don't need anyone killed today, thank you. I've had enough of that."

Her fingers tightened on mine. A low blow, but a direct hit. Funny that she was trying to mother me now. She'd never wanted to before. Always our father's daughter, obsessed with sword fighting, strategy, and law, she'd never even seemed to miss our mother. Ursula had always been studying or practicing in the yard, telling me to stay out of her way when I toddled after her. Andi had been the one to care for me, my substitute mother. Andi had always been the moderator between me and Ursula, too.

Andi, who had betrayed me and now was just as gone from the world as Hugh.

"I can't imagine the kind of grief you're feeling, Amelia, but you must think of the babe. Take care of yourself for your child's sake."

What in Glorianna's name was she talking about? I squinched my eyes open to glare at the lacy canopy and pulled my hand out of hers.

"I'm sick over Andi's betrayal and Hugh's murder, Ursula. I'm not pregnant. I realize it's not in your realm of expertise, but a woman needs a living man's member inside her to make a baby. It might have escaped your notice, but *my* husband is dead."

"I'm going to ignore that and write it off to you being out of your head. But you need to get a grip."

There was Ursula's usual impatience—and a shadow of hurt in those steel-gray eyes. I was on a roll today. Normally nothing pierced her heart.

"Hugh left only a month ago. You could easily be two or three months along. I realize it's not *your* realm, but I think you can do the math."

My ladies had discreetly retreated into the antechamber, giving us privacy to squabble, so I scooted my own self up to sit against the pink-satin-padded headboard. Ursula made no move to help me.

"You think I'm with child?"

She nodded. She'd cut her hair short for the campaign—all the better to fit under her helm. The ragged cut set off her sharp cheekbones. "More, Andi said you were. No, don't shake your head. This is one of the things Andi asked me to tell you."

"I don't want to hear it. I hate her. I'll hate her forever!"

"I don't care. Enough with the drama. Be your father's daughter and pull yourself together."

"I am, Ursula! I've held up for days and days and *days*. You have no idea what it's like! But I stood there and let you lay my husband's body at my feet and I didn't break. Now you want me to listen to the words of the woman who killed him in cold blood?" The poison wanted to rise again, but I choked it down. I didn't want Ursula to see me sick again.

"It wasn't cold blood." Ursula's voice was the flat of a blade. "It was chaotic and frenzied and horrible. Impossibly fast and excruciatingly slow. If I could take back that moment, if any sacrifice I could make would change that dreadful sequence, I would in a heartbeat. We could have hidden the truth from you, but Andi wanted you to know she takes responsibility for it. Even if it means you hate her forever."

She let the silence hang between us, full of the weight of expectation. She'd learned the trick from our father and wielded the weapon with the same mastery. I'd never been able to bear it. I plucked at my gray skirts.

"Fine. Then tell me and have done."

Ursula held up her blue-veined hand and showed me three points, as if I were still the five-year-old to her fifteen and she was explaining the three goddesses. "First, she said that you were with child and that she will bear the mark of the Tala also."

"How could she possibly know that?" The question ripped out of me. "I'm still not sure it's true! Besides—why in Glorianna's name would she wish such an evil thing upon her niece? That thrice-cursed mark brought her only misery and destroyed her life."

Ursula shook her head, seeming to notice her cold hands for the first time, because she rubbed them vigorously together, then stood and paced to the fireplace, holding them out to the fire.

"She's not wishing—she simply said what she believed to be true. Andi has changed. Whatever she's gone through, she's . . . more than what she was."

"How?" My throat felt raw. It bothered me how much I ached to know. I'd hated that she'd been forced to marry that demon spawn, hated that she'd done it to rescue me. I didn't want her to change. All I wanted was to go back and make it so none of this ever happened.

Ursula gave me a wry look over her shoulder. "She's uncannily like our mother now."

"I don't remember her. You know that." Hard to remember a woman who died giving birth to you.

"I do." Ursula spoke softly to the flames. "And Andi has that about her now. Something witchy. I saw her do things . . ." She shook it off. "Hugh told her you were with child because she didn't want to come with us and he thought that she would do that for you."

I scoffed at that, but she ignored me.

"Then, after he . . . Afterwards, I told her it had been a lie and she got that look in her eye—you know how she sometimes did? Like when we argued with Father that Hugh was for you and not for me. And she said, 'Pairing either of them with anyone else would be an exercise in futility. This is how it will be.' "

I remembered it word for word, just as Ursula did. Andi had always hung in the background, preferring to be invisible, but she'd stood before our father—who'd been so, so angry that my cursed face had distracted the match he'd planned for his heir—

and told him what he wanted was futile. *Nobody* told High King Uorsin what he wanted was futile.

No wonder he'd been so angry with her.

He'd recognized her disloyalty to the kingdom and the family long before anyone else. Maybe he'd recognized her murderous heart when I had not.

"She was like that, only more now," Ursula continued, as if I'd replied. "More confident. She said your daughter would bear the mark and—"

"Whatever *that* means."

"Whatever that means," Ursula agreed, "and that you should send the girl to her. That your daughter will need what she can teach her."

"Is she out of her mind?" Ursula didn't answer me, so I scrabbled off the high bed in a tangle of skirts and grabbed her by the arm. Her metal-embedded leather sleeve was still icy wet from the gale outside. "Why in Glorianna's name would I trust Hugh's child with his murderer?"

"I'm just passing along the message, Amelia." Her remote calm made me want to grind my teeth, as it always did. Princess Ursula the Heartless, they called her. No man would ever have her because she loved her sword the most.

"Then tell me the third thing and go."

"She said to find the doll our mother left you."

"Doll? What doll?" I shook her arm. The whole thing enraged me. Why would she taunt me in my grief with all this nonsense?

Ursula looked down at me and gently peeled my clenched fingers off her arm. "I don't know, Ami. She gave me the same message. Remember that horrible little hair doll Andi always kept, on the high shelf in her room?"

"No." I spat it out, like I wished I could spit out all this rage. But I did remember. She'd let me play with anything of hers but that. It was ugly anyway.

"She took it with her, I guess."

That surprised me. Andi had fled Ordnung disguised as one of my maids just after the Tala attacked. She'd been crazy acting, screaming about dogs howling. I didn't think she'd taken much. She'd been so heartbroken, so afraid our father would kill her mare. She loved that horse. More than she loved me. If she'd ever loved me. I hardened my heart against the sympathy. I should be more like Ursula. Funny, since now I'd be a widow—my bed as cold as my spinster sister's. So ironic.

"So?"

Ursula sighed, the hard smell of her impatience hitting me. She'd delivered her messages, done the requisite comforting, and was ready to be on her way.

"So, just that. Andi thinks our mother made each of us a doll and that we need them. She said to find yours."

"Hard for a dead woman to make a doll."

"I said the same thing, but I had a lot of time to think on the journey here." Ursula turned her head and pinned me with a pointed look. "I remember now—her making it while she was pregnant with you. She spent months on it. Singing and talking to you. I know it's a sorrow to you that you never knew her, and maybe I should have told you this before now, but she loved you and talked to you all the time. Maybe some part of you knows that, deep inside."

"I don't know that." It hit me then, unexpectedly hard, and I sank to my knees, not feeling the warmth of the fire. I was all alone now, with no one to love me. Not my mother, not Hugh, not even Andi. The pain of them all mixed together and a high keening sound rose from my throat. The people of Avonlidgh might not cry out at the ravages of death, but I was a child of Mohraya, a daughter of Glorianna, and we do wail out our grief.

"Amelia . . ." Ursula put her hand on my shoulder.

"Just go. Leave me alone for a while." I sounded like I was begging her. In fact, I was. I couldn't bear for anyone to see me this way. So lost and broken. "Dulcinor can show you your rooms."

Another person might have argued. Andi likely would have, as much as she hated my hysterics, but Ursula always respected someone's desire to be alone. Without another word, she left, softly pulling the door to behind her.

I sat on the floor in front of the fire, my dry eyes baking while soothing tears remained in some distant, cutoff place. Alone.